PRAISE FOR *DESTROYER OF SORROW*

"Vrinda Sheth's writing is brilliant. *Destroyer of Sorrow* is magnificent, riveting, and heart-wrenching. I really don't have words to express my appreciation. Reading it did something to my heart that maybe I'll be able to explain someday."

—JAI UTTAL, Grammy-nominated sacred-music composer, multi-instrumentalist, recording artist, and ecstatic vocalist

"I've read several versions of the Ramayana over the decades, but I have never read anything like this. What Vrinda Sheth has done with this adaptation is incredible. She writes with the pace of a thriller and the sensitivity of a poet. It's a combination that illuminates this classic with an extraordinary new light."

—MUKUNDA MICHAEL DEWIL, director, *Vehicle 19* and *Retribution*

PRAISE FOR *QUEEN OF THE ELEMENTS*

"The author adeptly fleshes these ancient mythological figures into rounded, relatable characters who feel as human as any other in contemporary YA fantasy. Sita, with her complex emotions and conflicted history, is an especially compelling personality, and Sheth gives her ample page time to tell her story in her own words. Whether readers are familiar with the Ramayana—an Indian epic that has been popular throughout South Asia and beyond for centuries—or they are discovering these characters for the first time, the novel delivers time-tested stories playing out against a distinctive fantasy world."

—*KIRKUS REVIEWS*

"My dear friend, the multitalented Vrinda Sheth, has written the best modern rendition of the Ramayana (the story of Rama and Sita), and she has written it from the perspectives of the women. This adventure-packed tale is also filled with sublime illustrations done by Vrinda's mother, Anna Johansson."

—SHARON GANNON, cofounder of Jivamukti Yoga, author of *Yoga and Vegetarianism*.

"Again, in this second volume, the work is richly illustrated with Johansson's lovely, dramatic, and colorful illustrations. Especially noteworthy here are her charming renditions of natural scenes in the forest and the various fauna (and bloodthirsty monsters!) found there. Once again, lovers of the Ramayana will find much to enjoy and to debate in this lively, creative, and provocative retelling of the Rama story."

—DR. ROBERT P. GOLDMAN, principal translator of *The Rāmāyaṇa of Vālmīki: An Epic of Ancient India*

PRAISE FOR *SHADOWS OF THE SUN DYNASTY*

"What especially stands out in this edition of the Ramayana is the celebration of the feminine voice: The female characters who would normally be overshadowed by their male counterparts are now invested with agency and power. The extraordinary positive contributions from such female personalities leaves the reader with a fresh view of this amazing tale."

—GRAHAM M. SCHWEIG, PHD, professor of philosophy and religion, Christopher Newport University, Virginia; author of *Bhagavad Gītā: The Beloved Lord's Secret Love Song*

"Reader, be prepared for a treat. Vrinda Sheth's Ramayana is far beyond routine storytelling. Her telling is full of the kind of personal detail and insight that comes from knowing her subjects at a heart level. Rama for her is not only an archetypal hero—he lives and breathes, radiating mystical power; Sita is more than tragic heroine or unearthly goddess—she is a powerful, self-aware human yet divine being. The Ramayana is a feast of emotion and grand inspiration: It calls us to experience life to the fullest, not shrinking from its tragedies or rewards, but giving ourselves fully to the whole cosmic drama. Immerse yourself in Sita's Fire, and you will find yourself doing just that."

—RANCHOR PRIME, author of *Ramayana: A Tale of Gods and Demons*

"The intrigue and mystery starts with the opening line—never have I been pulled so quickly into a book through a few simple yet tantalizing words. The art and magic unfold page after page through story and image alike. From injustice and savagery to heroism and beautiful princesses, the unique style of Vrinda Sheth's writing captivates the heart and mind, drawing one deeper into the burning intricacies of Sita's Fire."

—BRAJA SORENSEN, author of *Lost & Found in India*, *Mad & Divine*, and *India & Beyond*

"What an excellent retelling of the Ramayana! If sheer artistry, imagination, storytelling technique, and descriptive writing were not enough, Vrinda Sheth accurately conveys the emotion and underlying philosophical content of the story as well. With God as my witness, I went in a skeptic and came out a believer—and now I can hardly wait for future volumes in the series."

—STEVEN J. ROSEN, editor in chief, *Journal of Vaishnava Studies*; associate editor, *Back to Godhead*; author of *Holy War: Violence and the Bhagavad Gita*, *The Hidden Glory of India*, and *Black Lotus: The Spiritual Journey of an Urban Mystic*

"*Shadows of the Sun Dynasty,* by Vrinda Sheth, is rich with deep insights into the motives and emotions of the entire cast, which makes for an unforgettable entrance into the political intrigue and web of emotions in the kingdom of Ayodhya. For those who enjoy an unforgettable story, you have in your hands a unique book that will pull you in from start to finish. Anna's exquisite illustrations further enhance the story. I expect this beautiful book to enthrall the present generation, leaving its indelible mark in their minds and hearts, as other versions of the Ramayana have for countless generations."

—KOSA ELY, author of *The Peaceable Forest* and *The Prince and the Polestar*

DESTROYER
OF SORROW

THE SITA'S FIRE TRILOGY: BOOK THREE

DESTROYER
OF SORROW

AN ILLUSTRATED SERIES BASED ON THE RAMAYANA

VRINDA SHETH

ILLUSTRATED BY
ANNA JOHANSSON

Foreword by Dr. Vandana Shiva

MANDALA

SAN RAFAEL | LOS ANGELES | LONDON

MANDALA

PO Box 3088
San Rafael, CA 94912
www.mandalaeartheditions.com
Find us on Facebook: www.facebook.com/MandalaEarth
Follow us on Twitter: @MandalaEarth

This book was made possible by a grant from Bhaktiland,
a nonprofit supporting the expansion of quality bhakti art.
www.bhaktiland.com

Library of Congress Cataloging-in-Publication Data available.
ISBN: 978-1-64722-147-8

Publisher: Raoul Goff
VP of Creative: Chrissy Kwasnik
VP of Manufacturing: Alix Nicholaeff
Associate Publisher: Mariah Bear
Managing Editor: Lauren LePera
Project Editor: Phillip Jones
Senior Production Manager: Greg Steffen
Cover and Book Design:
Eight Eyes, www.eighteyes.com

Mandala Publishing, in association with Roots of Peace, will plant two trees for each tree used in the manufacturing of
this book. Roots of Peace is an internationally renowned humanitarian organization dedicated to eradicating land mines
worldwide and converting war-torn lands into productive farms and wildlife habitats. Roots of Peace will plant two million
fruit and nut trees in Afghanistan and provide farmers there with the skills and support necessary for sustainable land use.

Manufactured in India by Insight Editions

10 9 8 7 6 5 4 3 2 1

2020 2021 2022 2023

TO MY CHILDREN

Naimi, Luv, and Khol

Contents

SITA AND HANUMAN

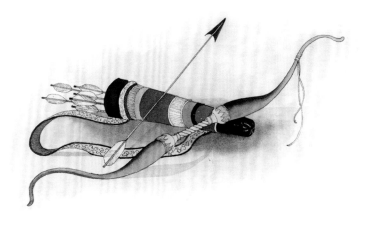

Foreword

Sita as Shakti

I am honored to write the foreword to Book 3 of Vrinda Sheth's trilogy based on the *Ramayana*, a timeless epic that renews itself in different ages according to the needs of the times.

Indian epics are always woven around the contest of forces of adharma—destructive power—and forces of regeneration, resilience, and dharma.

Vrinda brings out the agency of Sita in protecting herself, her integrity, and her autonomy while held captive by Ravana. While the battle between Rama and Ravana is part of the story, the real story is the contest between the violent, destructive power of Ravana and the creative Shakti of Sita.

Sita breaks many molds that define women as the passive, helpless second sex. Violence against nature and women is rooted in the assumption that both are objects to be owned, possessed, and exploited. In spite of being physically captured and held captive, Sita cannot be possessed. As Shakti, Sita cannot be conquered by Ravana. Her story is the story of power in feminine form—unconquerable, unmasterable, unreachable.

In Sita, the false dualism between the sacred and the secular, between divinity and dead matter, is transcended. Sita is of the Earth and returns to the Earth. The Earth is a goddess. Sita, as goddess, is of the Earth.

Sita is both an earthy, biological woman and a goddess. In contrast to the last few centuries of Western mechanistic, industrial thought, in the *Ramayana*—and in all indigenous cosmologies—the Earth is not dead matter. The Earth is sacred. She, and all her beings, all her elements, are an embodiment and expression of the Divine. The Earth is Mother Earth. She provides all sustenance to all beings.

Sita is of course the loving wife of Rama, who retains her unconditional love in spite of his doubt about her love and integrity. But Sita, as the Earth, has a larger family, an Earth family, in her larger home, which is nature. Her fourteen years in exile made her Sita of the forest. Even in her captivity over the course of eleven months, her family is the trees and animals, the leaves and a blade of grass.

As humanity stands at a precipice, staring at extinction, the story of Sita can inspire us to find our Shakti to resist the violent forces of greed and destruction and use our power in creative form to protect the Earth, her biodiversity, her life-sustaining potential. There is a Sita in all of us.

—DR. VANDANA SHIVA, founder of Navdanya and Diverse Women for Diversity, environmental activist, physicist, and author of more than twenty books

SITA AND HANUMAN

Gauging the Enemy

I cling to a karnikara tree. I will never let go! Bright yellow blossoms shelter me. The demon's fingernails stretch across my skull. I tighten my arms around the trunk, the bark tearing into my skin. Grabbing my hair by the fistful, he yanks my head back. Horrendous nightmares did not prepare me for this. His heads surround me; he has fangs like the tusks of elephants. Pendulous lips, wet with saliva. Hungry eyes that dart across every part of my body. Countless arms, eager to hold me. He has already trapped me, the princess. But that is not all I am!

The moment he touches me, I shatter. I will never be the same. My psyche ruptures; my identity cracks apart. All that I previously conceived of as *me* dissolves. The well-mannered princess, the reserved girl, the human woman: gone. Like molten gold from a volcano, I burst forth; like a sleeping goddess awakened, I soar up, explosive. My true form asserts its dominance, and I rise above the blood-drinker.

The sky is my hair, fire my eyes, the Earth my feet, wind my magic, and this expansive Shakti my very breath. All the animals of the forest have fled, but an owl with piercing green eyes witnesses my transformation. Not until this crisis do I know myself, and yet it's not enough. With one motion, he pulls his hand into a fist, closing me up and pulling me to him. Just like that, I'm silenced. My Shakti is new to me; his Maya is ancient and practiced. I'm bound with invisible cords, gagged by a ghostly force, held motionless by Maya beyond perception. I'm reduced again to a woman abducted, torn ruthlessly from my home.

As he pries me away, his hot breath threatens me. Like so many women before me, I have no choice: I stop resisting and let go. As he tears me away from the karnikara tree, the skin of my inner arms rips. Chunks of my hair are wrenched loose. Yellow blossoms rain down on us: princess and blood-drinker, woman and abductor, Sita and Ravana. I hate the heavens for marking his act with this sign of victory. The flowers flutter by me, caressing my skin, never to be looked at again without shrinking. I struggle against his Maya that binds me. I call out to the wind: *Stop him!* I call out to fire: *Burn him!* Earth, water, sky: *Save me!*

Only silence. The fire in my soul is doused. The elements bow to him, not me. I *need* Rama. I shout at the top of my lungs: "RAMA!"

No answer.

I feel broken, like a child ripped too soon from my mother's womb. The goddess, awakened so briefly, seethes with unspent Shakti. The fire is real, longing for release. I tremble with unshed tears. Can I survive? I don't yet know.

He flies into the air by his own Maya, taking me south. Having lured me from my husband, having slain Jatayu, the mighty vulture, Ravana trembles with excitement. We are both covered in brown feathers. Blood drips from his sword. Jatayu fought so bravely to save me. Now, he lies wingless on the ground. I begged him to fly to Rama, to find my protectors. Instead, he spread his wings and attacked with his claws. Dangling in Ravana's grip, I feel the Earth pulling at my toes. The clouds collude with him, filling my mouth with moisture, gagging me.

I cry out again and again, "Rama!"

All living creatures have fled. I see no one to enlist as a messenger until, finally, a monkey the color of honey leaps up from the treetops. Desperate to leave a trail, I fling my jewelry down. My cherished anklets, golden earrings, and necklace. Heirlooms from my mother. May these lead Rama to me! The monkey's howl is the last thing I hear. Then land disappears. The ocean spreads out in all directions around me. The waves roar in approval, hailing the demon king. I give in to self-pity, sobbing into the Cloth of Essence, this golden garment that reflects my core. It has already become less golden. The sun sets. A moonless night shrouds our destination in darkness.

I cannot stop my tears, for I already know that the life I cherish with Rama will never again be mine. I don't even know who I am. My Shakti has calmed, quiet against the bonds that bind it, but it will not be dormant for long. My agitation and anger are unsettling—dark, destructive, frightening. It demands action: *We will destroy him!*

But I feel helpless. I'm not used to being on my own. Rama, and my family before him, have always been at my side. Help me! Somebody!

I will, Shakti promises.

And the demon laughs out loud. He can hear my thoughts. I cover my face with my hands, fearing I may lose my sanity. The jarring forces within me respond to my fear. The invisible cords he bound me with have become a second skin. The pounding of my heart is more palpable, an emotion that takes over my entire being. A strange syncopation starts, settling my Shakti into me. It becomes me. Was always me. What is happening?

Ravana begins to descend through the dense clouds. Ornate golden domes shine in the haze. The structures are so tall that they pierce the clouds. I didn't know such a thing was possible. I cannot see beyond our landing place, a courtyard with high walls. Everything around me dazzles with gold, the walls whitewashed. I have no way to ascertain where I am, though I search for clues. Have I learned of this place? Heard of it? Past the ocean, obscured by clouds.

Ravana has not yet let go of me. He allows my feet to touch the ground, but I cannot take a step without him. He rushes me past gates guarded by monsters of his kind. I became aware of one thing: He does not want anyone to see me. A group of blood-drinkers awaits us, bowing as their king approaches. I understand their importance by their costly adornments. Clusters of servants and underlings stand behind each of them. Their likeness to their king is striking: the same bronze hair, the same night skin, the same gleaming fangs, the same arrogance. He shields me from them, hiding me behind his massive body. Am I a secret? A shameful act he wishes to hide?

He curtly acknowledges his people by their names, easy for me to learn because of their descriptive nature:

Virupaksha, Squint-Eyes

Vajradamshtra, Lightning-Fangs

Dhumraksha, Smoke-Eyes

Prahasta, Hands-That-Take

Mahodara, Mighty-Abdomen

Mahaparshva, Mighty-on-All-Sides

Akampana, Unshakable

He speaks to each of them through a different mouth, as if each serves a distinct part of him. I distantly record that Ravana possesses ten heads and twenty arms. Wisps of black smoke crawl across my feet and grow into a malevolent smog, staring at me with eyes that are just like Ravana's. It spits scorpions at my feet. The insects twitch their razor pincers and . . .

"Indrajit!" Ravana snaps.

The smoke vanishes. The spiders evaporate. I recognize the name: Ravana's legendary son. A predator. A wielder of the darkest Maya.

"Mother," Ravana then says.

A jolt runs through my body, the cleaving toward one of my own sex. I strain to see the woman in their midst. Is Shurpanakha, his sister, here? She instigated this. But Ravana forcibly turns me to the final male in the entourage. A blood-drinker matching Ravana's height and looks. A sense of heavy disapproval radiates from him.

"Brother," Ravana says.

The brother's eyes fasten on me as if I'm the terror among them. Without waiting for a

response, Ravana takes me away. My hand reaches out toward him, a silent plea. But Ravana's disapproving brother could be just as eager to consume me. I snatch my arm back.

When Ravana enters his private quarters, he finally releases me from his grip. I massage my wrists to regain feeling in my fingers. He visibly relaxes, eyelids drooping lazily over his eyes. I've entered a twilight realm belonging to the gods. The spacious hall is decorated for festivities, redolent with heavenly fragrances of aloewood and incense burning. Fire lamps flicker across the hall. Fresh flower decorations stand artfully by each pillar. Jeweled staircases lead up to skylights, open to the sky. I see a fistful of stars twinkle in the night. A backless throne dominates the center of the room, raised high on a marble dais. Mosaics of gems sparkle across the walls, and gold-spun drapes billow from the ceiling. A lush carpet, woven to resemble the surface of the Earth, covers the entire floor. Plush pillows are scattered in heaps on the rug. There are finely wrought beds everywhere, with gilded bedposts and flowing drapes. The walls are inlaid with pearls, coral, silver, and gold. I'm startled by the exquisite, tasteful, and luxurious atmosphere. I expected his home to be as grotesque as he is.

As we arrive, hundreds of women mill out from the women's quarters. My hope to kindle the sympathy of the women is drowned out by their eagerness. The consorts throng around us like ants around a dead cicada. They seem tethered to their lord, bound to him, controlled by him, dependent on him.

A woman steps forward, asking, "Shall I inform the queen of your arrival?"

He points at me. "*This* is my queen!"

But there *is* another queen, who doesn't care to greet me, the new conquest. May she come and reclaim her husband! And yet the sheer number of women make me wonder if I'm worthy of the queen's notice. Hundreds, if not thousands stand together in clusters, filling the hall. I see blood-drinkers with smooth midnight skin; Nagas, their elegant hips turning into coils brilliant with gems; Apsaras, gleaming with otherworldly beauty; humans, the crop of our kind. An extravagant harem. I don't understand why he adds me to his collection. Someone here must feel empathy for me. Surely, one of them can show me how to escape.

As he herds me up the steps to the throne, he transforms into another shape. I hear his arms and heads receding, an intake of air. Before abducting me, he fooled me with the form of an ascetic. Only when he wanted to prove his potency and power did he display his ten-headed form. What now?

I take one step at a time, trying to catch the eyes of the women standing on each step. They all look only at him. My bare feet are damp and slippery against the cold marble. I shiver, my teeth touching.

As we stand high above his consorts, they gaze up at us. *Us. We.* How pleased he would be by the feeling of union in those words.

The king gets down on his knees, and I step back, the cushions of the throne pressing against my thighs. He stares up at me with eyes that are not his. He stole the shape of them from my heart. I refuse to look directly at him, but I can see how much like Rama he looks. My beloved's royal features are a jest on this demon, mocking their nobility.

Ravana speaks as if we are alone.

"Sita, I will be your slave." His tongue darts out, wetting his lips.

"Only if I become yours first!" I retort. My voice is lost in the large chamber.

"Marry me." *As if I am not already married.* I press my lips together. He hears.

"I will do anything you want." *Except set me free.*

"I will make every wish of yours come true." *Except for the ones I actually have.*

"You can fly anywhere you wish on the Pushpaka." *But not away from you.*

"I will make you happy." *By forcing me to see happiness your way.*

"This kingdom will be yours." *If I come to your bed.*

"I don't want this!" I exclaim.

Ignoring my words, he rests his forehead on my feet. His skin is hot like coals. I shrink back, but I'm trapped against the colossal throne.

Where is Rama? I was so sure that he would be on our heels, his bow and arrows in hand. But I heard his death cry. Why do I fool myself he is alive? He was calling for me, for help. My name echoed across the trees, the cry of a dying man. My throat is sore from shouting for help that never came. No one will come to my rescue. That knowing forces me to stand tall. I will need everything within me to survive.

"Sita," Ravana says. His voice is pleading. Soft and gentle, and as false as his face.

I clench my fists. I don't want to hear my name on his lips. I don't know where on Earth I am, or if Rama is alive. I wrap my golden cloth around me tightly.

"Sita," he says yet again.

I want to cast off that name!

Now he stands up and towers over me. The torches flicker with his breath, casting shadows across the vast hall. With my mind, I reach for the fire: *Yield to me! Become mine!* But it is futile because the fire is already bound within me. And *that*, not these external flames, is the source of my strength.

He speaks again, but this time, I shut out his voice. I uncross my arms; the scratches on my forearms are rough to my touch. Flecks of blood cover the Cloth of Essence, which has never admitted stains before. I will not remove this garment until I'm reunited with Rama. I swear it. I look out at the gathering of women. They are impossibly silent, like statues. I cannot even see breath moving through them. How many times have they witnessed this very scene before?

I recall with cold clarity, thirteen years ago, just months before our exile from the empire, I stood in Ayodhya's library. The records told of a time when hundreds of women had been abducted by this very creature. One of my dearest maids, Rani, had escaped when the women banded together. With one voice, they lay a curse upon Ravana: "You will pay with your immortal life. A woman, just like us, the wife of another, will be your final death."

I look around for the woman Rani described as the Brave One, who had rallied all the abducted women together. And yet she didn't escape; she stayed. She could be one of the hundreds below, but I don't know a single identifying attribute of hers. I look at the woman closest to me. She avoids my eyes. They will not speak to me without his permission. He controls everything here—I feel that. Perhaps even the breath in their bodies.

"Please sit," he says, courteously as if I'm here by choice. "Let us show you Lanka's hospitality." With his slender yet muscled Rama arm, he gestures toward the throne.

My neck and shoulders are taut with defiance, and I say, "Your ploys cannot fool me!"

But my eyes betray me as they trail back toward him. The sun has not risen on my first day in captivity, and already I am being lured. Ravana was pleased enough to overpower me before, revealing his thick necks, heads, and arms, his chest covered in battle scars, held up by massive, muscled thighs and calves. Why does he pretend to be human now?

Before the question is fully formed, the answer is clear: He will use every tool, every weapon, every method at his disposal to break me. Now he cheats me with the best imitation of Rama he can muster, and my eyes are drawn in his direction. What else will he trick me to do against my will? I am up against an enemy so powerful, so manipulative, so full of Maya, I must be equally powerful to survive this.

He could ravage me before this audience. As he lifts his hands toward me, my body is numb, my throat tight. I can hardly feel my fingers. With a light nudge, he pushes me onto the throne. My knees buckle and I sit. I hate that my aching legs are relieved.

"Let us begin!" he cries out, as if all this has been orchestrated beforehand.

Perhaps it has, a million times before, for each of these conquests. I can see only the outlines of the women who stand on the far side of the hall. He sits down next to me and claps his hands. The women mobilize at once. A group of them arrange their instruments: vinas, mridangas, sitars. The musicians begin playing hymns praising Shiva, the lord of destruction. Dancers, decked out in flowers and jewelry, begin displaying their skills. In a bizarre unfolding, they twirl, leap, stomp their feet vigorously, and tell stories with their hands. I see and hear them, but I feel nothing.

A parade of women ascends the steps slowly, ceremoniously. They carry platters of fruit, sweets, and artfully prepared meat: peacock, deer, fish, buffalo, and goat. They smile at him, eager to be in his company and win his favor. They offer us chalices of water, crystal-clear spirits laced with spices, and various fruit wines. Without looking, he grabs the food and drink, his thirst and appetite insatiable. His human face is enraptured by the scene below. I sense his shadow faces around him like an aura, even as I avoid looking at him directly. What I see from the corner of my eye is more than enough. He devours the food, eyes fixed on the spectacle below.

With his attention finally elsewhere, I'm granted my first moment to myself. As I sit in the center of the Lotus Hall, all their eyes return to me regularly. Sitting on the backless throne, as far away from him as possible, I'm like a mouse in the jaws of death, my end inevitable. I force my mind to piece together the impressions I have gathered. I wrap and unwrap the ends of my garment around my fingers. Where am I? How can I escape?

The parade of women carrying platters continues. I touch nothing. I will *never* eat or drink in his house. The women seem hypnotized by him. Every one of them is a beauty, with glowing skin, lustrous hair, and a shapely body. Adored by so many women, why has he taken me? Is it to avenge the mutilation of his sister?

When Shurpanakha had raised her sharp claws and rushed at me, my intuition had flared. The warning had gone far beyond the immediate danger. When Lakshmana cut off her ears and nose, it had forged a new path for us. It was as if I had seen destiny split open an abyss for us to fall into. Shurpanakha promised revenge. Is this it?

I search for Shurpanakha, scanning the women's faces. When I think of her, I feel Ravana's Maya turn to me. He doesn't turn his face; he casually pops purple grapes into his mouth, but his attention is clearly on me. The Maya delivers a direct message: *I want you, Sita.*

The force of his Maya grows around me, as if he is using his invisible twenty arms to pry my psyche open. Like a demon in a nightmare searching for a way to possess me. I am surrounded on all sides by him. If he can penetrate my Shakti, he will gain control of my heart. As his Maya probes me—as palpable as actual fingers—I see a small leak in it, oozing quietly away. The totality of his Maya has been compromised, even if it's as hidden as an untold secret. That knowledge of his weakness gives me power. My reaction is instant, as if it's a weapon I've wielded a thousand times: My eyelids clench shut; I tense and inhale, holding my breath; then I exhale sharply in a small burst, just enough to fling him away from me. I blast out my Shakti like a golden halo around myself. I must be shining like the sun itself.

He is shut out. A bunch of grapes hangs limp in his hand. He turns to me. Slowly, he lifts his hand to his mouth and squashes a grape between his teeth. The juice dribbles down his chin. He smiles: *Impressive. Now watch.*

His energetic body swells and grows. First, I discern each of his ten heads, chaotic with constant processing of information, but that's not the end of his cage. I thought I had sensed his true form as a shadow faintly emanating from the human body he currently inhabits. How wrong I was. Not even his massive twenty-armed form can contain the swell of his Maya. Because I could not see it before, it seems to grow in front of my third eye, but perhaps it was always there. Within moments, he fills the entire chamber. It is built for this. Now I see how easily he holds these women in his energetic field. How erroneous to call the ten-necked body his true form. *This* is his true form—this mass of blasting, explosive Maya. It is imbued with his emotions and memories, but darker, more intense. He is prancing, displaying the extent of his power as a small child would: *Look how strong I am!*

I am content to sit quietly, my Shakti impenetrable. In his arrogance, in his absolute confidence in his Maya, he has not noticed the compromise, the way small amounts of him are constantly flowing away into the Earth, returning to their mother. He is, after all, made, in the end, of the elements. He too will return to dust. I will see to it.

His Maya now gathers force as he heads directly toward me. I see the indigo condense into dark violet, then black, and his dark power probes my bright-as-sunlight Shakti. Again, I use a small exhaled breath to shrug him off. The small blast of my Shakti sends a burst of light through him, illuminating him for a split second. His being is populated by souls, like people in a city. Parasites, or prisoners? A shudder runs through me. His violet Maya flits around me, then slowly fades into the shadows. Soon, all I can see are slight waves of color behind my eyelids. My Shakti flickers faintly within me, like grief suppressed.

The music from below reaches my ears. My arms loll to the sides, my breathing more laborious than before. I am truly exhausted. I'm weak here in his domain. But still, I *can* shut him out—a small mercy when my body is so vulnerable. I hear another grape being squashed between his teeth. As he lifts his hand to place it on mine, my hand darts away and hides beneath my golden cloth.

The dancers below are reaching a frenzied crescendo. They depict the goddess Kali slicing off the heads of her enemies. I almost smile. He sees the irony too, and with one small snap of his fingers, the dance changes. It now shows Kali transforming into Parvati, her more gentle self. Parvati runs into the arms of Shiva, and their lovemaking begins. A subtle message indeed. I raise my eyes to the ceiling.

The dome above reveals that night is still strong. I feel the presence of the elements up there. The ivory elephants, stacked on top each other to make pillars, glare at me with ruby-red eyes. With their trunks lifted, they look very alive. The moonless night is portentous; I have brought death with me to this cursed place. No sign of the rising sun that to me always signifies Rama. But does the sun rise in Ravana's kingdom? I don't know. I don't know if I am still within Earth's time and reach. I tap my chest a few times, patting down the horror that comes from not knowing and the horror that comes from knowing what's next.

I have challenged and repulsed Ravana's magic. He will tire of words and complete the violence he began when he grabbed my hair and pulled me away. I know what happens to women like me, but I refuse to think of it.

I can't sit still a second longer. I stand up and walk down the steps. I'm unsteady; I haven't had a drop of water or food since he stole me from our home in Panchavati, that beautiful single-room dwelling, with its thatched roof, built by Lakshmana. It was meant to be our final sanctuary in the forest. Lakshmana had been so certain Rama's death cry was a trap. It wasn't Rama's voice, he'd said. These blood-drinkers love schemes, he'd insisted. And I had walked straight into one of them. Just yesterday, on the fourteenth day of the spring month. I cannot think of my brother-in-law; we parted in anger. And yet I may never see him again.

I continue down the steps, but stumble. Two women rush up and take my hands to steady me. I grasp their hands gratefully. *Will you help me?* my hands ask theirs. When I reach the bottom of the stairway, they withdraw. *No, we will not.*

He has stayed on his throne. His eyes, which have not left me for a moment, tingle all over my back. I go straight to the dancers, where the music is loudest.

"Help me," I beg. "Help me."

I catch the hands of the girl playing Parvati. "Help me escape."

I grab the hands of Shiva, sending a prayer to the real one.

The music stops, the women falter. All eyes are on me.

"I am Sita," I call out, my voice strong. "Princess of Ayodhya. My body, heart, and soul belong to Rama, prince of Ayodhya, heir to the noble Sun dynasty. I have been abducted against my will. I beg you to come to my aid. Help me. Nothing good can come of this unrighteous and cruel deed. If you have ever loved, please find mercy in your heart for me. If you love your lord, help me. He plays with fire and will burn!"

I speak louder, wanting everyone to hear. My voice echoes against the walls. "If your king had won me in a fair battle, I would follow the rules of dharma and succumb to my fate. I would bow my head and accept surrender. I would become his wife. But like a dog, he has stolen me away. A true coward, he did not challenge my mighty husband in battle. Why? Because he knows of Rama's power! Rama will come here with his golden-fletched arrows. He will avenge me. Rama's arrows will destroy your king and your entire race!"

When I speak of Rama, tears begin streaming from my eyes. His cry rings in my ears.

The king of blood-drinkers is content to watch no longer. "Sita! Hold your tongue!"

I ignore Ravana and feel the energetic rise of his anger, yet I can suddenly take full breaths. I see that when he loses control, I gain it. Then I hear the rush of air behind me, and a second later, he hovers in front of me. As he lands on his feet with a loud bang, the women scatter to make way for him.

"Rama is dead," he hisses through clenched teeth. "Give up this farce."

The women quickly gather behind him. They are one entity. It's me against them.

"You speak of dharma?" he says, eyes narrowing to slits. "What do you know, ignorant woman! I have claimed you according to the laws that govern our kind. Your so-called valiant husband failed to protect you. He brought you to Dandaka! For thirteen years, he dragged you around those dangerous forests. That is no place for a woman, especially a treasured princess. Rama might as well have thrown you into my arms!"

He now comes nose-to-nose with me. I immediately look down. His toes are perfect, with rounded, shiny nails. This heartens me; he will never achieve a believable likeness to Rama. Ravana doesn't know that after thirteen years of walking barefoot, Rama's feet are calloused and lined with dust.

"No one here will listen to your foolish claims," Ravana spits out.

A murmur arises among the women, the first sound they have made in his presence. It must be assent on their part. His hand hovers around my chin, as if he means to force my eyes to his. Instead, he tugs my braid. My scalp, already so tender, flares in pain.

"You are mine now."

He flings my braid away so sharply, it lashes against my hips.

"Bring her to the Ruby Room," he orders them.

Shocked whispers erupt, as if I'm accorded a high honor.

"Give her the respect of the highest queen. Spare her no comfort or luxury. But do not speak to her. As you can see, her mind is befuddled."

He leaves, throwing me a look of desire and frustration. The ministers await him. He is a king, after all, even though he places his own whims first. If only I could be privy to their meeting, to understand why he abducted me. His Maya remains palpable around me, as if he's unwilling to actually leave me. I stare at the exit. Has he really left? The wives stare after him too, longingly. When I'm sure he is gone, my neck softens, my chest slumps forward, my knees buckle, and I sink to the ground, hands shivering. They gather around me silently, preparing to escort me to the Ruby Room. Someone among all these women must sympathize with me. I *must* find her, befriend her, and find a way to escape. The Brave One. She's here somewhere.

Daivi's Command

I was soaring away, wind on my tail staking out our path of escape, with Sugriva always a leap or two behind me. I crushed the treetops under my feet—leap-flying my best for Sugriva's sake. To convince him. To make him see that Daivi was with us. Destiny was on our side, even though Vali was hounding us, as terrifying as a raging forest fire. Howling his violence, he stalked us, our revenant king. Sugriva, also our king! But a king is one, never two. Vali would make sure of it, obliterating Sugriva. Obedience to king and clan was our greatest calling; every Vanara knew it. Every monkey knew it: our honor code. Disobeying the king was the gravest crime, but fleeing was Daivi's command. Destiny had taken charge when I least expected it.

We were close to the southern sea, far from our home, Kishkinda. But Vali had no intention of letting us live. His mighty roar in the distance, yet so near that it pounded against my eardrums, felt like a death blow. Vali was gaining ground, closer than he'd ever been. He menaced us, made triple powerful by our terror. My tail curled into a tense arch. Sugriva behind me, an anxious shadow. Grabbing Sugriva's hand, I aimed for the next peak of the Vindhyas, and then the next. We had to find a hiding place, a way to trick Vali, because we could not outrun him—not with Sugriva's will so deflated, so eager for his brother's mercy. Daivi had not yet touched my master. I held him, like a net does a fish.

The Vindhyas had a thousand peaks, and Vali pursued us across each one. We had crossed the Mekhala and Utkala regions, and the Narmada River, infested with huge serpents. The great river Krishnaveni offered us no shelter; neither did the smaller Godavari nor Varada. We tore through the human cities where Vanaras never went. The humans knew the menace of monkeys, however. Seeing us, so large and monkey-like, they froze. As Sugriva descended from the sky, those civilized people rushed from the streets in terror. They shrieked in fear; we crashed down onto rooftops, demolishing their buildings under our feet. The dust and rubble we left in our wake did not deter Vali. We jumped through windows, balconies, doors, building after building. Clothes left to dry tangled around our feet. We could not shake Vali off, even for a moment. There was a reason no Vanara dared challenge him.

We ran from the cities, pursued by arrows and javelins, the human armies mobilizing. But the only threat to us was Vali. City after city gave us no reprieve. From Avanti to Abhravanti. Vidarbha to Rishika. Mahishaka to Banga to Kalinga. We left human civilization for Dandaka, the terrible borderland. Nothing was worse than Vali with his fangs out, embodying death, the noose his tail. Like a starved blood-drinker, he was intent. How had this bloodthirst for his only brother come about? Even as I ran by Sugriva's side, I did not understand this enmity. In between the decision to leap left or right, I wondered: What made Vali so determined to slay his kin?

As we slid through the aerial roots of a banyan tree, Sugriva's tail tangled in the branches. He cried, "I cannot run any farther, Hanuman! I cannot!"

He steadied himself against the tree trunk, his tail unknotting itself. It had been five days. We had not stopped once since the great schism between the prodigious brothers. I was not as tired, being the Son of the Wind.

Sugriva's large body was loose with exertion, tight with tension. The fur on his body stood straight up, screaming. A snake hissed under his hand. A dire omen. "My brother is stronger! He shows no sign of tiring!"

It was true. We kept evading Vali, but he was as close as the next breath. Even now, a tree behind us groaned as he crushed it under his feet. Night was setting in, highlighting every danger, emphasizing Vali's awful nearness.

"Let me . . ." Sugriva could barely speak through his heaving breaths, "surrender!"

"Never! Vali has no mercy for you." I would carry him if necessary. "Think of Ruma, if not yourself!"

Hearing her name was like the lord's own. The love between Sugriva and Ruma was legend. He straightened. "For Ruma," he said, "I run."

Sugriva threw himself into the sky in his wife's name. Even an exhausted Vanara's leap was something to behold, and we had no need for stealth with Vali so close. Pursued by our enemy, we crossed another four regions: Andhra, Pundra, Pandya, and Kerala. The sun was again rising on the horizon. We had outrun night but not Vali, and Sugriva's feet were barely heeding his commands. Defeat flickered every time he blinked.

"Look!" I cried.

Up ahead, we saw the great mountain Malaya, the abode of Agastya, the Holy One. Sure enough, Vali quieted down. Even the craziest Vanara had sense enough to rein himself in before the sages, for with one look or word, Agastya could reduce our entire lineage to ashes, or frogs, or eternal torture in Patala's fires.

"Permission will be granted to us," I promised, "but not to Vali to cross into the next region!"

I could not know this for certain; Holy Ones were as unpredictable as the tempest, but they rarely turned away those in need. With shelter so near, Sugriva beat off his weariness, leaping with double speed. I could feel the hairs on my neck rise; Sugriva's eyes looked ready to pop out of their sockets. As we stepped into Agastya's sanctuary, we composed ourselves. Vali's anger clung to us, but he had to hold back. Unlike our monkey brethren, we could restrain our maddest impulses. Vali knew we would be as good as dead if we brought our strife here. The Holy Ones had no patience for us. To them, we seemed like spoiled children, squabbling over toys. Sugriva and I made sure to keep our anguish at bay.

The sacred fires blazed bright in every corner of the ashram. The sound of mantras lulled us into a sleepiness we could not yet afford. Half our size, Agastya dwarfed us. Physically, we were far more powerful than he. But can physical prowess ever trump the mind? We humbly requested his permission to cross into Tamraparni, the haunt of crocodiles. He detected Vali behind us, a ghostly shadow.

"Will you never learn," Agastya inquired, "that forgiveness is the path to peace?"

"I am ready to forgive," Sugriva said, "but my brother is not."

"Do not blame external forces for your plight," Agastya said.

Sugriva took a deep breath and hung his head. I admired his humility; it was a bitter drought. How was he complicit in his brother's enmity?

Agastya looked intensely at the glowing jewelry secured at my waist. I wanted to assure him I had not stolen them, but he spoke first, curtly: "You will find reprieve. It's as close as a forgotten memory."

Sugriva startled awake. Reprieve? Were we destined to live, then?

Agastya dismissed us, giving us leave to proceed. As soon as we could, we broke into a run. The few minutes Vali would spend with Agastya was our only hope. To find a place to hide and rest. The eyes of a hundred crocodiles peered at us in the light of the sunrise. Where could we go? We moved quietly, seeking a hiding place. Vali would expect us to run, so we did the opposite: We crept up a tree without even rustling a leaf, so close to Agastya's ashram that the fires painted half the tree orange with its flickering light. We flattened ourselves against a tree trunk, hidden by the greenery. I curled my tail around a sturdy branch and made sure Sugriva did the same. I had pushed him far beyond his own limits, and long after we settled in, his chest still heaved. Our eyes darted toward any noise, wary of Vali's approach, but Sugriva *had* to rest. Unwillingly, I admitted I did too. We had leaped farther into the southern terrain than either of us had ever been. Even in my sleep, we ran—and landed, my feet before Sugriva's, pushing down the Earth, a tree, a mountain. Jump! Run! Escape!

And everywhere I turned, I felt the iron current of my own life, urging me forward. So this was the heady scent of Daivi, one that every Vanara yearned for more than for a mate, honey

wine, or a fight between equals. Daivi was our goddess, the one we prayed to, the one whose call we revered. Like all other Vanaras, I had awaited the call, expecting it. I'd seen so many fall under her spell. She was the igniter of our pettiest squabbles and our grandest ambitions. When a lifetime friendship turned sour, Daivi was invoked. When two people fell in love, it was Daivi's will. Gods and humans followed dharma like slaves, their every action dictated by that law. But our Daivi was gut instinct. Commands from within. Who could dispute it?

I'd yearned for that command, but I'd never felt Daivi in the slightest. A full-grown Vanara, I'd grown resigned: I would not be one of the fortunate ones. It was my betters who knew that call. It was they who directed my life. It was those like Sugriva and Vali who spoke with an authority that only her touch could provoke.

Yet in the span of a few days, I now knew my goddess intimately. Two commands in less than five days. Her call was impossible to ignore. She commanded me to save Sugriva, and then she flung a collection of jewels from the sky directly into my hands. I kept the jewelry close to me, even when Sugriva eyed it critically. He did not press me, for there was no time. I was the wind under his feet, the compass of our flight. I was the servant, the leader, the advocate for his life. Without me, he would already have perished.

By running from our king, we were fugitives, outcasts, anathema. But I *knew*. Once we stood before our people again and spoke that one word, Daivi, they would know. I would spit it out from the depths of my being. Her name would ripple across their furs, would subdue their tails, and they would *know*. We'd acted only on her command. Or I did. And Sugriva followed. On his own, he would never have run, never broken from the clan. He was tied to Ruma, his wife. He would not have run from his brother, his king, his executioner. When I'd seen Sugriva's majestic back bending, accepting Vali's decision to execute him instantly, everything within me awakened. I'd gone to his side, whispering that one word that is sacred to us all. The breath he took was like his first. Ravaged, awakening to a new life. He turned with me, and ran. And ran. And ran.

Rejecting the death sentence was another death sentence. But all I knew was that we would live. Reason could not explain it. From then on, my trajectory was set. Or so I thought.

Then, midleap, Daivi's second command came to me, the answer to a prayer I never uttered. In my dreams, I saw again the sight of the crying queen in Ravana's grip. I felt the world's suffering. The millions afflicted. The life/death struggle. The next, our own, became the only one again. Sugriva and I had squeezed into the crevice of a mountain, grave as shadows, eyes fixed on the ominous sight. Sugriva had gripped my arm, detecting my Daivi cleaving away from him, toward the woman, glowing in a golden garment. But nothing could have stopped me from jumping up to catch the jewelry. The bells had tinkled and glowed, fit for the gods. I caught a golden anklet, a necklace, and a pair of earrings. Sugriva had looked at me, shoulders tight with panic. Two separate instincts now warred within me: to save Sugriva, to save the queen. To know these destinies was glory, but one was plenty; two was pain. How could I be pulled in two separate directions by the same goddess? Why did Daivi do this to me?

The agony made my eyes dart under my sleeping eyelids. The rest was not restful.

Sugriva and I woke up at the same moment. I felt the imprints of the anklets against my skin. Questions flooded me at once. Thousands. Two Daivis demanded answers. Our shelter from Vali was "as close as a memory." What did that mean? Where had Ravana taken the crying queen?

I had to stick to Daivi's first command. And so it was: I would live or die with Sugriva, my master. Sugriva and I began to confer in whispers. Sleep had restored some of his innocence, and he looked again like the king I'd known: valiant, with round, hopeful eyes, noble like the sun. He insisted that Vali couldn't possibly keep pursuing us. Vali had Kishkinda, an unruly kingdom. One didn't leave it long unattended. He had his wife, Tara, and his son, Angada.

The morning light made Sugriva's tawny fur shine golden. His amber eyes were unclouded. Our tails were still curled around the branches, keeping us anchored.

"Your brother must have a weakness," I whispered.

"None," he answered. "Why did you save me, Hanuman?"

"You are not yet saved," I reminded him grimly. "Why does Vali wish to kill you?"

"You heard his words: I left him to die. When he fought with Mayavin, that savage bull monster, I pounced on my chance and put a boulder across the cave opening. I betrayed him."

"But that is not true! You thought he was dead. You were devastated!"

Sugriva was silent, his tail drooping. Every one of us had thought Vali dead. The entire kingdom had mourned him, a Vanara so grand, so majestic, the rest of us had longed for just one word from him. I had not yet received a word of approval from our great king. Our race had been created for a very specific purpose, one we always searched for. In our minds, Vali was meant to be that heroic king, the very orchestrator of our collective Daivi, as persistent as hunger. And then he'd been dead. I'd grieved along with all the others.

I examined my memory. When Sugriva returned without Vali that day, had there been a hint of deception? Had his sorrow been a charade? But no. His grief had been true, his certainty real. Mayavin's great bull body, with its long, pointed horns, its sharp cloven hoofs, and its massive hind flanks, made it possible to believe that Vali had finally found his match. And yet, as I watched my master now, grim resentment lined his brow. Sugriva wasn't telling me everything. What was he keeping from me?

We had rested less than an hour. Agastya's ashram was quiet. Hundreds of sages in morning meditation increased our feeling of safety. Silent crocodiles basked in the rising sun.

"When Vali returned, you could have contested his claim to the throne," I said. "You could have had him surrounded and imprisoned. But you didn't."

Sugriva had acted impeccably in Vali's absence. He ruled with deference to Vali's system and took advice from Vali's queen, the astute Tara. Then, like a true disciple, he had given it all back to Vali the moment he reappeared. That's why he needed full support now to stand up to a brother he'd never before challenged. Sugriva sighed, exhaling so forcefully that the leaves trembled.

And that's when I heard something. I stiffened, moving only my eyes. Sugriva turned to see what I saw. Flat on the ground, not far from us, was Vali. He moved slow as a reptile, eyes fixed on our tree, and a large host of spider monkeys followed him. We were surrounded. They hoped to ambush us and kill us in our sleep. Sugriva and I looked at each other with dawning comprehension: Vali would not give up. Madness had taken hold of his mind. He didn't think of Kishkinda. He didn't think of his family. He had set everything aside to achieve one aim: Sugriva's death. For a moment, the desire to give up flashed in Sugriva's eyes.

"If that queen could fight, in the arms of Ravana," I hissed, "then you can too!"

Our tails curled together in solidarity. Pressing down into our haunches, we launched away from the tree, into the air. We had rested; Vali had not, and his reflexes were slower. We were about three seconds ahead of him, but the spider monkeys were everywhere. They rose up from the trees like bats out of a cave. A black storm cloud, they pursued us, using their long arms, legs, and prehensile tails to catapult forward. I prayed Agastya's wrath would not strike next, for the noise they made was no less than a chattering thunderstorm. Soon, handfuls of them clung to my legs. I leaped up the treetops. They crashed into my back, biting, scratching, shrieking. I flung them off, but they persisted. Soon, Sugriva was covered in spider monkeys, only his golden mane visible. Neither of us wanted to kill our own, but on Vali's orders, they would kill us.

I ripped them off my body, dashing them against branches, and prayed for their swift liberation. I slaughtered twenty, forty, one hundred. Sugriva's fight doubled that count. Still they attacked, and Vali was gaining ground. I held a handful of them by their tails and swung them around. Blood squirted from their nostrils and mouths, spraying on their kin. This finally gave them pause, their round, black eyes watching us unblinkingly. It pained me to kill those who were innocent and so much smaller than me.

"Hanuman!" Sugriva shouted.

Vali was so close, I could see the sweat darkening his fur. I let go of the spider monkeys, hurling them in Vali's direction. As they crashed against his adamantine chest, he growled, advancing. With unspoken agreement, Sugriva and I hurled ourselves into the mass of spider monkeys, shape-changing. Chattering in agitation, they leaped from branch to branch. So did we, now two out of thousands of spider monkeys, lost in the masses. Vali pounced, ready to extinguish every last one of them just to find us. As he slaughtered them mercilessly, they scattered in protest, shrieking and fleeing, missing limbs and tails. The tree trunks bled monkey blood. Sugriva and I swung toward the periphery, acting exactly as our borrowed forms dictated. We swung about in circles, as they did. We scratched our heads and armpits; we bared our fangs; we slapped our cheeks. The poor creatures were too confused to actually escape their so-called protector. Their death. As soon as we reached the outer edges, we resumed our forms; we needed our Vanara powers to maximize our leaps.

Vali barked, throwing himself our way.

"Father! Father!" I called out, begging him to favor us.

I seldom evoked my father's true support. The wind grew beneath our feet.

"Father! Father!" Sugriva cried. He seldom called for his.

The sun glimmered, casting a blinding light into Vali's eyes. He shrieked, understanding what we'd done. And the next moment, he called for his father. A crack of lightning pursued us. Indra, lord of the gods, was coming to his aid, but our godly fathers would not battle for us. They showed their love by small favors but would not intervene.

We bounded off, straining with all our power. I worshipped my father's forceful push against my back. He lifted Sugriva too, flinging us far beyond our own capability. We flew over Ayomukha, the great mountain embellished with metal ore. The fragrance of the sandalwood trees filled our nostrils for a moment. Then my father withdrew, setting us down gently on a majestic gateway of gold decorated with pearls and jewels and built in times long gone.

Best of all, we could not see Vali. It was the first time we had felt his absence. Sighing once, as if our bodies were one, Sugriva and I turned our eyes onto our path. Whichever way we turned, we saw only the roiling sea. Fueled by sheer desperation, we bounced on the heads of sea serpents and skidded on waves. We swam and somehow made it past the ocean to Suryavan, then to Vaidyuta, which had trees laden with fruits all year. We had not seen or heard Vali since our fathers' interventions: we began filling our stomach with the delightful fruits, when my tail snapped to attention. Truly, it was my sharpest sense. Vali again!

With fruit juice dribbling down our chins, we took flight to the Kunjara mountain, whose name we gleaned from what was below it: the immense and legendary city of Bhogavati. It was protected on all sides by the unassailable Vasuki, king of serpents, the streets guarded by sharp-fanged, highly venomous serpents. As we leaped across the vast expanse of this city, winged serpents spit poisonous gems out of their mouths that burned and blistered my skin where the gems touched. Thankfully, they assailed Vali in the same manner. We escaped onto Mount Rishabha, tumbling down into the dreadful world of the ancestors, a place no living being must visit. Yama's awful capital, enveloped by total darkness, stripped us of our mortal bodies.

In that moment, Daivi was ripped from me, the future ahead a glowing vision.

"Sugriva!" I shouted.

He hovered beside me, ripped from his body. It was too soon; we were not ready. Our mortal frames were toppled to the ground, as if dead. I was connected to my body through my tail alone. If I took another step, I could never return. I knew this—felt it especially in the desperate quiver of my tail. Beyond this, there was no path for the living. We had come to the very end of the Southern Quarter. That is how far Vali had pushed us.

We heard him now, falling from Mount Rishabha, as we had. Vali tumbled past us, rolling at such speed, he didn't know what was happening. We watched his powerful body lose animation as he too was severed from all of his Daivis and flung into the land of the ancestors. His speed was such that his spirit was flung deep into the land of the dead.

Sugriva and I were arrested, staring into the darkness. Was this the end? Was our enemy dead? If Vali was truly gone, we would make our way back to Kishkinda, and Sugriva would again become king. It was a place that badly needed a ruler. Left unguided, Vanaras would descend to their monkey natures. Even our great goddess Daivi would become a thing thrown around to justify ill ends. She would become the ill-used mistress of drunkards. Knowing the entire south so intimately now, we could make our way back quickly.

Sugriva and I carefully stepped back into our bodies, joining again with our destinies. The relief I felt was an ecstasy, for I could feel her need all the ways I was yet meant to serve. Never did our eyes leave the spot where Vali's soul had disappeared. We turned our attention to his slumped form. Sugriva had neither the courage nor willingness to touch his brother's unconscious form. Gingerly, I turned Vali over. His tawny skin was warm to the touch. I looked at our great king, whose punishment we had resisted. At any moment, he might lift his claw and slice at my throat, but his golden eyes stared straight ahead, his slack jaw displaying his four mighty fangs. The mane around his face was tainted with spit from his own mouth. Yet there was much unspent power in his body. I did well to leave him, taking a step back. Every instinct told me to run, but we had to be certain. If the ancestors had claimed Vali, we would be free. We retreated to the top of Mount Rishabha. Our eyes were fixed on Vali's body.

The sun set, and darkness surrounded us on all sides. Ghastly noises gathered strength, as if the spirits were agitated by our presence. Harsh winds began to brew. The darkness intensified, surrounding Vali. His body twitched once. Slowly, he rolled over, and a storm of spirits descended. Vali shook them off, like a lion scattering flies, but just like flies on a cow's hide, they descended again. Something ghastly was taking place. The borders were growing too porous, the line between the living and dead less defined. Weighed down by ghosts, Vali pulled his feet, one after the other, coming closer to us with every step. Sanity bid us surrender, flinging ourselves at Yama's feet to become one with the Ultimate Daivi that awaits us all.

Instead, we fled. As if Yama himself had arisen, we bolted. The anklets at my belt tinkled. Little by little, I was coming to know what a ruthless mistress Daivi was, for the days turned into weeks. Vali relentlessly pursued us as we fell into a cycle of rest-run-rest-run—the rhythm of life shorn of anything but survival. Leaving the south, we turned east. We crossed the rivers Bhagirathi, Sarayu, Kaushiki, Kalindi, and Yamuna. These rivers were deemed holy, but that did not help us in the least. We drank the water deeply from the Sarasvati, the Sindhu, and the Shona, then swam down the rapid current of the Mahi and the Kalamahi, always with Vali as near as our own shadows. Could it be that we were propelled by the same power, toward a goal only she could see? I couldn't bear the thought, for only her mercy made me go on.

As we reached the end of the Eastern Quarter, the broad summit of Mount Mandara greeted us. We were faced again with an ocean. The sea, black as a storm cloud, was infested with great serpents. Beyond it was the mountain with the abode of Garuda: the mightiest of eagles, the bane of snakes, and Vishnu's carrier. We caught only one glimpse of that most wonderful eagle, the king of his kind.

By this time, questions no longer haunted me. I knew there was something Sugriva was not telling me. We knew a forgotten memory would give us shelter. Daivi was all around me and nowhere to be seen. We just leaped on, hoping against hope that somehow, by some chance, Vali would tire. The mountains Karna-Pravaranas and Oshta-Karnakas, immersed in the ocean, helped us leap away from the mainland. We sought refuge in the islands. Yava-Dvipa, with its seven kingdoms, rich in jewels, was home to all creatures. This land was mired in its own politics; everyone was killing everyone else. Beyond Yava-Dvipa, the mountain Shishira loomed in the clouds, full of waterfalls and forests. There, evil blood-drinkers seized our shadows, arresting our escape. What a comical sight that must have been—us running for our lives, held in one spot. We resisted until sundown erased our shadows. The momentum of our resistance flung us away like pellets from a slingshot. We were tossed in the air, flung upside down. Disoriented, we landed in a fantastical place. Ahead of us was the Ocean of Milk, white as a cloud, shores lined with fragrant silver trees. We stepped unwittingly into the Sudarshana lake, crowded with geese and shining silver lotuses. The Gandharvas, Yakshas, and Kinnaras immersed in love play did not appreciate our intrusion. They rose naked, readying to assail us. No one cared that we were running for our lives.

Thirteen yojanas from the Eastern Quarter, there was the golden mountain Jatarupa-shila. On top of this mountain, the thousand-headed serpent Ananta rested, worshipped by all beings. A triple-crowned golden palmyra tree rested on a sacred mound. It was like seeing living symbols filled with meanings we could not decipher. In one voice, we mouthed a prayer to this great guardian of the realms: "Protect us!"

But in our hearts, we knew we were doomed, for Vali would never give up, and we had already traversed the south and the east. And so we headed west, hoping for shelter there. But there was nowhere in the world Vali could not go.

A Ghastly Golden Island

With my back against the bejeweled wall, I've become stone. Every inch of the Ruby Room is covered in gems, the color of blood. No windows. I'm alone save for two silent maidservants at the door. The torch lamps flicker across the gems, reflecting like a wolf's eyes in the dark. I refuse every comfort offered to me: the bed with its velvet covers, fresh clothes, food and drink. Every time my eyes blink close, yellow flowers land on my skin. I startle awake to shrug them off, to call for Rama. To hear an echo of his voice calling for me.

"Are you alive?" I whisper. My heart throbs wildly. I don't want to know.

My mind races. I cannot sleep. Ever. Again. The wrenching emotions are not directed only at Ravana. If I escape—*when* I escape—life will forever be changed. The women abducted from Ayodhya so long ago were not welcomed back. None of them were.

"Rama, Rama," I whisper to the walls of my prison.

So many years ago, I had asked him what he would do if I was abducted, like those other women were. He promised that his love would always protect me. That answer was enough for me then, sheltered by his arms. Yet here I am.

When sleep finally overcomes me, I stand in a silent forest; the leaves don't even whisper in the night wind. I'm in the secret grove at Sharabhanga's ashram, where I first encountered Ravana. In the first year of our exile, a lecherous spirit had latched onto me. In his attempt to violate me, I was pushed toward my true nature, for as my anger grew, the fire in my belly did too. I kneel on the grass, looking at the charred circle where I stood; the circle of fire I conjured kept him at bay. The Earth cracked open, and with a fiery exhale, I flung this spirit into the Earth and sealed it shut. A piece of Ravana. That part of him is lost forever, incorporated into the elements.

I pluck one blade of grass, looking at the blackened tip. Whatever transpired here was so powerful that it left permanent marks. I understood my Shakti even less then, and yet Ravana's energy body suffered permanent damage in the process. If I did that once, how can I do it again?

I go to the altar and touch the smooth stone of the Shiva-linga, offering a wordless prayer. Ravana's cloying Maya reaches for me. Icy manacles wrap around my wrists. *You are mine now.*

I rear up, just like I did when he touched me. I become larger than life, greater than anything that can be captured: *I will never be yours!*

Then Rama appears. I run to him, my beautiful, irresistible, kind-hearted husband.

He stops me before I can reach him.

"Rama, what will you do?" I whisper.

"I don't know," he says.

The shock I feel is my memory. It pushes me out of the dream. But I don't want to wake up. I don't want to see the rubies glitter menacingly in the torchlight. I cling to the dream, to the memory. But I'm awake. When I asked Rama what he would do if I was stolen away, his answer had shocked me. *I don't know*, he'd said. I'd never heard those words from him. I've never heard them since. He is so vastly knowledgeable on a range of subjects. From state-craft to the names of flowers, Rama always knows. Night-blooming jasmine had engulfed the silence with its fragrance. I long for that smell now, the assurance of the past. Rama's final words echo in my mind: *If I ever lost you, I would lose the way to my own self.*

We are both lost. I'm pulled under into the deepest darkness.

My eyes blink open to a canopy of ruby necklaces above. Silken sheets and velvet pillows swallow me. They've moved me onto the bed! I have not slept in one for thirteen years. I stand up immediately, shrugging off the soft covers. What else did they do to me while I was unconscious? I move away from the bed, looking down at myself. My breaths come in short gasps. *Rama, where are you?*

The rubies sparkle pink and red. The two maids are by the door, silent, unblinking. I cannot remember ever being so cold. A single blade of grass rests in my palm. I pinch it between my fingers while I inspect my body. The golden Cloth of Essence is secure around me. My arms and waist are tender with bruises. The scrapes on my forearms are crusty with dried blood. I secure my crest jewel at the nape of my neck, the only ornament I did not discard. My scalp aches, and my tongue is dry. I feel like a skeleton, stripped of all flesh. Did I always know that I would end up here?

But I do not know where I am! I turn to the women at the door.

"Where am I?" My throat hurts when I speak. "How long did I sleep?"

The women don't answer. I landed here on the dark moon night of Chaitra, the first month of spring. The fog in my mind tells me I've slept a long time. When I move closer to the maids, I see to my dismay they are merely lifelike statues. A chuckle behind me stiffens my back. I turn slowly, knowing what I will see. Ravana stands at the head of the bed, leaning against a ruby pillar. I'm alarmed at my own disorientation. I didn't see him or sense his presence. He clings to the handsome human form he's crafted.

"Stand before me in your true form," I challenge. My voice quivers.

"Princess, you know so little about what gives me pleasure. I can take *any form* you want," he promises.

He is decked out in gold jewels, a purple silk cloth sweeping across his bare chest. I look past him, over his shoulder. He smiles and pushes away from the pillar, walking toward me, a gleam in his eye. Tension shoots up my spine. I become acutely aware of the violence he longs to perpetrate. The fate of every woman captive.

I back away. Turn and run. I fling open the ruby-red curtains, out into a hallway. Both ways are the same, doorway after doorway draped with heavy curtains. I can't stop my instinct to run, however futile. I escape down the palace hallway, past room after room identical to the one I've left. Only the gems differ. I run past a sapphire room, a tiger's eye, silver, lazuli. Emerald. Diamond. Crystal. My run turns into a shuffle. I must find an escape. I must. Ravana follows me calmly. The hairs on my neck rise as I feel his proximity. I hate myself for being a woman, for being a pawn that he could just snatch away. I hate myself for being so helpless. The blade of grass is still between my fingers. I have a moment to wonder how it came to be there. Then he catches up to me and matches his pace to mine.

"Here," he says gently with that mock-friendly voice, offering me a chalice. "Water."

I have never been so dried up. So thirsty. But I distrust him vehemently.

"Return me to Rama." My jaw hardly moves as I speak.

He sighs, as if I'm being childish.

"Don't you see," I say, flinging my hands out, "that this will lead to your death?"

My fingertips brush against the chalice; it clatters to the ground, liquid darkening the mosaic floor.

"Don't *you* see," he answers, "that refusing me will lead to yours?"

His presence fills the entire hallway, full of shadows and spells. It is so tempting to look him in the eye as I confront him with reality: "I do not fear death. *You* do."

I'm right: He emanates a pulse of anger; his gems sparkle with lightning.

"But there are other things you fear," he retaliates, sliding a finger across my cheek so carefully, it doesn't actually touch my skin. I clench my jaw and turn my face away.

"Come with me," he orders. "I want to show you something."

I have a choice, but one so small that exercising it has already lost its point. Withdrawing my mind from the present, my body follows his command. He leads me into a hallway where a handful of his consorts wait. Why have these women been singled out from his extravagant collection? His favorites, I presume. I look at each of them and try to smile. The corners of my lips do not quite lift, as if the effort is beyond my ability. They appear to be one lively entity focused solely on him; I can't distinguish one from the other. Yet I'm truly relieved that I'm not alone with him.

He leads us through the palace, every detail heralding his wealth. The richness oppresses me. Naively, I've thought only the righteous would possess such splendor. My eyes water and redden. It feels as though even the air serves Ravana, worshipping his name and then sending it to my nostrils so that I can scarcely breathe. As we begin to climb a spiraling stairway, my thighs protest. The group of wives follows Ravana, eager to let me disappear among them. First, I think it's out of sympathy, but then I feel their desire for him: *Look at me. Love me. Choose me.* Each of them is eager for a drop of interest from their lord. If only his attention would waver and leave me in the illusion of anonymity. But like an insecure person gravitating toward the most unforgiving judge, Ravana seeks the love of the only unwilling one. It's as if he's examining every particle of every breath I exhale. Just like one of his queens, he emanates his need: *Look at me. Love me. Choose me.*

I cannot. I will not. Whether Rama is alive or not, he's the one I love, the one I choose, the one I look for. This knowledge invigorates me as we continue our ascent of what seem to be never-ending stairs. I hold on to Rama's words from the dream memory, but all I can capture now is the final word: *lost.* It fills my will with lead. I can barely lift one foot after the other. I cannot see the end of the stairway; the zenith seems to be the sun itself.

"If your human lungs didn't need time to adjust," Ravana says, "we could have flown up." As if he showed me that courtesy when he snatched me away. As if he doesn't savor this excuse to make me obedient. His wives drink his words as if they are compliments. His voice makes a pulse within me snap at my bonds and chew at them, like an angry feline bursting to be released. We finally arrive.

The stairway opens up to a titanic terrace without a roof. I step out and feel the freedom of nature immediately. The sky is like a large parasol, protecting me from the glare of the universe. The mist in the air clings to me eagerly. My lips and cheeks become moist with droplets of dew, declaring their love. The Cloth of Essence begins to glow, satiny under my fingertips. I feel the life here, the vitality of the elements. Wind tickles me behind my ears. We stand on the highest tower, a golden city sprawling beneath us. The mist settles on my skin; my hair absorbs the moisture, adding extra weight to my braid. The view would have been breathtaking if I had any breath left to give.

I fill my nose and lungs with air and breathe in the consorts' perfumes—fragrances stolen from flowers that mingle with their personal scents. I turn from them, and my next breath is tinted with salt from the ocean. I look out over the citadel, seeing far into the horizon. I see hills, lakes, and forests that end at the turbulent sea. I look over my shoulder: the ocean. I spin to the back: the ocean. Every direction I turn, I see it—and my life force drains from me: I am on an island, separated from the land I've always known. I press the back of my hand to my lips. I didn't even suspect. Bringing me to this high tower, Ravana has shown me how truly hopeless my situation is. If Rama lives, how will he ever find me?

My face is frozen. I stop breathing. The wind plays with my hair and my garment. If only it could blow me away. Ravana holds out his hand to me.

"Behold my kingdom," he says, "comparable to no other in its wealth and splendor."

What he means is that I can see there is no way to escape.

"Become my queen. Every pleasure awaits you. It is you alone that I desire."

I look at the pinched expressions of his consorts. They murmur wordlessly; their jewels tinkle as they shift positions. He certainly loves to conduct his drama with an audience at hand.

I hold up the blade of grass, still in my hand. "I will address myself to this," I say, pinching the little green spear between my forefinger and thumb. "It is worthier of my attention than you are."

I look at the blade of grass. "If you lay dead, I would not lift my hand to deliver your body into the sacred fire. Food for vultures is a fitting end for a coward like you. You are nothing but carrion in my eyes. A spineless, gutless lecher and liar. You shame your entire race, as you drag them to hell with your blind lust. Why have your yellow-and-black eyes not popped out of their sockets, the way you stare at me?"

His rage is instant. The wives gape. Despite his careless words, Ravana doesn't like being insulted in front of his women.

"Do you understand?" I say fiercely. "I would not touch you with the smallest toe on my left foot."

If there is one touch that signals scorn, it's the foot's. Yet he tries to be cavalier. With a chop of his hand, he disperses the mist and clouds and calls forth the sun. A subtle blur of twenty shadows accompanies his every move. Light raindrops spray on us like small flowers from a tree. Another chop of his hand, and a rainbow appears; the queens gasp and clap, delighted by his manipulation of nature. For the moment, I'm forgotten.

I watch his power, seeing how the rainbows stem from his navel and arch upward into the sky. It's magic, pure and complex. But his hunger for approval is poisonous. His arrogance, his flippant use of nature, is disturbing, like seeing a revered elder made to dance like a puppet. Everything I see belongs to the Earth itself and will remain hers once he and I are gone. The Earth is older than he is, even if he claims millions of years as his. The contrast between him and Rama could never have been clearer: Rama uses his prowess to serve, not to impress. Unassuming and gentle, Rama fills the world with light. Ravana fills it with darkness.

My anger draws Shakti into my body. It rushes up through my feet, and I feel my connection to the planet, to *my mother*, shooting through the building, down into the Earth. As I reach down, she reaches up, meeting me halfway, solidifying roots that can never be ripped out. While he is busy conjuring rainbows, I reach out with this power to his navel and throw the blade of grass into his Maya, impeding his movement. The rainbows fade away. He flattens his hand against his stomach, feeling the stagnation.

"None of this is yours, can't you see?" I ask. "Have you learned nothing?"

I let the Shakti rise through my body, unfolding the pulsating thousand-petaled lotus at my crown. I've never done it before. Anger courses through me, quickening my breath, and I say to him, "You who have lived thousands of years have forgotten that you too must die!"

The lotus at my crown grows like the hood of a cobra. The queens cannot see it, but Ravana does. In this moment of sheer power, I flare up with light and blast it across the ocean. *Here I am!* Like sunlight shining through a storm cloud, I send out my signal: *Rama, find me!*

I'm seen by one pair of round, yellow eyes.

"Empty threats, princess!" Ravana spits out. "But mine are not. And hear me now."

With a closing motion done by one of his invisible hands, he tightens the energetic cords around me. The power flaring at my crown wilts, the petals rippling back into me. He steps close, his false, sculpted features twisted.

"Like a slave, I've bowed at your feet, Sita. You forget who I am."

Black clouds gather above us. I will never use my connection to the elements for such selfish reasons! I fight against the cords of Maya. I push myself toward the sky, past my body's limits. My resistance is futile. I feel like I'm trying to stand while an aggressor holds me down. My challenge to his dominance is pathetic. A graceless struggle. I give up. His wives draw nearer, surrounding me. They are extensions of him, willing to do anything he bids. Their cloying perfumes mingle into a noxious fume.

"Twelve months, Sita," he says. "You have twelve moons to come to your senses." He turns away, but looks at me from the corner of his eye. "After that, if you remain stubborn, I will slice your bones from your body, drink your blood as it gushes out of your veins, and savor the taste of your still-warm flesh."

I see a vision of my body crushed to a pulp, only my face intact. Blood everywhere. It is not my thought but his.

"There is no one in this universe that can defy my command!" he growls. The clouds thunder. "Not even Yama, lord of death. Come to my bed or not. I *will* enjoy your flesh while you breathe or when you're dead. I *will* drink your blood, suck the meat off your bones, and throw the rest of you to the crocodiles in Lanka's moats!"

Horror tingles at the back of my neck. "Do it now," I challenge. Heat splotches my skin pink. "Twelve months will not change my mind."

He bares his neat row of teeth, and I see the shadows of his sharp fangs. He takes a step toward me, desire and bloodthirst throbbing in the vein of his neck. But the clouds stop rumbling as one of the consorts restrains him. Her black hair shines in the sunlight. Her lips barely move as she says, "A man who seeks pleasure from a woman who doesn't want him is doomed to suffer. But a man who seeks pleasure from a woman who desires him is granted the highest pleasures. Don't waste your time on her, my lord. I desire you."

Only his chest moves with his breath as they wait for his decision. But I already know that he will not follow through on his threat. Not yet. A cruel smile grows on his lips. He intertwines his fingers with his queen's and allows her to pull him back.

"You will change, Sita," he says. "I know your heart better than you do."

On the climb down, he speaks about what he has seen in my heart. He describes my sister Urmila. He talks about my anger toward Lakshmana. And on and on, like a fortune-teller. I am faint from hunger, thirst, and defiance. Noticing my labored breathing, a queen comes to my side, the one who restrained Ravana.

"Take my hand, princess." Her voice is kind, sympathetic.

I gratefully lean on her. She is of my height, and I notice through my fatigue that her golden complexion is the same as mine. She kindly helps me down each step. When I look at her, she offers me a shy smile, but her eyes dart to Ravana, and I understand that we are under scrutiny. I want to learn her name, but Ravana has not paused his soothsaying. She cannot show disrespect to her lord even through a whisper. As he keeps talking, his omission is clear to me—so obvious, I'm sure his consorts must notice it. He never once mentions Rama, as if he has not seen the emerald light that is the color of my soul.

As they deposit me back into the ruby prison, I hold the helpful queen's hand, wanting to know her name at least. That's when Ravana drops an image into my mind so suddenly that I'm unprotected. It's a vision of him ravishing me, using me for his pleasure. I discard the image and forbid it from ever entering my consciousness again. This I can do, even when bound by his spells. Like most other women, I have shielded myself before from a man's unwanted attention.

I recall clearly the first time a man assaulted me with his gaze: I had just turned thirteen. Kings from all over the world had gathered to win my hand. Their desire for me was uncomfortable to bear but only one among them violated me with his eyes. Before the king of Kashi even tried lifting Shiva's bow, he looked at my thirteen-year-old body, doing with his eyes what he could not with his hands. It prepared me for the way Ravana looks at me now. I see the value of that adversity: Kashi prepared me for worse evils.

And you will meet the same fate as Kashi did, Ravana.

Rama had returned from battle covered completely in Kashi's blood. When Rama's face had split into a victorious grin, his teeth had shone white against it. And so I know that victory can look horrific. May a gruesome victory be ours.

As the days pass, Ravana moves me from one luxurious chamber to the other, hoping to sway me with opulent surroundings. I didn't know what it meant to be tired until now. It's a sickness that eats life from my spirit and my body. I have heard the very old in my family speak of sleeping but never feeling rested, living but not feeling alive. I know what they mean now. Even at the beginning of our exile, walking for miles and miles in the scorching sun, I was not this exhausted. The twisting pains in my stomach help me stay awake.

Sleep is deceptive. I maintain my own vigil. The fasting invigorates my spirit but weakens my body.

I'm huddled in a corner on the gem-studded floor, eyes closed. The marble might have been a relief to my feverish skin if it had not been my abductor's floor. The water they splash on me might have quenched my thirst if it wasn't from the demon's fountain. Whenever my eyes close, I have flashbacks of the abduction. I cannot shield myself from it; the impressions are already within me. My reaction to his touch is seared into my being.

I explore the Maya, probing it, assessing my mobility. My physical body is unchained. I can move my arms and legs any way I wish. But he has tightened my Shakti so close to my body, that I am my body. If only he caged my physical form and let my spirit free.

I hear the movement of the drapes at the doorway. Through swollen eyelids, I peer up at the person approaching. She wears a cream-colored sari, the servant's uniform.

"On the floor again, princess?" she asks me, putting her hands on my arms. "Come to the bed."

"No!" I protest, but it's only a weak moan.

She strokes my hair gently. "Come, put your head on my lap."

I sit up. I can feel the patterns of the gems imprinted on my cheek. My suffering is not the maid's fault; I will not blame anyone but Ravana. I take hold of her hand.

"Help me," I beg. "On my honor, his end is near."

My lips are dry and cracking; even mumbling is painful.

She looks frightened and pries her hand free. *No one here will help you*. With her mouth she says, "Let us help you."

But I do not want the help they offer. They only want to bathe me, wash my hair, oil my skin, perfume me, put me in fresh clothes, and present me to their lord, a repackaged gift. No wonder I am so tired. Every hour someone comes to coax me into agreement:

Sleep on the bed, princess.

Come take a bath.

Sit in this hot water tub.

Rest on this pillow.

Wear this. Wear that.

Eat this. Eat that.

I refuse and deny, protest and resist. Whenever Ravana approaches, screams rise up my throat. I feel his Maya always nearby. I fear I will succumb to insanity.

I stand on my tiptoes to see outside the window. Thankfully, this chamber has one. I reach my hand up to the windowsill. Dried leaves from outside lay perched there. All I can see are the branches of a tree and the sky, but there is a forest out there. Every night, I watch the moon grow fuller. Rama will at any moment burst into Lanka, a rising sun on the horizon. That's the vision I conjure again and again. Especially as Rama's birthday comes and goes. He would have turned thirty-one. I arrived in Lanka on Amavasya, the dark moon. The full moon marks two weeks in captivity.

As the moon rises, I feel the response in my body. My womb works to cleanse itself, and my bleeding will soon begin. I've been so focused on keeping track of time, I didn't think about my approaching cycle. Humiliation fills me at the thought of sharing this private time with my captors. During the years in exile, Rama and Lakshmana were very conscious of my privacy and rest.

As the full moon shines in through the window, I focus on my womb. I refuse to bleed in captivity. I turn from the window, pressing my back into the wall, and slide down to the ground. I close my eyes. My body begins to shudder in response to my intention.

"What is she doing?" I hear the maids whisper. "She's strange."

As I restrain the cleansing in my womb, I feel the warning arise. *If you do this, your womb may never be suitable for a child.* I have two choices. Bleed, and face the humiliation of doing so in captivity. Two, seal my womb, perhaps forever. Hesitation confronts me with my yearning. My heartbeat knocks wildly at the treasure of my unborn. Their mother, I deny them life. Hearing their call, I refuse to heed it. Knowing the cost, I do it. I pull the energies upward and stop my womb from menstruating. I *refuse* to mourn my unborn children. Ravana has taken enough.

As the full moon glows in the night sky, the doorway drapes to my prison are drawn apart with fanfare. I turn to see an elderly woman step in. I'm relieved it's not Ravana, but suspicious. She has been allowed to see me, so Ravana trusts her, but I cannot. Her skin is dark like night; she's sheathed in lime green and lavishly decorated, with a thick gold belt around her waist. Her anklets and jewels tinkle as she glides inside, the green dress glistening. I'm reminded of a naga—half snake, half human. She is clearly someone important; four servants trail behind her. I stand with my back against the wall, the moonlight shining in from the window above. Two servants rush behind her with a cushioned chair, and she sits down close to me.

"Princess, fruits for you," she says, having her peace offering placed between us.

Perched in a golden bowl, the assortment of fruits looks heavenly. Mangosteens, grapes, dates, figs, and berries in all colors and sizes. A delicious fragrance wafts toward me. My mouth salivates; my stomach growls. I make no move to pick one up.

"You must wonder who I am," she says.

When she smiles at me, her fangs glint. Under normal circumstances, I would offer a respectful reply to any elder, but my skin crawls despite her age and alluring presence. She looks like someone who has spent all day tending to her appearance. Her hair is coiffed, not a strand out of place; her face is meticulously painted to make her eyes more slanted, lips larger, cheekbones pronounced.

"Can you guess?" she prods. "I heard you're far cleverer than you look."

She leans forward and examines me thoroughly, crinkling her nose. "You look and smell like a human, but my son tells me you're not. What are you?"

"You are his mother."

"But I just told you that," she says, displeased with my lack of cleverness. "I'm Kaikasi,

the queen mother." Though I haven't seen his true form since the first day, I see the resemblance in her domineering eyes, her angular features.

"It seems that you've put a spell on my children," she continues. "First Shurpanakha, now Dashagriva. They speak of little else than Sita, Rama, Sita, Rama." My heart quickens when she says Rama's name. "Lately, Vibhishana cannot stop talking about you either. I've never heard such a fuss about a human before."

She still calls her son Dashagriva, meaning "Ten-Necks," instead of Ravana, the name he's earned: the One Who Makes the Universe Scream. Surely, she was the very first one he made wail at the moment of his birth. Curse that day.

"Then again, it seems very likely that you're not human at all." She leans back in the plush chair, toying with one of her bracelets. She whispers over her shoulder, "Is this the one we've been searching for?" and then to me, "Tell me something about yourself."

I'm her entertainment for the moment. But who have they been searching for?

"Why are you here?" I ask, my voice whispery. I breathe through my nose, as even the air passing over my cracked lips hurts.

"My youngest son has asked me to intervene. Vibhishana feels that your presence is disrupting our kingdom. I'm the only one Dashagriva listens to."

Vibhishana must be the one who radiated displeasure at my arrival. Kaikasi lifts one of her eyebrows. "Perhaps we may just have you killed?" She shrugs pleasantly. "My son needs his toys taken away sometimes."

Why does she threaten me? Can't she see that I would welcome death? I can feel my body eating its own flesh. I cannot cross the room without seeing stars.

"The last time I saw that cloth you're wearing," she says, "Anasuya wore it, all white and bland, like herself. No cloth in the world can hide her ugly face."

I'm stunned into silence at her insult and her admission that she knows Anasuya, that aged holy woman who embodies grandmotherly wisdom. Anasuya is the opposite of Kaikasi, who resists aging as bitterly as a snake resists capture.

"I'm sure I don't need to tell you this," she says, "since you've seen it with your own eyes. Anasuya really needed all the tools she could find, like that precious cloth, to keep Atri's eye on her. As if you can ever keep a man's eye from wandering." She huffs bitterly.

I feel like my head has just been filled with court gossip.

"Tell me something about yourself," she insists.

"I was born from the Earth," I say.

"A foundling! How pathetic. Not even your birth parents wanted you. You humans have a terrible custom of killing your own girl children. Barbarians. Or do you mean something else when you say `born from the Earth'?"

I don't truly believe that she is interested in me. Most people care only for themselves. I pull my legs in and cross my arms over my knees. I turn up my own scrutiny. If she is the only one Ravana trusts, then she knows more about him than anyone else does. Her skin is shiny, like the green silks that flow around her. She smells like fresh flowers and sandalwood.

"You are beautiful," I tell her.

I cannot remember feeling like that myself, full of life and vitality. Ravana's ceaseless ploys to break me leave me feeling old and misused. I hadn't realized how much until I see the contrast in his mother. The compliment works.

"I feel terrible seeing your condition," she says, tutting. "It doesn't befit a servant, much less a princess. Come stay with me. I will not let my son near you without your consent."

Anger flares; I don't need her protection! I breathe carefully to clamp down the words that long to spill out. I have the power to obliterate Ravana completely. If I curse him, the Earth will hold my hand and join my cause. Together with the elements of nature, I can turn the ten-headed king to dust. Then why don't I?

I don't know how to yet! I feel the potential. I feel my dormant potency, just beyond reach. A river rushing forcefully underneath a thick layer of ice and fire smoldering at the center of the Earth, hidden by layers upon layers of sediment.

Kaikasi stares at me hungrily now, truly interested for the first time. "Now I see why you appeal to our lord."

Our lord. She is her son's servant. Her statement has provided a natural opening for the question I want to ask: "How did your son become so powerful?"

"He was born powerful," she says proudly. The fanatic gleam in her eye is unmistakable. She almost slithers with arrogance. "His father is the esteemed holy one, Vishravas Paulastya, grandson to Brahma the creator. Yes, my children have sacred blood in their veins, even if their father is weak." She waves her hand, indicating some defect in Vishravas. "But in fact, it was on my encouragement that my son began his penance. It was because of my advice that he pursued the path of greatness. My son has brought us all with him to the highest echelons."

Her eyes glow, the epitome of the proud mother. Concealing my curiosity, I say, "Every mother takes credit for her children's success."

"Ha! But in my case, it's true. I was a trusting little girl when I approached Vishravas for children. I didn't even know the words to articulate what I desired. Imagine! I told him to divine it through his own powers, which he did. But then," and here she tilts her lips dramatically downward, "he informed me that I'd approached him at the wrong hour and therefore my sons would all be defective. Even then, I understood immediately the cruel nature of men. I begged him not to curse my children because of my misstep. I didn't even know the details of the act that makes children, not to speak of the proper hour for such things, according to these holy people. And yet my unborn children were already doomed! No wonder I couldn't stomach that man after I'd gotten the children I wanted. You'll see—all marital relationships end in misery."

I hardly know how to absorb the unexpected turn of information.

"My point is," she continues, "I would not let any disadvantage mar my children's future. So I remember the day clearly, so many thousands of years ago, when I took Dashagriva aside and pointed to the flying Pushpaka, belonging to his half-brother, the lord of wealth.

'Why does Kubera have such a magnificent craft, while we are forced to walk like paupers? All that your half-brother has gained comes from a boon from Brahma.' My son was such a clever boy, he immediately understood and set out to seek his own boon." She chuckles fondly. "He was so eager, he didn't walk far from his father's ashram in the Himalayas. With his first sacrifice, he outdid my highest expectations. For one thousand years, he fed the blazing fire, praying to his great-grandfather, the creator."

As she speaks, a mountain peak appears in my mind. She stoked her son's envy, manipulated him to covet what belongs to others. No wonder I sit in Lanka now.

"At the end of a thousand years, my son severed his own head and offered it into the fire." She clutches her heart. My intuition flares along with the fire in her memory. "Oh, the pain I felt seeing my son wounded. He refused any assistance, wanted no help with his bleeding neck. As we watched his head burn, he didn't allow any of us to come near him. The pride I felt at his sacrifice and the awe I felt when he dismissed the boon that could have come to him then. No, he set his goals higher. For ten thousand years, he mortified himself, offering his heads one by one, sacrificing his own body to gain Brahma's boons."

I pick up a plump plum from the bowl. Once, he was just a jealous boy goaded by his mother. The place of his first sacrifice sits like a jewel in my mind. Somewhere in the Himalayas, there is an ancient forgotten firepit.

"I cannot stay with you," I say.

I carefully place the plum back and push the golden bowl away, praying she doesn't notice the abrupt change of topic. A few mangosteens fall, rolling to the ground, ripe purple. Kaikasi bends forward and snatches one up. Just like her son would, she throws it into her mouth, without bothering to peel off its leathery skin. She chews on it loudly, smacking her lips, looking at me. Her gaze is uncomfortably similar to Ravana's: dominating and deceitful. She spits out the mangosteen seed.

"You are beautiful too, Sita. Despite your insanity."

Let me always be insane by their standards.

As she stands up, the servants rush forward and pick up the dais. Her lime-green dress clings to her old body. She turns to me one last time, evaluating me.

"You don't know how lucky you are that my son has chosen you," she concludes.

Once she's gone, my thirst has grown so terrible that it creates magic of its own. Truly, it's not me but my dry throat that invokes the golden vessel. My gift from goddess Ganga. I hold the vessel with both my hands and bring it eagerly to my mouth. The crystal-clear liquid is sweet and nourishing like honey. When I'm done, I return the vessel to Ganga. It simply vanishes from my hand. The sweet water fills me, clearing my mind. Kaikasi has certainly given me much to think about. Did Ravana want me to know the source of his powers? Why else would his mother, his self-proclaimed confidant, speak of it?

It's dark in Lanka. The two maids by the door are dozing. My eyes fix on a small object on the floor: one of Kaikasi's purple mangosteens. It's black in the darkness, like a tiny skull. In boasting of her son's accomplishments, the queen mother has pointed me to his weakness. Like any mortal, he has won his powers through effort. There is a way to undo him.

As I close my eyes and settle my cheek on the floor, I wonder what terrors await me here. None as painful as a life without Rama. I stand up to peer at the moon again. I feel like a deer, afraid and skittish, weak from fasting. But I'm visited by a flash of omniscience. I know that I am the only thing Ravana does not possess, the only thing left in this universe that he can desire but never ever have, so of course I am the bait, Rama is the hunter, and Ravana is the hunted. Not me, not me! This insight fills me with vigor. All my personal suffering is to bring Ravana to his doom. He is the hunted, not I. Knowing this, I settle into my most peaceful sleep since the abduction.

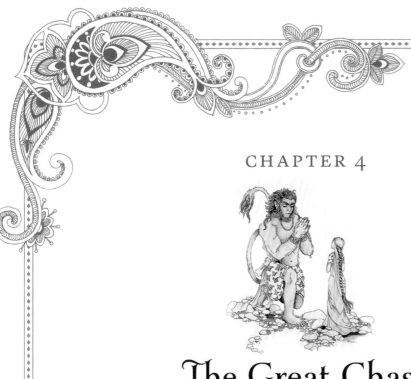

The Great Chase

Daivi made us run from Vali, but she gave us no sign! Half the world—south and east and no shelter. We plunged into the west with no plan, stumbling like dying men in denial. The hand of death rested on my shoulder, for to run with Sugriva made my spirit split in two. The cries of the queen echoed in my mind. Had I chosen the right Daivi? For the doubting soul, peace will be found in no direction.

Vali pursued us like an arrow released from a bow. What fueled him? Yet his initial zeal flagged, while our periods of rest grew longer. This was more excruciating; we did not know which shadow, which corner, which moment would reveal him. He was like the One with a Thousand Eyes, beholding us from all sides. We could trust no one.

We crossed through Surashtra, Bahlika, Shudra, and Abhira, with their lovely thriving countrysides. Certainly, we would feature in the nightmares of those regions. Leaping by, we grabbed their fruits, their other food—anything we could snatch on the run. We did not appear as benefactors. Children and adults alike were horrified by us.

We leaped into Kukshi, with its thick forest of trees and thickets, then onto a network of mountains and the western ocean, full of whales and crocodiles, and lined with coconut groves. After the cities of Marichi, Jatipura, and Angalopa, we crossed into the Alakshita forest. Where the mighty Sindhu River meets the ocean, we rested on Hemagiri, with its charming slopes. We saw a sight that might have astounded us in another lifetime: With apathy, we observed gigantic *simha* birds feed their young with whales and elephants. Herds of elephants trumpeted like storm clouds, grazing in the valleys surrounding this great mountain.

From there, we saw the western ocean and the Pariyatra summit, so rarely glimpsed. This was where the Gandharvas lived in the millions. We learned not to approach them too closely or take any of their fruits, for they would not tolerate it. Supernatural as we were, these beings of light had magic beyond ours. When they were angered, the glow from their bodies blinded us. The trick for us was to appear like ordinary monkeys. Then we could steal a small fruit here and there. If only that trick would work on Vali.

On the other side of that ocean was the mountain Chakravan, shaped like a discus with a thousand spokes. Next to it, the city Pragjyotisha, where the evil-minded Danava, Naraka, lived. There were enough caves there to get lost for a thousand years, but Vali had more experience than us traversing triumphantly through underground tunnels. We stayed clear of this tempting escape.

Beyond this was Meghavan, with ten thousand streams of waterfalls, full of boars and tigers that roared incessantly. We leaped onto the sixty thousand mountains, all the color of the rising sun, the foremost peak being Mount Meru. This was where the sun set, becoming invisible to all living creatures for a time. This was as far as we could go. Beyond it was an abyss of darkness, the end of the Western Quarter. We would not go near it, for the sight of the ghosts at the southern border had warned us. Something foul was unearthing at the ends of our world. The treacherous Kiratas had told us as much about the Eastern Quarter.

Again and again, I could see the dead bull Mayavin pawing the ground, hot air snorting from his nostrils. I demanded that my mind unearth one thing: the forgotten memory of the reprieve that the Holy One, Agastya, had promised us. It was clear to us now: Nowhere in the world was safe. Vali's fanatic single-mindedness inspired our own. We had traversed three-quarters of the known world. To give up now was not an option. It heartened me to see this new resolve expand Sugriva's leaps. He was twice as skittish as before but had but triple the determination to keep going.

"For Ruma," he often said, under his breath. She animated him even in her absence.

Part of me, I had to admit, enjoyed the Great Chase a bit too much. I had absolute faith in Daivi, even with her merciless ways. No one can sustain their path unless they find some form of sustenance in it.

As we turned to the final quarter of the world, the mighty north, whose crest jewel was the Himalayas, my obsession with the forgotten memory grew feverish. I could think of little else. I held up the jewelry dangling from my belt to examine every memory I had. Maybe the glowing jewels would share their magic with us. Then I'd quickly stow them away, hiding them from sight lest the two conflicting Daivis obscure each other!

But how to retrieve something you cannot remember?

The memory! The memory!

We ran through the countries of the Mlechhas, the Pulindas, the Shurasenas, and the Prasthalas. I begged Sugriva to quest through his mind, to remember the forgotten. We continued through the Bharatas, Kurus, Madrakas, Kambojas, and Yavanas. Wherever we went, humans cried out, "Monkeys!" only to choke on their own assessment. Were we monkeys, or men? A monkey would say, "man"; a man would say, "monkey." We did not stop to explain our divine ancestry, our mixed blood, our supernatural powers.

We leaped into the Shakas, Arratakas, Chinas, and Parama-Chinas. The Niraharas and Daradas. Everywhere, they reacted with the same amazed dread. Then we at last traversed the mighty Deva-Daru pine forest. Refreshed by the fragrance from the trees, I felt a memory skim close, just out of reach. It snorted at me like Mayavin, the bull, the very demon that had inadvertently caused all this. I couldn't understand it.

While I grappled with this, we reached the mountain named Kala, with its caverns and caves. Beyond it was an open space, without mountains or trees. The dust and sand in this horrifying wasteland prevented us from leaping. We were reduced to hopping like rabbits across the vast terrain. In my mind, I caught hold of the horns of the bull, looking into its eyes.

"Tell me!" I demanded. "Tell me what I've forgotten!"

"Hanuman," Sugriva cautioned in a dry whisper.

The sun pounded our heads. There was no water in sight, only dunes. I knew this was not the time to grapple with imaginary bull demons, yet I couldn't stop. As we walked, I could see the bull's mighty body disintegrating into a skeleton.

"Sugriva," I said in a hoarse voice, "I cannot stop thinking. About this skeleton. A bull skeleton."

He did not answer. And then our red faces, drenched in sweat, saw the most welcome sight rising before us: Kailash, where Kubera's majestic dwelling was. The foothills were bright as the moon. The lord of wealth proclaimed his bounty through every sprig and bud. We took refuge in the vast lotus pond, filled with red and blue lotuses, frequented by celestial beings. When I shook my mane, the water droplets were like blood from the bull's corpse. Was I growing delirious?

From there, we crawled inside the Krauncha mountains, home only to seers. Beyond this was Mount Mainaka, with the scattered dwellings of horse-faced women. The hermit's lake was there, covered in golden lotuses, frequented by Kubera's bull elephants and his cows. Beyond that region was Shailoda, surrounded by bamboo cane, and then Uttara-kuru. There were rivers by the thousands there, rich with sapphire and emerald. Mountains bright as fire. This was the land of lovers, and we found no one single. Everyone was coupled and delighting in sensual pleasures. Despite the undeniable pull this had on our senses, we did not get sidetracked. Sugriva had Ruma, and I had Daivi. Besides, I could think only of a bull skeleton. Now it sometimes flew across the sky above my head as if it had been kicked a great distance. Hallucinations, or a memory piecing together?

The sight of all those lovers gave us hope. Vali was known for his love of women. Perhaps

he would get enchanted and forget us. Such fantasies gave us false hope—enough to appease our exhausted minds. Quite fittingly, it was in this place of unions that the bull skeleton and Vali began to converge.

Then we arrived at the Northern Ocean, from where we could see the Soma-Giri, the source of radiance in that sunless region. There dwelled the blessed one, the soul of the universe, the creator Brahma. By no means could we go farther north, for no path lay ahead. Those who crossed beyond there had never again been seen. Untouched by time and sun, it was a place no one could return from. This was the end of the world. The end of our hope.

To my great dismay, Sugriva was drawn to it like a magnet. I understood the pull of the void. Sugriva's frame had turned lean and taut, every muscle and bone outlined. In many ways, neither of us had ever been so powerful, so vibrant, so challenged to the edge of our capacity. But as is often the case, neither had we been so mentally exhausted, so pushed to the edge of our faculties. As we had been pursued by Vali, his relentless presence had grown large in our imagination. We both feared now that accepting Vali's decree was the only Daivi.

Gazing at the sunless place beyond the northern peaks, I demanded answers. The time for sweet words, cajoling, and praying were over: "Tell us! Show us!" I howled. "DAIVI!"

That's when Sugriva said a name: "Dundubhi."

And the world shattered into a million pieces. A crack of lightning: the forgotten memory!

I saw it all then, as if I was the one who'd kicked Dundubhi across the forest, away from Kishkinda, hurling it a yojana away. I fought down the gigantic bull, crushing his neck and deafened by his dying bellows. I kicked his corpse into the sky. Then I became the sage Matanga, sitting in meditation, feeling Dundubhi's hot blood splatter across my face, seeping into my closed eyes. The corpse landed in front of me. Enraged, I pronounced a curse: "Whosoever did this will die instantly if he ever disrupts my ashram again!"

And of course, Vali had been the one. Vali slew Dundubhi and, later, Dundubhi's son, Mayavin. Vali was barred from Matanga's ashram: Rishyamukha. The place where Dundubhi's corpse had landed was just a few yojanas from Kishkinda—close enough to hear the nighttime revelry emanating from our great city.

We had run across the worlds, when the One Place Vali Could Not Go was so near our home. Sugriva and I looked at each other. Without a word, we turned from the north, back home to Kishkinda!

Clearly, Vali had expected this, for now he hounded us without pause. There was no rest, not even one blink. He chased us the way a leopard chases its prey. Any moment, I felt, he could reach out, catch hold of my tail, and throw me into the land of Yama. Behind us, he was a demon from Patala, our karma, our Daivi, our Everything.

We tore through the north, crushing everything as we fled. As we got close to home, our hearts beat with joy. After all the wondrous sights we'd seen, none compared to the ordinary gray slopes of Rishyamukha. Vali began howling thunderously behind us, chilling our blood. Blood pounded through my head, the channels for prana growing smaller and smaller. Soon, I could not breathe, but still we ran faster than any other being has ever run. The veins in my body, the muscles, contorted, changing shape, growing, swelling, dwindling, dying. The two of us, Hanuman and Sugriva, died a thousand deaths as we crossed threshold after threshold. Our minds were linked, our bodies doggedly obeying.

Run, run, run, run, run, run, run, run!

There was no line, no boundary, demarcating Rishyamukha from the rest of the forest, but we felt it. It was as if Daivi herself stood at the finish line, beckoning us. But Vali was gaining ground. The smell of him filled my nostrils. His breath puffed against my neck. His nails scratched across my back, ripping out flesh. His hands reached past me toward Sugriva, the weaker one. His true goal.

"Daivi!" I howled. I swung Sugriva forward, flinging him away with all my might. Then, with the last ounce of strength I had, I threw myself blindly into Rishyamukha. Leaves and branches crashed around me. Curling into a ball, I collapsed next to Sugriva, and we fell to the ground. Crushed, defeated. We surrendered and waited for the death blow, for Vali.

But nothing happened. Slowly, I opened my eyes.

Our king stood just steps away. His abdomen heaved and his fangs hung out, but he was unable to touch us.

We lay flat on the ground, looking up at the sky. Not believing our luck.

My whole body bubbled with glee, with laughter, with joy.

Daivi, you saved us!

The Great Chase was over.

CHAPTER 5

Sky-Fallen

Darkness is attracted to light, and Ravana's Maya fills my chamber like Indrajit's malevolent smoke did on my first day in Lanka. It catches my braid and flings me toward the marble wall as violently as I was pulled from the karnikara tree. I'm thrown into the wall and brace myself for the impact that will crush my bones. *Rama, Rama.* My heart beats. But only my soul is being violated, not my physical body. Ravana's Maya drags me through room after room, wall after wall, but it cannot enter me or compromise my Shakti. But like a ball, I'm flung about and dragged out into a courtyard. A fountain stands in the center, depicting blood-drinkers capturing young girls. When caught, the girls spray blood through their mouths into the monsters' gaping jaws.

I'm dragged onward and away against my will, like a slave. The more I resist, the stronger the force is. The path is direct, as when Ravana flew across the ocean. Where is this Maya taking me? The push and pull grows so strong that I see our destination as a blinding light. The Maya tightens around me, keeping me small, shrunken. Then I'm placed down gently, just the way Ravana deposited me on Lanka's cold ground. The Maya retreats, just like he took a step back in Lanka, secure in the knowledge that I had nowhere to go.

The dreamscape is vivid: A small valley surrounded by mountains. Snow decorates the mountains, the peaks obscured by clouds. Before me, noxious fumes ooze from a pit of poison. The vapors flow by me, as constant as a river, laced with a burning, sickening jealousy to seize what someone else has. The feeling stabs at me, prickling my skin, wanting to possess me.

I understand where I am from the queen mother's description. This is the place where Ravana burned his first ritual fire. This is where Dashagriva, driven by his mother, began his journey to monstrosity. But it was he who nurtured the feeling, stoking the fire of envy internally and externally for one thousand years. The ground, the air, the entire atmosphere are all saturated by this powerful driving force. This was his prayer after all: to become richer, stronger, more powerful than his brother, Kubera. This is where he sacrificed his first head, praying to Brahma. If I came upon this place awake, would I feel the strangeness and the urge to turn away from a haunted place? I suspect that I would see only a deserted valley, the firepit long since filled with dirt, overgrown by bushes and trees. His secrets are well guarded, buried in half-forgotten memories. Protected by the Earth itself. How ironic.

The seconds tick by as Maya's force flows around me. Ravana's Maya dragged me here. Does he know I'm here? The force that pulled me here doesn't know what to do with me. It parallels exactly my situation in Lanka: I'm captive, but my captor does not know how to control me. He doesn't know what to do next. He's never met someone like me before. My will to escape awakens. Perhaps I can travel into the dreams of a well-wisher and tell them where I am!

But the dormant aggression of Maya awakens and grabs my wrists and ankles. This is not an escape route, just another ploy of his to assert his will over mine. I draw closer to the ashen firepit, stepping across cinders in it accumulated over a thousand years. Resting inside the blackened cavern is an emaciated ghost just like the one that accosted me at Sharabhanga's ashram so many years ago. He fixes his eyes on me, looking for a malaise, a place where his envy can grow and take over my psyche, my life. I stare back into his eyes, neither of us moving. His forked tongue, bright red like his eyes, darts in and out. I can hide nothing from his penetrating supernatural glare. I go closer. My hand darts forward. I hook my fingers into the sockets of his skull, and his body evaporates. The skull falls into my hands, heavy as a boulder. I dash it to the ground with all my might. It bursts into pieces but immediately reforms intact. There is no end to the terrible Maya here. I stomp on it. It turns to ash. Then reforms. I pummel it into the earth, I . . . I startle awake.

Just beyond the drapes of my prison chamber, an unfamiliar man speaks: "How can you keep her like this? It has been eight weeks!"

Has eternity been only that short?

"Very good, Vibhishana," Ravana replies. His tone is like acid on the skin.

"She is slowly dying!" Anger smolders in Vibhishana's voice: "No food, no water!"

"Your knowledge reveals your spies in my private quarters!"

"Let her go."

"Withdraw your spies at once. Do you think your concern for her supersedes mine?"

"If so, honor her will. Return her to where she belongs."

"She belongs to me. I'm doing everything in my power to nurture her back to life," Ravana says. "She will surrender. I'm sure."

The certainty in his voice chills me. What is he planning to do?

"We do not interfere with your personal affairs—you know that," Vibhishana says. "But your behavior has been odd since you brought her to Lanka. The word *obsession* has come up in the council. Even Grandfather Malyavan is concerned."

"Tell them to speak to me themselves instead of sending you as their maidservant."

"King, though you are my elder brother, it is my duty to inform you when I disagree with your actions." The formal tone indicates that Vibhishana has retreated from brother to dutiful minister. "There is something dark brewing here. I am not alone in my concern."

Ravana remains bitingly dismissive: "What can any of you possibly fear when I am your king? The only darkness I see is your disobedience to my will."

"What of Sita's will?"

"No one may see her without my permission."

"I'm asking for it right now, my king."

"Put your fangs away. Neither your formality nor your preaching will take you anywhere. There is no reason for you to see her. That's final."

My heart beats erratically. My hope that someone on Lanka will sympathize with me has found an unlikely target: Ravana's own brother. I stand up and step toward the doorway.

The maids reach for each other's hands, obstructing my path. They will not let me exit, just as Vibhishana will not be allowed entry. The sounds of their footsteps retreating echo with futility.

The maidservants signal that now I must follow them out of the chamber. I look for a sign of Vibhishana, but they take me to a great archway with a paneled door. Like everything else here, it is built for people much larger than myself. One of the panels swings open to reveal a woman who stands before me completely unclothed. Her golden-brown skin gleams with moisture, slick and smooth. I cannot recall that I've ever seen a grown woman naked before. The etiquette around my life as a princess did not call for it. Even my sister and I wore simple cloths tied around our breasts and hips once our cycles started. The woman notes my expression and smiles—or maybe smirks, perhaps deeming me a prude.

Because I don't move, she grabs my wrist and pulls me within. The panel closes with a boom behind us. I could never have imagined the scene before me. Though we are inside, there are waterfalls, pools, and lakes. The waterfalls cascade down from openings in the ceiling, so I do not hear the voices of the women thronging here. It seems that every woman from the Lotus Hall is present, but the stilted atmosphere from that night is gone. I have entered a fantastical realm, an enchanted water park, where there are only women. There is no shame, no need whatsoever for clothing. The women are at ease, their breasts moving when they laugh. The water from the many waterfalls flows into large crystal ponds. Many women sit at the banks, washing their hair, chatting, and smiling. They soap each other, comb each other's hair, oil each other's limbs. They pay scant attention to me.

Steam rises from one of the ponds. The women in it are all pink-cheeked. Bottles of perfume and oils stand in neat rows against one wall. A slender girl smells bottle after bottle until she finds the one she likes. One woman sits alone at the top of a waterfall, brushing her black tresses that are as long as mine. She is the only one whose eyes are fixed on me. The atmosphere is sensual and intimate.

My eyes have moved but not my body. The woman by my side tugs at my garment.

"Come, princess. It's only us women here. Don't be shy."

I sink down to the floor, my back pressed against the door. She sighs but leaves me. My braid feels heavy with the extra moisture. I suddenly yearn to loosen my hair and redo my braid. But even here I don't feel safe. Freeing my hair is something I've done only around my most intimate friends. With Rama.

At the opposite side of the room, a woman enters and undresses, adding her billowing silk clothes to a large pile of costly garments. I look down at the Cloth of Essence wrapped around me. My magical dress has stayed spotless and glowing for the twelve years since I got it as a gift from the wise Anasuya. Now it's ripped in several places and is a dull yellow, a reflection of my inner state. I am determined not to part with this cloth. Rama last saw me in this garment, and I will return to him the same way!

The golden-brown woman comes back with a bowl full of steaming water. She places it next to me and directs her companion to put a basket next to it, brimming with an assortment of oils and perfumes. She kneels next to me. Her wet hair drips onto my thighs.

"We are your friends. Wash your face. You will feel much better."

I wring my hands. She takes one and begins to towel it with a warm cloth.

"No," I say drawing my hand away. "Please no. If you're my friend, tell me how I can escape from Lanka."

She immediately withdraws, giving her friend a look. Before she turns away, I impulsively say, "Introduce me to your queen." There is a clear hierarchy here.

That makes her laugh. "Queen Mandodari does not bathe with us!"

Mandodari. It means "soft-bellied." A name has power.

"If she does not, then why should I?" I ask.

"You do not have her stature! Even if you were in the Ruby Room . . ."

"Yes," the one behind her chimes in. "Don't you know how many short-lived women like you we've seen come and go?" The look she gives me tells me I'm falling short of their expectation. If only Ravana would look at me that way. "And how many of us has Queen Mandodari seen come and go?"

There is awe in both of their voices, even though they've just admitted Mandodari's indifference to the victims of her husband's appetite.

"The queen will never bother to see you."

"She doesn't mingle with us." They shake their heads.

"But Dhanya-Malini wants to speak with you," the golden-brown woman says. "She's the one who held your hand all the way down the stairs. Remember?" She points to the woman alone at the waterfall, combing and drying her hair in a breeze from a small window. "She is his favorite."

"But we are not actually allowed to speak with you," she whispers, as if suddenly remembering. "Later, when you become one of us, we will tell you everything."

"That day will never come," I say with forced dignity as I sit there, half-wet, my hands slipping out of my own grip. They shrug and leave me.

I remain seated, watching a stream of women come and go. They all enter and exit through different doors, only one of which I can see. This bathing hall is built so marvelously, I can't find a comparison, emphasizing again how otherworldly Lanka is. Some of the women take quick baths; others stay longer, playing with balls, swimming, jumping into the ponds, amusing themselves. It must be true that they are not allowed to speak to me, for no one approaches me again—not even Dhanya-Malini, who is not *the queen* but a queen among the consorts. And what does this queen want? It has not escaped my notice that some of them might carry ill will toward me. I know enough about harem intrigues not to be fooled. Despite their friendly banter, these women are rivals.

I examine the room carefully. Perhaps there is some avenue of escape. Although I know I'm stranded on an island, I cannot restrain these thoughts. There are stairs, platforms, and alcoves everywhere—many places to hide. Where is the water coming from? And where does it drain out? Just as I begin contemplating this, the door behind me swings open.

I nearly fall to the ground but catch myself quickly. It's the maids from my chamber, come to fetch me back to the room. Their master waits, and he will not leave me alone for long. Hardly an hour has passed. In the chamber, a handful of servants stand at the ready, waiting for me. Clearly, they've expected me to be fresh and clean. Each one holds an assortment of jewelry, dresses, and other adornment. A servant stands holding a large mirror. The objects gleam with ethereal power, designed for gods. Ravana lays on the bed, legs sprawled, eating a juicy pear. He glares at me, disappointed by my appearance.

"Why do you hate yourself?" he asks.

He sees my denial of his comforts as that. He gets off the bed and starts picking out jewelry, trying to tempt me with the most exquisite pieces, finely wrought crowns with large, sparkling gems. He dangles them in front of me, expecting my frivolous woman's nature to take over. Oh, jewelry! Oh, dresses! Oh, pretty things! He assumes these costly items will seduce me, call to me. I walk to the other side of the prison, standing under the window. It's true that the jewelry I'd worn since birth meant something to me. I wore the pieces faithfully even in the forest. I'm bare now except for the small crest jewel at the base of my skull. My attachment to this small jewel swells, the very last connection I have to my father, to my previous life. I wonder if Ravana has noticed it. Will he take it from me once he discovers its value? Immediately, I force my mind to think of something else.

"I want to meet Mandodari," I say.

I have my back to him but know he does not like my request. I hate how well I already know his subtle cues. Or else he just isn't very subtle. I hear him putting down a heavy piece of jewelry.

"Mandodari doesn't approve of my being here," I venture. "She wants you to let me go."

When he gets angrier, I know I'm right. His energetic swell is unnerving.

"You know a lot about Mandodari without having met her," he muses.

"She wasn't there on the night of my arrival. She never mingles with the others."

"One of these things you have observed. But the rest . . . her name and her attitude, these someone has told you."

"Yes, they told me that Mandodari is far superior to me!" I cry, turning around. "Why do you insult this great woman, your true wife, by dragging me here? Why do you covet me when you have Mandodari. Or Dhanya-Malini, your favorite!"

"Women!" He spits the word out like a curse and overturns one of the platters with jewels. "I send you for a bath, and you come back as filthy as before, your mind full of gossip!"

He flees—or so I imagine, until he returns with the two women from the bath. I'm sitting on the floor in a corner, as far away from his wealth as I can. When I see the two helpless women, I stand up immediately. They cower, naked, in his grip. The maids standing at the ready with adornments don't move at all.

"Was it these two?" he demands.

When I see the terror in their eyes, my own rises. I step forward but have to steady myself against the wall. My belly is empty. My throat parched. He has wrapped his hands around their necks. "Let them go!" I cry.

"I will," he says and slashes his nails against their necks. His nails grow sharp in the split second it takes to slit their throats. They sink to the ground, holding their necks. Gurgling. I run forward toward them. He stops me with a warning hand. His nails are short and harmless again. "Don't forget they die because of you."

The anger I feel is immediate and immense. "You will die for this! Rama may forgive you, but I will not!"

His hands hover over the dying women. Red blood spills out around their necks. The moment they take their final gasp, he pinches the air. Their souls hover in his grip, already tethered to him as they were. Shocked, I inhale sharply; his consummation of them wavers for a fraction. Their essence draws toward me and touches my Shakti. And then he swallows them.

Without looking at the servants, he waves his hand toward the two bodies and leaves. As the maids drag the bodies out and clean up the blood, I just stand there. I remember the way I cried the first time I saw a living being die: a great black buck killed by Lakshmana in self-defense. I have seen a blood-drinker die, a giant that tried to abduct me. But I've never seen a woman murdered, the most atrocious act, second only to killing a child. But I don't shed a single tear now. Instead, I make a promise that their deaths will not be in vain.

I have to escape. I have to escape. I have to escape. I know nothing else but this. I'm fixated on nothing but this. How? How? How? My initial instinct to make one of the consorts my ally is gone with one sharp flick of his nails. I cannot implicate any of them. I need to act now before he returns.

"Take me to the bathing hall," I tell the maids.

They look at each other but do as I request. They know it's their lord's desire to see me clean, after all. I've grown so weak, I need their help to push open the doors. "Thank you. I will heed your lord's wishes."

They accept my lie. The bathing hall is less crowded now. The women avoid me completely. They must know what happened to the two who talked. The less they look, the better chance I have. Because I have no grand plan, I follow my naked instinct. I walk across the hall, careful not to slip. I approach the waterfall where Dhanya-Malini was. Without looking around, I walk up all the steps to the place where I saw the favorite combing her hair. That breeze had to come from outside. Yes, the wind is strong here at the top of the waterfall. I can touch the ceiling with my hands. My heart thumps faster when I see the dainty window, open to the elements. I peer out and see a sorrowless tree with flaming red flowers in bloom.

I squeeze myself through the window. Hanging out by my torso, I reach frantically for the branches, catching only leaves and flowers. I push away the floor inside with my toes, and reach. Flowers fall to the earth. I start falling out and finally grab a tiny twig of a branch, enough to pull myself out. The elements greet me so warmly. I have the strength to grab onto a sturdier branch. I'm outside. I've escaped. My breath comes in short gasps, but the air is warm and breathable. I move closer to the trunk, deeper into the foliage of the tree. I try to hide from the window, but I have to move soon. Not much escapes the one with ten heads. But even he is not omniscient!

Between the branches, I see the white palace walls extending in front of me. I climb to the other side of the tree, hiding myself from the spying eye of the small window. On this side, I see an overgrown forest full of sorrowless trees, their red flowers like bursts of fire. The wind is warm and pleasant, and I long to bask in the sun, but I have to be fast. I climb down the tree, clumsy and awkward. As soon as my feet touch the ground, I run to the next tree, hiding under its flaming red flowers. And then the next. And the next. The flowers and leaves tickle my skin like the reassuring touch of a friend. I'm free. Birds chirp; wind rustles through the leaves. As I run for cover under the next sorrowless tree, I peer up at the blue sky. The sun, like Rama, gives me life. I look back only once, dismayed to see how close I still am to the whitewashed walls.

A small deer with white flecks pauses to watch me. My heart stops: The last deer I saw was the golden one with the rainbow tail. My doom. The trap. Quickly, I hurry before I can relive the moments leading up to the abduction. I begin to run more recklessly, ignoring the pain in my lungs, the utter exhaustion of my limbs. As I run, I call out toward the elements, blasting out my Shakti as I did to repel Ravana: Earth! Fire! Wind! Water! Sky!

To my immense surprise, the wind gathers around me, and I run more quickly. The fire at my core flares up. At the center of the Earth, I feel it roaring. The Earth trembles under my feet. I fling my Shakti up toward the sky, like an eagle about to soar to new heights. For a split moment, I am the sky, looking down on myself running through the blooming sorrowless forest. The next moment, I'm flung back down into my body, so harshly that I tumble and fall.

SITA.

He calls me, but not with his voice: with his cursed Maya. He flings me down. My face hits the ground. It softens around me, cushioning my fall. Still, I have dirt in my mouth and eyes.

SITA. Again his voice, so loud in my ears that I punch my fists against them. I start crawling away, trying to get on my feet.

Sita. My elbows buckle. The deer nibbles grass. Birds twitter. The hissing voice all around me that only I can hear. I scramble to my feet and run feebly now, strength expended.

"Sita!" His real voice, at some distance. My arms go numb.

I scramble for shelter, clinging to the nearest tree, just like I held the karnikara weeks ago. Tremors of excitement and terror wrack my body, like waves of a stormy ocean against the shore. The elements responded to me but then shut me out. His voice is still far away. The maids must have told on me. Yet why would they sacrifice their lives for me? For the sake of this foolish escape? Why blame those poor women when I know exactly what alerted him to my whereabouts? He felt me asserting my powers and expand into the sky. He threw me down.

Still, I am quiet. I hold onto the tree. My pulse syncs with it. *Hide me.*

He calls for me again. I hear footsteps by many pairs of feet. The sounds of weapons clanging. Harsh female voices. They walk in circles around my tree, and I dare hope that they will not detect me. Then a face appears through the branches, as hideous as Shurpanakha with her nose cut off. A terrible blood-drinker female.

"Found her!" she yells.

Was it by scent, luck, or deductive reasoning? I do not know. Others like her appear, parting the branches to look at me. They clearly find me as revolting as I find them. They use their sharp tridents to coax me away from the tree while shouting loudly, "Master. MASTER!"

Ravana has been flying to find me and now descends through the trees. For a fraction of a second, I see his ten-headed form before he assumes the human one. Looking at me up and down—I clearly feel the trail of his eyes—he exclaims, "Gods, you are beautiful!"

I stare at his feet. I'm covered in dirt, the taste of the earth still in my mouth. I cannot look anything but insane. But the elements were alive in me. A forgotten vitality still pumps in my veins. He sees it.

"Where did the power come from to command the elements?" he asks. "Keep asking the question, clever girl. You will understand."

Feeling the elements alive was sheer joy. His words taint my elation. Why did the elements respond to me now and not before?

Capturing me yet again excites him. My ignorance delights him. I take a step back, retreating into the tree branches. I will *not* go back into the palace. Ravana sees my resolve and orders the guards to put away their tridents. In his first act of true understanding, he allows me to stay outside. Before he departs, he ducks under the branches to stand under the tree. He smells like desperation and sweat. His hands are very restless, and I scuttle away.

"I'm growing tired of your reaction to me," he warns. "If I was going to force my way on you, wouldn't I have done it already?"

To prove his point, he tames his hands and leaves me alone. The blood-drinkers remain, weapons in hand. He gives them orders before he leaves. They tighten their grip on their tridents and turn toward me. It cannot be good. And yet I've escaped from the palace.

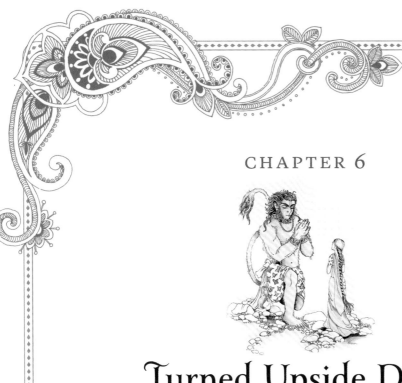

Turned Upside Down

Minutes after Rishyamukha became our only shelter in this world, the reality became clear: Vali's determination to kill Sugriva had just begun. His howls had alerted our Vanara clan. While the two of us still lay panting on the ground, they gathered behind him. All Vali had to do was point to us, and they came rushing. Our clan, our brothers-in-arms, our drinking companions, our childhood friends: they surrounded us unwillingly, giving us time to stand up. A terrible fight ensued while Vali watched. Prowling from side to side, he smashed his fists together again and again. But what Sugriva and I had lost in exhaustion, we had gained in mental power. We had traversed the entire world and found reprieve. Daivi's blessing stood between them and us. They saw it and knew they could not defeat us. We would kill every one of them. Vali allowed them to withdraw.

With their blood on our hands, we watched them retreat, but the warning remained: Vali had millions of shape-shifting Vanaras at his disposal, and they would come for us like extensions of Vali pouncing from every shadow. We had won an existence imprisoned in Rishyamukha, battling assassins. It quickly became monotonous. Holed up in a cave, Sugriva and I began to merely exist, day to day. My sole focus became Sugriva's spirit as he declined into depression. Without his wife and clan, he saw no future worth living. Shunned by our own felt like a slow death. How had we succumbed to this lowly feud, brother against brother? What could Sugriva and I do besides wait for Daivi to turn the tide?

And if there is one thing about monkeys, we have no patience for waiting. The worst part for me was that with Sugriva safe from Vali, the other dormant Daivi was forcefully awakened. Every day, I looked at the jewelry, searching for clues. Every day, I wondered if I should have acted differently. Could I have prevailed against Ravana? Unlikely. The demon king was immortal and undefeated. Still, I had daydreams about snatching the mystery queen from his arms. My mother would have said that I never stopped trying to swallow the sun. In other words, I dreamed of the impossible.

Days and weeks crawled by as slow as the Great Chase had been fast.

One day, as Sugriva stood basking in the sun, praying to his father, the fur on his skin started rising, his yellow eyes widened, and his tail hung limp. I knew not to touch him when he showed these signs of fear. Like most other animals, he had no discrimination in such moments. It was always uncanny to see him, so impressive in size and power, reduced to anxiety—not without cause, certainly, for there were assassins in every shadow. Sugriva pointed to something in the distance. I saw an unexpected sight: "Two humans."

"Yes, Hanuman!" Sugriva scratched his neck violently.

He went from initial paralysis to the next stage of agitation: restless movement. His tail moved rapidly. "Look at them! They cross into Rishyamukha, searching. Their weapons gleam in the sun. Sent here on Vali's order!"

Sugriva started moving in and out of the mouth of the cave: sunshine, darkness, sunshine, darkness. He waited for my assessment. The fur on my neck started rising ever so slightly. The two men were frightening indeed, covered in battle scars and loaded with weapons: bows, swords, and shields. One was the color of the moon, the other like the forest. If we became their target, I didn't doubt that death could carry us away before we could breathe, "So be it." Sugriva's fear was not unfounded, but I also saw an intense contradiction in their demeanors. They frequently backtracked to examine something they'd seen. Their method was random, aimless. I felt a pull toward them, as if they were masters and I a servant who had delayed my duty for too long. Suddenly, I relaxed completely as my body understood something that I did not. As Sugriva came out into the light again, he spoke, awakening me from a trance-like state. I shook my head vigorously. "Not assassins," I concluded. "But not ordinary."

"Why have they come? Go, Hanuman. Discern who they are!"

"As you command." I bowed.

If I had one undiluted joy, it was to leap from a great height, so even now, on a mission, I threw myself from the mouth of the high-up cave. For a moment, I felt my father's breeze raise me high into the sky. The next moment, the winds crashed against me with their natural resistance. I began my descent, pulled down by the force of the Earth that I had not yet conquered. I landed on a solid tree branch. As my toes molded themselves around the branch, a restless itch ran up my feet. "Not another leap!" I ordered.

No disguise would be convincing if they saw me leaping through the trees. Dropping down to the ground onto my forepaws, I began to sprint on all fours. Banana leaves swept my face and underbrush tickled my belly. What disguise would work best? What did I know about them so far?

The jungle was dense around me. The trees in high bloom obscured my view. As I got near them, I slowed down and stood upright. I thought of my father for good luck and stepped into the form I'd chosen. The gleam of their arrows flashed through my mind. Better to give them a good view of me first to allay the warrior's instinct to attack. But I was prepared to be shot, ready for anything in this unknown situation.

Cautiously, barely breathing, I stepped out from a cluster of banana trees. I had made myself similar to them, dressed like a sage but a foot shorter. No weapons. No muscle. Mostly just skin and bones. I folded my hands at my chest, as I took another step toward them. Before I looked at them, I wanted to make sure they saw me. Direct eye contact, I had learned long ago, could trigger paranoia. I couldn't risk it, so I waited, alert to a clue that they'd seen me. Monkeys chattered in the distance. I kept my ears shut to their banter.

One of the men inhaled suddenly, and both stopped. That's all. No weapons drawn. I smiled inwardly. My disguise had worked. I looked up to meet their eyes, to establish friendly contact. Like a magnet, my eyes were drawn to one of them. *The leader,* my mind said before it shut down. His eyes were like the bottomless ocean. My tail shivered. My disguise was slipping! What was happening?

Mental mechanisms activated, ensuring my disguise. I was vaguely aware of it, frozen in place by his eyes. Goose bumps rippled across my skin. I felt like the Earth was trembling under my feet with a coming earthquake, yet the forest was still. I was bound, as if by magic, looking into the stranger's eyes. I'd never seen him before, but he did not seem strange at all.

They waited for me to speak. What finally brought me back was a warning: The other man was not so patient, and I saw his fingers tighten around his bow.

Think, Hanuman, think!

I was running out of time. I didn't know what to say. I'd lost my faculties.

Look at the other one!

I followed this command, redirecting my eyes. That woke me up!

His eyes were blazing and reddish, intense and frightening. If I were a soldier, I would have saluted and gone marching. The strange tide of emotions abated. My intelligence came to the forefront. It chided me loudly: *Sugriva is anxiously waiting!* I kept my eyes firmly on the Angry One and addressed myself to him. A yellow karnikara tree behind him shone like a halo, giving him a godly look. I bowed to the ground. A little praise and a lot of humility were always helpful.

"O tigers among men, your appearance is extraordinary," I said. "From your broad shoulders and gleaming weapons, I surmise that you are warriors. Yet you are dressed as ascetics. Please tell me who you are and why you have come here?"

"I am Lakshmana," the Angry One said. "I am the servant of my brother, Prince Rama."

He looked at his brother before continuing. Maybe he was under the spell too, for that was the only reason I could fathom for my reduced faculties. I was stumbling along a dark

alley, hoping to emerge on the other side without falling. No being encountered during the Great Chase had reduced me to this. Not even Daivi's touch had affected me like this.

"My brother Rama is the crown prince of Ayodhya, the rightful heir to the throne."

Rama. The name the queen had wailed across the sky. I focused on Lakshmana. His language was refined and beautiful—the language of humans in its most distinguished form. Royalty, then. Lakshmana continued with many noble words about his brother. Rama did not move while his brother sang his praise. Yet he seemed bemused by my presence. Lakshmana glanced at his brother. He wasn't able to gauge him either.

"By destiny's will," Lakshmana said, "we have lived in exile from our kingdom for the past thirteen years. There is much more to say," he continued, stepping away from the blooming tree. "But first I must inquire about your identity and your purpose in approaching us."

Aha! They were wise in the ways of the forest, never believing even the most believable. I'd been standing still so long that a trail of insects was crawling up my leg. I swatted the insects away as I felt my disguise slipping again!

Silence ensued, and Lakshmana chided me, sounding like the voice of my mind, "Sage, my brother is eager to know who you are."

For the second time, I was broken out of a trance. I'd been standing mute far too long. Befuddled, I had no choice but to simply stick to the truth.

"I'm here on behalf of my master, Sugriva," I said. "You are now in Rishyamukha, the only safe place on Earth for him. As his servant, I too am limited to this area. Your arrival in our territory has greatly distressed him. He sent me here to ascertain your true motives."

"And what have you understood about us so far?" Rama asked.

I felt my tail go limp and my shoulders melt down, as if I was a shy boy in front of my esteemed father. My eyes were on the ground. And that was that: the end of my disguise. I could see my tail, right there between my feet, limp and humble, just as I'd experienced it. Lakshmana gasped and looked at me curiously, up and down, up and down. He'd never seen a Vanara before, that was clear. I had to look up at Rama then. How had he done it?

Rama smiled broadly, showing all his teeth. He had seen through my disguise from the first moment! Who was this being, and why was Daivi so incredibly quiet in his presence?

I fell at his feet, my forehead on the ground. My world with its straightforward ways was upside down. The musty smell of soil filled my nose. I stood up, chastened. The indentation where I had prostrated was a direct pathway to Rama. There were forces at work here, a dimension of fate that I knew nothing about, beyond my imagination.

"I know this much," I began, trying to answer the question Rama had put to me seemingly ages ago. "Your lives are dependent on finding something you've lost. Yet you have almost given up."

I knew I could say more, but the veil over my consciousness had not lifted, and Lakshmana beheld his brother with anguish. My words had unearthed a core of something unbearable. Rama underwent a transformation: His smile vanished. The atmosphere was no longer conversational. Even the tree blossoms seemed to droop. All amusement was gone from Rama's now severe features.

"We don't know who you are," Lakshmana said, putting an arm around Rama's shoulders. "I don't even know what you are. Yet you have understood our very essence."

I understood that I had gained their trust. Restlessness crept up into my every limb. I wanted to jump to the karnikara tree, shake its yellow blossoms, and leap to the coconut tree, then onto the great banyan, the largest tree in Rishyamukha. Stop! What was I searching for?

"Three months ago . . . ," Rama said, and went silent. His hand tightened on his bow.

Lakshmana continued when his brother couldn't. "Three months ago, my brother and I were lured away from our dwelling. Going against the order of my brother, I left his wife, Sita, unprotected. She is a princess of the highest character. She should never have been living in the jungle. We do not know for certain who abducted her or where she has been taken. But we will *never* give up."

He pressed the tip of his bow into the earth for emphasis. So few sentences, yet he had conveyed so much. He was the one who had left the princess unguarded, and he blamed Rama too, for having brought Sita to the jungle. My heart beat faster. I could clearly see how Daivi was silently weaving her web. But I had not forgotten Sugriva, who was still fearful and anxiously awaiting my return. Choosing my words carefully, I said, "Most respected brothers, I can only imagine the pain of your loss. Yet I am certain Daivi has brought us together. My master has also been deprived of his kingdom and his wife. He is in urgent need of an ally. I urge you to come with me and meet my master."

Lakshmana waited for Rama to indicate assent. Rama seemed elsewhere for some moments. I couldn't imagine how the impatient Lakshmana had dealt with Rama's despondency, a situation I knew all too well because of my relationship with Sugriva. The four of us had been destined to meet. And so the words just slipped out.

"Please," I begged. "My master needs you. Please come with me. Meet Sugriva. Then you can decide how to proceed."

A spark of life ignited Rama's eyes. "You have not told us your name yet."

"I am Hanuman, son of Vayu and Anjana."

"Hanuman, I trust you like a brother," Rama said. "Take us to your master."

My tail hit the ground several times. I could not quell my enthusiasm. I knelt down and expanded my size, so that they could easily sit on my shoulders. "I will take you to our cave, situated on the peak of Rishyamukha."

Once they were seated, I wrapped my arms around their thighs and chose my first landing. I flew through the air, feeling its support and resistance. Tree blossoms and leaves scattered in our wake. Then I touched the top of a coconut tree and leaped onward to the great banyan. I briefly traced the well-known path with my eyes, ascertaining that I could succeed without the use of my hands.

By the time we landed at our cave, I was still digesting the powerful impression Rama had made on me. Therefore, I was less conscious of Sugriva's state. I knelt and allowed the warrior princes to slide down my shoulders. When I looked up at Sugriva, I saw what Rama and Lakshmana looked like to one who could see nothing but potential enemies.

Sugriva was paralyzed with fear. Surely, he knew that I would never bring an enemy to his presence. Surely, he could not doubt me now. But in my own distracted state, I didn't recall that emotions are not rational. I fixed my eyes on him without even blinking and said, "I have brought *friends*."

I wanted a fitting welcome for the princes, so I stood in front of Sugriva, blocking him from our visitors in case he bared his fangs, which he did. I repeated my statement in our own language. Slowly, Sugriva became himself again. My tail curled itself around his for a long second in a wordless assurance, and his hands, shoulders, and tail finally relaxed.

With that disaster averted, I stepped aside so that the four of us could appraise each other. Sugriva's physique was impressive. It wasn't hard to imagine that he was the son of Surya, the sun god. A gentle glow enveloped Sugriva, but as he looked into Rama's eyes, alarm returned to his yellow eyes. He said something to me in our own language, a guttural growl.

"We come in peace," Rama assured him.

He was noticing Sugriva's distress, something not always perceptible to beings of other species. Rama pressed his hand. The handshake prolonged itself, and they began to

converse. I kept my eyes on Lakshmana, eager to discern what impression we really made on them. I was not disappointed. Unlike Rama, who was an enigma, Lakshmana did not hide his thoughts well or perhaps at all. Lakshmana was no longer the Angry One. Instead, he was full of curiosity. His eyes went often to our tails, whose movements suggested they had lives of their own. When Sugriva smiled, Lakshmana's stomach retracted minutely, a small admission of surprise. He hadn't expected the sharp fangs, which, of course, all monkeys have. I could understand it made us look dangerous—even like blood-drinkers.

Sugriva's round eyes glowed like small embers of gold, and his red face was flushed. When Lakshmana looked at me and then back at Sugriva, I knew he had seen the striking resemblance between us. With tawny skin, reddish faces, and golden eyes, Vanaras shared similar traits. To an outsider, we all looked exactly alike.

I had one distinguishing feature however: my chin. As long as I could remember, I'd been known as Hanuman, "Powerful Chin."

Lakshmana and I stood aside and let our masters do the talking. I noticed that Sugriva had shrunk, matching his height to Rama's. Few things were as powerful as eye-to-eye contact with a potential ally. Otherwise, we were a head taller than the brothers, who were tall by human measures. Suddenly, Sugriva turned to me: "This is about that golden lady we saw?"

Rama took two steps forward, eyes stormy: "You have news of my princess?"

"We think so," I answered.

Because I saw how much this meant to Rama, I was afraid to swear my life on it. Daivi made me meek before this man.

"Hanuman will tell you exactly what we saw," Sugriva said.

"Her golden voice reached us from the clouds," I said. "The Ten-Headed One held her as they shot across the sky. My tail beat against the ground and went limp, like a snake with its neck cut off. She threw her jewelry down. I caught every piece."

"Sita!" Rama cried out, pounding his chest. He had a wild look in his eyes. "Bring me the jewels!"

My hands trembled as I delivered the bundle to Rama. He sank to the cave floor. As he examined the golden anklets, tears sprung from his eyes. He pressed the anklets to his chest, sighing deeply, like someone struggling through his last breaths. He held each piece to his heart. The sight of her jewelry was evoking Sita's presence, as if she was here. Suddenly, I feared for Sita's life. If Rama was so distraught, how would she be, that delicate princess?

Next to me, Lakshmana whispered the significance of Sita's jewelry. Like all royals, Sita had worn heirloom pieces since the day she was born. Going into the exile, she had kept only the most essential jewels. They were like her limbs, extensions of her body. For thirteen years, Rama and Lakshmana had seen the golden anklets around Sita's feet. Seeing her jewelry without her was like seeing a woman's locks torn from her skull. Each jewel had gained value by its nearness to her over the years. Indeed, I had felt their immense potency when they fell into my hands, precious beyond their material value.

Seeing Rama's grief, Sugriva and I made soft yelping sounds, voicing our sympathy. For a long time, Rama couldn't speak. This was the closest he had been to Sita since her abduction.

"We thank you," Lakshmana finally said, "for safekeeping Sita's jewels for us. For inviting us into your protected territory. For honoring us with your friendship. We are less alone now and more hopeful that we will find what we seek."

The meager light in our dim cave had vanished as night came upon us. Rama's countenance was grave, his eyes dry. Darkness surrounded us, making the unspoken more ominous. The princess had been abducted by a ten-headed monster known to be immortal and invincible. My heart felt as dismal as the night around us. The chances of ever finding Sita were pitifully slim. Where on Earth could she be? Yet this was not the time for a bleak foretelling of the future. The potential alliance between the masters hung thickly in the air. Nothing truly concrete had been said. There was much to understand before an alliance could be sealed.

"Daivi, that most unpredictable force," Rama said, looking at Sugriva, "has been kind to me after all, bringing me to you. Sugriva, son of Surya, will you tell me your story?"

Sugriva's yellow eyes focused on Rama. Despite his prowess, Sugriva had the air of a defeated man. It was evident in his flitting eyes, the slight hunch of his shoulders, and I could see it especially in his tail, which curled in on itself, cowering.

"Your request is sound, king among men," Sugriva replied. "Will we fight for one another like true friends? Before we can answer that, we must understand each other. Yet I'm afraid to reveal my story. I'm far inferior to you."

"Let me make that decision," Rama encouraged.

"The person I fear most in this world," Sugriva began, "is my own brother, the mighty Vali. Once, we were the closest of friends. Vali, the son of Indra, is the strongest Vanara in the universe. He was rightfully enthroned as our king, and I was his most faithful ally and confidant. My brother can never resist a good fight. Eager for battle, he pulled his loincloth tight and set out to fight Mayavin, a mighty bull demon. They retreated to an underground cave, and my brother ordered me to wait outside. When one full year had passed, I heard my brother scream, a ghastly sound. I heard the demon bellow in victory. Fearing for Kishkinda, our kingdom, I secured the largest boulder I could find against the entrance of the cave, trapping the demon.

When I accepted the throne, I made sure his wife and son were given full respect, their high position in our kingdom unchanged. But then Vali returned, alive and victorious. I greeted him affectionately and immediately offered the kingship back to him. But he was convinced that I had willfully plotted against him. Nothing I said could convince him of my sincerity. He bared his fangs and declared his intention to execute me in front of all our people. I had to flee, leaving everything."

Sugriva paused. The four of us sat at the mouth of the cave, illuminated by the moon. Rama had not shifted once during the telling, intent on Sugriva. I had never seen anyone listen so attentively before.

"This is the official story," Sugriva continued, "one that you need to know. But now I will tell you the real reason for my brother's enmity." He sighed, glancing at me. "My brother and I fell in love with the same female, Ruma, the most beautiful Vanara. Even her name, 'Salty,' conveys how coveted she is among our people. Like salt, that precious spice, Ruma was recognized as exceptionally beautiful, even as a girl. The tawny fur covering her body is the color of honey. After she achieved womanhood, it remained soft as velvet, like a baby Vanara's. The pink of her face is like a lotus, never deepening into red. Her eyes are amber, flecked with gold. Because of her many suitors, the drape across her hips was always made of the costliest material, enhancing her station."

I couldn't stop staring at my master. How long had we run together? And never had he told me the reason for Vali's enmity. Now everything took on another hue.

"Leaving aside his own noble wife," Sugriva said, "Vali turned his heart and attention to Ruma. Everyone was sure that she would become the queen, that Tara would be displaced. But when it came time to pick a mate, Ruma chose me. And then our brotherhood changed. Vali was prepared to fight me, but Ruma spurned him repeatedly. She made it abundantly clear that she loved me. Ever since our marriage, Vali has sought a reason to snatch her from me. Finally, he had found his opportunity. He knows that Ruma will never truly become his while I live. I'm only alive today because of my faithful Hanuman, who is swift like the wind. There is no hiding place on this Earth that we do not know, for truly my brother pursued us to all its corners. Together, we have always managed to escape Vali just in time.

"My brother has taken everything from me: my possessions, my friends, and my freedom. But what I can never forgive is taking Ruma against her will. She is forced to live as one of his concubines. I can never forgive this! Yet I'm homeless and helpless, exiled from the Earth itself. If I face him in battle, I am sure to die. I have begged Hanuman to leave me to my fate. But seeing you, hope grows in my heart for the first time."

By the time Sugriva finished, night had wrapped us tight in her embrace. We could see only dark outlines of one another. Yet the mood was lighter. The similarities in their situations were astounding. They truly understood the depth of each other's pain.

"Sugriva, my friend," Rama said, "I vow to restore you to kingship by any means."

I sensed a jolt in Lakshmana. I understood that Rama's vow was unprecedented: He was vowing to do anything, righteous or unrighteous, in his determination to vanquish Vali.

"You will rule the Vanaras again," Rama promised. "You will be reunited with Ruma."

With a yelp, Sugriva held Rama's hand. "In return, I vow that I will use all the powers as king of the Vanaras to find Princess Sita."

I kindled a fire at the mouth of the cave.

"With the fire as our witness," Rama and Sugriva said, "we vow to be allies, and serve each other's purpose until our goals are attained."

They clasped hands above the fire, the smoke wrapping around them like a seal.

An alliance had formed between monkey and man.

CHAPTER 7

The Curse on His Heads

The chirping of birds wake me at sunrise. Four guards sleep on the ground around me. Several times during the night, they spoke in detail about how they'd go about eating me piece by piece. I saw the hunger in their eyes, the way their nostrils flared whenever they smelled my flesh. It's only the sight of them that disturbs the serene forest. But they look less menacing in the morning light. Maybe the innocence of sleep touches even them. Squirrels begin chasing one another across the branches. Rabbits hop out, only to retreat when they see us. Flocks of animals roam about freely. The peacocks preen and caw. A flock of green parrots fly up and away. If only I could have wings. The vivid red blooms, with their yellow pods, of the sorrowless tree have begun to wilt in the summer heat. It is said that the fragrance from these flowers wipes away even the grief of death. I can feel it—how my broken spirit yearns to pull itself together and become whole again. The sorrowless forest is so vast and overgrown, I can almost forget I'm in enemy territory.

The fruits here don't revolt me, as the food within the palace did. This food is pure, untainted by contact with the palace. I must regain the strength of my body. I will need strength for the task ahead. I see a vine on the ground with large honeydew melons growing. The earth is soft beneath my feet, something I hadn't noticed when I was trying to escape. I smash a melon open with my fists and hungrily dig in with my fingers. I sit on the ground with the melon in my lap, eating quickly but carefully. Each bite is an offering at the altar of survival. The sweet morsels taste like hope.

Initially, I'm too weak to move far from the whitewashed palace walls. The arched entrance seems to me the gaping mouth of a monster, ready to suck me back in. I feel safest under the branches of a tree, just steps away from the honeydew patch. From here, I peer up at the tiny window, the one I escaped from. Someone watches me, though I cannot make out her face. I'm eager to move away from the palace, deeper into the sorrowless forest.

Walking is familiar to my body, invigorating. The guards allow me to move about freely, a signal that a fence or enclosure surrounds me, so I'm not surprised when, eventually, I'm stopped by another whitewashed palace wall. It looks exactly like the one on the other side, and the feeling of being boxed in constricts my throat. I have to go sit under the shade of a tree for awhile. The guards lurk around me. Taking a handful of dirt, I approach the wall. I draw a thick line on it, and then begin to walk along the palace's perimeter. I will continue until I return to this dirt line. I should at least know the size of my prison.

On my way, I find a lotus pond with crystal-clear water, teeming with fish, frogs, and turtles. Blue and pink lotuses float on the surface. I splash water on my face and neck, the first time I've voluntarily done so. As I explore, I forage for edibles, as I used to do with Rama and Lakshmana. I find trees heavy with mangoes, cherries, and chikoos, and bushes with blackberries and vines of sweet green grapes. Such bounty clustered in one place feels unnatural, and I don't eat much. I cannot, because my belly has grown small from the starvation.

Wandering in the forest, I revive, minute by minute, hour by hour. My desire to live, to nurture myself, comes and goes. I imagine the elements awakening, responsive to my fingertips. But it feels like shouting someone's name through water. I mull over this as my body and entire living system slowly recover.

As I duck under trees, avoiding prickly thorns and wiping the sweat from my brow and walk, walk, walk, my mind works incessantly on all the unknown pieces that together form Lanka as a whole. Every armor has its weak links, and I need to find Lanka's. Is it in their food? How does Ravana feed the entire city? Who supports Ravana unquestioningly? Could I persuade someone to fly me back across the ocean? Which blood-drinkers can fly? How can I get a message to Vibhishana? Or Dhanya-Malini? Mandodari?

The determination to escape has not left me, though the obstacles are unlimited: I have to get past the guards, leave the garden, find my way through the city, get to the shore, and somehow cross the ocean—all this without alerting Ravana, he who compulsively visits me at any time, to my whereabouts. I feel extremely tense in his presence. What holds him back from violating me?

On some days, I feel sure: *I am the last woman Ravana will ever torment.* On days like that, I can think lucidly of the abduction, recognizing how meticulously crafted the scheme was. I recognize that Ravana's attempts to seduce me are a warfare technique. It's based entirely on his whim, fluctuation from romance to aggression, from affection to threats; I have read about it in the lore on warfare. He wants to remold me with new beliefs and new loyalties.

One day, he brings me to the dungeons and threatens to imprison me, along with others he disdains too much to kill. Death is mercy, he means. There is an old, old woman with dirty white hair chained up against the wall. She was a beauty long ago. Death is preferable to rotting slowly away. Another day, he pursues me in the form of various animals: first a bird perched on a branch nearby, then a deer, then a monkey, until he has taken the form of every animal in the sorrowless forest, until I can't bear to have my eyes open. He shows me that I cannot trust anything I see. Nothing is what it appears to be. Another day, he gives me the gift of being poisoned. The fruit in my hand rots, and the poison spreads rapidly in my system. Only when he sees me turn my thoughts inward, fixed on Rama, ready to die, does he withdraw the spell. But the truth of it remains: Even a fruit I pluck myself from a tree could be my last. And like this, he keeps me under duress.

I will not break.

But . . .

Other days, I cannot stop thinking about whether Rama is dead or alive. The guards poke my skin with the tips of their weapons and frighten me. On those days, I curl up on the ground, covering myself with the tattered yellow cloth. I remain silent and unmoving, no matter what Ravana says, no matter what he does. My heart beats rapidly in my chest. Rama's death cry echoes in my ears, seared into my heart like a wound that will never heal. On such days, I press my cheek to the ground. My hair and hands smell of the Earth and are streaked with dirt. When I wake up the next morning, Rama's name is inscribed in a circle around me. The guards kick the dirt, stomping on Rama's name, obliterating it. Kernels of sand fly into my face and eyes.

"Get up," the one with many eyes commands. "Time to eat."

When I don't move fast enough, she pulls me up by my hair. To me, it feels like Ravana's own hand doing it. These guards do nothing without his explicit permission, and yet not all the hideous guards are malicious. One of them brings me a banana leaf that has been sprinkled with water. She brings me mangoes and berries. I am surprised by her kindness. She has speckled white hair, bushy like the tail of a fox. The matted parts drag across the ground. Her skin is leathery and hangs loose around her asymmetrical face. I want to thank her, but she has already turned away, reaching for her trident. The others call her Trijata and regard her as a type of prophetess, someone with the ability to see the future in dreams. But I have only seen her take long naps.

During one of my walks, I see tender coconuts at the base of a coconut tree. I pick one up, knocking it to hear the hollow sound. I have no instruments to open it, but of course the guards do. I direct my request to Trijata. The coconut grows heavy in my thin arms. The other guards start grumbling, but Trijata takes the coconut from me and pierces a hole in it.

"Thank you," I say, and gratefully drink.

I'm elated by her small act of support.

"Would you like to have some?" I ask her, even though it's against etiquette and unclean to offer someone my remnants. But it can also be sign of intimacy.

I hold the coconut up to Trijata. I have to use both hands. It's still heavy with plenty of sweet nectar. Before Trijata can take it, the one with many eyes knocks it to the ground. The two others thud their weapons against the ground in approval. It strikes me, however, that they have been patient with me, just trailing behind me. The threats they make have started to ring hollow. I sense a softening toward me.

Another predictable visit from Ravana comes and goes. When he's gone, the guards become talkative.

"I don't know why he has not already just had his way with her," the one with the bulbous nose mutters. "He wants to!"

I know it too; it flashes through his eyes.

"If he did, his head would shatter into a hundred pieces," Trijata cackles.

"Quiet!" Many-Eyes barks.

"A thousand," Bulb-Nose says.

"Tell me what you mean," I interrupt, curiosity awakened.

"The curse," Trijata says.

"For that, I will slit your throat!" Many-Eyes lifts her sword.

"Stop!" I cry. "It was I who asked the question. I am the princess of Ayodhya. You are bound to listen to my command."

I draw myself up tall, my eyes unflinching, as I've seen Rama do in conflicts. The guards gape at me, and Many-Eyes drops her sword. It's the first time I've pulled rank on them, so Many-Eyes challenges me.

"You are a prisoner," she says, spitting at my feet. "We are free to torment you in any way we choose—"

"But not physically harm you," Trijata says.

"Silence!" Many-Eyes's red-shot eyes bulge from their sockets. She lifts her sword in warning again. Now I know their orders.

"Don't forget," I say, "that anytime I choose, I can become the queen of Lanka. Then one word from me would mean life or death for you."

Many-Eyes closes her mouth, and the other ones half-bow to the queen that I could be. Clumsily, they stumble through the story, telling me of a curse on their master's head. Once they get going, every one of them chimes in to put the pieces together.

"It was one of those girls from heaven, prancing around in her see-through silks, swaying her hips, and saying how expert she is in all the arts. But when our lord showed his desire, she ran away, teasing him."

"So of course he ran after her. And soon they were playing the yes-no game."

"We all know how that ended, ha-ha!"

"Yes is the only answer our lord accepts."

"That little creature never stood a chance."

"But then she ran crying to her husband, one of the gods. 'Boo-hoo, look what he did to me.'"

"As if she was so pure and innocent!"

"When everyone knows it's not a crime to take a woman against her will!"

"Women never know what they want anyway."

"But her husband couldn't do anything when he found out. Our lord is too powerful!"

"But the curse!" Trijata reminds us. "Now our lord cannot touch a woman if she says no."

"No more games for our lord."

"No more yes-no, which he was so fond of."

"Or his heads will shatter into thousands of pieces."

"But he *has* touched me," I say, "against my will."

He dragged me from our ashram and yanked me from the karnikara tree. He held me close to his body during the entire flight over the ocean. The memory of those hours make me feel ill. His arms encircling my limbs, a phantom wound. But what if that wound had been real? What if the unspeakable had been done to me?

"He can touch you as long as it's without desire," Trijata clarifies.

I understand the distinction immediately: as long as there is no sexual intent.

"He has to wait until you agree to become his queen before he can embrace you."

I am twice-protected now by my own resolve and by the curse on his heads.

"That day will never come," I promise.

"Why not?" Trijata asks, but all of them are listening.

"If you had ever seen Prince Rama, my husband, you would not ask me why. Rama is the upholder of justice. Bright like sunrise after a night of terror, he will arrive here. Then you will see for yourself."

All the demon women laugh at me then, a real cacophony.

"You are crazy!" they cry. "We have seen all the gods! Even Indra, king of heaven. He was subdued by Indrajit, our prince, the heir. There is no one more powerful than our king!"

I don't argue. Words will never be enough to persuade them.

"You will forget your little human when you become queen," Trijata promises.

"Remember us when you are queen," they beg.

Queen Sita, ruler of Ravana's heart and the golden island. "Mistress of the Universe," they call me. This stings worse than their insults. These are Ravana's words, the titles he offers me. And to my dismay, I can see not just that these guards think that it tempts me, but also that it is the inevitable outcome. But the curse protects me. For the first time, I fully face how much worse my situation could be, what Ravana's daily visits might have actually entailed. I put my hands on my heart and say a prayer for all the women *before* the curse.

The next morning, the guards are suddenly replaced by stranger-looking creatures. I hadn't thought it possible. The new ones are decorated with self-inflicted wounds. One of them has destroyed half her body: Her left eye is sewn shut, left breast missing. Even half her mouth is fused together.

"Where is Trijata?" I ask her.

"Which one?" she says, slurring the words through her half-mouth. "We know a thousand."

My heart plummets. It's a common name. When I press the new guard for information, she presses the tip of her trident against my neck and pushes me away. A small droplet of blood runs down my neck. They spit at my feet and tell me I'm so revolting, they would not eat me even if they were starving.

When Ravana comes, I demand, "Where are my guards?" *Where is Trijata?*

He pretends innocence and lifts his hand toward the new ones. *Right here.* He sits down on the low-hanging branch of my tree. He plucks a leaf, which turns into a flower in his hand and smells it before offering it to me.

"I have had the same guards for weeks," I insist, ignoring his little magic trick. My heart skips a beat when I realize I don't know exactly how much time has passed. "Why did you suddenly replace them?"

A tickling sensation creeps up my arm. Ants? I lift my hand to sweep them away. But it's him, trailing the flower along my arm up to my neck. I swat it away.

"All of my guards are hardened blood-drinkers," he replies. "They wouldn't think twice about snatching a newborn infant from its mother and eating it alive in front of her." He crushes the flower and flings it to the ground. "But your tears melted their hearts. One of them even dared suggest that I return you to your little prince. Imagine, you turned their hearts in your favor. Next, they would be plotting to set you free. You are too charming, my princess. Why can't you show a drop of that kindness to me?"

"When have *you* showed even a drop of kindness to *me*?" I say it with anger, but in actuality I'm fascinated by what he has revealed. They cared for me!

"You are the one rejecting every single thing I offer," he answers.

"Except for my freedom."

"You are free to go anywhere you wish in Lanka."

"You set your most menacing guards on me and tell me I'm free!"

"They would not be necessary if you took your rightful place as my queen."

"You coerce me in the name of love."

"Let me show you what it means to love a woman, Sita. That weak husband of yours did not even please you for thirteen years the way a man must please a woman. Celibacy is not for a married man. What was that idiot thinking? What a cheater he is. Mark my words, the name Rama will come to mean 'cheater.' It will mean 'weakness.' Rama is that man who cannot satisfy his woman. Rama is not a real man at all. He is a sexless, impotent weakling."

The words hurt. I wrap my braid around my arm. *He comes prepared*, I remind myself. "You worship at the altar of how much you wish you were Rama! You spend your days and nights composing this poetry about him. Your words mean less than the croaking of dying crow." I speak loudly so that the new guards will know the truth. "You have never even spoken to Rama. You have never even seen him."

Quietly, I thank the thirty gods for this. Now Ravana can conjure only a poor imitation of Rama, a composite of the impressions he has stolen from me. He cannot cheat me, as

Indra once cheated Ahalya, by taking her husband's form. Ravana lifts his eyebrows and crosses his arms across his chest. His scrutiny teases my actual reaction from me. I speak brave words. But I feel the lump in my throat, the pain I feel when he criticizes Rama. And these new guards do not know me at all. I hadn't realized the small bud of affection I had for the others, especially for Trijata—the hope I had that they would help me. Now I have to start from the beginning again. Ravana sees all this, sitting on that low-hanging branch that I never want to touch again.

"Sita," he says softly. "Rama is dead." Another one of his mantras. "You suffer unnecessarily. You can come inside the palace anytime. I will give you anything you want."

"Very well," I say. "I want to meet Dhanya-Malini and Mandodari."

The one I actually want to meet is Vibhishana, the only person that may be a potential ally to me. Trijata is lowest on the hierarchy, Vibhishana highest. I don't know how to contact either of them. I'll take one step at a time. Let me be crafty, like a blood-drinker, so help me Kali, goddess of all brave choices.

"The first one I grant you," he answers. "As for Mandodari, you especially will appreciate that she will not be summoned, neither by you nor by me."

He is suspicious of my sudden request. But he cannot read my mind. He is perceptive, but I have my natural boundaries, which keep him at bay as effortlessly as the shore does the ocean.

As soon as he's gone, the new guards close in on me. They surround me, as if I were attempting to escape. Their hatred is so intense, I cannot bear to look them in the eye. Their malice makes their deformities monstrous. They mutter to each other and lift my braid with their spears. How they can hate me so much, so instantly, I don't understand. Every so often, they tug my braid, gauging my reaction. They must know how terrible that particular act feels to me. Rama used to drape himself in my hair, cloaking himself in it, letting it run through his fingers.

My only recourse is to take shelter in memories. Ravana's insult, calling Rama impotent, pushes me to reflect on the parts that held some truth. On the day of Rama's coronation, we had joked about having hundreds of children. Or maybe ten, in the way of the young who don't know the labor involved in having just one. I'm still naive in those matters, exiled from the natural progression of most women's lives. But as we went into exile, we took a vow of celibacy, not wanting to raise children in the dangerous jungle. We had quietly joined hands, silently understanding each other. It was a serene moment, with the sun rising, a wild bird perched on Rama's shoulder, a small fawn resting her nose in my palm.

"Do you agree with this decision?" Rama had asked. And because I was a girl of seventeen, the yearning for a child of my own had not yet begun. My answer was simple: "Your affection is all I need."

The vow was also to honor Lakshmana at our side. How unfair that we might revel in passionate love play while he was alone, while my sister was forced to be childless. I laugh a quiet, bitter laugh now, remembering that my sister's worst fear had been to marry an old man, like our distant uncle, Shigraga, who had long hair growing from his nose. Both of us

had been too innocent to understand the true sacrifice of love: to always be tied to those we love, desiring them, yearning for them, even when they aren't present. Urmila's life might have been easier had she married someone like Shigraga. He might have been a doting husband. She might have had a brood of children occupying her heart, demanding her time. Instead, what did she get?

Like me, Urmila had one year with her husband before her life was shattered, and a year in Ayodhya, that great city, did not yield much private time. Now she's been alone for close to fourteen years, waiting for a husband who might never return. Most women of our age already have grown children. Like me, she may never experience the joy of having any. Even so, I had never regretted our decision. Rama's love has been so immense, I feel fulfilled completely by his affection. I don't need to know if Rama lives or not. His love is alive within me. My captor cannot fathom love for love's sake. And for that, his head may burst into a million pieces. I'm protected by a curse on his heads. May that protection pave the path to his destruction.

In the Name of Sita

As the sun rose, the last embers of the witness fire glowed orange against the flaky ashes. As I awoke, I kissed my tail and turned my eyes to the sun. It seemed brighter than usual, blessing the alliance between Sugriva and the prince of the Sun dynasty. Whether the sun was truly beneficent, I didn't know. But I did know this: Our lives had taken a drastic turn. Sugriva's survival was not in my sole care anymore. The thought of Rama's presence lifted a burden from me. But Vali was held in high esteem by all of us. How would Sugriva really feel seeing his brother dead?

The royal brothers had woken before me and gone for their morning baths. Now they ascended the mountain wall to our cave, navigating the cliff easily. Water from the river glistened on their skin, dripping from their long, matted locks. I jumped from the mouth of our cave to pick the best fruits and berries. As I leaped through the sky, I barely felt my usual sensations of joy. I was intent only on returning to the cave quickly. When I returned with my arms full of bananas, berries, and mangoes, Rama and Sugriva were already deep in discussion. I spread banana leaves on the floor of the cave and piled the fruits on top. Greeting them wordlessly, I sat down and listened.

"It's too late for reconciliation," Sugriva said. "But you have not seen my brother. He is unimaginably strong. Though I see that you are mighty, I've never known any-one to match Vali's strength."

Challenging a warrior's strength was not something done lightly. But if ever someone was in a position to ask this question, Sugriva was. The success of their alliance depended on Rama's ability to vanquish Vali. Lakshmana had told us about Shurpanakha and that Rama had slaughtered fourteen thousand of her kin. The "massacre," he called it. But Sugriva needed more than words to assure him. Rama's face lit up; Lakshmana brought his bow and quiver. Picking just one arrow, Rama went to the entrance of the cave.

Sugriva and I followed. What could he possibly do with this one arrow? Rama placed the arrow on his bow and drew the string to his ear. He aimed at something only he could see and sent the arrow flying. It disappeared into the jungle.

I felt my tail curl around my ankle. Rama dropped his bow to the side and didn't move. A sudden noise made Sugriva jump. A sala tree in the distance cracked in half. The two pieces crashed into the jungle just as the sala tree next to it split. And the next. The noise was deaf-ening. Rama had picked the tree with the hardest timber, and each tree gave off the sound of an explosion. Sugriva held up his fingers to me. Seven! One arrow. Seven sala trees!

Rama glanced at us with a slight smile. Next to me, Lakshmana crossed his arms over his chest. Their eyes were still focused on the jungle. As if anticipating a doubt that wood was a breakable substance, we watched as the arrow flew onward and into the faraway moun-tain. Of course, we could not see the arrow, only its effect. As if someone had drawn a line across the peak, the mountaintop was shaved off and flung away. I could not stop myself from investigating!

Tracing the path of the arrow, I leaped past the sala trees and onto the mountain. Just as my feet landed on the flattened peak, I saw the arrow burrow into the Earth, creating a large cavern. This sudden commotion near Kishkinda would not escape notice. I needed to get back to Rishyamukha immediately. I was capable of defending myself, but now was not the time to fight. We wanted to draw as little attention as possible to Rama's presence. As I leaped away from the peak, I saw a host of Vanaras in the distance, leap-flying toward the mountain. They would not be able to understand the source of the mountain's sudden transformation. No one would believe the power of Rama's arrow unless they, like us, had witnessed it. Once I returned, Sugriva told me he had watched Rama's arrow return to its quiver. Thus, the question of Rama's power was settled.

"But if you challenge Vali," Sugriva said, "he might send out the formidable army amassed within Kishkinda. They will attack you, just as the blood-drinkers did on that day that you refer to as the massacre."

"You don't want this to happen?" Rama said, settling down to eat again.

"No," Sugriva said, sitting down. "It brings us no closer to Vali. It drains Kishkinda of her resources. If our best warriors are killed, how will I make good on my promise to you?"

"Challenging Vali to personal combat is the only way," Rama insisted.

"Yes! But if *you* win, Rama, then *you* will be the one entitled to the throne. Also, if you fail—though I hate to think of it—then my only hope will be gone. I will be exiled to Rishyamukha for the rest of my days."

"We need a plan of action that will not fail," I said.

In Vanara terms, this meant that we would have to resort to dirty tactics. We went back and forth in this way, crafting our plot. Rama and Sugriva would have to collude as warriors to conquer Vali, who had never been bested in battle. The plan was not without faults, but we set our minds to execute it after the next full moon, a night Kishkinda celebrated with much honey wine drinking. It was our best chance to attack Vali when he was weak.

"If we succeed," Sugriva said, "we will have one month to find Sita before the monsoon rains begin. One month is exactly the amount of time I plan to allot the search parties."

We watched the rise of the full moon in silence. While we sat in our cave, Sugriva and I knew full well the revelry taking place in Kishkinda. Every Vanara would be in the grip of honey wine. Vali, a lover of drinks, would be especially muddled.

When the sun rose the next day, there was a chill in the air—or perhaps it was in our hearts. We snuck through the bushes, approaching Kishkinda with stealth. We were counting on most of the guards being too drunk to take their jobs seriously. Indeed, the two guards posted at the entrance did have their loincloths tied on backward. Kishkinda looked ordinary from the outside, like any large mountain. But inside, there was an almost unimaginable abundance of riches. I whispered something of this to Rama and Lakshmana, a detail that was irrelevant at the moment. I wanted them to know that we were not just foolish monkeys bickering over caves. The look Rama gave me informed me that he knew very well that we were not simple-minded monkeys (although I might have been behaving like one at that moment). I fell silent.

Sugriva was extremely agitated, scratching his tail repeatedly. The first step depended on him and his nerve, and he clearly he did not feel courageous. I turned my full attention to him, speaking to him in our language, assuring him of his powers, reminding him of his many brave feats. Growing taller by my words, Sugriva tightened his loincloth. With a prayer to the rising sun, he left us and proceeded alone. I said a prayer to my father the wind. From our hiding place, we heard Sugriva roaring like a bull, and my heart cheered. That was the master I knew! Within minutes, we heard another roar from inside Kishkinda. Vali had taken the bait!

Though we could not yet see them, we heard the brothers crashing together like two thunderbolts. Trees were uprooted and hurled through the skies, and boulders smashed against the grounds. But I was not worried, for I could hear that Sugriva's shrieks were just as loud as Vali's. The noises of their fight were steadily coming nearer to us. I looked at Rama and saw that he was ready. A golden arrow gleamed on his bow. I prayed Vali would not notice Rama's blazing weapons. Demolishing the forest as they moved on, my master and Vali came into sight.

"There they are!" I whispered.

I was unable to contain my agitation. I could see bite marks bleeding on Sugriva's shoulders; Vali had none. I shuddered, my fur bristling: Sugriva was already badly wounded. My toes dug into the Earth. Rama's arrow was perched and pulled tautly to his ear. It followed the movements of the two fighters, who were locked in a deathly embrace. What was Rama waiting for?

"Hanuman," I heard Rama say urgently, under his breath.

I went as near him as I could, avoiding his bow.

"Who is Vali, and who is Sugriva?" Rama whispered.

His eyes never wavered from the two Vanaras, and then I saw the scene as he was seeing it: two supernatural monkeys, both with tawny skin and long tails and of the same size and musculature wearing red loincloths that draped their hips. I cursed myself. In our determination to execute our plan, we hadn't thought of Rama's unfamiliarity with us Vanaras. We had not considered how alike Vali and Sugriva were! Even a Vanara might take a moment to tell them apart. To a human, they were as inseparable as identical twins. I pointed out Vali several times: "That's him!"

But the fighting monkeys were moving so swiftly, my pointing finger was of no use. Not until Sugriva's tail coiled and he ran for his life did Rama know which one was his ally. He could not release his arrow, for then he alone would be deemed Vali's killer. Vali shrieked in a crazed rage, hurling scathing insults at his brother, but he didn't pursue him, for he knew that Sugriva would run into Rishyamukha and be safe. Beating his chest in a show of vigor, Vali turned back to Kishkinda. He hadn't noticed us.

Sugriva had been crushed physically and mentally. Lying at the entrance of our cave, the great monkey was bruised and bleeding from bites that covered his arms and shoulders. He had stared into the jaws of death, yet he was seething. All the trust he'd had in Rama had vanished, and from his limited perspective, I didn't fault him for this.

"Calm yourself, Sugriva, my friend," Rama commanded. "You did not warn me that your brother is your twin. I feared sending my arrow into the wrong heart! Rouse yourself once more. Wear this flowering *gajapushpi* creeper and challenge your brother again. The red flowers will help me distinguish you two. I will not allow the battle to go on long. Let us accomplish your goal, for it is mine too."

Sugriva breathed heavily, slowly regaining some of his strength. None of his bones were broken, so another fight was possible. I admired Rama's cleverness. My thoughts had been with Sugriva; I had not yet considered how to overcome that obstacle. But Sugriva had not challenged Vali to fight since the Great Chase. And now, twice in a day? It was incredibly suspicious. Only a fool would ignore the smell of a trap. But I kept my mouth shut. This was between Rama and Sugriva. They would have to call it off if they saw fit. Summoning his last bit of power, Sugriva went roaring again at the gates of Kishkinda, hurling foul words at his invincible brother. Vali answered at once. Either he had no dependable counsel within Kishkinda, or he ignored it. The awful battle began again, two brothers fighting to the death.

Rama had his arrow poised, following their every move. Like last time, the Vanara brothers blurred together, tawny skin, big builds—indistinguishable. But there was the red creeper around Sugriva's neck. Yet Rama did not shoot. My heart dropped in anxiety. Sugriva would not survive much longer.

"Release your arrow!" I urged Rama.

Now! Vali's chest was visible.

Now! Vali's back was turning to us.

Now!

Now!

The shrieks of the dying Sugriva rippled through me. We were running out of time. But Rama was in distress.

"I cannot do this!" Rama whispered urgently. "Killing a man engaged in combat is forbidden."

This was not the time for Rama's conscience to assert itself!

"But Vali isn't a man!" I stressed. "He is a Vanara! A monkey! He has claws! And a tail!" I was saying anything to release Rama from his paralysis and shoot his arrow from his bow to split Vali in half like a sala tree. "Slaying a beast is forgivable!"

"Not forgivable to Sita," Rama said. "She would not approve!"

"She is not here!"

And that fact snapped Rama out of his dilemma. I could see his mind sharpen. He saw his goal clearly: Sita.

"In the name of Sita," he said. His arrow flew.

The next moment, the mighty Vali fell to the ground. Rama's arrow pierced his heart. Rama put his bow down, looking grim. Sita would not approve. He had violated his code of honor. This was not something he carried lightly. My ethics were a lot more flexible than Rama's, yet I was not unmoved seeing Vali on the ground, dying. As a supernatural being, life unwillingly left his body. The red on his face darkened. His yellow eyes searched for his slayer. To honor the dying Vanara's wish, Rama stepped out from our hiding place. I followed him to pay my respects to the one who had chased us across the world.

Turning his blood-burst eyes onto Rama, Vali spoke harshly, "Who are you, coward?"

Blood seeped from the corner of his mouth. "You cannot be Prince Rama, held in high esteem in these lands and beyond. That Rama would never transgress like this." Blood flowed profusely from the arrow wound in his chest, but his fury was immense. "Answer me, weakling! If you wished to slay me, why did you not challenge me to combat?"

Sugriva was stricken, silent in his dubious victory. At first I thought Rama would not answer. Remorse was not an option, after all.

But Rama said, "I have punished you, it's true, for I value loyalty above all else. When my father exiled me, I accepted his command without question. When my brother Bharata insisted on returning the kingdom to me, I gave it back to him. When I went into exile, my brother Lakshmana followed me. Such is the power of brotherly loyalty. But you, monkey, have turned against your own brother. Proud of your power, you've turned on the one who deserves your loyalty, your affection. You took his wife, transgressing against the laws of love. Tell me, is there any difference between you and Ravana, king of blood-drinkers? Like him, you've stolen the wife of another. You've misused your brute power for your own gain. For this, your life became forfeit."

Rama gritted his teeth against his personal anger. He would not admit the breach of the warrior code. Vali's breaths grew laborious, but he clung to his life.

Our clan began to pour out from Kishkinda, some wailing openly, others quiet in deference to Sugriva. It seemed like everyone but me had known the real reason for the clash. The beautiful Ruma came running, the bells on her waist belt jingling. Sugriva clambered to his feet, calling her name. As she threw herself into his arms, he stumbled backward clasping her tightly, but then they immediately separated, conscious of Vali, breathing his last. Their fingers intertwined tightly as Tara came running.

The Vanara queen stumbled to the ground in her hurry to her fallen husband. She beat her chest as she ran, crying loudly. This emotional display was highly unusual for the wise and restrained queen. Tara had been on the king's council long before she was Vali's wife; her intelligence was superseded by none. Indeed, her first words to her dying husband were, "Why did you not heed my words, my love? I told you not to fight Sugriva a second time! Were you so eager to make me a widow? Beloved, how can you leave me like this?"

She placed her head on his chest and cried, wiping her tears only to call her son forward.

In our desire to accomplish our own ends, had we really considered the devastation we were causing? Making Tara a widow and Angada fatherless. The young Vanara boy, who looked so much like his father, had grown several feet since I last saw him. His tawny coat was still velvet smooth, softer than a grown Vanara's. His sorrow was all the more terrible to behold; he could not sob openly like a little child, yet his whole body trembled with emotions he could not express. Vali held Tara's and Angada's hands as his eyes began to close. Forcing them open, his last words were directed to Sugriva: "Appoint my son heir, and our enmity will be forgotten. If you swear to protect him, I will bless your kingship."

I heard Lakshmana sigh behind me: Appointing Angada heir would rob Sugriva's future children of that right, but the unspoken threat was that Vali would curse Sugriva's kingship.

A curse by a being of Vali's stature was potent. Sugriva finally nodded, eyes on the ground, Ruma clinging to his arm.

Vali indicated his readiness, and one of my oldest friends, Nala, came forward. He would have run with us in the Great Chase if I'd allowed it. Nala bowed to the dying king and put his hands on the fatal arrow. With one great pull, he dislodged Rama's mighty arrow. Vali gave a great final roar; his eyes rolled back into his skull, and his soul departed for the land of Yama.

Holding onto Vali's dead body, Tara turned her wrath on Rama. It showed her shrewdness, even in her grief. She chose her target well, for Sugriva could not have silently withstood her words. Could Rama?

"You go about showing a righteous demeanor, Rama, and yet you are not righteous! You are the worst kind of impostor, for you claim to be kind and noble, when indeed you are cruel and ignoble! Alone, neither of you could have survived my husband's power. Together, you have become the embodiments of deception and deceit. Sugriva's reasons, I understand. But what crime had Vali committed against you, Rama, that you executed him?"

Rama was silent, eyes full of compassion.

"Your future victories will be soiled by his blood," Tara cursed.

Tears pouring from her eyes, she stood up and raised her arms to the heavens.

"The mighty Vali is dead!" she cried. "Your son is dead!"

Tara swung her hands down. Using her own formidable powers, she invoked the Lord of Heaven with her grief. Clouds rumbled above us, turning blackish with water. The first drop of rain smattered against my cheek. The king of heaven would not be silent after the killing of his son. The monsoon rains began pouring down. Sugriva stood with Ruma and I with Rama.

Not until the fight came to an end could I admit the change in my heart. Daivi had known it all along, withholding her whispers until I was in a place to hear. Sugriva had depended completely on me. I had served him with all my capabilities. Now, as king, Sugriva had endless resources. He had been reunited with his dearly beloved Ruma. He had the entire Vanara race at his disposal. He did not need me anymore. I could finally acknowledge the inevitable: My heart had found a new master.

The Brave One

I sit under my favorite sorrowless tree, the canopy of branches the roof of my house. Most of the sorrowless trees are small and erect, with dense foliage. There are only a few that have grown large like this one. The dark green leaves are pointy and long, like Shurpanakha's nails. I sit cross-legged and meditate, my only sanctuary. I hear a voice speaking to me.

Have heart, my dear, have heart. You will not be forgotten. You will lead a worthy life. You look back on what you've accomplished thus far and stare into a blank space—a blank space filled with pleasant encounters, quiet mornings, kisses from the one you love. A good life. While you were in it, the need to reflect simply did not exist. That is the gift of happiness: to be fully present in the moment. That happiness has been torn into shreds, replaced with a blank space. But it will fill with purposeful colors—colors of your own choice and making.

When I open my eyes, I see a mongoose sitting directly in front of me. They are bold but shy animals, and they are fearless, the natural predators of cobras. She looks up at me patiently, looking way too sweet to ever crush a cobra's skull. Her nose is incredibly pink, her eyes light green. She stares at me, and I stare at her. In Ayodhya, we kept pet mongooses in the nurseries to ward off snakes and rats. I offer my hand to her.

One of the guards steps forward threateningly, lifting her spear, and my heart stops. Before I can intervene, the mongoose turns to the guard. She stands on her hind legs, hisses, opening her mouth wide, showing her pointy sharp teeth. With a curt wave of my hand, I shoo the guard away. Though I rarely use it, the gesture is imbued with years of royal training. The guard shrinks into the shadows. The mongoose sinks down on her paws again and turns to me, aggressive display all gone. I reach out to her again, and she shyly sniffs at my fingers.

She settles in by my side as if she's always been there. I name her Sharduli, which means "tigress." Whenever our eyes lock, a wordless communication takes place. Later, I watch her as she tries to catch fish in the lotus pond. I laugh out loud when she falls into the water, shaking her head furiously as she emerges. That night, Sharduli curls up at my feet, her speckled fur and bushy tail soft against me. Her presence brings me a warmth I've been missing—and something more: Her loving presences allows me to finally face aspects of myself I'd been avoiding.

A bright moon illuminates my dreams.

"Sita, you're thirsty," Lakshmana says.

He hands me a small jug of cool water, fresh from the river nearby. The clay pot is hand-painted and smooth against my palms. The cooling water soothes my parched throat. How did he know I was so thirsty? He always knows these things. *Oh, Lakshmana, what did I do?*

When I turn to him to plead for forgiveness, he disappears. I wake up with dry, cracked lips. The hare-marked moon beams brightly. But my dream questions are stronger than my thirst. Like a stubborn friend, they demand an answer. I alienated Lakshmana, my loyal ally. Why?

The minutes before Ravana came to kidnap me are shrouded in a burning haze. I remember different things at different times: the weight of the water jug as I carried it to the false visitor; the way the Cloth of Essence stuck to my chest, drenched in tears; the fear that gripped me when I heard Rama call for me; that I could hardly breathe; that Lakshmana wouldn't budge until I spoke the way I did. I cannot bring those words to the surface now. They were accusations that hurt him terribly—something I ought not to have said, words I've chosen to forget.

Every time the words begin to form

in my mind, I'm mortified and turn away. I busy my hands with the texture of the Earth. Whenever my eyelids close, I see Lakshmana at the periphery of my vision. Sleepless or awake, what I long to escape from haunts me. Guilt tells me all this is my own fault.

If I had not asked for the golden deer.

If I had not pushed Rama to capture it for me.

If I hadn't suspected Lakshmana.

If I hadn't accused Lakshmana of . . . of . . . of . . . ?

Just say it!

"I accused him of desiring me," I whisper. "I told him he had followed us into the forest, biding his time. I accused him of wanting Rama dead. I accused him of wanting to enjoy me."

I cover my face with the golden cloth and weep softly. "Lakshmana, my dear brother, forgive me. It was so unworthy of me to speak that way to you. Fate punishes me every day. I accused you of desiring me, and now I live imprisoned by Ravana's desire. It wasn't you, but him. Forgive me!"

I'm wide awake now and can't stop staring at the moon: round, perfect, glowing, serene. Starkly opposite to me. Even if I lose track of days and weeks, the full moons endure. This is the fourth. I wipe my cheeks and look out into the night, starlit and bright; my eyes are full of tears as I send my apology across the sea.

"I'm sorry. I'm sorry. Forgive me. You are the brother I never had. You are blameless. Your intuition was right from the very first second. Come to my rescue!"

I was so wrong, dancing into the trap, as unconscious as a fish swimming into a net. My adoration for having a pet deer of my own ruined me, along with my conduct toward my brother-in-law. After I face my own behavior, my own allegations, I relive that scene with Lakshmana countless times, recovering every word I said to him. I cringe hearing my words. I see how twisted my intuition became. I desperately try to intervene: "Do not leave me! Stay with me!"

But no matter what I say, Lakshmana runs off, disobeying the order of his brother for the first time in his life. I'm left to my fate.

The disturbing recollections connect me to a life I've lost. I peek at Sharduli's pink nose, which sticks straight up to the moon, her mouth open as she breaths deeply. I am closer to this little creature than I was with Lakshmana; he never seemed fully at ease with me, nor I with him. Even holding Rama's hand was sometimes awkward in his presence. Had I been resenting Lakshmana secretly, all those years, for depriving me of the fulfillment of Rama's passion? If Lakshmana was not with us, we might have changed our minds. We would have grown comfortable with the idea of raising children in the wilderness, which, after all, grew more familiar as the years went by. The forest became our home, and children would have been welcome. How terrible that I turned our sacrifice onto Lakshmana, suspecting him of desiring me. But none of this was Lakshmana's fault. Finally, my moon-bright confession allows me to slumber.

In the early morning after this nearly sleepless night, I hear laughter, women's gleeful shouts, the sound of heavy anklets tinkling. Without opening my eyes, I crawl to the protective branches of a sorrowless tree, the leaves moist with dew. The unfamiliar sounds disrupt the familiar. I've become a creature of habit, and this disruption unsettles me. The sun has hardly risen. The noise has awakened my guards too, but after they have located me under the tree, they are merely disgruntled. What is happening? Who is intruding into my gardens this early? Sharduli is sleeping soundly in the little burrow I dug for her. My guards stay seated, holding their weapons erect. Half-chewed bones lay scattered around them.

The laughing women swarm the sorrowless forest. This unexpected visit must be prompted by my request to see Dhanya-Malini. The laughter is like birdsong from a heavenly realm. It's not all of his consorts—not even half of them. But many. By the wild, overgrown look of the gardens, they have not visited here often, but this is their domain too. They pick flowers and talk gaily, draped gorgeously in all possible materials and shades. Rich velvet skirts sweep the ground; sheer veils trail from their sparkling crowns. Their upper bodies are bare; most wear only an embroidered silk cloth tied artfully across their breasts. As they enjoy their morning exploit, they are also searching for me. I expect them to notice me at any moment.

To my surprise, they do not see me beneath the tree: I've become one with the forest. But the presence of the guards should alert them to my whereabouts. I expect my guards to declare where I am or prod me out with their spears, as they sometimes do when I'm not quick enough to greet their master. But my guards have become gargoyles in the garden. The consorts look at them the way you look at rotten leftovers, making no effort to hide your revulsion. So, they have a silent little battle going on.

"Where is she, then?" a dark-skinned beauty with dimples asks.

A blood-drinker with luxurious copper hair tentatively calls out, "Sita?"

"Shush!" She gets a slap on the shoulder. "What disrespect! Only *he* can say her name."

Their talk has woken up my mongoose. Sharduli's nose twitches as her round eyes blink open. She yawns and manages to look grumpy too when she notices all the commotion. She shakes the dust off her coat and promptly comes to me.

"What if she's escaped?" I hear them say. "Remember that day . . . ," and they whisper among themselves a tale that has gone through many hands and become a legend. Me, flying out from the window at the bath, with wings like a *vidhyadhara,* shooting bright light out from my hands, blinding everyone. They speak of how powerful I am, how gorgeous, how extraordinary, how spectacular. Otherwise, surely their lord would not prefer my company to theirs. They have made me into a living goddess.

Oh, Sharduli. I shrink back into the branches, actually hiding now. She turns to look at me. I cannot live up to their expectations as a goddess or a woman. I'm just a sad, desperate, lonely prisoner. Sharduli crawls up to my shoulder and starts licking my face. I pat her head, tracing her half-moon ears. I feel that she is grooming me for my debut appearance.

The sun is visible now, a dazzling and comforting spectacle as it sparkles on the lake. But the women's excitement has settled down; they are turning sulky, like spoiled children. They pluck grass from the ground or leaves from the trees, and discard them without a glance. The flowers they've picked lay forgotten, exuding the spicy fragrance of dying blooms.

"Dhanya-Malini!" someone calls out.

Do something, they seem to demand. *Where is that goddess for whom we have woken up so early, for whom we've dressed with special care?*

Hearing her name, the favorite stands up. She's been sitting quietly by the lotus pond. Ravana's name is etched across her lower back. The scar tissue is pink. She stands up and turns around, and it so happens that her eyes are drawn directly toward mine, half-hidden as I am behind the branches. She freezes, realizing that she alone has set eyes on me. The favorite consort emerges now as a person of her own, when so often I see them as one. Her eyes are haunted, her demeanor gentle.

I take a big breath, gathering my wits; I was the one who summoned her. I place Sharduli carefully on the ground. *Stay here.* Not one to obey, she slinks off behind the vegetation. Steadying myself on the branches, I take a step forward. I wait for the favorite to say something, do something. It's true that I've requested this meeting, but I did so because she wanted to meet me. Two women died for telling me this.

"Our lord's chosen one is here," Dhanya-Malini says.

Her voice carries to all the consorts. They look first at her, then all around, still not seeing me. Pulling the Cloth of Essence across my chest, I take a step forward. They gasp, as if I'm a daylight ghost. I hear my guards snicker. They are following the development closely. No doubt they are starved for some action, when all they have is the stalemate of Ravana versus me during his daily visits. The consorts come toward me, becoming one cohesive whole again. They even move in a synchronized way. The favorite is lost in their midst. I was right to be worried I wouldn't live up to their expectations.

I cannot hear their whispers, but I see their eyes large with concern. They take in my unwashed face, my unkempt hair, my tattered once-golden cloth, my protruding collarbones, my uncertain stance. I'm the most pitiable creature they have ever seen, a half-drowned kitten in need of rescue—certainly not a goddess shooting dazzling light from her fingertips.

In a move that seems practiced, they bow before me. One of them speaks: "Gracious one, bless us. Take your place as our queen. We want to see you free and happy like us."

They grow silent, waiting for my response.

"But are you free?" I ask. "You dance for him all night." A slave is superior to these women, recognizing her enslavement!

They burst out laughing and say, "*He* dances for *us*! All night, he dances for us." They giggle and clap their hands. Their ornaments chime in with them. "Has he not danced for you?"

I see how clever that tormentor is. By allowing the women to dominate him, he makes them feel superior and strong, powerful in their ability to subdue him. I shudder and then notice how the women's laughter subsides abruptly. All at once, they stop laughing. So they are performing for each other, confirming their belonging, their hierarchy. I turn my face from them: We have nothing in common.

But the favorite steps forward. She is exceedingly beautiful, even among all these beauties. She wears an odd necklace about her neck; not one of the beads is the same. She is of my height and coloring: hair dark as night, complexion like the glowing moon. Her features are symmetrical, her eyes large. Her resemblance to me is uncanny. Her womanly appeal is intensified by an expression of tender sadness.

"I am Dhanya-Malini," she says in a gentle, whispery voice. They look at her, as if she is their guru. They acknowledge her high position, next only to Queen Mandodari's.

My hand lifts, and to my surprise, she bows down, so that my fingers rest across her head. It seems that I am bestowing blessings upon her. Dhanya closes her eyes. Her hair is soft and silky. A rushed whisper flow through the throng of women, their jewelry tinkling. I bend down to face Dhanya. She brushes away a tear.

"Tell us why you won't become one of us," she says.

If only they could see me with Rama. Then they would understand. I armor myself with knowledge of Rama: his superiority, nobility, and selfless love; his promise to love only me. I take a deep breath and say, "I was fifteen when I met Rama. He was on the precipice between boy and man. Luminous like an emerald, his skin smooth, his chest broad. The moment I saw him, I memorized his every feature, shocked at my own audacity. I had never before seen anyone so perfect, so young and yet so ancient. Someone I knew before knowing."

The consorts thirst for my words.

"When Rama broke Shiva's bow, winning my hand, I felt that the pieces of my soul had burst, scattering across the sky like unseen stars. As you know, we women are often married without regard to our hearts. But I was so happy I could scarcely breathe. I told my little sister that I felt I'd wandered the whole universe myself to find Rama. He made a vow to love only me. I do not have to share my husband with cowives, a harem, or thousands of women. He is mine!"

They begin to whisper. Dhanya-Malini stands and sweeps me into a tender embrace. Her mouth is by my ear, and her breath tickles as she whispers fiercely, "This was the necklace we used when we gathered our strength to curse him."

She presses the odd necklace into my hand. "A bead for every woman who spoke the curse. With one voice, we decreed that a woman, the wife of another, would be the cause of his final end."

The hairs on my neck tingle. A premonition rises up from my feet.

"You are the Brave One!"

"You are the one we invoked," she whispers. "You must be!"

I pull her back into my arms, my heart flooding with emotion. That's when the blood-drinkers intervene: "No touching, whatsoever!"

I hear them mobilizing behind us. "Stop, at once!"

"No one but the king can touch that skeleton!"

"Only Kamadeva on his sick days knows why he'd want to!" Half-Mouth shouts. The four of them come charging at us.

With an exaggerated roll of her eyes, Dhanya steps away from me. She is not afraid of these half-mutilated guards, and she wants me to know that. But the night stalkers do not miss a chance to retaliate at once, poking the little queens with the dull ends of their weapons. A few tumble to the ground.

"We eat one of you for breakfast every so often!" they cry. "Don't forget that!"

"That will be the fate of this skin-and-bones bag too." Pointing to me.

"Pity the one who must eat that shriveled carcass."

On and on they continue, insulting me, until Dhanya and I lift our hands at the very same time. The royal gesture. *Enough!*

"Then leave," the guard orders. "You fluffheads have pestered us all morning."

Dhanya briefly interlocks her fingers with mine, then they hurry away without looking back. I stare at the necklace in my hands, feeling its hidden potency. First, Ravana's brother turns on him, and now his favorite consort. Something is happening in Lanka right under Ravana's nose—or noses, I should say, since it's more impressive to evade all ten. Perhaps he is so invested in convincing me that he has only one nose that he's dulled the faculties of his others. Perhaps his other noses are offended at his insistence that they do not exist. I almost feel like giggling with these thoughts. For just this moment in the sun, I envision Ravana's ten-faced, twenty-armed form as a drawing in a fairy tale.

The sun has now properly risen. I have not had a chance to even rinse my mouth, much less drink water or eat, but like a true yogini, I have not felt the pulls of my body. Sharduli hasn't forgotten. She comes my way, pushing an egg along with her forehead. For a moment, I admire her light eyes, their black, oval pupils, and the rusty color of the fur around them. The blue-speckled egg tumbles to my toes. As I weigh it in my hand, I wonder if there is a life growing in it. The egg is incredibly smooth, as marvelous as a gemstone. Sharduli runs away into the vegetation. A honeydew melon peeks out from the underbrush and begins rolling toward me. It thuds against my feet, and Sharduli races to me, standing on her hind legs. Now that she's provided me with a melon, she wants her egg back. I pat her on the head and hand her the blue speckled egg. She's content to hold it between her paws and crack the shell with her teeth. I don't know why it fascinates me to see her do this.

The honeydew is sweet and tastes like early morning, fresh and cool. I sit on a slope near the pond, eating in silence with Sharduli. The guards take turns visiting the pond, gurgling and spitting, splashing their necks with water, and squatting to urinate. Like me, they never undress to attend to their body's functions. I have more in common with the lowest hierarchy in Lanka than the highest. This is our morning routine, even if we are performing it later than usual. But I notice that the guards are angry with me. They whisper and glare. Several times, they point to Sharduli. Trijata and my first guards would have never hurt her, but these belligerent ones might.

They wait until it's dark to attack. A spear flies past me, hitting the ground where Sharduli sits. I cry out, but Sharduli has moved, rearing up on her hind legs. I reach for her. But another spear comes flying.

"Stop!" I command.

But they don't heed me. They surround us, jabbing their spears at Sharduli, who dodges them and shows her teeth. I throw myself on top of her, protecting her. I clasp her tightly to my bosom. Her little belly moves like a bellow, the air rapidly going in and out. Sharduli cradled to my chest, I stand up and face the guards. Their weapons are still lifted, as if they will kill her in my arms. Their teeth are bared, and they growl at us.

Gritting my teeth, I say, "Do whatever you want to me, but do not dare touch Sharduli with even the dull side of your weapons. Or I swear upon my honor that I will curse you to burn in the land of Yama for a hundred lifetimes."

They spit at my feet and continue to glare. How easy to spit back at them!

I retreat under the sorrowless tree with Sharduli in my arms. She drapes herself across my shoulder, her little heart beating next to mine. The guards hover around us, weapons still aloft. I whisper into Sharduli's ear the need to hide sharp teeth until we have a strategy that will ensure victory. Showing our power too soon will bring their weapons down upon us. We have to be ready first.

Right Side Up

When Rama finally had a great search party ready to scour every corner of the Earth, the heavens opened up and the monsoon rain started. It came much earlier than expected and drenched us so fiercely that none of us could recall a season so terrible. The rain was so thick, we could not see even a foot ahead. There was nothing any of us could do, except for absolutely the last thing we had patience for: wait.

The rumbling clouds released their heavy loads again and again. My clan had retreated into Kishkinda. Sugriva had offered Kishkinda's abundance to the princes, but Rama had vowed not to enter a kingdom for the duration of his exile. Lakshmana and I had found a cave on the outskirts of Kishkinda, and the brothers had retreated there. It reminded me of the Rishyamukha cave, which I knew Sugriva would never again enter. The rainfall steadily poured down in such heavy streams that fish and other aquatics must have swum out of the rivers to claim the entire Earth as their domain.

Once the dark cloud of Vali's death dissipated, Sugriva went on a rampage of enjoyment, making up for lost time. Kishkinda was filled with Vanaras amusing themselves with drinks and pleasure. The fact that they could go nowhere during the monsoon gave them further license to indulge their fancies fully. I did not

speak of it to Rama and Lakshmana, disliking the unfavorable light it placed on my clan. In tune with Rama's mood, I couldn't justify the boisterous celebrations in Kishkinda. The Vanaras knew there was a search pending, but there was nothing they could do now, so why waste days sobbing? They enjoyed every moment heartily, foremost among them my master, Sugriva. Such is the nature of monkeys, but I could not join in the mischief.

Most days, Rama sat on the floor of the cave, saying nothing and hardly moving. There was no reason to. He reminded me of a mystical sage who had access to higher planes and levels of consciousness. I doubt Rama even saw me there. He sat cross-legged, gazing at the big eye of the cave, which cried and cried. Lakshmana's breaths were more rapid than Rama's; he was not able to subdue his impatience. The quieter Rama got, the more active Lakshmana needed to be. They were like opposite manifestations of the same disease.

Lakshmana polished their weapons until they gleamed and then did a long, strenuous routine with his swords until he dripped in sweat. Next, he would sharpen each arrow, offer wet flowers to the altar he had built, and practice yoga that stretched the flexibility of his body to its limits. Then he sharpened the arrows again. He talked almost incessantly about various options before us. Should we notify Ayodhya about Sita's abduction? Should we seek help from the wise sages about ways to kill Ravana? Should we supplicate the heavens to stop the monsoon?

I watched Lakshmana but attended to Rama. I rubbed his feet, fanned him with a banana leaf, warding off swarms of mosquitoes. Rama didn't notice them or Lakshmana's frenzy. Unable to tolerate Rama's despondency, Lakshmana would plunge into the heavy rain and disappear, returning hours later drenched and with a handful of fruits.

"Eat, brother, please," Lakshmana pleaded.

Rama wouldn't unless Lakshmana forced him to. Later, Lakshmana begged, "Let's do the warrior routine together."

But Rama did not accept the weapons that Lakshmana tried to hand him.

And the next day, he'd say, "Set aside this grieving, brother; it doesn't befit you!"

And then, "Rama, please . . ."

But Rama's face remained grave and silent.

There was no solace for Rama in the here and now. I had never loved or lost anything the way Rama had, so I couldn't imagine the depth of his frustration. We had been so close to purposeful action. So there we sat, two human princes and a monkey.

One evening, when Rama had been unreachable all day, Lakshmana sat down next to me. I immediately knew he was going to confess something. Every so often, he flinched or shook his head, as if discarding a word or phrase; he was formulating his thoughts before he spoke them. I smiled to myself. Rama was the thoughtful, articulate one. Lakshmana was spontaneous, often repeating words or sentences to get his point across. I hadn't given Lakshmana's inner life any thought. Lakshmana was, in my mind, like an extension of Rama, not someone with an independent existence. And yet, as he silently formulated his words, I began to suspect what he'd say. He had left Sita, after all, against Rama's orders.

"All this is actually my fault," he said, enunciating each word carefully, looking more certain as the words were spoken. Then it all came out in a rush.

"The very first day when Sita was gone," he said, "my brother changed before my eyes, summoning powers that I did not know he possessed. He launched his bow and arrow and said, 'I will destroy this entire universe.' As he drew the string to his ear, I felt the energies of all the elements draw near, and I understood that he meant to blast them and us away.

"I—Lakshmana—would be gone. Rama would be gone. Everything would be gone. I knew this with dreadful certainty. Rama has the power to end the world." His whisper was fierce, daring me to challenge him.

"I ran to Rama, locking my arms around him, screaming in his ear, begging him to stop. With just my own strength, I could never have held him back. But he stopped. He dropped the bow to the ground, and he has not been the same since. I lost him. How could I think I knew better than Rama?

"If I had not stopped him, we would not be sitting here now. Sita would not be gone. None of this would be. And maybe that would have been better."

Helplessly, he gestured toward the silent figure of Rama and grew quiet. I stared at Lakshmana without blinking. I felt skittish by the gravity of his words. I didn't want to think of Rama as the Destroyer of All. I didn't want to think that he was the Lord of Everything, capable of retracting this creation, and me, within seconds.

"Speak," Lakshmana said, nervous by my long silence.

"If you had stopped Rama, we would not be here," I blurted out. "And that would not be good at all!"

I scratched my head. It was my turn to formulate my thoughts. And to think I had pegged Lakshmana as impulsive!

"The moment I saw Rama," I said, "everything changed. It's hard to explain. I felt like I was turned upside down. Only now, I'm beginning to see that it was right side up. Lakshmana, your instincts were right that day. This world is meant to go on. Your cause has become mine. Daivi leads us all. We will find Sita."

I spoke of Daivi to him, but found that Lakshmana put little stock in the idea. He did not mock me or her. But it was Rama's submission to fate that made him accept the exile from their kingdom. Lakshmana still held some bitterness toward Daivi, I could see.

"If only I had not left Sita unprotected," Lakshmana said, "she would not be missing."

"No, Lakshmana. You would be dead," I answered, which is what I'd longed to tell him. "No one can face Ravana and live to tell the tale. Whatever made you leave Sita in that moment protected you. Maybe it was Daivi herself that directed you! Ravana would have killed you. Never doubt it."

Lakshmana looked at me with half a smile, considering this. *All right*, he seemed to say, *we can leave this subject behind*. Now that he was unburdened, he was eager to return to safer ground. After that day, Lakshmana greeted me with affection.

I spent my days with the brothers rather than with my own Vanara clan. The reason was simple: My universe had a new center point, a new center of gravity. I was bound to Daivi: to Rama. His joy was mine; his sorrow was mine. I could not celebrate with my kindred.

On a good day, Rama accepted his brother's invitation to practice weapon routines, swords gleaming through the air. I watched them moving as if one, twirling their swords and shields in the air, jumping, kicking, slashing. I could see why Sugriva had been so frightened when he first beheld them walking into our territory. Although the brothers were smaller than us, they had skills that we did not. They crossed the swords and shields over their chests, bowing to each other, panting. Sweat poured down their faces, just like rain outside the cave.

"You did the right thing, brother," Rama said, "when you stopped me from releasing that arrow. You reminded me of who I am. If everything we've heard about Ravana is true, *he* needs to be destroyed, not the universe. When I could see nothing but Sita, you saved me."

"When you're silent," Lakshmana replied, jaw clenched, "I fear for your well-being."

"Didn't I just beat you at swordplay?" Rama said.

I had not been aware that they were competing, but Lakshmana's face split into a wide grin. "Yes, you did, my brother. You did."

I was heartened by this exchange. I did not wish to be anywhere else. I felt like the luckiest Vanara on Earth that they didn't shoo me away. Strange, that I could feel content while Rama was overcome by his misfortune. When he did speak, he spoke of himself as the most cursed of men. He berated himself for shooting Vali in the back, for being lured into the trap of the golden deer. There was no end to his self-recrimination. Was there ever a man as unlucky as him? All my time with Sugriva had prepared me well to support one so crushed by destiny. My mind seemed to be an endless valley, and Rama's voice echoed from one side to the other.

"As soon as the rain ceases," I promised him, "King Sugriva will immediately send out all our monkey forces. There are millions of us. If anyone can find her, we will!"

The fourth person in the cave was Sita. Though Rama's exile was in its final year, he could never return to Ayodhya without her. Even in his sleep, he murmured her name. Like raindrops, Sita's name clung to the walls of the cave. She had never once complained during the many years of exile. Her manner was simple yet profound. When she spoke, everyone listened. She had a deep compassion for all life. But the sweet reminiscences were always followed by darkness: He had failed her, not protected her. His worst nightmare had come true. Where was she? What was she being subjected to? Was she losing hope? Did she curse him for taking so long?

One night, when the brothers were sleeping, an unexpected visitor arrived: Angada, the crown prince. The brothers slept shoulder to shoulder, with arms intertwined. It was the only time I saw either of them without worry. But even in his sleep, Rama would frown.

"I want to speak to you, Hanuman," Angada said. "I cannot speak freely in Kishkinda. You know how impulsive the king can be."

This was true for any Vanara king and not a dig at Sugriva, I hoped.

"Why do you trust me, prince?" I asked. I was Sugriva's closest ally.

"You are loyal," Angada said. "While everyone else stayed, you ran with your master. We all admire you."

I hadn't known that.

"Is it true," he asks, "that Prince Rama wants to kill Ravana?"

"Yes," I said. "His main aim is to find Sita. But Ravana will be punished."

"I want to help," he said. "We all must use all our powers to accomplish it!"

I was surprised by the determination in Angada's voice, the hint of powerful knowledge.

"Why did my father have to die?" he asked, expecting no answer. "My father told me that despite Ravana's faults, he is a brilliant warrior, a masterful strategist, undefeated in battle. But he sought out my heroic father. My father had never been defeated in battle either. The Ten-Headed One snuck up on Father during his morning meditation. To teach the demon a lesson, Father caught Ravana with his tail and stuck him under his arm and leaped forth to this next destination. In that way, Ravana was dipped into the four oceans, where Father worshipped, dangling from my father's armpit like a rag doll!"

I assessed Angada's impassioned claim. It sounded like a mighty exaggeration—a son's glorification of his deceased father. I couldn't imagine the enormous Ravana dangling from anyone's armpit. Yet after a moment, I remembered that Sugriva had mentioned this episode. It was not a commonly known fact, for our race did not approve of consorting with demons.

"Indeed," Angada continued fiercely, "once my father arrived back home and released the demon, the Ten-Headed One bowed his proud heads at my father's feet. He accepted my father's superiority. Ravana marveled, my father would say, at the Vanara ability to leap so high and far. And none was more gifted than my father. My father was Ravana's superior!"

Angada opened his mouth to continue, but instead, a look of great sadness came over him. He turned into the young boy that he still was. His tail curled around his ankle, and he cast his eyes down. I felt a momentary pride in his restraint, for I knew he could have said a number of accusatory statements here against Sugriva. Or against Rama. Perhaps not everyone in Kishkinda was drowning in honey wine; clearly, Angada had given the subject matter deep thought.

"Your father would have been a true asset against our enemy," I said in an effort to console him.

But Angada's yellow eyes filled at once with outrage. "My father would never dishonor his vows! This is what I came to tell you. Father and Ravana made a pact with the fire as their witness. They would be friends unto death and never cross each other again."

When I heard this, understanding rippled through my entire body. Something that had puzzled me was illuminated so brightly that my fingers and toes started twitching. Sugriva truly was Rama's only hope! I took hold of Angada's hand.

"It is truly a rare one," I said, "who can set aside his own grievance for the greater good. You are destined to be a great leader, Angada."

Angada sat tall, looking very much like his mighty father.

"What you must know, Hanuman, is that something dangerous is happening to the world. Father called a meeting after the Great Chase. He foresaw great troubles at the Ends of the World." Vali battling ghouls at the Southern Quarter flashed before me. Even then, I'd known something was off. "He said Ravana was preparing to demolish the borders between the living and the dead—that he planned to make death the highest privilege. No one will be allowed to die without Ravana's permission."

Daivi gripped my heart, clenching it. This was one of the higher stakes. What would a world without death be? It seemed that every empire told tales of rotting corpses coming back to life. Was that to be our true future? All of us reduced to skeletons? Restless spirits?

Rama and Lakshmana stirred; Angada pressed my hand.

"My father's hands were bound. Mine are not. I will serve with you."

He slipped away into the dark, rainy night. And yet, what he had told me changed everything. I had to share this knowledge with Rama when he awoke. It was Daivi that pushed Rama to kill Vali. An alliance between Rama and Vali would have been for naught. Ravana was Vali's ally. Vali could never have led a charge against Ravana; my entire clan worldwide would have been accountable to that warrior's truce. Sugriva, on the other hand, was not. And if Ravana meant to subvert the very structure of the world, then he was a greater evil than any of us had imagined. As soon as the rain ended, we would gather our forces. We would not be stopped.

Outside, however, the rains still raged, as if controlled by the demon's will.

You will never find her, the winds howled.

You will fail, the rain promised.

And the terrible truth was that I could not with conviction declare them wrong.

SITA

CHAPTER 11

Sharpen Your Claws

Dhanya-Malini's conviction that I'm "the One" feels heavy, impossible. It was one thing to imagine my power in private, another to be held responsible by another. Can I see my circumstances differently? Can I gather the courage to be just as smart, villainous, and ruthless as Ravana is?

My only comfort is my friendship with my sweet mongoose. As I go foraging for my daily portion of fruit, Sharduli trails across my shoulder, light as a dream. I scratch her rust-colored neck, and her fluffy tail tickles my waist as I walk. When it comes to our diet, Sharduli's name suits her, and our needs diverge. Like a little tiger, she hunts ground birds like peafowl and partridge, or lizards, insects, and snakes. She brought me a cobra once. She goes hunting, and I go picking. I've given up the tender green coconuts for now. I am not brave enough to ask the guards for help; they've maintained their animosity. If they lift their weapons at me, Sharduli always comes to my side, little as she is. The fur on her neck sticks straight up, as mine would if I had any; I stroke her back, calming her. I always turn my attention to Sharduli, who fixes them with her tiger eyes. She puts herself protectively between me and them. She strikes me often as not just a pleasant companion but also a real ally.

After we eat, Sharduli sits in front of me, holding me entranced with her eyes: *Don't you know that you have so many choices? At this moment, the paths*

Anna 2018

you could take radiate from you like rays from the sun. This is true for every human being, but especially for you. Have you forgotten who you really are?

I turn away from her uneasily, unsure whether the words are hers or conjured by me.

Don't turn away, she says. *No one but you can save you from this situation. Never think otherwise. Only you can raise your hand. Only you can take that step.*

But all I see is the same old forest, the same old guards, the same old me. I remain a prisoner in the sorrowless forest. It's one thing to be bold in the privacy of one's own home, and quite another to step out into the world with it. Dhanya-Malini and Vibhishana, my two allies, are helpless too. No one has ever challenged Ravana and lived to see the next sunrise. Sharduli never once blinks to show that she agrees with my reasoning.

Such is the state of my mind when Ravana regales me with a solo vina concert. I'm less resentful than usual because Dhanya-Malini is with him. He seats himself on a large cushion. Dhanya comes to sit next to me on the grass. I greet her without smiling. We know not to reveal our affection in front of him. Self-absorbed as he is, he still has a possessive eye on us. But when he begins playing, I'm spellbound despite myself. It is absolutely melodious. Haunting. He is skilled the way only a dedicated artist can be. Devotion to an art form cannot be feigned in its execution. His fingers dance across the strings. Sometimes he hums along, eyes closed. The most beautiful thing is that he forgets me when he plays. I wish he would play that instrument all day. Dhanya-Malini and I take advantage of the moment and begin to talk quietly. We have so little time that I immediately go to the heart of the matter.

"Why didn't you leave when you had the chance?" When the others escaped, she chose to stay.

"Then I wouldn't be here with you right now!" Dhanya says with extra heat in her soft voice. It's a touchy point. She does love him, after all. She is like a trained spy whose sole mission is to deceive the one she seduces. It is a dangerous game.

"There are no rules for what you do," I whisper, "no maps."

She squeezes my hand gratefully and looks at her lord with a beguiling emotion that cannot be feigned. Her appeal is intoxicating, for she has the air of a lover who has transgressed, whose sole purpose is to make amends, to be forgiven. She has been living in the paradox of deeply loving someone she is preparing to kill.

"As soon as he took me," she says, "I knew there was no going back. My destiny was to stay with him. To wait for you." She emphasizes this with another firm squeeze. This time, an electric current runs up my arm. "I never expected to become his favorite. Never quite knew how I earned that honor." She looks at my face. "Now I understand perfectly why."

She has noticed our uncanny similarity and has drawn the same conclusion that I did: He has been looking for *me*. I wonder how many others have made the same connection. Then again, the two of us may be the only ones eager to orchestrate his downfall. Others will not see what we see.

"But why, Dhanya? Why has he been so eager to find me even before I existed?"

Her fingers play in the sand. Then, "By forces beyond his own reasoning."

It's my turn to feel pinched. I'm troubled by her conviction. I feel too ordinary. So I say, "You could have invoked one of the gods?"

Her finger draws wildly in the sand. "All my life, I learned that I would be safe as long as I was obedient. I was the perfect wife, Sita, the perfect mother. I did everything according to my husband's will, and before that my father's. But my husband failed to protect me. My father failed to protect me. My son was too young. Such was the case for all the women my lord abducted that day. I was filled with futility, with the arbitrary nature of those rules. I just *knew* that it had to be one just like us. That's all I knew in that moment."

A crescendo in the melody silences her. She turns her face to him but continues: "When I held the hands of the other women that day, I was channeling golden light. I did not direct our words; they came to us naturally."

The melody of the vina stops, and we both stiffen, aware of the threatening nature of our talk, speaking of all this with Ravana so near. But the pause is merely one that the melody requires; he throws his shoulder into it, manipulating the string with more vigor. But perhaps he senses our conspiratorial bond, for he plays louder and louder, overpowering the space, drowning out our whispers.

"But how can he be destroyed?" is the last thing I manage before we are swept away by the melodious raga, by the force of his dominance. We close our eyes in absorption; I can hear his other arms reaching for the strings. One instrument, twenty hands. The intricacy is astounding. The morning sun envelops us, as if shining brighter in response to his song. The parrots begin to caw, the cuckoos chirp in tune, and other birdsong complements his playing. He has created an entirely new style of playing, a new form of music.

The melody awakens something in me, and Sharduli's voice reaches me again:

There is no such thing as a crossroad. There never was the choice between good or bad, right or wrong, righteous or evil. "This or that" was invented by someone with poor imagination. At every moment, the choices available to you are limitless. You weave the course of your life by your own hand, your own magic. It takes effort to reach for other paths, other magic. But it can be done. You can reach beyond what you were given. You are the one who is responsible for the life you've created. The last one you made burned up in a flame—a fire of your doing. That was your choice. What will you choose this time?

Her words and the music are so intense that I squeeze my eyelids tighter. I don't want to see the creature that can produce such strangely intriguing melodies. I don't want to think about my choices. I sense Dhanya swooning next to me, her breathing quickened. It reminds me uneasily of the line between us, when otherwise we have everything in common.

When he's done, the silence hums with his art. We sit like that until he claps for himself—two hands clapping together. I cannot fathom why he insists on fooling me with that human form: We both know it's not real. Ravana looks at me eagerly. I cannot lie. "Lovely," I admit.

His whole being lights up as if I've just agreed to become his. One innocuous word. Nothing is casual in his presence. Everything means more to him, less to me. Now that his attention is back on us, Dhanya and I relate stiffly. It is hard to see her go without giving her a final embrace. She smiles coldly at me. As she leaves, she drags her toe lightly across the sand.

Only then do I notice what she has drawn skulls. Nine skulls with a firm line across them, erasing them. She looks over her shoulder, giving me a meaningful look that chills me in the sunlight. She even lifts an eyebrow. But that's a mistake, for he stiffens, hands tightening on her arm. He turns his gaze sharply to me. I summon all the innocence I have, eyes wide and distracted. She cocks her head and looks up at him. Then they're gone. His departure is always a relief. My spine loosens. I'm left with the sensation of ash on my hands.

I quickly erase Dhanya's sand drawings. Then I retreat to the sorrowless tree, which has become like my home. I can be at relative ease the rest of the day. I can think in leisure about what Dhanya has shown me. Usually, my guards even take naps as the long hours pass slowly, but they take turns sitting near me. I'm far too dangerous to take naps around. Sharduli is warm against my thigh, digging her nose between the earth and my leg. Just as I sink my back into the tree, one of the guards comes into my bower. Her flaming bronze hair gets stuck on branches. She yanks her head free, leaving strands of hair behind. It's like a thief has intruded into my house. The blood-drinker charges up to me, putting her nose to mine—only she does not have a nose. I don't dare push her away.

I get up to seek a place where I won't smell the breath of this intruder. I scoop up Sharduli and kiss her little nose. She licks my neck. I hold her little body to me, reflecting on Dhanya's words. Sharduli's musty smell on my shoulder is comforting. Hidden behind a cluster of bushes, there is a grotto just big enough for Sharduli and me. We settle in, but the noseless one stands before me, star-ing furiously. I sigh and start going to the place where I've marked the whitewashed walls. Sometimes, when I'm agitated, I circle the parameters of my prison, beginning and ending at this place. It usually takes me all day. It's soothing to have an achievable goal.

As I go, all the guards follow, knowing the routine. But I get the uneasy sense that they are guarding the noseless one from me. As I walk, the angry guard insists on facing me every few minutes. I avoid her as persistently as she pursues me. All day it's like this. The others don't intervene, as they sometimes do when one of them harasses me too much.

After a while, she finally desists. I sigh in relief, taking in the sorrowless forest that makes my existence bearable. The foliage is green and bright, without any of the humidity of the approaching monsoon. My eyes are drawn to movement behind a tree. The greenness of the forest begins to take form and, without warning, my deepest dreams manifest. Rama stands there, magnificent and majestic. His hands are empty, his bow nowhere in sight. How has he gotten past the guards?

"Rama?" I whisper, heart beating fast. I cannot believe my eyes. And I shouldn't.

But the emerald luminescence of his being draws me toward him. I run into Rama's strong arms, locking him into my tightest embrace. With my ear pressed against his heart, I begin to melt, and then I hear a heartbeat that is not Rama's. A cackling laugh bubbles up from his chest and makes my insides squeeze tight. I'm in the embrace of the noseless woman. I cry out loudly and stumble away, repulsed by the illusion. Rama is gone, replaced by the aggressive demoness.

"You don't recognize me, do you?" she demands.

And when I hear her voice, I instantly do. "Shurpanakha."

With only slits for a nose and no ears, Ravana's sister is unrecognizable, but her nails are as sharp as ever, pointy at the tips, like claws.

"So you know my voice but not my face," she says. "I don't recognize my own face either, thanks to those so-called righteous brothers."

I'm still frantic from the encounter with "Rama." He looked so like himself. How did I not recognize the illusion? *Because I wanted so much for it to be true.*

"You tried to kill me," I say.

"They taunted me!"

"But you rushed toward me with your claws lifted."

"They should not have played with me!"

I agree. "They should not have taunted you."

Though her face is distorted, her eyes have not changed. She looks malicious, explosive with rage. Every time she squints, her pockmarked skin yields a grimace.

"You really think Rama will just be able to walk into Lanka and appear in front of you?" she asks. "What a fool you are!"

Shurpanakha's words reach me like a distorted echo. The apparition of Rama has fraz-zled me completely.

"You are the only one on Lanka who has actually seen Rama," I say.

It makes her one of the most dangerous people here. She can appear as a perfect Rama, an illusion I am not immune to.

"You would not have been able to conjure such a flawless imitation," I continue, "unless Rama made a strong impression on you."

Strangely, this makes me feel close to her. But dismay lingers in my belly, to have seen Rama only to have him snatched away, a mirage. Even that false moment was a blessing.

"I'm the one who told my brother about you," she says, and then she transforms again, flaunting her skills as a *kama-rupini*, her ability to assume any form she desires.

Now I stand face-to-face with myself. The Sita facing me is pristine, glowing with vitality, the golden garment an extension of her inner glow. I do not look like that anymore. My Cloth of Essence is now torn and colorless. If anything pleases me these days, it is the fact that my external appearance reflects in some measure my inner world, where vast stretches of barren lands yield one little flower that sighs *Rama* before it wilts.

"I requested to be on guard duty," Shurpanakha says, "so that I could watch you. If your so-called protectors hadn't attacked me, you would still be an unknown little princess roaming around in the jungle. But, no, they punished me because I'm a woman who chooses my own mate. They laughed as they brutalized me, cutting off my nose and my ears." She reverts to her mutilated form, pushing her face close to mine again. "It would have been kinder to kill me!"

I take a step back. I can't defend myself against her accusation. I knew that her mutilation would have consequences for us. Still, it didn't happen the way she tells it.

"We did not laugh at you."

"Did you not? Rama and Lakshmana sent me back and forth between them, mocking my offer as if I'm some ugly slut! For that alone, I demand revenge." She looks me up and down. "Would my brother have bothered with a few humans? No. He wouldn't have avenged me. But I only had to show him you, as bait. How tiring to show him this form of yours again and again. Then he crafted his clever plan to steal you away, to leave Rama half-dead without you. He thinks the plan was his, but it was mine."

She fingers the pink scar tissue where her nose was.

"The plot was to leave Rama half-dead?" I ask.

"As soon as I saw the way Rama looked at you, I knew he would be devastated. What a pathetic man he is! Wandering around Dandaka, completely lost without you." Here, she turns herself into Rama, calling out in a high-pitched, squeaky voice: "Sita, Sita!"

But my breath stops. "Rama's death cry was false!"

Whatever grudge I hold toward Shurpanakha is washed away in the flood of this revelation. He's alive! Even though she set this plot in motion, I'm filled with gratitude to her for bringing me this news.

I grab her hand and press it to my cheek and say, "Thank you, thank you!"

The other guards began to approach us. She dismisses them with a flick of her wrist. Years of royal training. She is a princess too. My genuine gratitude shifts her just a little.

"I loved a man like that once," she says, begrudgingly. "Vidyujjihva, my first husband. My brother killed him in a battle. Accidentally."

She pulls her hand away, scratching her long nails against the surface of my palm. "I thought I would enjoy Rama's suffering. But instead, it's my brother's discomfort that pleases me. Scorned by you, he suffers. I enjoy it a lot."

The sudden movement in my gut tells me this is an opening. She knows more about the abduction than anyone else, save for the wretch himself. What information can I extract from her that will lead me in the right direction? Like Queen Mother Kaikasi, Shurpanakha must know things.

"Every time I refuse his advances, his humiliation increases," I say. "If I were to escape from under his nose, he would be embarrassed beyond words." I hesitate, and then finish boldly: "You, I'm sure, move about freely from here to the mainland."

Her eyes dart across my face, turning into narrow slits. I cannot predict her response. Slowly, her lips curve into a sinister smile. The pink flesh around her scars strains against it. "Trying to escape from here? You are going to need to sharpen your claws for that. Does he know that you plot against him?" She waves her sharp nails in the air. "How can a woman be a threat to him? Do you know that even the strongest human was never able to draw even a drop of his blood?" She adds, under her breath, "That's why he didn't ask for immunity from humans."

"Tell me about his boons."

"I made him abduct you, and now you ask me for help?"

"I'm sorry about your husband," I say. "I truly am. I know how it feels."

She turns on me, eyes burning. "Do you know how it feels to have your nose and ears cut off?" Her voice rises. "Do NOT think you know me!" Her spittle sprays on my face.

I try to catch hold of her hand again, to regain the moment of gratitude, but she throws her claws into the air and howls. Offering her empathy was the wrong thing to do. Now she shakes her flaming red hair like an enraged hyena, and the scar tissue on the slits of her nose turns livid. She charges toward me, arms raised, just the way she did that day so long ago. The guards rush to us, preparing to restrain her. She stops right in front of me, her face so close to mine that her features blur, and says, "I hope he eats you. If he doesn't, I will!"

She turns and runs. She was the bearer of good news. Knowing that Rama is alive, my intense desire for our reunion awakens forcefully. But it soon makes room for something disquieting. I retreat to the grotto, feeling the earthen walls all around me. Sharduli meets my gaze steadily with her round, light-green eyes. She crawls into my lap, putting her nose against my cheek. I caress her half-moon ears and stroke her head all the way down her back. The ugly emotion snakes around my heart and tugs it out of my chest. Knowing Rama is alive only highlights his absence.

"Five months!" I say out loud. "Is there another reason you haven't rescued me, Rama?" I scratch a likeness of him into the dirt wall. "Have you given up, my love?"

I know my husband's power and capability: "You can destroy the worlds with one arrow, revive a dying deer with soft whisper, melt the coldest heart with a glance, and find a kidnapped princess by sunset." One full moon at the most.

Unless he doesn't want to. My hand flies up to suppress a cry, flinging dirt into my mouth.

"You promised to hold me in your heart forever!"

And how many men have promised the same thing, only to cast their women away?

"But Rama would never do that!"

Didn't Dasharatha denounce Kaikeyi? Wasn't she his favorite? Maybe Rama is quietly glad to be rid of me. No one will blame him. He must have halfheartedly searched for me. When he did not find me, the desire for a new wife might have ignited in his heart. He doesn't love me anymore. My joy is replaced with this heart-wrenching doubt. He should've come by now. I rub my palm against the poor Rama likeness, erasing it. It's my own doubt I cannot bear. Rama's love is so much a part of me that I cannot envision who I am without him. I understood myself as a beautiful woman only when Rama came into my life. With him, I became a woman. With him, I became a wife. With him, I would have become a mother. Without him, who am I?

My birth stars always predicted that I would be a queen. I was promised that my husband would live long and prosper. I would have children, be fortunate, and change the world into a better place. How unreliable the stars are! How cruel the gods! I don't experience myself as a woman without Rama. Without him, I drift in darkness, unaware of my own light.

When, finally, I quiet my mind and descend into my inner sanctum, I hear Sharduli's sweet, relentless voice speaking to me again:

Don't give in to grief, to terror, to impotence. You are imprisoned, it's true. But who can limit that which is limitless, that which can never be bound, cut, burned, kept, owned, enslaved? Yes, I speak of your soul, dear child. And I call you "child" only because you behave like one. You can choose that, certainly. But some choices lead down and others up. Some lead forward and others backward. Those of poor imagination did have a hand in creating the structure of this world, after all. It is bound by a certain duality. Thus, when you're not a child, yet you act like one— petulant, entitled, irrational—where will that lead?

It does not befit you to be so bewildered, to act like a tree with no branches, no fruit. I feel compassion for you. Yet you linger there too long. Remember that some emotions seek to trap you; they long to feed on you, to make you theirs. Those urges, those feelings, those thoughts within you are not so different from external forces that long to do the same. It is therefore that I tell you, princess of my heart, rise. Rise! You've been docile for too long. It is time to claim the upward path. It's time to reach out and take what is yours. It's time to be who you are.

I take Sharduli's paw in my hand and look into her light-green eyes. "Who are you?"

When you accept who you are, then you'll know the answer.

I'm a seed, sinking deeper into the soil. When I bloom, my roots will bind me.

CHAPTER 12

Intuition, or Illusion?

The sun is setting, and Ravana has not yet come. In these weeks and months, not a single day has passed without his harassment. I hope today he will break the pattern. I hope he will stay away. And yet, because my hope is wrapped around his absence, he is present in my mind. When he isn't accosting me, I'm preparing myself to rebuff him. Noticing this tinge of obsession, I start pacing around my tree, determined to reroute my energies. During our exile, I found small tasks soothing, like crafting clay pots and painting them with natural minerals. I decide to gather flowers for an offering to the thirty gods. I hum as I work, keeping my mind on the flowers and fragrances. I imagine that I'm in Panchavati and that Rama is just a glance away. My bouquet grows beautifully, but I cannot resist the pink and blue lotuses I see floating in the pond.

As my feet touch the water, I remember that on the first day of our exile, my feet swelled with heat, prickled by thorns. Rama carried me to a pond, pulling out the thorns and ministering to my feet. How loved and cherished he always made me feel.

Sharduli paces at the shore as I wade deeper into the pond. Though the sun has almost set, sweat trickles down my neck. The wind plays with my hair, and the muddy bottom is squishy between my toes. The water feels wonderfully cool as I submerge myself completely. When my head goes under, startled fish swim

away. I savor the complete hush under the surface. I come up for air next to a fully bloomed pink lotus. Bees buzz around us. The petals are perfectly shaped and pinkish, the color of my palms. I inhale the sweet fragrance of the lotus and look up to see the sun disappear.

The day is over and Ravana has not yet visited. The make-believe is over. I'm suddenly anxious and scan the forest. He must be on his way here. The guards linger on the banks. The pond ripples from my movements. The Cloth of Essence clings to my body, heavy with water, making my movements effortful. If I emerge from the water now, my garment will be like a second skin. With my luck, Ravana will appear just as I reach the shore. The way he looks at me is chilling enough. I cannot bear to have him see me like this.

The water that was a refreshing friend, aiding my fantasy, becomes another prison. My feet are rooted into the mud. A cold breeze rushes through the tree crowns. The water grows cold around me. The fish swim closer, nibbling at my skin. The guards start shouting for me to come out, but I feel sheltered by the water, no matter how chilly it is. I try to recall the shape of the moon, gauging how much it will illuminate the night.

Let it be a moonless night, I pray. Darkness can replace the water as my shroud. Submerged in the pond up to my neck, I perform my evening prayer, offering the water back unto itself. I glance at the abandoned bouquet on the shore. The submersion begins to feel like a penance. My legs feel burdened, light as I may be in the water. I have little flesh on my body; I feel it in the way the cold attacks my bones. I have not eaten anything all day, not even my usual austere portion. If I stay in the water like this, how long will it take before my body collapses?

"Come out now!" bellows the one with no neck.

Sharduli has retreated to a tree branch. I sink farther into the water, my chin touching its surface. My braid has come undone, my hair floating behind me like a long cape. The guards have lined up on the shore, shouting at me. But their threats are hollow; no one dips as much as a toe in the water to retrieve me. I stay where I am, submerged in a misery that is not altogether unpleasant. The moon rises up in the sky, round and shining, a sun without rays. How could I have forgotten? It is a full moon. Tonight marks seven months in captivity. For seven months, I've kept my womb sealed.

Suddenly angry at myself, I splash to the bank and rise from the water. I will not let fear dictate my entire life! The night breeze makes goose pimples all over my body. My cloth clings to me. My fingers and toes are wrinkled like dried-up jujubes. I gather my hair into my hands and wring the water from it, twisting it around and around. I am just about to do the same with my garment when I hear that voice from hell. Ravana barely finishes uttering my name, and I've flung myself back into the pond. The water embraces me with its coolness. If only I could stay below the surface with the fish and lotus stalks. When I come up for air, Ravana sits at the shore, dipping his feet into the pond. He has removed his silk shawl. The guards are nowhere in sight. Oh, I hate, hate, hate how helpless I feel!

"Pleas-s-s-se," I say through chattering teeth. "Please go away."

"That's no way to say you've secretly missed me all day."

Words are meaningless. But the sooner he gets what he's come for, the sooner he will leave. "What do you want," I ask, without a single inflection.

"You," he says, and gets into the water.

My calm turns into terror. I duck underwater and flee. The dread of being seen is replaced by the fear of being touched. I scramble up on the banks and away from him. Now he is in the water, and I am on the opposite shore. When he stops moving, I do too. I hug my legs to my body, hiding myself as best as I can. He slowly swims toward me, eyes intent on me. I dig my heels into the earth and push away. He stops. I stop. He advances. I retreat. I know I cannot truly escape him; I just need a safe distance.

"Am I so repulsive?" he asks, his wet skin shimmering in the light.

I choke on my response. This moonlit night is too reminiscent of another treasured night with Rama, where love was the very air we breathed.

"It doesn't have to be this difficult, my princess," Ravana says. "I suffer seeing you like a wild animal."

I stare at his shadow and say, "Only because you've reduced me to one."

"I will never hurt you." His tone is different this night, almost despondent.

He patiently waits for my next move. The moon shines down on us, softening the dark night. In another life, in another place, in another dream, I might have been able to concede his handsomeness, the way that Lakshmana and my father are handsome. Ravana says no more but gives me a longing look before turning his eyes to the moon.

"Beautiful, is it not?" he says.

It seems like it will be a long night ahead. "It reminds me of Rama."

"Everything reminds you of Rama."

"I'm glad you've noticed."

"I notice everything."

"But understand nothing."

"What do you mean?"

"No," I say sharply. "Do not pretend that you care what I think or feel."

Ravana looks at me, genuinely baffled, before turning to the moon again. When I'm quiet, the words flow from his mouth, soft as

flower petals. It is a tactic he has not yet tried. I know how to parry with the aggressive Ravana, but this is a new face—hesitant, confused.

"You don't understand, Sita. I *only* care about what you think, what you feel. I can't sleep at night. I spend most of my waking hours trying to understand you. There is nothing I want more than to please you. I'm alienating those close to me for your sake. I'm losing the love of my family for you. The hope for your favor is the only thing that drives me."

There is something genuine about him. He is asking nothing of me. He isn't even glancing at me. I've never seen him more benign. It seems as if he has forgotten I am here. His nine missing heads might still have their eyes on me, but I don't feel them as I usually do. The two eyes I can see are gazing at the moon.

Careful, careful, I think. He is weaving his spell more masterfully tonight: He has come to understand me more and is appealing to my empathy. I look at him sharply. Has he moved closer?

"Haven't I proved that I will not harm you?" he pleads.

He is dangerous because he believes his own words.

The wind sweeps over us like a cold blanket. A cloud covers the moon. It is true that he has never physically harmed me, but I have seen his desire to do so many times. Despite the invisible barrier he cannot cross, he is a man of dangerous moods, a predator. May I never forget it. Since he isn't looking, I wring the water from my garment and my hair. Sharduli hoots from a nearby branch. *Use his mood to your advantage.*

He stands submerged to his waistline, where the water ripples around his navel. He seems to be in deep contemplation, unguarded. The moon travels to another place in the sky. Direct questions will not work.

"Tell me how you became immortal," I say.

Ravana looks at me without turning his face, a sidelong look. "Only I know the full extent of my power. It's only fitting that I trust you more than I've trusted anyone else."

I almost smile. Divulging his secrets to me is like confessing his crimes to a cat or a mouse. I'm his captive and no threat to him. Let him think it's in the name of love.

"Through the power of my arms, I've conquered my enemies," he says. "But the source of my immortality is the boon granted to me by Brahma, the creator. My mother has already spoken to you of this. Like all others in my family, she knows one or two locations of my penance. I had not yet reached manhood when I offered my first head into the ritual fire.

"With blood still spilling from my neck, I traveled to the edge of the world, seeking a sacred and secluded place for my next sacrifice. I finally found it in the desert between Earth and Yama's abode. I spent one thousand years there before offering my next head."

A chill of horror spreads over my skin. I have heard of the insane hacking off their own limbs. A special power is needed for such intense self-mutilation. A special madness. As he continues speaking, I find it increasingly difficult to stay awake. A dark Maya flits around me, a ghostly presence eager to show me the source of its power. The pull to fall into unconsciousness is strong. Whenever it touches my damp skin, my teeth chatter lightly. Is he conscious of this singular force?

He seems too absorbed in his tale to notice; he savors this rare opportunity to speak candidly. Describing his austerity in detail, he reveals three more locations: at the Ocean of Milk, at a cliff shaped like a cow's ear, and at the bottom of the red clay canyons. Now I know half of the locations where he acquired his powers. He must really judge me harmless, else he has no inkling that my knowledge could have any consequence. And I see why: I'm a prisoner and a woman. Can there be anyone more pitiable? And yet it's at this precise moment that I glimpse that my womanhood is an asset to me: I'm willing to listen. My compassion and openness is precisely what encourages him to speak so freely, and so I learn the emotional cost of his penance.

He had to leave everything behind, very much like leaving this life for the next. He did not bring his family bonds with him. He had to shed every single attachment, every desire, in order to open himself to the possibility of what was to come. That required singular determination. His mother thinks he did it for her, for their clan. But she was left behind too, as were all of them. All he held to was himself. That is where his ultimate loyalty lies.

"You are tired," he says, finally noticing. "Sleep. I will not touch you."

Is his promise anything to rely on? Yet I curl up into a ball and fall asleep within seconds.

The Earth rises up to embrace me. The exhaustion and chill in my bones melt away. My clothes and hair dry in the gentle breeze of the night. I fall asleep. But my spirit is fully awake, ready for the onslaught.

The sand banks begin to shake, and I'm pulled into the water, dragged under by an invisible force. I plunge to the very bottom of the ocean. I focus all my faculties on the element of water, praying to make it mine. The escape route opens up to me, a trail across the ocean floor. I don't dare feel delighted yet. The sea water molds around me, and I begin to swim at the speed of thought. When I emerge from the sea and step onto the mainland, Rama waits for me. He throws his bow aside and runs to me. For months, they have camped on the shores, seeking the means to cross it and rescue me. The joy I feel is so immense, I'm sure I will explode. Only his strong embrace holds me together. I cry out loud with tears of joy. Lakshmana stands next to us, smiling broadly. All is forgiven, and it's time to return to Ayodhya. The exile is complete; our family waits. We can put this tragedy behind us. I'm free from Ravana! I'm so exhilarated, I ask no questions.

The entire journey back to Ayodhya, I never once let go of Rama's hand. I sleep holding his hand; we walk through the jungle hand-in-hand. As the mighty empire comes into sight, we nearly sprint, so eager to be reunited with our family. The entire city glows, decked in flower garlands, redolent with costly fragrances, and lit up by fire lamps. The royal family stands ready with all the sacred instruments to crown Rama king. We rush into their arms, forgoing all formality in our unspeakable joy. Finally. Home!

Rama never lets go of my hand, even when his matted hair is shorn and the crown is placed on his head. He sets me on his lap, and we are showered with flowers. The streets are crowded with our beloved people, celebrating our homecoming. I bite my lips, restraining the intense joy I feel meeting my people whom I love so much. It is the happiest day of my life.

As time goes by, I give birth to beautiful twin girls. I never thought I could love anyone more than Rama. The months in captivity withholding my cycles seem like a faraway dream. Thoughts of Ravana haunt me only in occasional nightmares. Rama and I are blessed with ten children: five sons, five daughters. Lakshmana and Urmila, with their children, are our closest companions. The queen mothers dote on us, adoring their grandchildren. The only one we miss is Rama's departed father. Time flies so quickly. My girls grow into beauties and are married. Our eldest son is groomed to take his father's place on the throne. The exile becomes a hazy memory, a hardship that only made us closer. Every night, Rama and I offer prayers of gratitude for the blessed life we have.

That is when terror strikes.

In the dead of night, we are abruptly woken. The kingdom is in chaos and hundreds of women have been abducted. The terror I instantly feel tells me I never faced my own darkness. The queen mothers have been killed, my daughters taken. My sons were slain trying to protect their sisters. Howls of sorrow and despair are heard everywhere. Ravana appears in my chambers, my daughters in his grip. He has not aged a moment. "Your daughters are just as beautiful as you, Sita," he says, "with none of your powers to escape." His cruel laughter rings in my ears.

Rama straps on his bow and quiver, but it's too late: Ravana is gone, leaving chaos in his wake. The citizens' agony turns to anger at their king. The devastated homes fester; the people grow harsh with envy, arrogance, and illusion. Darkness sweeps over the Earth. Kinsmen kill kinsmen. The women who are left are ravished. My lord's army is in mutiny. Ayodhya is broken.

I sit alone in the empty palace. A mongoose scratches at my knee, urging me to look into the mirror before me, but I cannot bear to see my own face. I'm the cause of this. I escaped from Ravana when I had the chance to undo him. I had the opportunity to save my people from this. I could have ensured that no women would be abducted by Ravana ever again. And yet what did I do? I spent my days plotting how to escape, and when I saw my chance, I did. Without looking back. Without one thought about womankind. Without one thought about humankind.

I force myself to look into the eyes of the self-absorbed woman I've become. I have valued my own happiness above all else. I've placed my desire above the world's well-being. I scream in agony and smash her face, shattering the mirror into a thousand pieces. The palace around me melts away. My mind reels as I begin to understand the web of illusion I've just experienced. I need no mirror to see that I've been confronted with my own selfishness. My strongest desire has been to escape from Lanka, from Ravana. Now, I've seen where that would lead us: into the same terror again and again. And so I shed that layer of illusion.

I force my mind to clarity. I find myself standing in a desert—the place where Ravana sacrificed his third head for his own selfish gain. The vibration here is so saturated with it that I hear the echoes of my daughters' laughter, smell the scent of my sons' newborn heads, feel Rama's devotion to us. I close my eyes and savor it for just a moment, knowing it will never come to be, and then I open my eyes and turn to the monster before me. The spirit that guards the firepit and the skull within it stands before me in the form of Mithuna, twins. It immediately morphs into ten children: five girls, five boys.

"You will have to kill us, Mother," they say with one voice.

And so I do. I kill them with the love of a mother, burying her dead children. They match their power to mine, pressing my strongest desire on me: reunion with Rama, children, family, peace in the empire. I hold still, neither accepting nor denying.

I look at my firstborn twin daughters, undoing them through the power of my gaze, reducing them to what they truly are: desire. My cherished dreams. The girls become children, then babies, then melt into the Earth. No essence remains when their bodies are shed, for they were never alive. Still, the roots of my longing are pulled out with the tug of grief I feel as the last one of them disappears into the Earth. I may never see Rama again. I may never have children. I may never be truly happy again in this lifetime. I accept it. I accept it.

The skull lies at the bottom of the firepit. I hold it up to my face, peering into the eyeless sockets, then crush it between my hands, my fingers turning black with ash. But the next moment, it re-forms, just as resolutely grinning as before: Ravana's sacrifice was greater than mine. His attachments were shorn; I cling to Rama.

I wake up with a start. It's morning in Lanka, and Ravana is at my side. True to his word, he sits at a safe distance. He beholds me fondly, as if we've grown close through the course of the night. This is the first full night we've spent together—and the last, I hope, though I cannot cling too tightly to any of my hopes now.

"You are even more beautiful when you sleep," he says.

He seems entirely unaware of what has occurred on the energetic plain.

"It is said," he continues, "that when a man stays a full night in submission to a woman's will, she becomes his master."

"Sounds like another invention by you to further your own plans." I want to yawn and stretch my body out, but I will not do such casual and familiar things within his view.

He smiles. "Maybe so, and yet it's true: You are my master." He leans forward suddenly: "What are those smudges on your hands?"

Tension spikes in my belly. The ash from the skull! I rub my hands into the dirt.

"I'm your master," I say, "the way a dangling carrot is the master of a donkey."

His eyes return to my face. "I don't underestimate you."

My tension increases. Does he suspect, after all? Does he know I've found the skulls?

Without closing my eyes, I carefully inspect his energetic body. On a being of his stature, the compromise is as minor as a cut on a child's knee. The droplets are tiny but steady. Left untended, even a small wound can be deadly.

He makes a sweeping bow, and the next time I blink, he is gone.

Out of nowhere, the throng of female guards surrounds me, mocking me. They remind me that I have to contend with them when he's gone.

"Spent the night with our king, did you?" No-Neck leers. "Don't act so holy."

"No use talking to her," another one says. "She loves his games."

"His other queens should take lessons from this one," No-Neck says. "By day, they pretend to hate each other. By night, they coo like lovebirds."

They coo mockingly and turn their weapons to poke me with the tips. They never tire of doing so. I yawn and stretch out my body. I beckon Sharduli to come down from her tree. If only they knew how I truly spent my night. I feel surprisingly rested.

CHAPTER 13

Salute Your Queen

I cannot leave Lanka as long as Ravana lives. Safety is an illusion. This knowledge sits heavily in me, right beside the knowledge that Rama is alive. Every time I think of Rama, I etch his name into a leaf with my nails. The ground where I sit is scattered with them, as if it's autumn and the trees have shed their bounty. Shurpanakha has come to sneer at me a few times, but always from a distance. Dhanya-Malini is my most precious connection. I never summon her, for fear that Ravana will harm her, but she visits me frequently. Most often, it's in his company. She always clings to his arm, as if she's there for him, but when he isn't looking, she gestures to me with her hands, eyes, and mouth. Both of us are trained in the use of mudras, and the gestures are our secret language. We feel the thrill of communicating right under his nose.

It is from Dhanya that I learn that Vibhishana's pressure to let me go has only intensified. When asserting his own opinion was not effective, Vibhishana rallied others on the council. Together, they have spoken to him. From this I understand that I have risen above being a mere conquest. An ordinary woman would not have this leverage. Vibhishana and the others feel the threat I pose. They may not understand it, but they feel it and know they are headed for destruction. The final night is coming for them.

On Dhanya's suggestion, I have asked to tour Lanka without Ravana. Vibhishana cannot gain entry to the sorrowless forest or permission for an audience. We hope that the tour will grant us the subterfuge we need. On the indicated day, dawn wakes me. Rays of light come in through the branches. I gather a handful of leaves to my bosom, pressing my beloved's name to my heart, and press my nails into a new stack of leaves, arranging them into neat piles. I eat a few pieces of honeydew melon to fortify myself.

When I hear the noise of a royal arrival, I gather the stacks of leaves and hide them in the pleats of my cloth. I draw the Cloth of Essence across my chest, hiding and pressing the leaves to me. Ravana has sent his mother as my chaperone, and her palanquin is gaudily decorated. Though I'm not delighted to see her, I'm glad that he honors my request to go without him. A long trail of maidservants lines up behind the palanquin, holding the usual: perfumes and oils, dresses and garments of various colors, towels and steaming water, mirrors, jewels, refreshments. It is not enough that I've said no a thousand times. Still they insist. I want to slap my forehead, the universal mudra for exasperation.

Kaikasi sticks her head out from the palanquin's sheer curtains. Her earlobes are weighed down with giant pearls, and her hairstyle is so elaborate, I'm surprised she can hold her head up. By way of greeting, she says, "Can you really summon our lord with your magic?"

Somehow, even that has been added to the gossip around Lanka.

"There is no reason for him to come," I say.

The queen mother crosses her arms, pouting, and says, "I'm tired of hearing how special you are. Show me."

It's like having an obstinate child on my hands, only it's a million-year-old grandmother. I cannot imagine that my stubbornness exceeds hers. As I lift my hand, her gaze hungrily follows my movement. I flick my hand through the air, pulling the wind to me. But so weak is my pull, so pitiful my power, that it barely responds. Yet, like a ripple in a lake, it grows and spreads so that he feels it as a gentle touch. I detach my sensory perception from him, which is to say, I pull my Shakti into my body and tightly around me. I don't want to feel his response.

"That's it?" Kaikasi asks, slouching stiffly back into her seat.

I drop my hand and shrug. She waits, suspicion scrunching her brows into a frown. Every so often, she scans the sky as if her son will come flying. It takes longer than usual, as if he knows the exact urgency of my summoning, containing merely his mother's need for entertainment. I do not know what the lord of Lanka does when he isn't stalking me. No king can spend all his time in the women's quarters.

Ravana arrives, followed by an entourage of servants and wives. An ivory umbrella with tassels shields him from the sun. Red silk is wrapped around his waist, and a matching shawl is across his bare chest. He wears a crown with lightning-bolt spikes, shark-shaped earrings, and a golden breastplate with matching armlets. Fancy.

As he approaches with great pomp, the chatter of his consorts announces, *We love him. He loves us. We don't need you.* Today, he is the heroic lover, granting me his favor, allowing me to see how desired he is. His wives hang on his arms and trail behind him. Still, he looks at me with wonder, as if he is seeing me for the first time. It's been only a few hours.

Dhanya-Malini's arm is slung around his waist. Her dress is exquisite, spun from pure gold. She smiles her sad smile, managing to look helpless and wise at the same time. With her hand at her side, she does the mudra for *It's done,* lifting her pinky and extending her thumb. When Ravana turns to the side, I do the mudra for *Perfect,* index finger and thumb touching.

"Everything has been arranged," he says, "according to your desire."

Dhanya gestures *Not exactly* and gives me a meaningful look. I make sure my crest jewel is secure at the nape of my neck, a reminder that I am my father's daughter. The leaves with Rama's name are pressed against my chest, covered by my garment. I leave Dhanya-Malini's necklace hidden in Sharduli's burrow. I walk past the maids holding paraphernalia for my beautification.

"At least clean your face!" Ravana argues.

I feel clean, streaked with dirt, soil on my hands. It would be amusing if he was ashamed of me, this coveted prize he's so mad about.

"Stop this bickering, children!" Kaikasi hollers. "Let's go."

She points at a sheer veil, beautifully embroidered, luxuriously studded with gemstones. It molds itself around me, hiding my unkempt state. He will not suffer anyone to see me. When I climb into the palanquin, Kaikasi wrinkles her nose and moves away. "You're worse than an animal. At least they groom themselves."

"My greetings to you, Queen Mother," I say.

She huffs and moves farther away so that I won't sully her dress. The blood-drinkers heave up the palanquin to their shoulders and carry us away from Ravana and his entourage. They have their own day planned. Dhanya has arranged a troupe of actors to enact Ravana's most famous exploits.

"Why interested in a tour of Lanka now?" Kaikasi asks.

"If I'm to be queen," I say, "shouldn't I see the kingdom?"

"That's what my son said. Sounds like you are repeating his words."

"If he's to be my master, shouldn't I make his words mine?"

"Enough! Do not squabble with me."

She chews the left side of her bottom lip and talks under her breath as if I'm not there. The folds on her neck jiggle as we're carried up the steps into the palace. We are sucked into the mouth of the monster, entering his belly. I hold my breath and sit up straight, pushing away the panic. *May I not be trapped in here.* I pat my shoulder, the way I'd caress Sharduli if she was perched there. I miss her small claws pressing delicately against my skin. I hug the stacks of leaves closer to me.

When we leave the entrance to the Lotus Hall behind, I breathe more easily. We glide through high-ceilinged hallways held up by mighty pillars of gold. The sun flows in through the high-up windows, casting the hallways half in shadow, the other in bright light. Finally,

we exit the palace and come out into the open. As we descend the stairway, a shower of flower petals rains down on us, along with the cheer, "Sita! Sita!"

Thousands upon thousands of people dressed in their finest, carrying banners and flowers, have gathered in the courtyard, which has been decorated with strings of mango leaves and jasmine. Torches with fragrant oils burn in the breeze. Conch shells blow, bugles and drums resound; *shehnais* play sprightly melodies. The people wave flags in the air as they cry my name. They throng around a large fountain in the center, one that I recognize with a jolt: It's the fountain I saw in a dream when Ravana's Maya pulled me to the first firepit. In daylight, it's made of solid material; blood-drinkers hold the girls tight. The liquid that gushes from their mouths is clear.

We move out among the people, the guards making way for us. Youngsters run up to the palanquin, holding gifts for me, eager to please. I stick out my hand and give them a stack of leaves. The rest, I scatter into the crowd. Hundreds upon hundreds of green, shiny leaves shower on them. They cheer loudly, jumping to catch this token from their presumed future queen. Kaikasi snatches the last one from my hand.

"What is this?" she demands. A question that needs no answer.

She glares at the leaf, reading the beloved name:

राम

"Rubbish," she says, crushing the leaf in her hand and throwing it out. "So, this is why you wanted to come out of hiding. What do you think a handful of leaves will do?"

We keep going moving through the chanting crowd. The chaos outside is in my honor yet has nothing to do with me. It's Ravana's voice, magnified by the hundreds. What has he done to incite this reaction? What has he told them?

"You think your husband is coming to rescue you," Kaikasi sneers, looking like her daughter. "You think he is on his way, that he will cross the ocean that no human has ever crossed. You think he will somehow break his way into this fortress, which even the gods cannot penetrate."

She is both right and wrong. I do pray for that day, but I don't think of the obstacles the way she delineates them.

"Believe me, he has forgotten you. How long has it been since you came here? You must have kept count. Seven months."

"And fourteen days. The monsoon should have been here." But the skies are clear.

She waves her hand impatiently. "If he was coming, your prince would have been here by now. Men forget so fast." She huffs out air from her nose, knowing this all too well from personal experience. "They tire of their wives. They seek their own pleasures. Just this morning my daughter-in-law, Sarama, revealed to me how unhappy she is with Vibhishana. He thinks he can manage the kingdom when he can't even satisfy his wife. Husbands!" As if she's illustrated her point expertly, she concludes, "The best course for you is to embrace your life here. It's beyond anything you could have imagined."

"Is it so glorious to be one of seven thousand women vying for one man's attention?"

I've learned the size of the harem from Dhanya. Kaikasi holds up her hand, as if she's heard enough from me already. The two bangles around her wrist clink together. Her fingers are manicured, the veins protruding. She grabs one of my hands, shooting chills up my arm.

"Sita, time runs out for women like you. My son's patience runs out. You don't have much time. He has never been this patient before. You will say yes eventually. Why wait?"

I pull my hand away. She starts counting on her fingers, "Some are persuaded by jewels and costly cloth. Others, when they see the other happy wives. Some need to be in the dungeons for a few weeks. Others need to see their former husbands and families killed. Don't think you are so special. One or two have been stubborn like you. Do you know what happened to them?"

She leans very close to me. "We ate them."

The portion of honeydew I ate rises to my throat. I grit my teeth and push down the nausea. She feels like a python, snaring me. Even the way her neck swivels reminds me of a snake. I keep my eyes on the city. We proceed onto a large thoroughfare, the streets lined with people, but the chanting is quieter. Will Vibhishana find a chance to speak with me? But what about Kaikasi, who favors her eldest son?

"Take us into the city!" Kaikasi calls out.

A chariot yoked with four white horses waits for us at the end of the courtyard. Like the palanquin, it's draped in sheer veils. The servants deposit the palanquin in the chariot, and we begin our descent into the city. Guards unknown to me march next to the chariot, one in each corner. For the next few hours, I see every stratum of Lanka. This is a city of opposites, full of the deepest horrors and the most auspicious endeavors. Side by side, I see hideous demons and beautiful perfected beings, shining with power and asceticism. And they are all Ravana's kin and people. He is lord to such a variegated mix of beings. He appeals to the lowest of the low and the highest of the high.

Our presence is noted, but the elaborate celebratory mood has not been constructed. I get to see the real Lanka, where all-too-familiar daily affairs are negotiated. I see great ritual fires blazing, mantras being chanted loudly. The bazaars are full of goods, and women haggle and fill their baskets with fruits and meats. The horses neigh as we navigate our way out from a busy marketplace. Every so often, Kaikasi points to a building, explaining its significance. But she doesn't seem like a person who mingles with commoners. The city appears in every way to be just like Ayodhya. The only thing missing is throngs of children; I've not seen even one.

"Where are the children?" I ask.

She shakes her head. "Our young attain youth immediately after birth. Within hours, they are ready go out into battle if needed. My ancestral grandmother Shalakatankata procured this boon for us. We've never needed to tend to helpless infants since—unlike you humans. Your lives are so short, yet half your life, you need your mothers to wash your bottoms."

I'm astounded by this news. I knew that was the way of the gods but not blood-drinkers.

The chariot turns a corner and begins the climb back up the mountain. My heart plummets. The urge to stand up, scramble out of the palanquin, and run into the crowd is very strong. Vibhishana has not yet made his appearance. Have I suffered this old woman's company in vain? The only useful thing I've learned is that Lanka has no children. If there will be a war, this appeases me. If Rama comes . . .

A great commotion ahead of us brings the chariot to a halt. The horses snort, and Kaikasi narrows her eyes. The horses lift their tails and begin to defecate. A crowd has gathered, blocking the road. I have not seen the likes of them before; they have the heads of boars, goats, bears, and other animals.

"Queen Mother!" they grunt, hailing her. "Queen Kaikasi! Most benevolent queen! Bless us!"

"Pisachas," she grumbles, but looks pleased enough to grant them an audience.

She slithers out from the palanquin. They chant her name even louder, growling and yipping. The guards around the chariot turn their attention to the spectacle. The one closest to me scratches her arm with her spear. Then her head turns sharply to the sky, and she cries out. The guards point at something I cannot see because the layers of sheer curtains obscure my view.

I get out of the palanquin, leaning on the railing of the chariot to gaze up. A few people stop to stare at me, but most are enthralled by the spectacle up ahead. The queen mother is occupied with the Pisachas. An eagle soars in circles above our chariot. One of the guards sprouts wings and takes flight. She's not quite a bird but not a blood-drinker either. Brown feathers flutter down in her wake, awakening memories in me of Jatayu, king of vultures. That valiant bird gave his life to save me so long ago. I hold up my hand to catch one of the feathers, as if reaching for that brave ally.

The guard swats my hand down. "Get inside!"

Instead of forcing me, she speaks in aggressive whispers to the other two, beating her chest. They point their spears at the eagle and the winged blood-drinker in pursuit. Their eyes never leave the sky. I stay where I am so that I can see exactly what is happening. They circle the chariot, anticipating a ground attack. This is proof of an internal threat to Ravana's power. It had truly never crossed my mind that they were guarding me from others within Lanka; I always thought they were here to prevent me from escaping. They fear nothing from me. Even if I had a weapon, perhaps a small hidden knife, I could never so much as poke anyone with it. That is not my way. Will I die because of it?

The eagle soars out from a speck of a cloud, chased by the bird guard. I pray for the victory of the eagle. Their enemy is surely my friend. This simple logic rings true. I feel the strong impulse to reach out for the elements, to grab hold of at least one and wield it. There must be something I can do to sway the wind in our favor. Just as I move my hand in the air to pull the wind to me, I remember: That would summon Ravana.

And so I rejoice when the eagle grows in size and swats the other bird with its wings. The brown bird starts plummeting to the ground and disappears behind a building. The guards hop in agitation, not noticing the blood-drinkers materializing behind them. The stealthy assassins attack. The guards are killed, their necks twisted, all at once. I stifle my cry. Though they are nameless strangers, their sudden executions fall heavily upon me; they are just servants. Kill *him,* not his servants! But I know I'm naive. The eagle soars in circles above us.

The Pisachas push forward an offering to Kaikasi, a creature with a chain around its neck. The eagle tucks in its wings and begins to plummet toward me. I retreat into the palanquin. I'm fairly certain I know who the eagle is, but nothing is as it seems here. The drapes flutter as the bird swoops down and lands on the railing, just outside the palanquin's curtains. It has fine brown feathers and a white neck. Just as I note the piercing yellow eyes, it begins to morph into a man. He has a warm energetic pulse, the kind one instantly trusts. An unlikely blood-drinker. I sit still and behold him. He is protected from outside view by the chariot's curtains.

"Princess, my heartfelt respects," he says.

If I had a doubt, his voice confirms his identity.

"You risk your brother's wrath to see me," I say.

"I cannot see you," Vibhishana points out.

I smile slightly. I'm grateful that he does not pull apart the drapes. "Vibhishana, your difference is as discernible as a flower's fragrance."

"A flower without fragrance is like a man without character," he says, understanding me exactly.

I glance at the crowd, just long enough to see that Kaikasi is bent over the chained creature.

"She will be occupied a few more minutes," he assures me.

He speaks quickly, knowing how little time we have. "My brother's life is protected by Grandfather Brahma's boon. My boon is trivial by comparison. My intuition always aligns with the highest powers of good. The day he brought you to Lanka, I dreamed of Kalaratri, the goddess of the dark night. She appeared to me in a shining golden cloth and a single black braid. Your presence in Lanka does not bode well for my people."

"Yet your pressure to release me has been unfruitful."

"Princess, open allegiance is impossible until a proper path opens up. We do not know the whereabouts of your prince. We are not yet confident in his ability to reclaim you. The means to overthrow my brother have not been revealed. But you, Sita, are in a unique position. You have rare access to the Ruby Room. He can only be destroyed from the inside."

I press my hand to my heart, where a green leaf is stuck between the pleats. I hand it to Vibhishana. He takes it just as Kaikasi glides toward the chariot, followed by her grunting admirers. Vibhishana instantly becomes an eagle, perched on the railing again, the leaf in his beak. Kaikasi lumbers up and shoos the eagle away, unaware of its identity. The eagle lifts, disappearing into the sky. Kaikasi's mouth and chin drip with blood. I expect her to notice the new guards, but the queen mother isn't one to pay attention to servants. Vibhishana has been clever. Will it be enough to avoid Ravana's notice?

"Go!" Kaikasi shouts as she slumps down next to me.

The chariots jolts into action. My temple slams against the side of the palanquin. I rub it softly as she wipes her mouth and chin clean.

"Go, go!" she orders, making the chariot speed up. My legs slam against hers.

"Really, he should force you to bathe!" She waves her hand in front of her nose, as if I've suddenly started stinking awfully. "I will not endure this again, I tell you that."

She has become very eager and excited. She tells me how delicious the chained creature was, a rare delicacy, a half-breed born from the union of a sage and an animal, captured in the wild. She does not care how distasteful her words are to me. In Ayodhya, it was Rishyashringa—half sage, half-deer, who performed the legendary ceremony that produced Rama and his brothers. Her appetites will never be acceptable to me.

She ignores me, tapping her fingers against her knee. The streets are strangely deserted now, and the sound of celebration has abated. Flower petals are crushed to the ground. But my tour of Lanka is by no means complete. The streets are empty only because the entire populace of Lanka has gathered elsewhere. A throng of guards, however, meet us to escort us to our next destination. Vibhishana's agents deftly mingle with them and then disappear.

The noise as we enter the court is deafening. The throng at the courtyard was just a handful compared to this gathering. Their greetings pierce my eardrums. Conch shells and bugles blow, drums begin to beat, and flower petals shower on me. The size of the court eclipses that of the Lotus Hall. The pillars are so massive that they have staircases and gilded balconies. The golden latticework and the abundance of gemstones display Lanka's signature style. All of Lanka's elite are here, attired grandly. At the far end of the hall, I see the dazzling stairway that leads up to the throne, where the king will preside. Ravana proudly waits for us there.

The royal family stands on elevated platforms next to the throne. Here is a diagram to Lanka's power, displayed in the hierarchy of thrones. The first one I take note of is Vibhishana. He stands to the right of Ravana's throne, just one step down, indicating his high status. He holds an ivory conch in his hand. The fearsome ministers, adorned with sacred clay, chant mantras and hold various articles ready. A ritual is underway.

The palanquin stops at the base of the stairs. The queen mother takes her stand next to Shurpanakha, right below Vibhishana. I have never seen Shurpanakha dressed in finery; her hair is brushed back, and she wears a crown. She displays her face before the mutilation, her nose long and warty. Not even her mother's sly beauty has made an impression on her features. Kaikasi presses her lips together repeatedly in the unconscious mannerism of the old. She has grown tired of me, of all this.

A hush descends as Ravana speaks.

"My beloved Sita, here we stand before you, ready to consecrate you as the queen of Lanka." The blood-drinkers lift their conch shells to show their readiness. Strained smiles display their fangs. "You will be our ruler, we your servants."

He introduces me to each of his ministers. The leaders of this nation bow at my feet. As each blood-drinker kneels, his entire entourage follows suit. With one name, a whole section of the room shows its obedience to my queenship. Ravana names only one son, Indrajit, but as many as a hundred kneel. Finally, "Vibhishana, my brother, acknowledges you as queen."

Vibhishana hesitates for a moment, then kneels.

"My mother, sister, and wife accept you," he goes on.

I behold Mandodari for the first time. The queen shimmers with youth, her skin, lips, and hair glowing. She wears a crown so large, it eclipses any other adornments. But her eyes are puffy and red, evidence that she's been crying. The crown and her tears both call out: *This honor belongs to me!* How I wish that were true, after all.

Ravana turns to his people and declares, "Faithful people of Lanka, Sita is the one we've been searching for. The Goddess of all Goddesses, superseded by none. I, your king, bow at her feet. Today, Sita will become your ruler. Put your hands together in prayer and salute your queen."

"Yes!" They roar, hungry like a firestorm.

Those who are not already kneeling follow the instructions of their king. Placing their hands at their heart, they bow to me. The sight of so many bowing down to me has an overpowering effect. They want me to feel awe at their meekness, humbled by their subservience to me. I clench my fists, my neck hot. The hall grows silent. The tension is heavy. I think quickly, *How can I turn this situation into an opportunity?* I take a deep breath and connect to my heart. It's time to make my will known.

I ascend to the top of the stairs and go to the head priest. I take the pitcher brimming with holy water and hurl it away. As it clatters down, the assembly looks up, gasping.

"Citizen of Lanka," I call out. "The best of Ravana's people, hear my voice. My will is in direct opposition to your king's and will always remain so. Save yourself while there is time! Reject Ravana and surrender. My husband prince Rama is noble and forgiving. You will be forgiven. Your clan, your children, your wives, will continue to live happily. Make someone worthier your king. If you do not heed my words, your entire race will—"

"ENOUGH!"

The Maya Ravana throws at me covers my mouth and takes my breath away. I sway on my feet. But I force my next words out: "Now is the time to act!"

These words are directed at Vibhishana. Again, Ravana silences me with his energetic hand. A shiver runs down my spine. The ministers are on their feet, their faces flushed with emotion. Their animosity is not unanimous; many of them look at me with animation, almost greed. Ravana rises up in the air to face me, his fangs bared, his eyes wide, his Maya vicious and vengeful. The insults he wishes to say aloud press on my psyche. He withholds them, wanting his people to see me as their queen.

"Behold the noose around your king's neck!" I cry out.

Half of the court shouts, "Release her! Release her!"

The other half cries, "She's the one! She's the one!"

Ravana swoops in and seizes me like a bird snatching up its prey. I dangle in his arms as he departs, leaving his people, leaving the consecration behind. He could fling me down to the ground and kill me instantly without any damage to his heads. Curse upon his curses! But like the lowest of humankind, he uses his brute strength to overpower me. Roughly, he drags me back to the garden, throwing me back under the sorrowless tree. This way, he can cling to the illusion that I am merely his prisoner.

CHAPTER 14

The Goat Blood Prophecy

It is dangerous to worship anyone but Ravana on this island, but rumors of me are spreading. Through the muttering of my unwilling guards, I hear them as the tiniest of trickles. It seems that my status has grown since the consecration debacle, or so rumor has it. But I have no privileges beyond the sorrowless forest. Dhanya cannot visit me now without sparking Ravana's suspicion. She is as captive as I am, just on the other side of the divide. Ravana's efforts to break me continue at their usual pace. I have not been able to discover more about the source of his powers. I don't know how to destroy his ancient skulls. Frustrated, I dig my fingers into the ground, the dirt jamming under my fingernails painfully.

If we were on the mainland, the monsoon rains would be here, drenching the world in cleansing rain, but not a drop falls from the skies. Only the full moons ground me, even as I restrain their force on my cycles. I go to pick mangoes, and Sharduli scampers along, straight to the pond, to see if she can cheat a fish of its life. She is happy to frolic in search of them. The pink and blue lotuses look so graceful in bloom. Nature does not yield to humankind's evil. The lotuses will bloom and wilt according to their natural course, regardless of what happens in my life. I find the mango trees, plucking off ripe mangoes, and begin sucking on one as I walk back. I gather the rest to my chest. Sharduli might like to have one.

Without any warning, the guards surround me and tie a cloth around my eyes. They drag me away. "Where are you taking me?" I cry. I can see nothing.

No answer but their cackling. I'm restrained by rough hands. I feel us rising into the sky. My stomach lurches as we lift off, their grip tight around my arms and waist. The last time I was airborne, I was trapped in Ravana's arms. I must *not* think of it; the lines of time distinguishing *now* from *then* blur before my darkened eyelids. With shallow breaths, I keep my emotions at bay. After long minutes, I'm shoved forward. My bare feet make contact with a cold, slippery surface, uneven under my toes. I concentrate on this, on each breath. They could be pushing me off a cliff. The darkness intensifies as I'm pushed into a narrow enclosure.

Someone takes my hand. The chill that shoots up my arm is familiar.

"Queen Mother?" I ask, my voice trapped in darkness.

She grunts and leads me into the tunnel. *He needs his toys taken away sometimes*, she's threatened. She pulls me by the hand and begins to chatter as if we are on a stroll. Her voice is amplified by the narrow enclosure. My fingers trail the uneven surface of a mountain. It is damp and cold. I take the blindfold off. It's only the two of us. When my eyes have adjusted, I let go of her hand.

There are many twists and turns. She curses once and pulls me back the way we came, turning in the opposite direction. I wonder if she is taking me to a place like the House of Wrath, where the royal family in Ayodhya would go to release intense emotions. Being sixteen and newlywed, I'd never been angry at Rama. But my mother-in-law had passionately described the house in detail to me. Cast in total darkness, the rooms became so dark, one could see nothing. You had to stay in the dark, seeking no distraction. In the final room, sunlight bathed you in its healing rays, cleansing you completely. From darkness to light, indeed—everyone's ultimate trajectory.

The tunnel is illuminated by a flickering torch up ahead. It opens up into a spacious cavern, decorated as a temple, with a big shrine at its center. We are the only ones here.

"Goddess Nikumbhila," Kaikasi says, bowing to the altar.

Nikumbhila is made of polished black stone and resembles Kali, weapons in her hands. I reverently touch the kusha grass they've spread around the altar. Red hibiscus flowers are everywhere. The soft petals haven't wilted; someone was here recently.

"This is Indrajit's place of worship. Only those he trusts are allowed here."

Hearing his name is enough to repulse me and remind me of scorpions.

"Ever since I saw you, Sita, I couldn't stop asking myself why my son is so fixated on you. He would never jeopardize his family, his sons, his fortune, all that we have won over millennia. How do you fit into our future?"

She tugs me away, her hand gritty and damp, like the surface of the mountain. "I've come to Nikumbhila again and again with this question," she says. "Shine light on this, Devi. Who is this woman? Why has my son developed this attachment to her?"

She pulls me to a somber area of the cave. It is dark, illuminated only by one torch. Her

face is covered by shadows. This corner feels like the secrets of a rich man who's won his wealth through devious means.

"I asked you what you are, remember? You could not answer. "

Can she not see that I'm just a woman abducted, torn from all I hold good and holy? She pulls me to a pool full to the brim with opaque liquid. The dark maroon ripples slightly in response to my breath. It has a pungent, salty smell.

"I have sacrificed three hundred goats in your honor," she continues. "Indrajit wielded the sword, as eager as I was. Nikumbhila appeared in the blood, showing us Lakshmi, goddess of wealth. With you as his consort, my son will truly become the one god. The gods will all accept his supremacy instead of contest it, as they so foolishly do."

I don't see anything but goat blood. Kaikasi takes a drop of it and smears it onto my forehead. "You are the one we've been looking for."

I wipe it off with the back of my hand immediately and back away from the pool of goat blood. Her insistence that I'm a goddess firms up my boundaries, but otherwise it means nothing to me. It must be like discovering you have a renowned father you've never met. It's fascinating but not deeply meaningful.

"You can capture my body but not my will," I tell her, knowing my words will be drowned out by goat blood prophecies.

The queen mother imagines that her son and I will join together, creating a new world order. But they ignore the most important aspect of a partnership: It must be mutual.

"The faults of the child will fall on the mother," I say.

Her shoulders slump forward. My captive mind longs for the bare earth, my sorrowless tree, and Sharduli, who by now must be pacing back and forth, awaiting my return. I take shelter in these small comforts, denied as I am any true knowledge of my identity.

I'm returned to the sorrowless forest as unceremoniously as I was snatched. I smell smoke as I approach my usual place by the tree. The three guards stand over a fire. The sun is high in the sky, and it's balmy in the air. I see that they are roasting something in the flames. A bushy tail lies on the ground. There is blood and a speckled coat of skin tossed on the ground. No!

"Sharduli?" I call out.

They turn to me with malicious expressions. Half-Mouth declares, "Your so-called tigress didn't even give us one scratch before we snapped her neck!"

"No!" I cry.

"Yes, what a disappointment," she says, gloating. "You should have named her Little Weakling, after yourself."

They turn the spear over the fire, roasting the small carcass, charring the flesh black.

"We will eat this little creature and enjoy your wrath," one of them says, "both far too small to satisfy any appetite."

"Curse us now!" Half-Mouth jeers. "Do your worst, pathetic human!"

"Short-lived, like this vermin!" another one shouts.

I cannot bear it. Sharduli's pink nose. Her unblinking eyes. Her soft, bushy tail. Her

intelligence. Her affection. Her understanding. I burst into tears. I turn to run away from this stinking spectacle, but the fourth guard is right there behind me, spear lifted.

"You are going nowhere," she says, showing her fangs.

"You cursed us, remember," Half-Mouth calls out. "We are eating up that threat."

"And you will eat up your own words," her friend says. "Curse, pah!"

They pick up the skewer and tear the carcass into four pieces. They blow on the flesh, tear chunks of it, blood tainting their lips, smacking their lips, all the while looking at me. My breath comes to me in short spurts. As on the day I was abducted, I'm blinded by my tears. I thought my heart was broken, but this is so gruesome, so cruel. My chest starts heaving with sobs, like when the Earth disappeared under me and all I could see was ocean.

"Curse us!" Half-Mouth exults, poking me with Sharduli's bloody bone.

"We will roast you up next," the others say.

They throw Sharduli's bones at my feet, licking their lips.

"You loved her little tail so much, here you go."

One of them throws the bushy tail at my face.

"I curse you," I say, between sobs. "I curse you."

But I can say no more. I'm not coherent. I can't talk. My little tigress. Sorrow, grief, anger, and pain erupt from me like bursts of lightning. The blood-drinkers are too dull to fathom my Shakti. But *he* feels it and is summoned. Within seconds, Ravana descends from the sky, flying to me, as he does only when in a hurry.

"Master!" They fall to their knees, weapons on the ground.

He looks at the smoldering fire, the bones at my feet, Sharduli's blood on me. He may not have known Sharduli at all, but he knows my pain.

"What have you done?" he demands of them.

More than ever, I can see the shadow of his true form, threatening to erupt from his human one. His dogs need to see him as he is.

"Master, master," they chant.

He turns to me. "Sita, tell me!"

In my grief-stricken state, I magnetize toward his compassion, the promise of revenge in his voice. He will do anything for me. My chest heaves. "They killed my pet mongoose, Sharduli, just to spite me."

"You have angered my queen!" he yells. "You have caused her pain!"

"But master!"

"Stand up," he orders.

"She threatened to curse us!" Half-Mouth cries. They cower.

As he lifts his arms, his energetic body swells. Their discarded weapons fly into his hands. He flings the spears at them, impaling them with their own weapons. They scream for mercy. Four thuds and it's over. The ghastly smell of their bodies final purging mingles with the smell of Sharduli's burned flesh. We're in the land of Yama, a hellish reality.

Their souls exit their bodies. I am vibrating with grief, and their essences begin to link with mine. Their souls rush toward me, animating my Shakti, compounding it, building it, fueling it, pushing me higher and higher. I rise into the sky. I fill up the sorrowless garden with my presence. I see the four walls of the premises I've so meticulously mapped. I see the city of Lanka, its streets thronging with blood-drinkers of all kinds. The fire that burned Sharduli grows and begins to burn the dead guards.

All this happens in an instant, and in the next, Ravana has grown to match my size. I know his body remains in the garden below, but his Maya, dark and powerful, approaches mine. And that is when I know: *He* killed Sharduli. *He* ate her flesh. *He* threw her bones in my face. He pretends to come to my aid when his obedient servants only act out his will. He is my only enemy.

I gather my fire. I will shatter his Maya. I will fling him into the dirt. I will end his immortal existence. The fire at my core flares, and I am about to lash out when I feel myself darken, my golden Shakti tinged with poison. How has this evil come into me? He watches, pleased. These dark flames are not his; they are mine. There are four dark flames latched onto my core. I instantly understand: This is not me, but them. The four dead souls are trapped in my Shakti, forced to do my bidding. Carefully, I unlatch them from me, as if I'm plucking fruit from a tree. I trace their outlines, giving them back to themselves. Their color softens, lighten. I release them. *Journey to your next destination. Go.*

With each one's departure, my power diminishes. When I release the fourth and final soul, I can see my physical body's hands moving. I'm back in my body again. A soundless sob runs through me. Sharduli's tail is in my hands.

Back in his false human form, Ravana watches me, smug.

"We are a match, Sita," he says. "Do you understand now?"

Deflated, I do. When I escaped into this garden, when I called out to the elements, it was on borrowed power. He killed those two women from the bath hall, inhaling their essence. In my shock, I inhaled just a tiny bit of their essence, and it gave me power—borrowed power.

"These souls want to be used," he says. "You could have kept them in your service for a later time when you need them. Or does it please you to be powerless?"

It's a dark power, a terrible power. It's not mine to wield. I understand perfectly that he orchestrated this scenario. "You did all this! To teach me how to trap them the way you do!"

"You are powerful, Sita. The most powerful woman I have ever met."

Like a large carrion opening its wings, he displays his form. He is full of souls he's consumed over countless millennia. If I could expand beyond the garden with only four souls, his potential is limitless. His entire body is a hellish torture chamber, a prison for the innocent. He is willing to kill his own people just to teach me a lesson. I've seen firsthand the power emanate from the sites of Ravana's sacrifices. Now I've seen his other vampiric power source. I know that his destiny is tied to mine and that his power can be undone. But how long can I find the sustenance to keep living this hopelessly captive life?

Even if I walk or run as fast as I can, I would never make it out from the gardens. The exits lead to other palaces, other prisons. Killing the guards did not give me Sharduli back. Their deaths give me nothing. It only affirms that violence begets violence, darkness more darkness. I would rather be powerless, but I'm not.

From somewhere far off, or as close as my heart, Sharduli whispers: *You are Ayonija, born of no womb, without birth, without beginning.*

I know that as my mother's daughter, I'm not all lotus blooms and bursting summer trees. I know the taste of blood, seeping into the earth, the dirt of decomposing bodies, the silent witnessing of brutalities. My mother does not interfere, and yet I've sprung up from within her to embody her defiance. When I do, will I qualify for Rama's love? It all centers on Rama for me. Rama's love.

I fall asleep with Dhanya-Malini's necklace in my hand and begin to dream. I float on a lotus like a sleeping baby. I hear voices echo underneath me and awaken at the sound of their prayers. A hundred women say my name, and I'm drawn to them. I grow from the lotus into . . . me. My devotees have invoked me. I'm exactly as they've made me. They've called me, and I will answer.

When I look down, I see a large, sprawling city, shrouded in night, covered with sleep and dreams: the perfect time to attack. Like mist descending to the Earth, I sink down, covering the entire citadel. I become the air they breathe; I descend into their dreams, their consciousness. It's the fire in their hearts I'm attracted to. It's my entry, my way into their beings. Nothing is hidden from me as I see their dreams enacting unspoken desires, appeasing daytime worries, enacting hidden fantasies. I obliterate their dreamscape, taking over entirely. There is nothing now in their minds but me. I don't say anything at first; I just want them to know the prayers of my supplicants have been answered: *I have come*. I lift my hand and bless them. And whisper, "I'm here."

I'm startled awake by a loud cry. It's my guards crying out: "Sita!"

They sit up, staring at me, as if they don't know whether they are awake or asleep, whether I'm real or a dream. A palace window lights up. Then another. We watch in silence as candle after candle, torch after torch, is lit. The entire palace is awake. Somehow, I know the entire city is too.

The next morning, I find out that all of Lanka, including its impervious king, was visited by the same dream. A dream of a lady with a long, black braid, draped in a golden garment. Every person woke up with a name on their lips: Sita. She lifted her hand in benediction. Some say darkness spewed from her mouth and hands. But that part came not from me, but from those who have something to fear, which means everyone in Lanka who is on Ravana's side. Those who love me found the dream auspicious, heartening. Those who hate me feel they were visited by a ghostly demon in the alluring form of a goddess. But I know: I don't have to choose either aspect. Both are mine to give, according to their desires and hopes. I will spew darkness or light in accordance to their most deeply held notions. Nothing is hidden from me. Nothing within their hearts is beyond my reach. Ravana thinks he brought me here, but I was summoned, and so I've come.

CHAPTER 15

Destroyer of Sorrow

The dream visitation elevates me to the top of the blood-drinker pantheon. No matter how many times Ravana replaces my guards, they remain sycophantic. Every time I stand up, they stand. When I speak, they fall to the ground, hands outstretched. They fear and adore me—all because of the dream. All because I've had the courage to deny the throne, a prize beyond their imagination and grasp. Ravana sweeps through the gardens like a brooding shadow; he has heard about the guards being slain while his mother was distracted by the Pisachas. But Vibhishana has covered his tracks well. Still, Ravana suspects it, like an itch he feels but cannot reach. His own kingdom is in upheaval. That must be a good thing, the blood-drinker kingdom unraveling. And yet darkness is growing in the world. I feel it at the edges of my dreams, as if some important boundaries may dissolve forever.

An unexpected visitor comes unannounced. After eight months in her kingdom, Queen Mandodari deigns to visit me. She comes without an entourage, declaring her confidence. The guards don't even need a signal from her to scatter. Mandodari stands silently at a distance. Her shoulders and belly are bare, a gem-studded cloth tied around her breasts. She has shining black hair, a gift from her mother, the Apsara Hema. Her skin is golden and her aura shimmering and so sweet of face, one would never guess her demonic nature. Among seven thousand women, she's kept her place as Ravana's primary wife, mother to his heir. Like Ravana, she has seen ages come and go. A year ago, her glow may have fooled me, but my perception has grown keen. No one can be his queen without matching his capacity for evil.

His other women look at me and wonder, *Why not me?* But Mandodari holds herself proudly, giving me a long, appraising look. With a husband like Ravana, her cunning has evolved. She must have presided over countless abducted females. She too is culpable. She certainly has not come to befriend me.

"I'm here because of the dream," she says. Her voice is low and steely, a sharp contrast to her feminine appearance. "Something must be done about you."

The way Mandodari says it informs me that her solutions are like the queen mother's: *Take away his toys.* But I am not just another helpless victim. This is a discussion, queen to queen. The words I form sound like prophecy.

"We *will* kill your husband."

Red spots appear on her neck. She feels threatened by this truth.

"If I allow his infatuation to continue . . . ," she responds.

With that, she leaves. Mandodari is no ally of mine. And yet Ravana does not come to see me the next day. Or the next day. Or the next. It turns into a week, then two. A stark change from his daily visits. At night, the windows of his quarters glow with merriment, bright in the darkness. Women's laughter, music, and shouts of celebration continue past midnight. I understand that the chief queen has rallied the consorts together.

As the eighth full moon of my captivity begins to rise, the party begins to spill out of the palace. Torches are speared all around the lotus pond. The fires glitter on its surface. Just like other evenings, I hear laughter and other sounds from the palace. But servants scurry about, setting up tables with food, the garden their obvious destination. As the crowd of blood-drinkers grows, they completely forget their deference toward me.

I leave and settle into Sharduli's and my grotto, hoping to avoid the revelry. But the servants set up Ravana's throne directly in front of me. Indeed, the consorts stroll along until they see me and then settle down in groups, drinking from their goblets. I close my eyes and keep my mind to myself. I see no opening for useful action. Gentle fingertips touch my hand. It's Dhanya with her soulful eyes.

"I tried to put a stop to all this," she whispers, kneeling by me. "But Mandodari has more power than I do. Forgive me."

Quietly, we hold hands until Ravana summons her. He's seated on his throne, drinking wine. She touches my cheek, her hand soft and damp. A dark sense of foreboding sits heavily in my belly. Night surrounds us, throwing ghostly shadows across those around me. Even the pretty queens look like demons, their lips glistening with red. As another group arrives, herded forward by a throng of guards, a chill slides over my skin. The cold I feel is recognition. Like me, these prisoners have no hope of escape. Their beings are numb. The old woman from the dungeons reminds me of Manthara, Ayodhya's notorious hunchback, her hair gray and dirty, her body gnarled. The blood-drinkers spit at her and pull her chains, making faces, indicating how gross they find her. Her thin arms wave in the air like twigs. They string her up on a branch, forcing her to witness the fate of the other prisoners.

To my left, a group of consorts drink copiously, giggling and talking. Their beautiful clothes are arranged around them carefully. They have no empathy for the prisoners. How many events like this have they attended to grow so callous? The food tables brim with meat: partridge, jungle fowl, porcupine, goat, buffalo, venison, rabbit, peafowl, roasted fish, and even *chakoras,* those rare moon-gazing birds. The other tables have venison, buffalo, and boar, sprinkled with spices. Heaps of rice laced with lemon slices and roasted cashews fill the air with their aroma

Shurpanakha stands by the food, sampling the various meats, spitting out morsels that don't meet her liking. She ignores me, yet her exaggerated behavior indicates she's putting on a show—for me or the queens, who knows? The maids walk about with crystal vessels full to the brim with various drinks: clear spirits, rum, and fruit wines flavored with fragrant spices.

Mandodari walks among the consorts with great authority, smiling as she moves from one group to the next. Clearly, she is the host, presiding over the debauchery, ensuring that everyone is pleased. The chalices of wine and liquor are never empty. She glances at me often but otherwise does not indicate that she knows me. So many of her problems would be solved if Ravana simply picked me as his choice morsel. He has threatened to do it. She's created a perfect setting for it to happen.

Ravana stands up. The cluster of women close to me stop giggling. As he walks past me toward them, their nervousness turns to fear. They clutch their goblets. What I mistook for flippant callousness was pretense. They knew all along one of them would be next. They clump together, eyes looking up at him, pleading. Some of them try smiling or sitting straighter. One titters drunkenly. They are young and beautiful, with long, shiny hair. The drunken one flashes her dimples as she smiles nervously. They are all humans, living as consorts to a man-eater.

"You," Ravana says, pointing at the one with dimples.

Her cheeks are smooth, and she glows like the moon. The others release a small sigh of relief. She seems too intoxicated to care. She stands up, swaying on her feet. He holds out his hand, and she takes it, smiling prettily. As he yanks her toward him, he looks at me. He smiles, wiping wine from his mouth with the back of his hand. The girl reaches up to his face and helps him, her finger tracing his lips. He looks at her approvingly, plunging into her with his Maya, obliterating her will, replacing it with his own. She grows momentarily slack in his arms and then perks up, a willing lamb at his side. "And you," he says, pointing to another.

Raucous laughter from another cluster of consorts demands my attention. They are throwing food into each other's mouths, seeing who can catch it between their teeth. One of them has fallen over into the table, platters of food crashing down on her. The laughter is uproarious as she sits up, a half-eaten peacock on her head.

Next to me, Ravana selects eight more women, and I unwillingly understand the significance of this number. One for each of his mouths. I cannot see his other arms or heads, but the women are pulled up, gripped in the air by invisible manacles. Returning to his throne, he sits two of them on his lap, one on each knee. The rest surround him in a circle, staring wordlessly up at him. The blood-drinkers around him cheer. They are waiting for their turn to feast.

"This can stop at any moment," Ravana calls to me.

All this a horrific ruse to get me to surrender? No matter what I do in this moment, it will continue. I clench my jaw and cleanse the sweat from my brow with a handful of dirt. As the victims scream, the band of musicians plays louder to drown out the sounds. Ten women are dying. What can I do? The blood frenzy grows so intense that I cannot watch. Ravana throws the half-eaten bodies to the guards, who lustily devour them. Shurpanakha snaps and growls, claiming her share. They chew and suck on the raw meat, snapping off bones, hacking off body parts, distributing it among themselves. The naga and blood-drinker consorts turn on the remaining humans. The Apsaras put dainty little bites into their mouths, plucking from the assorted collection. Without thinking, I attend to the souls that erupt from the murdered bodies, releasing them to the sky. In death, at least, they will be freed from him. I make sure of it.

The sound of a child crying turns my eyes back to Ravana. He has a boy no more than eight years old on his lap. I clutch my belly and stand up. He trails a sharp nail across the boy's neck, down to his stomach.

"Ma!" the boy cries, reaching out to me. "Ma!"

The crone in her chains howls curses, her voice brittle.

"Release him," I order.

The boy goes quiet, eyes glassy with terror. His arms dangle in the air.

"Take me instead," I say, stepping forward.

Ravana's eyes are unfocused, drunk. He licks his lips thirstily. His hunger is not satiated. Mandodari teasingly throws flowers petals on him. His skin shivers where the petals fall. He stares at me. All these months have been leading up to a moment like this. How will our story end? His impatience has hounded us since my first denial. He puts the boy on the ground and starts coming toward me. Blood drips from his fingers. He is so drunk that his human form starts slipping. His other heads appear and disappear randomly, a halo of flaming hair and fangs. He sighs hotly, coming to me. But Dhanya rushes forward and places herself between us. Her long, black braid sways at her knees as she lifts her arms to him.

"Pick me," she says.

Mandodari's hand flicks through the air, ordering her away. Her pretty brow knits furiously. So I was right: She wants him to devour me. This was the endgame for her. I try to push Dhanya aside, but she doesn't budge. Her hand drops, dismissing me, just as Mandodari dismissed her. Ravana comes closer, wrapping his hands around Dhanya's shoulders.

"Let her go," I insist, wrapping my arms around her waist.

Ravana turns Dhanya around so that she faces me. I'm struck again by the similarity of our appearance. He laughs and pushes her toward me, releasing her. She immediately steps back into his arms. Her dark eyes are empty and full of emotion.

"She chooses me," Ravana says. "Isn't that so, sweet lady?"

Dhanya squares her shoulders. Mandodari's flower petals rain over them, taunting him. Ravana pulls Dhanya closer. I refuse to believe that he will harm his favorite. Like a sacrificial lamb, she is held to her post, his hand gripping her waist. He caresses her neck, gathering her hair gently, exposing her skin. She meekly tolerates it, smiling nervously. He doesn't look at her; he looks at me. I don't believe he will do it. He positions her slender neck before his mouth. My heart beats faster. He won't!

When he bites into her neck, her eyes widen in fright. His fangs sink into her flesh. She yelps. Bright red blood runs down her shoulder. He sucks for a moment, drinking her blood. I'm paralyzed with terror. Then like a beast, he clamps his jaw together, shaking his head, tearing out a chunk of her neck. Her eyes grow glassy; Dhanya is quiet but alive.

I throw myself at them. The laughter around us spikes. How pathetic they find my effort to save her. They are too drunk to remember a silly dream about a goddess. I fearlessly push my fist through his lips, dislodging his fangs from her flesh. I wrap my arms around her body and pull her away. He grasps for her one second too late.

I pull her with me, running as fast as I can. We will find a place to hide until the blood madness has stopped! In his right mind, he will not attack her. Her wounds can be healed. Dhanya runs with quick feet behind me. No one has pursued us. They're too busy drinking blood. I slow down and turn to her.

"Where can we hide?"

She knows the palace better than I. She watches me quietly, eyes sadder and wiser than ever. Blood flows from her wounds. The gash in her neck is the worst of all. She puts her hand on my cheek. I barely feel her touch.

"Wear the necklace," she says. "It will cloak you in the strength of a hundred women."

Dhanya's body evaporates, turning into a glowing bright light. I'm alone. I cover my mouth, tears rolling over my fingers. It is her soul that I've saved. I hear the noises in the distance clearly. Screams, laughter, song. And I know what I must face: my own body in a trance. Dhanya's dead body. What's left of it.

I have never felt so strong, so real, in my spirit form. I could not even distinguish the difference. I was certain I was pulling Dhanya to safety. The shadows of the leaves are outlined starkly on my skin. I don't appear invisible at all. I reach up to pluck a flower from a tree, something a spirit cannot do. The flower comes off easily and rests in my hand. I close my fingers around it and think of fire. The flower bursts into flame. A startled bird hoots.

How easy it would be to engulf my body in fire and burn it, just as I did in my last life. The memory of being Vedavati, a powerful ascetic woman, enlivens me. In that life, Ravana was the cause of my death. Or, rather, having been touched by him, I chose death. This life, I must choose differently. I feel the Earth's power course through me. Ravana is occupied with drinking blood; I'm unfettered, and I know what to do.

Seething with Shakti, I return to face my enemy. Licking his fingers, Ravana pushes Dhanya's body aside. She thumps to the ground and rolls away. One of the guards grabs her arm and pulls her to the side. A group of them descend on her. Her limbs shake as they eat her. They tear off her clothes, flinging pieces of jewels over their shoulders.

I stand directly in front of Ravana. I clap my hands together, demanding his attention. Dazed, he lifts his head. The victim in his arms moans. He looks at me standing in front of him, then at my real body, cross-legged in deep meditation.

"Look at me," I command. My spirit voice crackles with unspent power.

I lock eyes with him, holding him with my gaze, like a lioness its prey. He begins to smile, enticed by the fact that my spirit looks him in the eye. Blood trickles down his fangs. Eyes locked, I glide backward into my body. His anticipation is palpable. He rises from his seat, eyes fixed on my closed eyelids. My spirit syncs with my mortal frame, giving my body a jolt. He backs up one step. My energetic pulse has never been stronger. But he waits, eagerly. The ghastly noises of the party continue, but his attention is fixed completely on me.

I sit up and open my eyes. Striking like a queen cobra, I latch onto his gaze. From there, I enter his body. He welcomes me with devouring fervor. All these months, I have never looked at him directly, never sustained eye contact, never allowed this connection. It has been as instinctual as reflex, a certain way to protect myself. Now I will use it to my advantage.

His body shivers with excitement as I plunge down into the core of his being. An enormous amount of light emanates from his core, the edges tattered with bitter black poison. The black tendrils stretch through his eyes into mine. Like him, I cannot look away now. His eyes are hypnotic. I merge my Shakti with his. There are altars everywhere to a woman who looks like me. Everything he has dreamed of doing to me lives here within him. Vicious erotic scenes unfold. "No!" I scream, panic rising like vomit.

His memories surround me, but one stands out. He howls in savage pain as he saws off his last head, blood dripping down his elbows. Then Grandfather Brahma appears. This is where it all started. I behold the network of power that holds him up. Standing in the center of it, I see the ten sites, spinning around me. This is the source of his true power. I cast my Shakti into the ten directions, ensuring that I can find these places.

Then I turn my attention to my purpose. First, I seek the two women he killed on my first day in Lanka. I owe them an apology. I treated him flippantly, and they paid with their lives. Hearing my call, they come to me at once, naked as on that day. Their faces are drenched with tears. Like neglected children, they look at me with apathy. They take me for one of them. I reach out to them both, bringing them into my embrace.

"Bless you," I say, releasing them from the trap.

They explode with joy and relief, their souls shooting up and away, but the dark landscape is dotted with shining souls. I've stepped into Yama's underworld, a hellish planet. There are so many souls here. Countless holy ones and women who cling to the forms they died in. I hear their names, their desires. Some simply sit and weep, not noticing me at all. Madness is their only shelter.

I cup my hands, and Ganga's golden vessel appears. I spiral up and grow large like a rain cloud. I shower down the holy liquid on them. The souls dance around me for a brief moment, before continuing to their next destination. They burst into the brightest light and then disappear. Thousands upon thousands are freed. Another set of souls bubbles up from the depths. For eons, Ravana has done this. I release them all, cleansing layer after layer of trapped souls until I'm the only one left. The space around me shrivels and collapses. Ravana's powerful form has been drained.

I focus on returning to my body, but I'm sucked into the very core of his being, blinded by the darkest of darkness. I feel as though every membrane of his body wraps tightly around me, absorbing me into itself. I cannot move; I can hardly breathe. But then I imagine I'm in the House of Wrath. I don't need to *see* to be safe. I trust that my path will be illuminated. Fear fills me, urging me to run, but I don't struggle. Fear fills me like water does a drowning person's lungs. I'm alive with fear, letting it flow through me. I'm self-contained. Free.

I open my real eyes and look into the eyes of Ravana. With one sharp jab of my real hand, I cut through the dark light from his eyes. My body sways backward, released from his force. I withdraw the Shakti between us and settle my spirit back into my body. I blink rapidly, returning to the present. The sounds of blood-drinking fill my ears. Judging by the uninterrupted revelry, hardly any time has passed. The blood-drinkers chew on bones, and the consorts walk about throwing dainty pieces of meat into their mouths.

I take in all this, but my focus is on Ravana, this lost, lost soul. I need not fear the eyes of my enemy. He is like a child, a lost child. I look into his eyes with the compassion of the primordial mother. He cannot stand it and has to look away. He blinks and turns his chin, and that's when his true form takes shape. He can no longer fool me with his false form, though he tries, for he is not ready to accede to my power. As I look, the false form he's assumed melts away, and one by one, his heads appear. All the while, I hold him in my fierce gaze. Again like a child, he wishes to assert his power and take control, unable to realize that his power is nominal.

His smile has vanished. His face has grown pale, and his eyelids are dropping. I've deprived him of his vampiric Maya. He is not the same as he was. I see in a flash of rage what he envisions doing: killing every one present and consuming their souls to fill himself up. I straighten in my seat, challenging him to do it. It will only prove that he is weak, that he needs others to be strong—he, who prides himself on his power.

Without a word, he stands up, his heads and arms drooping with deadweight. He stalks off, footsteps heavy. He pushes through the crowd of blood-drinkers, dragging his feet across the ground. The signal is as loud as a blaring trumpet. The party is over. As it ends abruptly, the queens look at me. They don't know what I've done, but they know it's my doing. The crone is let down from the branch. The children are led away with the other prisoners. I swear I will free them. The servants begin clearing away half-eaten platters, and the blood-drinkers claim the remaining bodies.

Ravana leans on his wives as he thumps up the palace steps. His radiance has dimmed. As he stands on the final step of the palace stairway, he turns to me. The light of the palace surrounds him, casting his face in darkness. I feel the full force of his twenty eyes. Slowly, his lips curve up. My shoulders fall forward, my spine pierced with a question. *While I cleansed his soul, what was he doing in my Shakti?*

CHAPTER 16

Defeated

Ravana's arrogant smile hits me like a double-pronged arrow. My victory will not conclude with a shower of flower petals. But his hulking form slumps forward into the arms of his wives. For once, having so many serves a purpose. He lets them lead him away. With him weakened, every second matters. Now is my chance. In his psyche, I saw the sites of his penances, clear as a map. Having cast my Shakti into them, I can access them like my own memories. I crawl backward into the burrow, deeper into the shadows. My guards are content to chew and suck on bloody bones. I lean my back into the dirt, sinking my toes into the musty earth. Fueled by my grief over Dhanya's slaying, made all the more brutal by its casualness, I close my eyes and leave the cursed island.

Ravana forgets that I'm the Daughter of the Earth and the Queen of the Elements, come here for the sole purpose of destroying him. All my identities fall away like a cloak on a warm day. I shrug them off: Rama's wife, Janaka's daughter, Urmila's sister, daughter-in-law, woman. No more. Nothing defines me except this moment. He is Darkness; I am Light. He is the destroyer, but I'm the one who destroys him. He is the screamer, but I'm the source of all sound.

When I soar away from my mortal frame, I feel more solid and real than when I'm embodied. The veils around my consciousness cease to be. I am

Kalaratri, the Dark Night of cosmic destruction. I know myself as Lakshmi, though I can never be confined to a few syllables. Even those who worship me can never know me in full. I spin the dreams of all beings. I hold them safe. I send them whispers of comfort and guidance. I send them nightmares as warnings, and I send one to Ravana right now.

Your time has come. As he sinks into the dream state, even he is my subject.

From this state, I behold the ten firepits that yoke his power. I stretch and spread myself into the wheel that is transposed across the Earth. Like spokes, they are connected to each other, a web woven across the sky. But that is just the foundation. The scope of his Maya is beyond imagination. It extends into the stars, wraps itself around planets, holds the sun itself in its radiance. The vibrations of power extend out from the Earth into the galaxy. No wonder Ravana has the power to summon the elements and conjure rainbows. And yet I feel the asymmetry instantly: ten sacrifices, but only nine heads. Ignoring the imbalance, I survey the network.

The cosmos is tethered to the ten sites of his worship. Everything in the universe is interrelated. The stars respond to the desires of all souls. But Ravana's desire has dominated and eclipsed the yearning of all beings. He has become the Dreamer, the Dominator, the Death of Free Will. The boundaries between the living and the dead are dissolving. He holds the balance of the world in his hands, and so he must be stopped.

I separate the sites of his penance from the planets the way a girl untangles the strands of hair on her doll. But at the ancient firepits, the skulls resist me. Like great magical objects, I cannot destroy them, for I do not have the right weapon. No matter what I do, they re-form whole again.

That's when I sense that Ravana has awoken. He has disentangled himself from the unconsciousness of sleep. Trepidation fills me. Every second matters. I approach the tenth site, where no skull exists—the place where he became immortal. I feel my energies rise around me, as if there is a threat ahead.

Ravana himself stands at the firepit. I half suspected it,

and yet the sight of him pulls me into the shape he knows me as. I'm Sita, with my single black braid touching my knees. The shadow he casts, the menace he exudes, it takes up half of me. There are no tricks, no games here. Just him against me. Next to his dominating ten-headed form, I feel dainty as a deer. His bronze hair shines like a lion's mane. His is the darkness at the end of the world, pulling everything to it, drowning out all else.

So, as Ravana strides toward me, I run. I cannot break free from the wheel and escape, for it is the entire universe. As if haunted by a nightmare, I run back to the Ocean of Milk, to the Cow's Ear Cliff, to Sharabhanga's ashram. At each place, the skulls shoot up in the air, challenging me, their teeth clicking. His voice follows me, snaking around me. I feel his dark shadow at my heels, almost catching me as I run in circles from site to site. He wraps my name around my neck. I'm yanked backward, forced to the ground. He pulls me back to the tenth site, the mountain where Brahma offered him unparalleled power.

"Why, Great-Grandfather?" I cry out. "Why did you do it?"

He stares at me from all directions. His ten heads surround me from all sides. There is nothing he cannot see. When he touches me, everything burns bright, and the circuit of Maya tightens. He smiles at my question to Brahma and shows me the truth. We all thought the grandfather came to Ravana as a result of his penance, but the story Ravana tells is different.

"Brahma came to interrupt my final sacrifice," he says. "He tempted me with immortality."

He shows me what would have happened. If he'd flung his last head into the fire, with the last strength of his mortal body, his spirit would have risen from the fire, consuming even Brahma. He would have become all-powerful, eclipsing the grandfather, usurping his position. There would have been no loopholes, no way to compromise his power. And I see it then: the weakness in his armor, the way a well-placed arrow at the right time, by the right person, can kill him. He who cannot be slain by a weapon, by god, beast, or divine creature. The scars on his body prove that they've tried: the scars of Vishnu's discus and Indra's thunderbolt.

Ravana's re-creation of the world would certainly place blood-drinkers at the top of the hierarchy. He throws an image of a lion at me, fangs bloodied, mane stained, eating his prey. *King of the animals,* he says, preying on other creatures, his people naturally at the helm. I twist the image, pushing the lion to the periphery, and focus on an elephant, peacefully pulling leaves from trees. She's the matriarch who came to Rama's aid in the massacre in Dandaka. *Queen of the jungle!*

He shreds the images and continues his tale.

"Had I resisted, had I thought more clearly," he says, his anger coursing through me, "I would have seen the devious nature of Brahma's appearance. If I had not taken Brahma's boons, my power would be complete, uncontested!"

Now it's incomplete: ten sites of penance, only nine heads. Ten sacrifices, one soul. But with me here, there is a balance that he has never been able to achieve on his own. He holds the ten sites in his soul, embodying the eleventh aspect. I am the twelfth element, the missing piece. As it stands now, he can be slain.

"Do you understand now that your quest to destroy me is pointless?" he asks. "Do you understand now that your desire to return to Rama is doomed?"

And he shows me what will happen. Just like every woman before me, I'm held with greatest suspicion. Behind my back, the people whisper. The servants attend to me but drop their smiles when they think I cannot see. The citizens hail me, but only when Rama is present. Otherwise they ask me, *Why are you still alive? Why haven't you killed yourself? Why haven't you flung yourself into the Sarayu? Why haven't you consumed poison? Why haven't you put a noose around your neck and jumped from a tree? Why haven't you abstained from food and drink and met your proper death? Why haven't you doused yourself in oil and set yourself on fire? Why have you avoided the proper ending for a woman like you? Why have you come back, rending asunder the very fabric of society? How dare you set this example?*

A defiled and impure woman like me should know better. Because I'm queen, because I'm a princess, I think I'm above it, better than others. But I will always be a woman first. I'm not meant to live after being defiled by another man's touch. Ravana drops the mirage. His hands hang by his side. His face is motionless: *Can you deny this truth?*

I've seen only that Ravana will be killed and Rama and I will be reunited. Now Ravana shows me what I've avoided. I know Ayodhya, after all. I know human society. I know what faces me if I ever return there.

Then Ravana raises his arms again, showing me my future in Lanka: I'm on his right side, Mandodari the left. My daughters and sons stand at my side, featuring their father's bronze hair, my golden skin. Here I have power, honor, my husband's devotion—everything a woman could want. I sit on the council by his side. He and his ministers are attentive as I speak. I'm a queen with unparalleled power. Sipping on the nectar of immortality, I live forever as Sita.

I throw my hands up, shredding the reality he purports to show me. As I do, I bring him to the underbelly of Lanka, to the ways of the blood-drinkers. While I, Sita, supposedly rule from the throne, Ravana roams the Earth, searching for another hapless woman to abduct and ravish. His desire for thrills has only grown more erratic, more uncontrollable. He disappears at any hour, returning with a new victim. His people capture Earthlings, sages, holy ones, children, and they feed on their blood and flesh. The half-dead inundate the Earth; the dying pray for death. The despair and screams of suffering of creatures across the world are constant.

"Can *you* deny this truth?" I challenge.

He turns his lips down in a frown.

From the corner of my eye, I see another possibility. It's the vision I had during my first days at Lanka, the evidence of my despair: I could invoke the Earth herself, wielding her powers of destruction to swallow up Lanka and pull down the entire island into her gut. I bring this to Ravana's attention.

The quake would be over within minutes. So easily done. But an earthquake of that magnitude would affect every innocent person on Lanka and the entire planet. The mainland would be compromised, ensuring certain death for countless creatures. Rama and Lakshmana, my family in Ayodhya and Mithila: Everyone would suffer the consequence.

"You are the only one who deserves punishment," I tell him.

And so I'm confronted with my final illusion: I thought I could destroy Ravana, but I cannot. I cannot do it alone. My heart aches with my love and need for Rama. Ravana does not know my certainty. He lingers on the visions. His lips have moved into a grimace.

"You choose them over yourself? Why do you want to protect the very people who will cast you happily into a fire? Why do you want to save the world when you cannot even save yourself?"

"My people will learn," I say. "By my very life, by what they do to me, they will learn. They will never persecute their women again, knowing that by denying, disavowing, and limiting their women, they destroy what they hold most precious: their own selves. Only in a society where all people are protected and empowered will harmony prevail."

He laughs at my naive understanding.

"Daydreams," he says. "You are mine, whether you accept it or not. You have tried destroying me, but you cannot. You alone know me fully. You alone know the source of my power. You alone have met me in this place, where no others can come, not even Grandfather Brahma. You are destined to be by my side."

"But a woman belonging to another will be the cause of your destruction!" I say, invoking Dhanya-Malini's curse. For killing her, he will die!

But the words ring hollow. I'm not wearing the necklace she gave me. It lies hidden inside Sharduli's burrow beneath my tree. But that is not my only assurance. I throw the memory at him. Just one lifetime ago, I sat in meditation. He intruded, pulling me by the hair. I transformed my hand into a blade, cutting the braid off. While he stood dumbfounded, I burned my defiled body, promising to return just to destroy him. And so I have.

"I will be the cause of your destruction," I say, conjuring Vedavati's dying words.

"Like everyone else I've battled with, Sita," Ravana says, "you disappoint me."

He inches closer to me. "What is the point of these words when there is no power in them?"

I can't go anywhere, for he is everywhere. I've done so much, but I can do no more. Unceremoniously, he chokes me with his power and drags me back to Lanka. He flings my ethereal body back into

my physical body. With a jolt, I awaken in the sorrowless forest. He stands above me, hands on his hips. I can see the dark night through his spirit form. Not one star is in the sky.

"If you try that ever again," he says, breathless, "I will not show you this kindness. I will not let you return to your own body."

To prove his point, he takes me by the throat and yanks me out again. My physical body jolts and thuds back to the ground unconscious. I'm hurled away. He steps between me and my body, claiming the latter for himself. I'm denied entry to the body I own unless he wills it. He shoves me back into my physical frame, and then it's like on the first day: I'm bound. I feel as though a cruel master suffocates me slowly to death.

"Accept your defeat," he says.

He puts his foot on my chest, pressing down, squeezing the air from my lungs. "If you go to my site of penance again, I will bind you eternally. You will become the guardian of my skulls, having no other joy, no other recourse, in that cursed world."

He lifts his foot, and I inhale sharply, gasping. He stands over me for a while, embodying the spirits of the skulls: skeletons, twins, scorpions. All the planetary energies will resume their place at the skulls. He has truly defeated me. I cannot escape, nor can I match his power.

"I've spared your family until now, Sita," he says. "I will kill them all. Your sister, Urmila. Your mother, Queen Sunayana. Your father, the esteemed Janaka. I will kill Rama's mother. His brothers. Every last one of them. I will destroy Ayodhya. Have no doubt that I will do this. Just for you."

He glitters with malice. "I will capture your essence, be sure of it."

I see myself leached of all Shakti until I'm just a memory, the tiniest of small seeds, the rarest of jewels, that he keeps in a small amulet around his neck. His ten necks glow with Shakti. Wars are fought for this amulet, the source of his absolute dominance. No one knows that I'm held captive within it.

Lying at his feet, a true victim, I see one final recourse. One forbidden path. Repulsive to me, fatal to him. He can destroy himself. I could never muster the deception required to play at seduction, but I can offer myself. His eyes have raped me many times. My purity will be compromised for all time. But as he has shown me, it already is. Whether he consummates the abduction or not, I am a defiled woman. The heat of his eyes prickles my skin. This is the final way: My body invites his touch by its very existence.

My hands reach to the Cloth of Essence to fling it off my chest. A thunder of paws fills my ears. Claws bite into my skin, pressing the garment back down. A tigress, shimmering like a dream, growls at Ravana's hand. Sharduli has come back! The two face each other, Sharduli and Ravana. She has come back just in time. He crouches, showing his fangs. He wants to throw her back into oblivion. Yet his instinct for self-preservation trumps all else. If I bared my body, he would not be able to resist. He retreats. Sharduli backs down and licks my face, standing guard until he's gone.

That is not the way he dies, she assures me.

With shaking hands, I adjust the Cloth of Essence, draping it securely across my breasts. I was ready to cross a terrible line. He has defeated my body and my spirit. I'm bound into

compliance by my helplessness, by my desire to protect those I love. I turn my face into the earth. Hot tears are my only offering. I receive nothing in return. I thought the day I was abducted was the worst one of my life, but now I feel like I'm burning alive. Vedavati's end is so seductive, the fire so near me. I must make her words come true. My words. I must destroy Ravana. But how?

I cannot do what I promised.

Mother, please.

Open up and take me away.

If no man but Rama has entered my heart

then open wide for me, mother

take me home into the Earth.

HANUMAN

CHAPTER 17

Southbound

As the last drop of rain hit the Earth, monkeys from all over the world convened for the search. It was hard to believe that there was darkness in the world when the forest around us was sighing with joy, completely satiated by the rains. The grass was still wet when millions of monkeys arrived. We gathered outside Rama's cave, our numbers extending toward Kishkinda and beyond. Rama stood at the mouth of his cave, his long bow beside him like a mighty pillar. The princes were adorned with their armors and weapons. Sugriva wore the golden breastplate of the king, as well as a gleaming crown. Rama shone like the sun, as did Sugriva standing next to him. Together, we beheld the troops before us.

Sugriva pointed out the monkeys from Mount Meru, black as coal; the monkeys from the Vindhyas, red as Mars; the pure white monkeys from the Himalayas; the golden ones from the sunset mountains. There were monkeys with lion's manes from Kailash. Monkeys with rainbow tails, who slept with their tails curled around rainbows. There were squirrel monkeys, owl monkeys, and howler monkeys; snub-nosed monkeys with bright blue faces; langurs, drills, and mandrills with bright red snouts. There were the apes with no tails: gorillas, orangutans, chimpanzees, gibbons. And finally: ten million glorious Vanaras, all leaders of our simian followers.

While the smaller monkeys chattered and moved constantly, the Vanaras had their orb-like eyes trained on Sugriva, waiting for his command. I beheld the reddish faces and the sharp fangs of my brethren, the anatomy of our bodies of human proportions but covered in tawny fur. I couldn't suppress my smile when I noticed the Vanaras' tails; here, we couldn't hide our restlessness. A million tails swept the ground beneath our feet. My tail was telling the same story: Time to go!

Although we were only servants deployed by our master, we did not think that way. Even the monkeys and apes who were not closely connected to Rama were eager to set out. It was as simple as this: We loved having a mission, a purpose, an objective. We loved sticking our noses and tails where they didn't belong. We loved snooping around. We were ordered to do it, turning everything upside down, leaving nothing as sacred. We were thrilled by the havoc we would leave in our wake.

Sugriva leaped from Rama's cave onto a large rock in our midst and roared loudly. We all turned to him, quieting down. There was no trace of the fear that had haunted him while Vali was alive. He commanded our attention, like the sun after many cloudy days. Hardly a tail moved as he spoke. As he directed us in detail where to go, I was impressed by the amount of geographic detail he had retained. He had been terrified during the Great Chase, yet it

had heightened his perceptions. His authority impressed itself clearly upon all of us. Mainda and Dvivida, the gorilla kings, rose onto their hind legs and pounded their chests as Sugriva spoke. But as he concluded, our king imposed a strict time limit on each search party.

"One month," he warned. "If you do not return within a month, you will be found and put to death."

As he said this, his body swelled in size, and the soft light around his body increased. Mainda and Dvivida blew air through their nostrils in a huff. They did not pound their chests in approval. But no one dared object to this decree. As king, Sugriva had the authority to kill any one of us right then and there. Of course, he would not. I knew that. But many knew him only as the killer of his brother and the son of Surya. We needed a ruler with an iron hand; we were not a species that succumbed easily to authority. Every monkey thinks himself king.

"Why only one month?" Angada asked. If anyone could ask, it was him.

"Leave a monkey to his own devices," Sugriva said, "and he will get so distracted by his own schemes, plans, and mischief that only the gods know when we would see him again. The second reason is our urgency. Eight months have passed since Princess Sita's abduction. We can waste no more time. I know the boundaries of the Earth, and how much time a Vanara needs to go there and back. If you are not able to find Princess Sita within a month, you never will."

Pleased by the answer of their king, the monkeys cheered and began milling about again. Rama and Lakshmana watched from the mouth of their cave. Neither of them interfered; this was a matter between Sugriva and his subjects. Sugriva divided us into four parties, headed by the most competent leaders. Vinata would go east, Sushena to the west, Shatabali to the north, and Angada to the south. Because Sugriva trusted me more than anyone else, he placed me in the southbound party. Jatayu, the deceased king of vultures, had pointed Rama south, the direction we'd seen Ravana fly.

I left my place by Rama's side to join my assigned search party. I walked among the hundreds in our party, pleased to see my old friends Nila and Nala. They both had special skills inherited from their fathers: Agni, the lord of fire, and Vishvakarma, the divine architect. I saluted the brothers from the Vindhya mountains, Gaja, Gavaksha, and Gavaya, all three the color of red clay. Their familiarity with the southern terrain would be a great asset to us. Certainly, I had been south, but only with Vali pursuing us. I bowed at the feet of Jambavan, son of Brahma and the eldest among us. Mainda and Dvivida, the mightiest of apes, were with us too. Their deeply set, red-rimmed eyes were inscrutable. Were they peeved at Sugriva's decree? Would Angada, who had not yet grown into his fur, be able to command such formidable apes? I prayed that our urgent mission would eclipse internal politics.

On Sugriva's signal, three of the search parties dispersed. Millions upon millions of monkeys followed their group leaders and leaped away, quick as arrows from Rama's bow. Streaks of white, black, and gold shot through the trees and ground like rivers breaking through a dam. For a few moments, the shrieks were deafening, until the three parties were out of sight. Sugriva looked pleased by their efficiency. He signaled me to join him at Rama's cave. Our collective spirit was already afoot and immersed in searching for the princess. My

desire to stay with Rama and my desire to find Sita were two opposing urges. One was from my heart, the other Daivi's command.

"Hanuman, my faithful friend," Rama said, "if anyone can find my princess, it will be you."

My ears flattened. My tail wilted. I was far from assured of our success. Rama held out his hand. The object in his fingers gleamed, and I recognized it at once, since I had seen it on his ring finger all these months: an ornate signet ring, engraved with his name.

When he dropped it into my palm, I felt a small jolt because holding it in my palms was like holding a piece of Rama. How marvelous that an object could be infused with such power. I felt unworthy of his confidence and did not want to give him false hope. I quietly attached the ring to my belt, tucking it away safely.

I fell at his feet. "Bless me with success."

As I met Rama's eye for the last time, I was infused with his blessing. His penetrating gaze did not feel intrusive. Instead, I felt that every dream I had could come true, that I was an indispensable part of the universe, that the worlds could not function as it did if I were not part of it. Everything suddenly made perfect sense, but I could no better explain it than a baby Vanara in the embrace of his parent. I was buoyed by intense vitality. The thrill of the impending search returned to me full force.

The last thing to do was bid farewell to our king, my dearest Sugriva. We had scarcely exchanged a word since the slaying of his brother. As I approached him, his shoulders sagged ever so slightly. If we were back in our cave at Rishyamukha, just the two of us, he would have asked me, "Did they compare me unfavorably to Vali? Do they miss him?"

But many eyes were watching our movement, and I would not betray the weakness I saw in his demeanor. We stood face-to-face, communicating without speaking, in the way of old, old friends. He knew my heart had found a new master. He, who had been bound to me by Daivi, could feel the pull of my other destiny. Otherwise, he would have called me to him in the past four months. He would have kept me at his side. As we held hands one last time, our relationship settled into friendship, freed from the constraints of the servant-master bond.

Then my search party took off, leaping through the trees. We were not concerned with the areas in the vicinity of Kishkinda, because we knew every stone, tree, and animal here; it was completely Sita-less. Most of the monkeys did not consider how very improbable the search really was. To find one woman among the millions of women on Earth! The best hiding place would be in a large crowd of people, for we scarcely knew what the princess looked like. Rama and Lakshmana had described her carefully several times, intent on sharing any outstanding characteristics. But how does one describe someone lauded as the most beautiful woman? Beauty was subjective, after all. Certainly, the Vanara ideal of beauty was different from the human one.

With Angada's approval, I quizzed our team, etching Sita's features into our minds. Flinging myself from a branch with one hand, I called, "What color is her hair?"

"Black as night!" they shouted, swinging all around me.

"And how long?" I cried, throwing myself to another branch.

"To her knees!"

Hair was of course easily altered and cut. But if Ravana had stolen her for her beauty, he would not have cut her hair. Or so we reasoned.

"What color is her skin?"

"Golden!"

"What color are her eyes?"

"Dark like the ocean!"

As we continued to leap-fly, we talked about her demeanor. She was a princess of the highest order. She would be regal, like Prince Rama. She would be known by the circumstance she was in. Truly, however, we were searching for Ravana. Being abducted by the king of blood crazies meant something significant. That ten-headed villain clearly valued her. It would have been far easier, and more characteristic, to have someone else do his bidding or to devour her immediately. Sita would be somewhere near him, in his palace. Jambavan, the eldest among us, recalled rumors of a golden palace that had once belonged to the gods. Yet the legends had become hazy. What was real and what was imagined?

There was one place that we never mentioned: Ravana's stomach. Blood-drinkers were infamous for their love of human flesh and blood. If this had been Sita's fate, we could only hope to find proof that she once had been alive. These were dark and unwelcome thoughts. Lakshmana had forbidden even Rama to speak of it. He had adopted the fanatic's unbending certainty that *we would find her*, willing it to fruition. This was the tactic we used, hence our overdone excitement as we set out: We felt as though we'd already found her!

We returned to all the haunts Sugriva and I had traversed during the Great Chase. We interrogated every being capable of speech that we came across. No one had answers. No one was willing to speak. There was a pervasive illusion that Ravana no longer existed. Most people acted as if we were conjuring fantasies as real. But we came on our first clue a week into the southern terrain. A small cluster of yogis huddled together when we said Ravana's name.

"Did you see him flying through the skies eight months ago?" I asked. "He was carrying a beautiful princess who was crying."

"He makes the sun rise and set," one sage said, and added in a whisper, "He can probably hear every word we are saying right now."

"Did you see him abducting a beautiful woman?" I pushed.

"Eight months is a long time ago," they answered. "We keep our eyes closed in meditation."

We knew they were withholding information. Nila and Nala had their eyes fixed intently on the sages as we bombarded them with questions:

"What do you know about a golden palace?" Angada demanded.

"Where is Ravana's residence?" Nala pressed.

"Where does he live?" Nila pressed, repeating the question rapidly.

Finally, one of them said, "It floats on top of the ocean."

"Hush! Hush!" his fellows said, and he fell silent.

They moved back into their austerity, standing on their toes, balancing on one foot,

sitting cross-legged, and refused to acknowledge our presence. The small monkeys pressed in behind us, itching to make life unbearable for the uncooperative sages. Their little minds were full of wicked plans. If we unleashed them, there would be lots of hair pulling, fruit throwing, and peeing—essentially harmless but terribly annoying and disrespectful. But these sages were simply scared. They had helped us as much as they could, so I held our restless friends back.

Next, we went to Panchavati, the forest where Sita had last been seen. Rama and Lakshmana had already searched the area, but they had been distraught. We hoped to find a clue. When we scoured Rama's abandoned hermitage, I felt a bit awed at being in their previous domicile. Here, the princess had been safe until she disappeared with almost no trace. The bamboo roof of the cottage had caved in, but the rest of the structure stood sturdy. A collection of clay jugs in the corner held stale water. A basket with fruits had nearly decomposed. Angada picked up the leathered skins on the ground, observing Lakshmana's handiwork. Little monkeys crawled in and out of the windows, unable to share my fascination with the cottage. But we all agreed that something strange had happened here. There was a hush in the air, an abnormal stillness. Stepping outside, I pressed my ear to the Earth, hoping for a residue of something, a telltale whisper.

Instead, I heard the faraway hum of heavy feet on the ground. Two-legged creatures! My pulse quickened because I knew all too well what that meant in parts like this: blood crazies. Clearly, the noise we had been making was summoning them. This could not be a coincidence. Angada signaled for us to scatter. The little monkeys happily disappeared into the treetops. Soon, eight blood-drinkers came into the clearing. Four of us stepped out to meet them: Angada, Nila, Nala, and me. They were not the usual blood-drinkers. I could tell by their scars, their weapons, and their big-as-elephant egos that they were higher ranking.

"We know your kind!" one of them sneered.

"We know your kind," Angada answered.

"What are you doing here?" the blood-drinker demanded.

"What are you doing here?" Angada echoed.

"Are you servants of that beggar?" the leader asked, pointing at the ruined cottage.

They were in search of information too. The four of us crossed our arms.

"What is your interest in Prince Rama?" Angada asked.

"Where is Rama?" they demanded. "Where did he go?"

"Where is Sita?" Angada demanded in turn. "Where did she go?"

"Say nothing," the second-in-command said.

And then they started bickering as if we were not right there—a common behavior when you deem someone else inferior.

"We've been here for months," the leader said, "with no trace of that prince."

"But these stupid monkeys know nothing!" the second one insisted.

"But what are they searching for, snooping around here?"

"Ask a monkey why he does something, and soon you'll be serving him bananas."

They laughed at this not-clever joke.

Angada stepped forward. "We will tell you if you tell us."

They quieted, looking him up and down, then said, "Tell us where Rama is, and we will tell you where Sita is."

We looked at each other, eyes wide. She was alive! They knew where she was! My tail wanted to throw itself at them and drag the truth out.

"The human brothers went to the Himalayas," Angada lied smoothly. "To propitiate Lord Shiva. They hope to destroy Ravana that way."

A believable lie and a good ruse.

"Your turn," Angada demanded.

Would their answer be in the same currency? I was alert for a lie, as the eight of them peered at each other. The leader bellowed, and they charged toward us.

"Catch one of them alive!" I shouted. If we could get one of them to speak!

They lifted their weapons, we our claws. I focused on the leader, intent on capturing him. He twirled his spear in circles around his body as he ran toward me. Hearing the noise, all the monkeys in our party rushed out from their hiding places. They swarmed into Panchavati in the hundreds, shrieking as they rushed at the eight blood-drinkers.

Seeing Mainda and Dvivida, the blood-drinkers understood immediately: They were outnumbered. The leader whistled, and the demons shape-changed into small brown birds. I was quick to follow, turning into a sparrow. The birds flew in a practiced pattern, diving through trees and evading me. They navigated the foliage with such ease that it was clear they'd flown this route many times before. As I got closer and closer, my wing snagged against a branch.

Another loud squawk, and their forms blurred. I saw that they shrank but not what forms they took. They disappeared completely. They hid in plain sight, shaped as some kind of insects. They could be ants on the ground, or moths on the bark, or slugs. I perched on a branch, watching the forest carefully with my bird eyes. For blood-drinkers, they were patient. Whatever forms they'd chosen, they were not budging. As the minutes ticked by, I had a choice to make: Match my patience to theirs or return to my people. I started attacking anything alive, devouring slug after slug, insect after insect, flying around the clearing. A buzzing noise caught my attention as five forms morphed and again took flight. Only five! I'd eaten three insect demons!

I pursued them hotly.

They swooped into a clearing, landing on the ground as they assumed their actual shapes. Aha! Their reasoning was clear: five against one. Thinking of Jatayu, I expanded into a giant vulture form and pelted them with my wings. With my father's power fueling my wings, I flew faster than any bird can, but I knew my ability to fly in this form would not last indefinitely. My talons and beak were deadly, and I killed three of the blood-drinkers, who died ghastly deaths. The remaining two leaped up and caught my talons, dragging me down. I resumed my true form. Pounding me with their fists and kicking me with their legs, they soon grew perturbed because their blows could not harm me, for they were truly like children to me, pelting me with weak hands. I threw myself to my feet, knocking their heads together. As the two skulls cracked, I cursed my rashness. I needed them alive. I carefully placed them down. One was still breathing, struggling through his last.

"Fulfill your promise," I said, "and you can leave in peace."

They had told us nothing in exchange for our lie.

"She has gone mad," he whispered. "She is beyond saving."

Truth or a lie? I could not decipher.

"Where is she?" I insisted.

"Lost to . . . insanity." And then his eyes rolled back.

I put my hand on his forehead for a moment, blessing his soul. When I returned to my search party, I kept the demon's words to myself.

"We must be on the right track," a little one said hopefully. "Prince Rama said so."

I had not shown the signet ring to anyone, but they all knew about it.

We went deeper south. There were thousands of us, but we moved together, as if we had trained for this undertaking. The extra confidence we had of our eventual success gave us incredible zest. It carried us through three weeks of finding nothing. We scoured all the southern cities: Dasharna, Avanti, Abhravanti. Vidarbha, Rishika, Mahishaka. Banga, and Kaushika.

At first, the cities appeared to be our biggest challenges. They were full of humans, thousands of them women. It was easy to get distracted, but not so easy to know if we had found anything of value. How were we to know if one of these women was Sita?

After scouring the first three cities, we felt all the more certain that Sita would not be found in a human city. It was not a man who had abducted her. The knowledge of blood-drinkers seemed all but extinct in these cultivated areas. After the first few cities, it felt like looking inside a cupboard, already knowing what was inside. The only confusing aspect was the presence of a female population that partially fit Sita's description. We were not there to harass innocent women, but we didn't dare overlook the female residents within the cities.

I was the only one who had caught a glimpse of Sita months earlier. The only clue we had acquired was a golden city floating in the ocean. Only one city left: Kalinga. I felt confident about this: If Sita was anywhere in the south, we would find her.

CHAPTER 18

It Was Not Sita

As we approached Kalinga, the last southern city, we spread out, looking through all the rooms of each house, scanning all the people for anything that might lead us in the right direction. As night set in, we had turned the city upside down. Our bellies were full of stolen food, but our minds were empty of hope. No Sita here either. We all were animated by Daivi, but it was not a fierce tug. As the moon made its appearance, we gathered on the outskirts of the city, hidden by the trees, waiting for our numbers to regroup.

We still had the Vindhya mountains, a mountain range known to host many supernatural wonders, to search. The red monkeys from the Vindhyas cheered up; they would be our guides. I wondered how the other search parties were faring: Vinata in the east, Sushena in the west, and Shatabali in the north. Had they found anything? They could have found the princess by now, and we wouldn't know until we returned.

We had only one week left.

All of a sudden, a huge rush of excitement swept through us. I felt the hairs on my body rise as I heard her name.

"Sita, Sita, Sita," the voices chanted, growing louder as they approached.

The doubt in my mind was as large as the Vindhyas. I was more frantic than usual as I waited for the news bearer, a little squirrel monkey.

"We found her!" he squeaked. "We found her!"

But then the rest of the little squirrels amended, "We *think*, we *think*, we *think*."

"It's better if I go alone," I said to Angada, who sat unblinking by my side.

He agreed: Sita might be in a delicate condition and didn't need a host of unknown Vanaras suddenly rushing toward her. Taking the shape of those little ones, I scurried off, following their lead. They brought me back into the city, past many houses, and into a maze-like alleyway.

"This way, this way, this way," they told me, slinking into an abandoned house.

We traveled into the underground cellars of the house.

"You have been very thorough," I complimented them as we turned yet another dark corner. Then, I heard the soft cry of a woman. We all stopped; here she was. Whoever she was.

"In there, in there," they urged.

"I will go alone," I told them. "Stay here."

I realized the woman was not crying but singing a haunting melody full of tragic undertones. It made me think of the blood-drinkers' insistence that Sita had descended into madness. Containing my eagerness, I cautiously peeked into the room. A young girl with black hair and creamy skin sat perched on the bed in the dark room. She was more alluring than any woman had a right to be. The room was desolate and nearly empty save for her. What a strange place to be—unless she was a captive like Sita. I slipped back into my own form. If this really was Sita, I wanted to approach her as myself. Shape-changing in front of someone rarely inspired confidence. I made myself smaller so I wouldn't tower over her. Tapping lightly on the door, I entered.

"Oh!" she cried out, completely startled. But she remained seated.

"Do not be afraid," I said softly, kneeling eye-to-eye with her.

"I'm not," she said with a short laugh.

That was not the answer I had expected. Even so, she was what I'd expected: not Sita. I looked at her intently, making sure I was right.

"Why do you gaze upon me so?" she asked. I immediately lowered my eyes. "And who are you? You are not a monkey."

Yet the fact that she had to say it meant I was. I could see the question playing across her face as she quickly looked me up and down.

"Oh, I've heard of your kind," she concluded. "First time seeing one of you."

"You are not a human," I said to her, finally understanding what set her apart.

The little squirrels had detected something unusual, and she did fit Sita's description. If only she had been the princess!

"No, I'm not," she admitted.

She looked hardly older than sixteen, a blossoming young woman. But depending on her true race, she might be much older. With an appraising look in her eyes, she held my eyes as her willowy body lifted off the bed. She floated up into the air, her posture unchanged. Hovering in the air like this, she looked at me. When I didn't react, her tiny smile uncurled again.

"Not easily impressed, are you, silent stranger?"

"Excuse me for coming upon you like this," I said, feeling suddenly nervous.

She started to impress upon me as a much older woman. By floating up into the air, she had already told me that she was an Apsara, a heavenly damsel. It was not entirely uncommon for her kind to play on Earth.

"Who are you looking for?" she asked, her brow furrowed. She slowly fluttered down onto the bed again.

"How do you know I was looking for someone?"

"You expected me to be someone else," she noted.

I sighed. With a whisper, I called the squirrel monkeys into the room. This young woman did not need our surreptitious approach. She smiled when they answered my call, invading her sanctuary. Aside from the bed with its white sheets, the room was bare.

"Our mission is not secret," I said.

Quickly, I told her of Rama and the missing princess. When I said the name Ravana, the room grew cold and quiet.

"You know him!" I exclaimed.

She was innocent and pure, not someone to be embroiled with the likes of Ravana.

"Yes," she admitted. "He is my beloved's uncle—not that he respects such relations."

My heart beat double-time. She knew him! Not even Rama had met his enemy.

"I am Rambha," she said.

I was astonished. Of all heaven's beauties, she had acquired the highest reputation, the first among four legendary Apsaras. The names came easily to me—names one might use to flatter or compliment other women: Rambha, Menaka, Urvasi, Tilottama.

"My beloved is Nala-Kubera," she said, "son of Kubera, lord of wealth."

"And Kubera is Ravana's brother," I stated.

She half-smiled at my knowledge, but there was something dark in her eyes.

"He doesn't respect those relationships," she repeated.

A chill around my heart told me what this might mean for a beautiful woman like her. The melody she'd sung was so lonely; it would surely haunt me on a moonless night. She carried a deep sadness. Now, I suspected it had to do with Ravana. A storm brewed in Rambha's eyes. When she articulated her fingers into a mudra, the feeling was transmitted to me. My tail curled into my back. Rambha stood up, tightened her garment around her waist, and began to dance. I had no inkling what she was up to, but my eyes were caught. The squirrel monkeys sat dazed on the floor, beholding her. I could see why she was foremost among the famous four. Every movement of her body was magical. Unlearned in the art of dance, I nevertheless comprehended clearly what she was enacting.

She sat at an imaginary mirror, fastening jewelry around her limbs, beholding herself with a pleased look. She draped herself in a dark-blue garment, sprinkling perfume on her wrists and neck. With girlish eagerness, she twirled before the mirror. I could see the flowers in her hair, the jewelry around her neck, the thick golden belt that chimed with each step. She clapped her hands and danced on, filling the room with her dazzling movements.

While enacting a woman strolling forward on a full-moon night, she embellished her gait with bold, excited eye movements. She thought of her beloved waiting for her and hurried her steps. When she neared Mount Kailash, Kubera's abode, she saw an encampment of soldiers. She slowed down, and her feet drew circles in the ground as she decided how to proceed. She knew this was Ravana's army, on its way to challenge Indra, lord of heaven. She chewed on her lip and then smiled. *He is like my father*, she reasoned. *Ravana would never let harm befall me. If any of the soldiers were to accost me, he would reprimand them immediately.*

Thinking this, Rambha did another twirl and proceeded past the encampment. Her steps were more cautious. No more bold dance moves. She carefully placed one foot after the other, not quite sneaking by yet not proclaiming her presence either. Once, she turned around quickly to stare into a corner. Was someone staring at her? She shrugged it off, holding herself proudly, sure of her safety. Some of the soldiers looked her way, bursting into song upon seeing her, but no one dared approach her.

She looked at the beautiful Narmada River, the moonlight dancing on her gentle waters. Swans swam together, beaks touching. *Chakora* birds cooed to the moon. A breeze, heavy with the fragrance of night-blooming jasmine, wafted by. Groves of karnikara trees clustered on the banks, their yellow flowers in bloom. She turned her back to the encampment, finally leaving it behind her. Rambha jumped into the air, articulating her fingertips with joy. Nala-Kubera was waiting: The night was brimming with the promise of love.

Suddenly, everything stopped—her breath, her dance, her movements. She stared ahead of us with eyes full of fright. I could not resist the impulse to turn and see. Who was at the door? How did the enemy arrive without a sound?

The doorway was empty. The next moment, Rambha stood there, but she was not Rambha. Before our eyes, she sank into a wide-legged manly stance. Her facial features transformed into a man with predatory hunger. She showed her ten heads, her twenty arms. He just stood there, emanating arrogance, staring over our heads, eyes locked with the frightened Rambha. He started walking toward her.

My eyes returned to where Rambha had stood. She again stood in that place, enacting herself. Her hands started to shiver, along with the bells on her belt. No words had been spoken between Ravana and Rambha, but her fear told us that she already knew what he meant to do. She put her hands together at her chest.

Please. Be merciful. You are like a father to me. Please let me pass. I'm like your niece. I deserve your protection. I belong to Nala-Kubera. It is for his pleasure I've adorned myself. His wrath is like Agni's. Don't do this.

"Young maiden," Ravana said, "you have enchanted me with your body. Your thighs are round and your waist thin like lightning. Your hair glows in the moonlight. I have never seen anyone so enchanting as you. On this lovely night, who will drink the nectar from your full red lips? Against whose chest will your breasts, like golden jars, be crushed? My loins burn with desire for you."

I wanted to cover my ears, hearing him speak so lewdly, yet I marveled at her ability to conjure him and his words so clearly through her mudras, her facial expression, and the heavy emotion she channeled. His carnal desire emanated from her, grabbing hold of us, making us squirm. The squirrel monkeys covered their eyes with their long, delicate fingers. I knew I did not want to see this scene, but we had no choice: We were part of the magic she was weaving. We were the swans on the Narmada, the monkeys in the trees, helpless witnesses to this scene. He stepped over us, walking toward her. Rambha twirled, becoming herself. Twirled again, becoming him. He cut off her plea for mercy with his vicious arms.

"Who is worthier than me to enjoy you?" he demanded, dragging her to a flat rock. "How can you insult me by denying me your body?"

Rambha burst into tears, struggling in his arms. *Stop, stop, stop. Please, please, please.*

His excitement growing, he began tearing her clothes off. He pushed her down on the hard rock, violently raping her. When he was done, he stood up, fastened his belt, and left her crushed. She lay in front of us a long time, limbs splayed and blood trickling down her thighs. Her hair was in disarray, her jewels broken. Her clothing was so torn she could not cover herself. Her flower garland was crushed against her skin, emitting a wilted fragrance. She drew her knees to her chest, sobbing into them.

I had to close my eyes. How naive I had been. I had thought countless times about Ravana devouring Sita, but this could have been her fate, again and again.

Rambha stood up. All her confidence was gone. Like a ghost, she slunk through the shadows, avoiding the touch of moonlight. She went straight to her paramour, running to him, trembling with shame, confessing everything, begging him to forgive her.

I could not stop him, Rambha cried. *Do not hold this against me, my lord.*

Rambha rose, embodying Nala-Kubera, a majestic, benevolent man. As he listened to her story, anger swelled in his body. To ascertain the truth of her words, he closed his eyes in meditation. In a split second, he saw the entire scene as it had unfolded. Seething, he gathered Rambha into his arms.

"Auspicious woman," he said, "since he forcibly took you, he shall never again have the power to do so!"

He took a sip of holy water and pronounced his curse. "Ravana, the next time you violate a woman, your head will split into seven pieces!"

He flung the curse out into the three worlds, making sure all the elements heard, that Ravana himself felt the manacles around his wrists. With the force of Nala-Kubera's curse, the laws of nature pried open Ravana's skulls and inserted their influence. The wheels of energy in his body were bound to the new dictum. Wherever Ravana was in creation, nature would bear witness. If he transgressed, the invisible web around him would pull apart. The force would be so intense that his heads would instantly explode.

Rambha sat in Nala-Kubera's lap, some of her dignity restored. But not all of it.

Her movements ceased. The room went quiet. We were once again in an abandoned house in the city of Kalinga. Now, I understood why she had to be alone sometimes. Not even her powerful lover could undo what had been done to her.

She held my eyes, daring me to show pity or judgment. She would tolerate neither.

"Because of me," she said, "Ravana cannot do what he wishes to do. Ever again."

There was a satisfied smile, but I could see the rage underneath.

"Wherever she is now," Rambha said, "your princess is protected. From my fate, at least. But that monster cannot be killed. My commanding father-in-law Kubera was vanquished by him. So was Indra, the king of the gods! Sita's fate is hopeless. Her only hope of escape is in death."

I warded myself from her conviction. With Rama at our side, we were forging a path ahead, unknown to the gods. It had to be so. Rambha turned away from us, her lips pressed together. Then she resumed her singing, beginning to untangle her long black hair with a comb conjured from nowhere. I didn't dare press her, demanding to know more. It was not wise to cross someone with her power.

Backing out of the room, I whispered, "Thank you."

Turning into a squirrel monkey again, I bounded off. Out in the night, I looked up at the moon. I prayed that Rambha's words were not prophecy.

Do not seek death, Sita. We are coming to rescue you!

Pure of Heart

Time was running out. The Vindhya Mountains were our last hope. Once we reached the shores of the ocean, we would have reached the southern lands. There, we would have to turn around, with a clue of Sita or without one. Only a few days of the allotted month remained. The content of Rambha's performance had spread like wildfire among our troops, from squirrel monkeys to the apes. It shifted our mood considerably, bringing Sita's plight to us more viscerally. We were ferocious in our methods; the Vindhyas had never been beleaguered like this. We surrounded each mountain, turning everything upside down, searching for secret doorways. We disturbed thousands of Apsaras and Gandharvas, who flew away as we intruded. Nala built bridges from one peak to the other, contraptions that floated on thin air. Other times, he mystically intertwined tree branches, creating tunnels. Nila conjured balls of fire to illuminate the caves and grottos we discovered. If we'd had the strength, we would have lifted each mountain to turn it upside down and shake it.

But we found nothing. The closer we got to the sea, the saltier the pools of water grew. Drinking water became scarce. The winds smelled like fish and sea creatures. Foraging produced few roots and berries. Soon, all the streams were contaminated with salt water. We drank it nevertheless and grew thirstier still. Our skin clung tightly to our bones. We had pushed hard and slept little. We were reaching the limits of our endurance.

We heard the ocean before we saw it. It roared with the vigor of hungry lions. We had to raise our voices to be heard. Not a creature was seen on the sandy shores. Clusters of sharp rocks jutted from the sands. The water sprayed high every time the waves slammed into them in a relentless battle between land and water. Neither element would ever give up. Would we?

We stood looking out at the endless sea. Sugriva had handpicked the best of us to go south. Because of that extra faith, we had been overconfident. We could push against the one-month time limit only if we returned with news.

A troop of monkeys flung themselves into the ocean. They would swim to the other side to find Sita. Their ruckus disrupted the steady motion of the waves. Then a massive wave rose. Glimmering fins surfaced. A serpent opened its jaws and snatched two Vindhya monkeys. The lash of its coils created violent waves, throwing the returning monkeys into the air. The serpent raised its hood ten feet high before plunging back into the depths. It was ten times larger than any of us.

I leaped from the dunes to the rocks, salt water splashing into my eyes. A nest of serpents weaved up and down through the sea, the gems on their hoods sparkling. The turbulence of their coming was enough to pull every monkey under. Angada threw himself toward them, swimming with quick strokes. The monkeys on the shore screamed in agitation. A female snake, without the telltale forehead gem, surfaced above Angada and opened her gaping jaw over his head.

"Angada!" I screamed.

I launched myself into the air, aiming for her gaping mouth. Diving into her maw, I shrunk to the size of a fish. She snapped her jaw closed. I expanded, blasting through the roof of her mouth. Scales, blood, and bone burst into the air around me. I shook the innards off as I plummeted into the ocean. I landed on slithering coils and flung myself back into the air. The waves clung to my feet like shackles. I pressed my feet down on a coil but the foothold was slippery and gave me no purchase. I flailed back into the water, bounding off another coil.

Angada swung his fists at a slick, black serpent. Nila used his claws to gash its scales. The den continued devouring anyone within reach. Monkeys were thrown into the air only to land in the jaws of sharp-toothed death. I leaped from one coil to the next, grabbing little ones and flinging them to shore. A flashy red serpent snapped at my heels, pursuing me. He lunged at my neck, a blur of red. I smashed his head away. One of his fangs lodged in my knuckle. He plunged into the sea but reared up again, a monkey dangling from his jaw. He threw his gullet back, gulping it down. I plucked out the fang from my knuckle and launched this dagger at him, just as I was swallowed into the ocean by a rising wave.

Hundreds of us were pulled under as a serpent of gigantic proportions rose from the depths. Gems the size of my head outlined his icy blue eyes. Angada and I grabbed the monkeys around us, herding them to shore. Nala, our bridge maker, threw a boulder into our

midst, drawing up an overpass. The rock grew into an arch toward the land. The monkeys near it scrambled to safety. Vanaras ran onto the makeshift bridge, pelting the serpents with rocks and boulders.

With cold intelligence, the father serpent wrapped his tail around the base of the bridge, crushing it. The bridge began to collapse. Angada made land, dragging out two sea serpents by their tails. They hissed frightfully, spitting out blue gems in anger. The father serpent let go of the bridge. With a hiss, he recalled his nest of children. Each of them spit out one gem. Steam rose from the heat of the venom. Snatching the remaining corpses into their mouths, the serpents sank below the surface. The father serpent beheld us coldly, eyes on Angada. The crown prince let go of his slithering conquests. As they disappeared, the last line of boulders suspended in the air collapsed.

We sank down onto the sand. The little monkeys lay splayed out on the shore like starfish, thrown up by the waves and left to die. We looked out at the ocean with a despair just as deep. Angada's anxiety was the most evident as his fingers wrestled each other. His velvet fur was plastered against him, outlining his delicate boyish frame, at odds with the power he could exert. Waves played against our toes, pushing us away and pulling us in. Our time was up.

"I cannot go back to Kishkinda," Angada said, speaking for all to hear. "What awaits us there? A sure death! Even if King Sugriva decides to forgive all of you, he will never forgive me, son of Vali."

I disagreed vehemently. "Sugriva is not a petty-minded monkey!"

But Angada mourned for his father and feared his uncle's retribution.

"I will take the yogic path and fast to death," Angada said.

"Be brave like Jatayu," I insisted, looking at them all. "That great vulture was alone! Yet he did not hesitate for a second before attacking Ravana! We must be willing to die. Yes. But not out of despair! A product of the mind alone!"

No matter what I said, Angada did not trust Sugriva.

"Do you wish to be executed publicly?" he challenged. "We will be subjected to ridicule and humiliation before death comes. We will be tormented so terribly, death will become our most cherished goal!"

Angada recounted the various ways traitors could be tortured, beginning with the mutilation of their tails. Threaten a monkey's tail, and he'll be convinced. All of us gripped our tails in horror as Angada spoke. We could lose a leg or an arm, but not our tails!

"Pray to Daivi," I implored my people. "She will guide the way."

Even her powerful name couldn't buoy them. Angada's conviction brought our misery to its rock bottom. Capricious as we were, he swayed us. Soon enough, all of us decided we would end our lives by fasting to death. I had a different vision of Sugriva. I didn't fear his unjust punishment, but I couldn't bear to disappoint Rama. I couldn't return to him with nothing.

Overcome by our failure, we followed Angada's example. He sat cross-legged on the ground, regulated his breath, and drew his attention inward. Nila sat next to him, extinguishing his inner fire, second nature to him. Nala too; those capable hands would not create more magical bridges.

I sat on a rock facing the ocean. This was a pitiful way to end my earthly life, especially since I would never see Rama again and Rama would never see Sita again. Taking inventory of my life, I felt guilty for my extravaganzas—the way I enjoyed simple pleasures, like leap-flying through the trees. Had I lived a worthwhile life? Was I ready to meet my final end? Now, when it truly mattered, I had failed. I had never been so disappointed in myself. I took out Rama's ring from its hiding pace. It was portentous in my hand, and I pressed it against my eyelids.

"Where are you, Sita?" I prayed. "Give me a clue. Give me a sign."

The ocean rumbled steadily, but Daivi was quiet. I lost all hope. I closed my eyes, shutting out the world, drawing my senses inward. But an animal instinct sent me a loud warning. Someone was standing near me—a thing I would not have noticed if I truly was intent on leaving the mortal realm. I realized quickly that only my mind had lost hope—not my heart!

I opened my eyes and beheld a gigantic vulture standing in front of me. Instinct made me swell in size. He could have gulped down ten of me. He looked hungry, his beak sharp like a bear's claw. I looked into his round, yellow eyes, so similar to my own.

I will not eat you, he said. *Or your friends.*

The vulture's words settled into my mind. His ability to speak like this signaled his extraordinary status. He was celestial. A gust of ocean wind blew past us, ruffling my fur. He was unruffled, for he was nearly featherless. His body bore the marks of surviving a fire, his wings reduced to stumps. I saw that he was very, very old. Hearing my thoughts, he laughed, as only a vulture can, in loud squawks. Several monkeys jumped up in agitation. Not so keen on embracing death after all!

"Don't fear," I told them. "He will not attack us."

You said my brother's name, the vulture said.

My faculties awakened. I didn't realize how far I'd withdrawn them, after all.

I've been watching you since you arrived. It's not often that my food comes to me. I planned to eat you one by one. I too have flown too close to the sun, Son of the Wind.

I shook my head. I could not fly. I had never been close to the sun. No Vanara could leap that high. Was he speaking in a code I didn't know?

He squawked again. *I am Sampathi, Jatayu's older brother. When I heard you speak my brother's name . . .* A shudder ran through his large body, and his talons dug into the ground. *I have not heard his name in many, many years.*

"Jatayu was a true hero," I said. "He was the first witness to the abduction of Princess Sita. He came to her rescue. He bravely fought the ten-headed demon!"

Where is my brother now?

"In the realm where the bravest warrior goes."

Dead.

"Yes. Prince Rama speaks of him often."

Sampathi's neck dropped. He pecked his wingless sides in distress. He had clearly hoped for a reunion with his brother one day. When Sampathi recovered, he said, *That ten-headed parasite!*

"You know Ravana?"

My talons left their mark across his chest. Protected by the creator's boons as he is, I could not kill him. I hope my brother injured him well!

The mention of our common enemy made my heart surge.

My brother and I were proud of our strength, Sampathi told me. *With great wing strokes, we flew up toward the sun. We wanted to test our strength, to prove how unstoppable we were. But our wings caught on fire and began to melt. I spread my wings over my brother, protecting him. But my wings burned off, and my brother was badly burned. We fell down from the sky and were parted, never to meet again. I have been at this shore ever since. Useless. Until now . . .*

"Sita!" I cried out loud. He knew something!

A throng of Vanaras gathered around us, my eagerness like a healing drought.

I saw a woman, clad in a shining golden cloth, captured in Ravana's arms. She was crying out "Rama!" ceaselessly. He took her to his golden island.

My mouth went dry. Would Sampathi guide us to this elusive place?

My eyes are not as sharp as they used to be, the great vulture said. *But if you look in that direction, even a weak-sighted creature can see the palace towers.*

I looked in the direction he indicated but saw nothing. Perhaps a faint shiver, as if the sun was rising on the horizon.

It's about one hundred yojanas from these shores. I saw her standing on the highest tower of Lanka. She shone like a sun.

I had been loosely translating Sampathi's words to the others. They were lining up at the shore. I felt their excitement ripple behind me.

Now I have told you all I know, Sampathi said.

As he uttered those words, feathers burst forth on his body. Two large wings sprouted. With one swoop of those wings, he could have tumbled us into the sea. He was being rewarded by cosmic powers beyond our understanding. The ancient vulture spread his wings and took flight. As our mental connection severed, I cried out, "Thank you!"

Never again would I turn my thoughts to suicide. I rushed to Angada, shaking him alive, and then to Nala, Nila, and Jambavan. I shouted at the top of my lungs, "We've found her!"

This wasn't strictly true. But I knew where the golden island was. As the news reached their ears, I could see their faculties slowly returning. I knew the feeling of retrieving myself from a deep tunnel. From the disorientation in Angada's eyes, our prince had traveled far. I pressed his shoulders. I stroked his cheeks. "You must live! You must stand up! Make your father proud!"

He looked at me without blinking. "Are you certain?"

"I'm sure! I'm sure! Look, look!"

I pointed his eyes to the faint, faint glimmer, just barely discernible over the horizon. Many waded waist-deep into the waves, peering at the horizon, forgetting the threat of sea serpents. Now we knew where the princess was. But how could we get there?

Lanka was built in the middle of the sea for a reason. It was at least one hundred yojanas or more from our shore. We had found out the hard way that even a strong swimmer would not live long in the monster-infested sea. It was impossible to reach Lanka by natural means. It was lucky for us, however, that we were not really natural monkeys. We could leap-fly unnatural distances. In fact, it was not long before this idea was presented. Every Vanara began to declare how far he could jump.

Gaja said, "I can jump ten yojanas."

Gavaksha said, "I can go over twenty."

"I can jump forty," Nala said proudly, and a Vanara's jump is something to be rightly proud of. Even then, Nala's jump would not take him even halfway to our destination.

"In my younger days," Jambavan said, "I could fly around the Earth three times. But now, I'm afraid I can jump no further than Nala."

Then Nila chimed in, "I can leap up to fifty yojanas."

Gandhamadana said, "I could do fifty, no doubt."

To which Mainda responded, "And I sixty."

"Eighty!" Dvivida cried, though Mainda looked affronted at this.

Impossible as that sounded, it was still twenty yojanas shy. A prolonged silence descended.

"I can do it," Angada declared.

We believed him. He was the son of Vali, who had been known to leap-fly to all the corners of the Earth. But an uncertain look crossed Angada's eyes.

"It would push me to the ends of my power," he said. "I don't know if I would have the strength to return."

"We cannot risk that," Jambavan said. "You are the crown prince. Sugriva will want you alive."

Angada turned away abruptly, but he did not argue. Jambavan turned to me: "Why have you not said how far you can jump?"

The white mane around his face was gray with salt water.

"You of all people should declare how far you can leap-fly," the old Vanara said. "Don't you remember at all?"

Jambavan told me that as a baby monkey, I had seen the sun glowing in the sky and taken it to be a ripe fruit.

"You wanted to eat the large orange, and you flew up into the sky and swallowed it, casting the world in darkness. Indra, king of heavens, struck you down with his thunderbolt, forcing you to open your mouth and release the sun. Unconscious, you were hurled down and fell onto a mountain. The mountain cracked, but so did your chin."

I rubbed my chin, thinking it had been slightly crooked as long as I could recall.

"Your father, Vayu, was furious," Jambavan continued. "He blocked the air from flowing in the entire universe. To appease your father, the gods came forth and gave you blessings. You can never be struck down by Indra's thunderbolt again. Agni granted you one percent of his brilliance, full knowledge of all scriptures, and the ability to speak eloquently. Yama granted you immunity from death and freedom from disease. Kubera blessed you with the wealth of energy; you will never get fatigued in battle. Lord Shiva promised that neither he nor any weapon invoked in his name can slay you. Vishvakarma promised that none of the weapons he has crafted can harm you. And finally Brahma, my father, granted you a long life, magnanimity, and immunity from Brahma's weapon, the most powerful of all missiles."

I stared at Jambavan; my mouth must have been gaping. With each power he mentioned, I felt an awakening within me, but my incredulity was stronger still. How could I have forgotten all this? The salty wind ruffled our manes, stinging our cheeks.

"You have inherited your father's ability to go anywhere," Jambavan continued. "You can become large or small, as you wish. Like your father, you can fly in all respects. Fast, like the wind."

"I don't understand, Jambavan!"

"You were a real nuisance as a baby Vanara," he answered. "You used your powers to play pranks. It became intolerable, and the wise ones were not amused. They checked your powers by a decree: You would forget your strengths until you became pure of heart."

I stared into Jambavan's black eyes. My dormant powers were bursting like firecrackers within, and I could hardly sit still, yet I did, because his final admission probed into me. Was I pure of heart now?

Mostly, I felt like the same Vanara that I'd always been—ready for adventure and mischief. But there was more. When I looked into my heart, I could see Rama's dark eyes. I heard Sita's molten voice cry for me. With a recognition so fierce it made me actually jump to my feet, I saw: My only desire was to find Sita!

My heart swelled, and my body began to expand too. This was a sensation entirely different from shape-shifting. Growing was as easy as a thought—easier, for I hardly articulated a desire to grow. It happened spontaneously!

Swift like a blowing wind, I outgrew the mountain I stood on. My valorous friends became tiny specks at my feet. The mountain was crushed under my feet, causing mountain lions and serpents to flee their lairs. Now I could clearly see the peaks of Lanka ahead of me. The largest middle peak was made of dazzling gold. My doubts vanished. I didn't think about what I was about to do. It was clearly outlined before me, as if it had already happened.

Crouching onto my haunches, I prepared to launch. I felt my huge weight smash the mountain underneath me, my toes crushing the hard rock into pulp. My monkey friends yelped and ran for shelter, protecting their bodies from the avalanche of rocks and mountain peaks. I threw myself into the air, into the fearful unknown.

"Rama!" I shouted into the expansive space around me.

SITA AND HANUMAN

CHAPTER 20

Protector of Tails

Ravana's pressure used to surround me only when he was physically present. Now it's constant—a reminder that I'm always under his dominion, no matter my resistance. My Shakti never rests. Every moment, I push away the darkness that threatens me. A larger threat hangs over me. If I don't relent, he will hunt my people down. My family. He will kill every single person connected to me. *Just for you*, he says.

I've seen his plans: To open the gates of the dead. To obliterate the cycles of birth and death. To make individuals' souls his own. To wield them for his own purposes. But I've accepted defeat. I have no more fight in me. Any influence I'd gained on Lanka died with Dhanya-Malini. Even the menial guards have thrown me off their self-made pedestal and turned me into a piece of meat. They want to chop me up and divide my flesh among them.

"How delicious she smells," they say, sniffing my unkempt body.

I'm emaciated, my skin taut over my ribs. I'm pouring out Shakti to protect myself. My weakened state makes me susceptible. Vulnerable. I start rocking back and forth, calming my body, but my hands tremble, and tears pour down my cheeks. I'm approaching a threshold and don't know what will happen at that juncture.

The sun has barely risen when Ravana comes. His first waking thought is of me. The darkness gathers the closer he gets, pushing against me forcefully. He wears the same silken clothes he slept in, still creased from the night's sleep. The cloth around his arms trails behind him, snagging on thorns. His women fan him, hold a large umbrella over his head, and carry his wine goblet. All I can see is the space where Dhanya-Malini would have been. She died for me, for her conviction that I would be their savior. Sharduli, my brave mongoose, is dead. I have no one to offer me comfort. I wrap my golden cloth protectively around me—a golden shield, the same cloth I wore when Rama last saw me, infused with his gaze of love. I will die with it on. When all the layers of my being are removed, the wounds on my psyche will be revealed. As Ravana comes nearer and I feel the sting of his eyes, I draw my knees to my chest to hide myself. I still hold my own, however, though I'm seated and he stands above. I would give more attention to an insect lumbering by. As I resist the darkness, I'm filled with light. I am the center of the universe, the one who holds it in balance by my very presence. He hates it when I show him how small he really is. Seething like a mad serpent, he reminds me of the ultimatum.

"Twelve months, Sita," he says. "Ten have passed."

I feel the ten sites of his sacrifice press upon me, as if they were my own accomplishments. If I wait until he kills me, what will happen to my soul? Will I be trapped in his body forever? Will I turn into a haunted guardian of his skulls?

His impotence revealed, Ravana leaves. A little monkey crawls out onto a tree branch and urinates on his path. Ravana almost steps in the puddle. This omen should hearten me, but it doesn't. Tears, hot and rapid, pour from my eyes. Two months feel too long. Rama has forgotten me. Only great Garuda, with his mighty wings, could cross the ocean. There is no reason to take another breath in this body. And yet I keep breathing, forced to endure through the body's partiality to survival. My hands find a solution before my mind does. My long, thick braid is heavy around my neck. It is thicker than a strong rope, long enough to coil around my throat and tie around a branch. I pull at this noose and feel the tightening around my throat. The passages of air constrict. It will work. My intelligence protests: *Suicide is not for a princess!* But, I think, *suicide is for anyone whose breath hurts this much.*

And that is the end of my resistance. I wait until my guards have feasted. Drowsy, they take a noon nap, secure in my docile behavior. There has been no better time than this. It is easy to disappear into the sorrowless forest to find a tree with a supple branch—my final friend in this life.

"I cannot do this anymore," I whisper. *Rama, forgive me.*

Months of turmoil melt away as I feel the end near. I tighten the grip on my braid. I will be free at last. The moment is grim, the end not yet accomplished. To steel myself for what I must do, I begin quietly repeating the beloved name.

And just like that, the trees join me in the song, startling me so profoundly that I twirl around. The melody moves me, loosening the hold of my noose. Within the melody, I hear songs about Rama. Songs of love, so soothing, I forget the braid coiled around my neck. I look about in wonder, my spirit arising and dancing among the treetops, resounding from top to toe with the names of Rama. When the song ends, I'm face-to-face with a golden monkey that shines like the morning sun. The last notes of the heavenly hymn vibrate on his lips. And then it's silent all around us. His eyes are round and honey colored. He looks into my soul, telling me without words, "*You must live!*"

He falls to the ground, touching my toes. I recoil from his touch, instantly suspicious. The first time, a golden deer. Now, a golden monkey!

"Stay away!" I cry.

I step away, walking backward from the impostor. Pity flashes through the monkey's eyes. He understands how devious Ravana has been in his attempts to seduce me. But no one knows this better than Ravana himself. He is a master actor. He knows what emotions will melt my defense.

"Shameless wretch!" I spit out. "Drown in the blood of the innocents you've killed!"

Interrupting my next curse, the golden monkey resumes the prayer to Rama. The meter and rhythm are familiar to me, a sacred hymn. The monkey composes the poetry as he sings, episodes from my own life with Rama. Stories that only Rama and I know. Not even Lakshmana knew about the crow that pecked at my chest. The monkey sings of a golden trail of jewels. My spirit soars again, but I stay where I am, my eyes assessing the golden creature.

With his song, the little one creates an impression of Rama in my mind. A Rama I've never known: a desperate, half-mad Rama, who says only one thing, and that is my name. I understand that my very anguish and desperation are perfect and necessary. They signal to me the eternal truth of my being—not only that I am incomplete and half-alive without Rama, but also that he too needs me to live. So many months I've strained to find a solution to Rama's absence, so many hours seeking the truth, and not even once have I imagined that he is as desolate as I am. I feel my wisdom flowing. *Yes, yes, yes, of course. How come you didn't know?*

I see Rama alone in a cave, the rock wall sharply pressing into his back, darkness surrounding him. He does not respond to anything in his surroundings. Outside, millions of golden eyes look eagerly up at him. Then the millions are gone, their eyes turned to search for a lost princess, a cause so hopeless, there is nowhere to begin.

"And yet here I am," the monkey tells me.

And I see the miracle in it. Then he says, in the refined language of royals, "I am the messenger of Prince Rama. We have searched every corner of the Earth for you, Princess."

I *want* to believe him. And now I recognize that he is the same little one that polluted Ravana's path. But I've been fooled many times. The monkey senses the change in me and takes a cautious step toward me.

"How am I to know you are truly Rama's messenger?" I ask.

"How lucky that I actually have proof," he answers.

The object is not even in my hands when I feel the current of recognition. So few material objects are infused with Rama's presence. His bow is one of them. Here is the other, his signet ring. A ring that has been on Rama's ring finger since the first and last day I saw him. I cannot see the ring properly for the blur of tears in my eyes. I feel the solid weight of it as I squeeze it into my palm. I trace the golden outline of his name with my fingers. Such a small thing can mean so much. I bring the ring to my lips again and again. My heart feels like it will burst with pain and joy!

"I trust you now with my whole heart," I tell him.

"I am Hanuman," he says. He does have a powerful chin. "Your husband is my master, and every simian creature is loyal to him. His cause has become our cause. I'm delighted that we do not have to end our lives in disgrace, unable to find the only thing he truly cares for: you, princess."

Hanuman assures me that the billions of monkeys in Rama's service will swarm Lanka and destroy the blood-drinkers and their king. I allow myself to be swept up by these tales of courage, even if my intelligence objects. How can monkeys challenge the immortal power of Ravana, who rules the elements? I silence my mind; I will put all my trust in these golden monkeys. They are led by Rama, and he is my lord. I feel like I am born into a new life, a new being. Now, I will have the strength to face Ravana again.

"But Ravana's words are no idle threat," I say. "He has given me his final ultimatum. Two months."

"Stay alive!" Hanuman says. And then, as if the thought just struck him, "Jump on my back. I will leap back across the ocean this very moment. I will reunite you with Rama within hours!"

To convince me of his prowess, he swells in size, large as a tree. I hear my guards stir in the distance; they've finally woken from their naps and noticed my absence. They will come searching for me now.

"I can grow much larger still," Hanuman assures me. "We can sneak away before they know you're gone!"

But he is wrong. Ravana is the sneak. I will not be like him.

"As long as Ravana is alive," I say, "I will not be safe. As long as his presence lurks in the shadows, neither Rama or I can return to the life we had."

Chastened, Hanuman nods. "To convince Rama that I've truly found you, I feel that I need some proof. A secret word, a token, a story?"

Tucked away in one of my pleats, I unfold the one jewel I did not discard: the crest jewel from my father. It does feel like a piece of me. Infusing the jewel with a prayer, I hand it to Hanuman. I long to detain him, to be a little longer in the company of someone who knows Rama. But I say, "Do not linger. Go straight to Rama."

The wind playing across the treetops is my only answer. Hanuman is gone.

Nothing matters more to me than the golden ring pressing firmly against my heart, impressing into my flesh what is already writ on my soul: Rama. Hanuman's coming has changed everything. I have Rama's ring to prove his existence, his love. I begin to daydream of the moment I will place this ring back on Rama's ring finger. I have not felt this happy since the day Rama promised to fetch the golden deer for me, for I was happy that day. I was certain that Rama would return, placing the deer delicately into my arms. Our story could have ended so happily, if not for . . .

Shurpanakha wanting Rama as her mate?

My desire for the golden deer?

Lakshmana leaving me?

Stop!

Ravana's very existence is the *only* reason. As long as he lives, there can be no happy endings. Even with him dead, happy endings are not guaranteed. This world is not permanent enough to comfortably contain happiness for long.

A loud crash startles me. A gazebo is hurled into the lotus pond, then another. Hanuman, tripled in size, leaps through the sorrowless forest, uprooting trees, crushing everything under his feet. Debris covers the lotus pond. Any thoughts of secrecy and stealth are shattered. Guards herd me back to our usual place; others frantically rush about, reacting to Hanuman's destruction. Only the area around me is left intact. Our eyes follow every plunging object, watching our world crash down around us. Hanuman jumps away from my guards, snatching some of them up in the process. He tosses them down to the ground, crushing them. I cringe, seeing their brutal deaths. But that is just the beginning. A terrible battle ensues just south of the garden. I can hear it all. How Hanuman resists them, how he jeers, how he kills one of Ravana's sons: Prince Aksha. None of this is good. This violence comes too soon. *Hanuman, why didn't you leave as quietly as you came?*

I hold Rama's ring tightly, praying that Hanuman escapes and returns to my lord. But soon Indrajit, the heir, arrives. I hear him declare his presence in a booming, domineering voice. Moments later, Hanuman is bound and dragged away. With Hanuman captured, I walk about in circles, like a trapped animal. The toppled gazebos stick out from the lotus pond, half-drowned. I'm plunged into fear, though it's not as bottomless as my suicidal one. All hope is not yet lost. I press Rama's ring to my heart again and again. Blood-drinkers do not honor the lives of messengers. What if Hanuman is not able to return to Rama?

I was prepared to kill myself. Now I prepare myself to protect Hanuman. I will fling this entire island into the ocean if need be! A drastic measure I've avoided until now. But I'm at a breaking point. Something must change.

A guard comes running. "The monkey was to be beheaded at court," she cries. "But Vibhishana put a stop to it. Now they're setting his tail on fire!"

My heart starts beating explosively. I must do something to help! I must gamble everything on Hanuman. If Ravana retaliates by going after my family, annihilating each person I love, I must wager that risk now. This is my only chance. Hanuman is the only way, leading me to Rama, my only hope. I do not let the reality of my situation invade my awareness at all. I just go. Away from the guards. I sit down cross-legged. I press Rama's ring to my heart and enter a deep trance. My consciousness leaves my body. Within seconds, I'm plunged into the center of the Earth. Every cell of my being is molten. My awareness spreads like a net encompassing the intense heat of the center. The chains placed around me by Ravana are nothing but his thoughts. Like a dragon rising from its den, I rear up, explosive, fire in my mouth. I burn those limits with my anger. My body becomes like the soul, the silent witness, and my true form asserts it dominance.

With precision, I feel every single source of fire in Lanka. There are hundreds of fires:

firepits where mantras are chanted, torches illuminating corridors, candles by love beds. Of all the fires, only one is moving, held in the hands of a malicious blood-drinker. I bring the full power of my presence to this little torch. And so *I* am brought to a tail wrapped in ghee-drenched rags.

Unable to resist my nature, I flare up in contact with the flammable substance; immediately I expand and possess the new territory, eating the rags, growing in size. From a small torch to a blaze on Hanuman's tail. The layers of rags quickly dissolve. Just as the flame touches the skin of his tail, I retract. Now we will blaze on our own merit, with our own power. I do not need oily rags to live. I don't need offerings of ghee to thrive. And certainly I will not consume a loyal monkey tail. Hanuman is willing to sacrifice his tail for me. Therefore, I seal his tail, protecting it indefinitely against the fire.

The flame on his tail burns brightly. He leaps away from his captors and becomes the torch that ignites Lanka. He had the ability to escape all along! As he runs along a wide balcony, the silk drapes at the windows instantly catch on fire. Following Hanuman's torch tail, I leap with him, as swift, as graceful, as powerful as the wind, and more, for I am fire—the element that ultimately will destroy the world and unto whom the other elements submit. I leap from Hanuman's tail. My form grows a hundred times larger, and the inferno is born.

I become a firestorm. I am a leaping flame that flies through the wind. I flatten against a rooftop, only to rise up like a wave in the ocean, sweeping down across the buildings. The golden domes melt like candles. The metal sighs and melts in my arms, submissive to my touch. Molten gold flows down, softly, gently, toward the Earth. Timber roars back when I clamp my jaw around it, only to quietly succumb to my anger, charring black and disintegrating to ash. The linen, silks, velvet, and cotton whimper in protest only for a second and go quiet. The cloths dance in the flames as they become my sustenance. I wrap myself around smooth marble banisters. They groan and slowly succumb to my pressure, crumbling and cracking and breaking into pieces. The marble emits a high-frequency hiss, its last breath, before crumbling down. The crossbeams take the entire edifice down with them. The substances I consume protest—hissing, groaning, crying—as they crash to the ground or turn to ash. I grow brighter in the face of resistance, eating, burning, engulfing. In the furnace of my embrace, *everything is transformed.*

Growing larger, I roar like an enraged lioness. The tips of my flames crackle against the clouds like lightning. I'm unstoppable. As I approach the people, I hear their screams. I stop and turn away, sparing them. The flames singe the hair of a sleeping man. He wakes up and shrieks as his skin blisters. Only then does he clamber to safety. Burning everything at my base, I hungrily leap to the next building. The rooftops crumble in my wake. I can only hope that the people have the wits to escape. Leaving charred rubble in my wake, and the murmurs of dying materials, I rage forward.

Raindrops begin to pelt my fire skin. I crackle at the pitiful showers, no doubt conjured by the king. The drops of waters moisten me, soothing my ragged edges. It does nothing to stop me. Then Hanuman leaps in the direction of the ocean, and I watch him go. The dark rain clouds above grow furious in their downpour, slamming my flames down. I continue to devour everything within reach. Suddenly I halt; my Shakti is spent. It coincides with the moment I feel Hanuman's torch tail extinguish in the ocean. He is on his way to Rama.

I open my eyes as Sita, and a hot sigh escapes from my mouth. My body is clammy, cold with exertion. *I did it. Hanuman is safe. Rama will be here soon.*

CHAPTER 21

The Ultimate Obstacle

When I was closest to the truth, I felt the most lost. When I was closest to what mattered, my instinct was to give up. The bodily urge was overpowering: Turn back. I had scrutinized more than ten thousand sleeping women in Lanka. Being so near my goal, I felt increasingly disoriented. The battle between Daivi and the evil forces of the world grew intense. Sita wanted to be found. But the forces that had captured her fought this. It was indeed a war between goddess and blood-drinker!

In the center of this battle, I found her. She was the center of the universe, the one who held it in balance by her very presence. All my notions of Daivi dissolved. Daivi was never mine. She never belonged to my Vanara clan. I beheld Sita, as if looking through water or the sun in the sky. Sita was a giantess, larger than Lanka. The beauty she displayed was frightening in its intensity. She glowed like the midday sun. Full of unparalleled Shakti, she embodied Daivi-Shakti. It magnified every sensation.

Once my eyes adjusted to the awesome shock of her presence, I began to see. Sita was so emaciated that her ribs were visible. Her hair was unkempt, her pale skin streaked with dirt. Unadorned, wan, and depressed in spirit, she had entrenched herself in stasis. She had little strength left. Finding Sita was the most astounding accomplishment of my life.

When Rama heard the news, he became powerfully present, as if awoken. The same was true for everyone in my clan. Sita, whom none of them had ever seen, transformed from a lost princess in need of rescue into the goddess herself, our very own Daivi. Her Shakti filled us all with certainty. Her need bound us to her so tightly, not one of us could breathe. We'd spent our lives dependent on her, waiting for her, praying for her help. Never before had we imagined that Daivi would need us! That the relationship was reciprocal! This changed everything. Everything.

With arms as encompassing as the universe, Rama held me to his heart, which pounded erratically against my ear. My hair stood on end; I felt that I was one with the cosmic rhythm of the universe. After Rama released me from his grateful embrace, his face was frightening to behold. I remembered Lakshmana's words that Rama had the power to destroy the entire universe. I believed it.

Millions of us crowded on the southern shore. Simians of all colors and shapes sat on the sand and the rocks, clustered in trees. I couldn't estimate how many apes, langurs, monkeys, gorillas, and Vanaras there were. We outnumbered the blood-drinkers a thousand to one at least. Yet this only exacerbated our problem: How could we cross the sea? Surrounded by the Vanara generals, Rama leaned on his bow, the tip plunging into the sand. He peered at the horizon at the destination we could not see. We stood like that so long that my fur was damp, my lips salty.

"I can take you on my back," I said to him, "and leap across."

"But our army would be stranded," Lakshmana said. "Success would be a gamble."

"As long as my enemy walks unpunished," Rama said, "I cannot be at peace."

Something materialized on the horizon, coming directly toward us. We must have been spotted on this side of the sea. Immediately, we formed a protective shield around Rama. Rama pulled his bow out and stood with both feet firmly planted, gripping the center of his bow. Lakshmana held his vertically, arrows ready. The blood-drinker came to a stop. He hovered in the air, eyeing us warily. He was bejeweled, with burnished copper hair. His clothes and hair flew around his muscular limbs. His features were noble, his eyes pleasant. I recognized him immediately.

"Vibhishana," I said. "Ravana's brother and counselor."

Vibhishana's eyes darted to me, lingering on my chin and the singed fur on my shoulders and arms. He too recognized me. His eyes focused on Rama as he spoke.

"Of what use is counsel when it's dismissed?" he asked. "I have advised my brother to return Sita to you. In his anger, he has cast me out. I have come to seek an alliance with you, Prince Rama."

This announcement caused a stir. He was not a messenger but a traitor!

"I pledge to serve you with all the knowledge I possess," he concluded.

"Seize him!" Sugriva called out.

Several Vanaras jumped up. Vibhishana immediately flew out of their reach.

"Peace," Rama commanded.

Sugriva acceded, and the Vanaras settled down.

"Allow him to descend," Rama said.

Monkeys screeched as Vibhishana landed among us.

"This blood-drinker has put his life into our hands," Rama said. "Do we accept him? Let Sugriva and all the leaders speak their minds."

"I do not trust him," Sugriva said. "We should imprison him and interrogate him."

"Having betrayed his own kind," Angada said, "surely he will turn on us too!"

"What will keep him from slaying us in our sleep?" Jambavan asked.

"Delaying his death would be foolish," Nila agreed.

"Yes!" others shouted.

Their voices were loud, competing with the roar of the ocean. Vibhishana's eyes followed our words. He displayed no fear but kept his distance. If approached, he would soar away. None of us had spoken for him. I had to, as he had done for me at Ravana's court.

"This blood-drinker is different," I said. "When Ravana ordered me to be executed, Vibhishana intervened. These were his words." I took a deep breath and recited his words verbatim: "'According to the laws of kings, a messenger must never be killed. If he has transgressed the boundaries of a messenger, his own master will punish or reward him. Since he has entered enemy territory alone, he deserves leniency. Let our rod of punishment fall upon our real enemy. According to the laws, you may inflict harm on a messenger only in ways that allow him to report to his master. His tongue must remain intact and certainly his head. Everyone knows a monkey's most prized possession is his tail.'"

I turned to look at Vibhishana. "That's when they set fire to my tail."

My tail was mortified by the memory but also proud because it had been protected.

"Brothers," I said, addressing them all, "those who come to us seeking asylum should not be rejected. And consider this: He knows the enemy better than any of us do."

Rama beckoned Vibhishana closer. As he approached, Vibhishana's footprints were swept away before the next step was taken. We watched him closely, determined to divine his true allegiance. Rama looked at him with piercing eyes. When Rama looked at you like that, there was nothing he couldn't see.

"Why have you come to me?" he asked.

Vibhishana's eyes grew soft and open. "When Sita first arrived in Lanka, a cloud of darkness descended on us. After Hanuman delivered his message, I implored my brother, 'You must give Sita back or engage in pointless hostility with a powerful and righteous man. Rama will lay waste to our city. You must give Sita back before the vast army of monkeys, equal to Hanuman in power, destroy us. For the sake of our dynasty, give her back.'"

"What did your king respond?" Lakshmana asked.

"I will tell you," Vibhishana said, "although some of you may agree with his judgment of me. 'Vicious kinsmen conceal their true feelings,' he said. 'They turn on you in times of trouble. Full of jealousy, you cannot bear to see that I've risen so far above you, that I've placed my foot on my enemy's neck time and time again. You covet the throne for yourself and therefore speak these foul words. To hell with you!' Those were his last words to me.

"My brother cannot see that a true well-wisher speaks unwelcome words! Yama's snare lies around his neck, depriving him of the power to think. I cannot be a silent witness to this. I have left everything—my wife, my family, my kin. Please accept me."

He surrendered at Rama's feet. I looked around at my fellow Vanaras. Were they moved by Vibhishana's testimony? But their arms were crossed, round eyes unblinking. Angada's anger was the most visible. He could not accept someone who had betrayed his own brother. Rama raised Vibhishana from the sand and said, "If Ravana, my sworn enemy, surrendered to me, I would accept him. I will not turn away anyone who seeks my shelter. Vibhishana, you will be one of us now."

Rama's next words surprised me but showed his forethought: "I divest Ravana, the ten-headed king, of his right to rule. I declare you, Vibhishana, the rightful king of Lanka."

Vibhishana seemed surprised but pleased. Angada and others murmured resentfully.

"Bring me fresh water," Rama ordered, "I will anoint Vibhishana as king, here and now."

Vibhishana dropped to his knees, head bowed. Lakshmana poured the water on his head as Rama said, "After I win back my princess, you will sit upon Lanka's throne."

Vibhishana had gone from traitor to king within minutes. His copper hair flattened against his skull, dark with water. Rama smiled at him for the first time. "With you by my side, I feel that we have already won this war. Tell us, how do we cross this ocean?"

Vibhishana was silent for a moment. "Varuna, Lord of the Seas, must be persuaded to cooperate with us."

Leaving us under Sugriva's authority, Rama set aside his weapons and approached the shore. Would Varuna part ways for us and allow us across? Rama turned the full power of his mind onto summoning the Lord of the Seas. He sat erect, a command blazing in his eyes. The hours passed by uneventfully. I was greatly shocked that the ocean lord did not rise up at once. But my master continued his patient supplication on the shore. The sun set and cold winds rippled across our bodies. Lakshmana covered Rama with the hide of a black antelope, then stood at his side, impervious to the winds.

All along the shore, small fires lit up the night. Vibhishana stood alone, like an outcast. Hostile yellow eyes followed his every move, so I invited him to our fire to share our meal. Nila had stoked a fire, Nala had arranged logs for seats, and Angada had assembled a large pile of fruits. My friends barely managed to hide their stiffness as Vibhishana settled down with us. As the darkness grew thicker, it seeped into his pores, making his body swell. It was known to us that demons came into their power at nightfall, but I'd never been this close to one of them; I was fascinated by the palpable change. Angada noticed it too. His tail twitched restlessly. He sat as far away from Vibhishana as he could. He couldn't openly repudiate him, but there were other ways to make your feelings known.

"What will you eat, blood-drinker?" Angada asked. "These fruits don't have the kind of meat you thrive on."

"The only blood I share with my kind," Vibhishana retorted, "is the one running in my veins. Not everyone is attracted to the taste of blood."

"Do you expect us to believe that?" Angada demanded, with the impudence of the young. "All of you are obsessed with human flesh!"

Vibhishana's fangs glinted in the light of the fire, seeming to agree with Angada's words.

"Never," Vibhishana said, with pride. "Since my childhood, I've followed the footsteps of my father, Vishravas, a self-realized sage. I have followed the highest principles that govern the worlds. Why do you think my brother has kept me so long by his ear? Thousands of mighty warriors vie for that position."

"Why did you leave his service?" I asked.

"For the throne?" Nala injected.

"My brother has never had a worthy opponent before," Vibhishana admitted.

"What makes you believe that you've found one in Rama?" I asked. "'A mere short-lived human,' as you'd say."

"Are you a mere monkey?" Vibhishana asked. "Hardly. And yet what did we call you?"

I nodded quietly, understanding what he inferred. Ravana's court had been eager to reduce me and my message by calling *monkey, monkey* repeatedly.

"That does not answer my question," I said.

The fire flickered across his eyes. I made sure to radiate warmth too. His answers were for all of us.

"To risk everything for a man I've never met," Vibhishana admitted, "seems like a fool's gamble. But consider whom I do know. Princess Sita."

"No one—man, woman, god, enemy—has ever influenced my brother the way Sita has," he said. "He is entirely focused on her. It's hard to explain. My brother's power has flung gods to their knees. Now he's on his. Many in Lanka are convinced that she is the goddess incarnate. I count myself among them. When she called on me to be her ally, she pointed me to Rama. She gave me this." He produced a bright green leaf and showed it to us. Rama's name was imprinted in the dark green. "I infused it with freshness, so I wouldn't forget what I felt that day. No intellectual query could have convinced me to your side."

Angada stood up, casting a large shadow. "Your words are very noble for one with two faces." He stalked away, unable to bear the demon's company.

Vibhishana stared into the fire, absorbing the insult calmly. So unlike Ravana.

"Why does Angada harbor such contempt for his uncle, King Sugriva?" he finally asked.

Neither Nala nor I had expected that question.

"That is not a matter we easily discuss," I said.

"Yet a child could easily discern the tension between the king and his heir."

"Maybe a blood-drinker child," I said with a smile.

In public, and especially as we prepared for battle, Angada and Sugriva worked together, setting aside their strained feelings.

"Even if it is as you say," Nila remarked, speaking up for the first time, "what is your interest in our inside affairs?"

"Soon, we will be at war. And mark my words, it will be a clash of such magnitude that those who live will sing about it until the end of all that is. The forces of evil and good will fight such a battle, unlike anything seen before. This battle will ask each of us to die and die again, in every sense of the word. The victor will be glorified and hailed until the end of the

worlds. Considering this, I want to know as much as I can about those with whom I fight. I want to know everything I can about my allies so that I may better assist you at each turn. There will be many strategies and setbacks."

Nila and I stared at one another. We had not thought as far ahead as he had. I was moved by his vision, his conviction that we had to be united in spirit.

"Success is not certain," Vibhishana continued. "Far from it. But I have never felt more confident. Not in their wildest imagination have they ever envisioned fighting with monkeys! My kin cannot see past your appearance, your tails."

Hearing itself mentioned, my tail did a little flourish. As the conversation continued, I held it in my hands.

"I'm glad to see your tail intact," he said with a puzzled look in his eyes. And it was a miracle indeed. "Family bonds run strong in all species. We harken to our kin more quickly and naturally. Thinking of my brother's defeat, I feel pain, even as we pursue that very goal. My actions are not motivated by hate toward my brother. Let me explain clearly why I took this step."

"Because you want to be king," Nila said under his breath.

"Because I want to protect my people! The current king heeds no counsel. He refuses reason. I am not alone in my dissension. More than half of the council agrees with me. We greatly fear that our king is willing to sacrifice us all for the sake of one woman. Would obedience to him win me your admiration? Or that I stand up and challenge him? It is for the sake of my people!"

Nila nodded once and looked away. I wish Angada had stayed. Vibhishana was winning us over to his side. As the fire died down and the others settled into sleep, Vibhishana and I lingered. We stayed awake, and I shared what I knew. I told him who, in my opinion, were the strongest warriors, who could be trusted with anything, who was fickle, too much monkey. As we spoke, a strange realization hit me: I had never seen Rama fight. I had seen his skill with his bow when he had shot down the sala trees with one arrow and when he had killed Vali. But I hadn't seen him in battle. How could I justify my confidence in him? As long as I relied on logic and proof, I couldn't, I realized. Like Vibhishana, I was following my intuition. So were all of us. And it was enough.

After three full days, the Lord of the Seas showed no sign of responding to Rama's summons. Rama's patience was exhausted. He stood up, shrugging off the antelope hide.

"Bring me my bow, Lakshmana!"

We crowded around the brothers, watching Rama tighten his bowstring. With red-eyed rage, he released a volley of arrows into the sea. Sea serpents were thrown into the air, spewing blood. The water turned red and the waves crashed into each other. Rama's arrows churned up whirlpools, and waves crashed high into the air. Muttering mantras as the arrows flew, Rama pushed the waves into the ocean, forcing them to retreat. Within seconds, Varuna rose up, a massive blue-colored being. Hands in salute, his voice rumbled like the ocean itself: "I cannot part the sea for you, my lord. My inherent nature cannot be reversed. But I will bring my creatures to the bottom of the sea. I will still my surface so that you can build a bridge across me."

He disappeared into the waves. It became calm like a forest lake, blank like a mirror. Every Vanara turned their eyes to Nala, our bridge maker, the son of Vishvakarma, the very same architect who built Lanka. Nala swelled with excitement at this vast, inconceivable challenge, doing something that had never been done before!

"I can sense my father's design of the island," Nala said, eyes closed. "There is a half-formed plan to build a bridge to the mainland. I will fasten my own ideas to it and build this bridge!"

He leaped onto a rock, crushing it with his landing. He directed the shards into the ocean as only he could do. Calling out orders, he set thousands of monkeys to work. We rushed into the forest and back to him with boulders and trees. When the boulders were hurled into the water, the sea shot up and cascaded back down. Yojana by yojana the bridge took shape, and with every boulder and every inch, we began to see it could be done.

As the building project proceeded vigorously, Rama retreated. After his three-day vigil, his body needed sleep. Lakshmana stood guard as his brother rested. I threw myself into the bridge building. I leaped to mountaintops, wrenching off their peaks and leaping back to the shore, hurling them where Nala directed me to. Like a great conductor, he stood at the helm, drenched in seawater, shouting, pointing, splitting, making, building.

It started as a narrow path, straight out from the shores in the direction of Lanka. But as it grew, it curved and took shape. As it grew long, it grew wide, reaching ten yojanas in width. Only Nala knew the reasons why, working as he was from the bottom of the sea up, ensuring a sturdy bridge. He directed us to jump up and down on it to make sure it could hold all of our weight. Hundreds of us stomped on the bridge. Small rocks and sand dislodged, tumbling into the calm sea. The bridge shook, but the structure held. It grew and it grew. I could not see its end from the shore.

When I returned inland at dawn, I sought Rama's sleeping form. The sun was about to rise. Rama sat up, brushed his matted locks from his face, and spoke to Lakshmana. Something about the way he gestured, pulling the deerskin around his shoulders, made me hurry to his side. When they heard me approach, Lakshmana rearranged his features. Something troubled him.

"I had a dream, Hanuman," Rama said.

I held his gaze as long as I could—just a few seconds—but I sensed the shift in him as clearly as if it were my own. It felt like being without shelter on a stormy night. Rain drenched and shivering with cold. I waited for him to speak. I felt the rise of his words, like water drawn up from a deep, dark well.

"After the Lord of Oceans Varuna acceded to my demand, I fell into a deep sleep."

He clenched his jaw. Lakshmana shifted uneasily. "I dreamed that I was a newborn child in the arms of my father. He was holding me for the first time. He kissed my cheeks and forehead. His mustache and beard were drenched with tears of joy. He held me to his wildly beating heart. 'My son,' he said, 'you will be the one. I pass this legacy to you. May you make the words of our great ancestor Anaranya true. May you be the one to slay Ravana, the archenemy of all things good. May you be the one who fulfills King Anaranya's dying words that a son of the Sun dynasty will destroy Ravana. In the name of Anaranya, go forth into the world, my son. May you be the one.'"

Rama whispered, "May you be the one," as if it was a curse.

My hands twitched into claws. What I felt was so forceful that I bent on one knee and dared to look up at Rama again. My heart beat wildly, like King Dasharatha's must have done that day. I was certain what Rama told me was not a dream but a memory—a memory appearing now to encourage us, to cement our intuition that the forces of destiny were at work here.

"May every father have a son like you, my lord," I said, throat clogged. "You will certainly make your father's words come true."

"Do not kneel yet, Hanuman," Rama said. "Victory of my accord is not certain."

His agony was more perceptible, forming like an arrow. Finally, we came to the kernel of what ailed him.

"My powerful ancestor, King Anaranya, was slain by Ravana thirty-six generations ago! The one who has become my archenemy has been relegated to legends. My esteemed father never saw him. Nor my grandfather. None of these powerful warriors had the opportunity to match their strength to Ravana's. This prophecy has been passed down from father to son for generations. Legend tells us that Ravana laughed while Anaranya took his last breath. When he uttered his curse, Ravana kicked dust into his mouth."

Rama made as if to spit the dust out of his own mouth. And it was fear of failure that came out as he did. I wanted to catch that dark gust, pull it out from his heart, and fling it into the ocean. But Rama took a deep breath and inhaled it back into himself. I was fully reminded of the state he was in during the monsoon. If this doubt, which in human terms was reasonable, took root inside him, would Rama's arrows swerve off their path?

"May you rise to the truth of your father's prophecy," I said. "May you avenge the death of your noble ancestor."

I hope he felt the conviction in my words.

A Vanara leaped up from the horizon, coming toward us. His honey eyes were filled with wonder as he shouted, "It's done! It's done!"

He bowed at Rama's feet. It was time.

The bridge was truly a marvel, ten yojanas in width and one hundred in length. Nothing like this had ever been done before. Walking on it was like walking on the rainbow to the moon. We marched forward, pounding our feet against the bridge, banging trees together, advancing like a monumental parade. The ocean was as peaceful as a forest pond. The coils of sea serpents flashed in the sun, but they did not rear their heads. We were ever vigilant against the approach of anyone from Lanka. They could have flown over us and toppled us easily into the sea. But hours went by, and we sang as we marched. When Rama tired, I carried him on my shoulders, and Angada carried Lakshmana. The crossing took us four days, and those of us who could did it without resting. We made it onto Lanka's shore completely unhindered.

We inundated the island, claiming it as if it had no masters. The golden city loomed large on top of the middle peak, touching the clouds. It appeared to me like a silent spirit, watching our every move. But Ravana ignored our arrival. There was complete chaos as we reached the shore. The monkeys felt the enchantment of the island, as I had on my first arrival. The abundance of flowers in full bloom, trees heavy with fruits, and sweet water in crystalline ponds enchanted us. My clan reveled in nature's abundance as if we were here to feast, not fight. But every time my eyes fastened on the golden city, my tail shivered: We were in enemy territory. Did Sita feel our presence? Did she know we had come?

CHAPTER 22

The Prophetess Speaks

Rama has come. Everyone I ask denies it, but suddenly I have more guards than I can count. All my lone plotting must now come to fruition—everything I know about Ravana, his weaknesses, his power sources. The nine skulls must be obliterated, his Maya vanquished. But all I can think about is Rama, so near that I feel him on the breeze. With Rama's ring in my hand, our reunion is no longer a fantasy. The impossible has happened: Rama is on the island. Yet Ravana's warning is true: A woman is only as good as her spotless reputation. Only as good as her submission to her lord. As good as the men in her life allow her to be. Can our love survive this wreckage?

The blood-drinkers are divided. Having seen the power of Rama's messenger, Hanuman, they fear Rama. The guards whisper that the ministers want to return me to Rama. The ash and stench from Lanka's ruins have turned the tide in my favor. The masses of monkeys that even I can hear from my place deep within Lanka have impressed them. But I know better: Ravana will not yield.

Crowds of deformed guards take turns taunting me, hissing at me, spitting at me. Trijata, the old prophetess, joins my guard. She doesn't speak to me, just sits perched on a rock with her face toward the sun. Then Queen Mother Kaikasi comes, telling me I can stop a war. She insists that I write a letter to Rama, sending

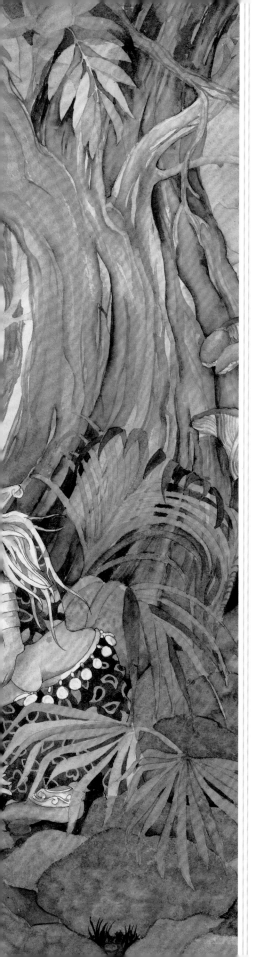

him away. I refuse by saying nothing. One of them pulls me by the ear, tossing me to the ground. I have not been treated so roughly in ten months. They keep chanting that they will sacrifice me to Nikumbhila, their goddess. The escalation convinces me of their desperation. My thin arms tremble as I cross them over my chest, protecting myself.

"I had a dream," a voice calls out.

It's Trijata. Her approach is enough to quiet them down, though their tridents still lean against my body, pushing me down. Her thin, silvery hair sways at her knees. She looks down at me with her one good eye and holds out her hand. I help her down next to me.

"I saw Sita," Trijata says, "dressed in purest of white, standing on the peak of a snow-capped mountain, surrounded by the sea. This lady mounted the back of a four-tusked elephant, which was ridden by her husband, who was bright as the sun. She rose from her husband's lap to stroke the sun and moon with her hands."

Their tridents thud to the ground as they take a step away from me.

"Then I saw our lord and master, Ravana," Trijata continues. "He fell from his flying palace Pushpaka onto the ground. His garments were black and his head like a skull. Then this woman, Sita, smeared in the blackest of ash, danced as she dragged him along the ground with a noose around his ten necks. All of Lanka fell into the sea, all while we were playing musical instruments and dancing. All of us blood-drinker women were there, laughing and drinking oil.

"Do you understand what this dream means? Do you? Before you taunt this noble lady ever again, you must think prudently of what I've said. This lady does not deserve to suffer. Her desires will be accomplished. My dreams have never failed to show the way."

As Trijata speaks, the entire left side of my body begins to tremble, an auspicious sign. The guards look at each other, grimaces twisted deeper. They want to sacrifice me to Nikumbhila!

"I will stay with you from now on," Trijata says.

She feels like a grandmother to me; she sees my pain

but doesn't dwell on it. She lies down on the ground and promptly falls asleep. I sit near her, straining to hear what is happening down by the shore while my mind races. Vibhishana has left us, which makes his guidance more urgent—the Ruby Room, he said. But I spent my first weeks captive there. It held nothing of import. The sun sets when Ravana enters the gardens in a hurry. He has dark circles under all his many eyes. The guards stand up, holding their weapons. Only Trijata remains seated, dozing against her spear.

"Sita, I bring you news," he says with a grim smile. "Rama is dead."

I cross my arms over my chest. He reeks of treachery.

"Come!" he commands.

A man steps out from the shadows. He is the first male Ravana has ever allowed near me. Indrajit's face is chiseled, and his black hair flows past his knees. He walks bare-chested, a heavy golden breastplate adorning him. He displays none of the curiosity that others have had toward me. He holds something in his hand, covered by a veil. He bows to his father, and his slanted eyes meet mine coldly.

"A gift for you, queen," he says, walking toward me.

I slowly back away until I feel the pointy leaves of the sorrowless leaves against my back. With a flourish, Indrajit bows. He unveils the plate and offers it to me. At first, I don't look; it's just a magic trick. But from the periphery of my vision, I see something so gruesome, I lose control of my eyes. They dart to the plate, seeing Rama's severed head; the blood still flows. His brow is knitted, his eyelids puffy and shut. Every detail is that of my beloved. The perfect mouth, noble cheekbones, high forehead. It's just a trick, and yet I cannot stop my wail.

"Rama! No!"

As Indrajit waves the plate in front of me, Rama's dreadlocks trail on the ground.

Tears flood my eyes. "Thirty gods have mercy!"

How can I speak, how can I breathe, when Rama is no more?

With two steps, Ravana towers over me. Indrajit makes way, stepping aside with Rama's severed head. Blood spills onto the ground. My hands lift toward it. It cannot be real.

"Become my wife," Ravana says.

He slides his hands in the air around my shoulders, as if caressing me. He looks down at me with tender devotion. "Rama is dead. But if you become my wife, I will pardon the Vanaras. Every one of them. I will pardon my deceptive brother. Resist, Sita, and they will all meet the same fate as your husband. Their heads will be offered at your feet, just like this one."

My eyes never leave Rama's severed head. Indrajit places it at my feet.

"Just say yes, my princess."

Under my gaze, Rama's head begins to disintegrate. The matted locks fall to the Earth. The skin melts away, revealing bone. Then a white skull grins up at me. Rama is so near, and still I'm subjected to Ravana's whims. Indrajit snatches his hands through the air, trying to catch the apparition. The golden plate disappears. Father and son glare at each other, both annoyed.

"So it's true," Indrajit says. "You have powers."

Before I can reply, he walks up to me, scrutinizing me with an intensity that is hard to bear. His eyes are full of dark magic. I want to retreat immediately, but I intuit that if I cooperate, this will be over more quickly. Indrajit's gaze surrounds me, laying itself on my body like a second skin. Unlike his father, he probes no deeper. It's just the shape of my body he wants. I stand absolutely still, hardly breathing. He starts circling me, scanning me from head to toe from every angle. His eyes are burning embers of fanatic passion. Indrajit's gaze has a physician's precise detached touch. I feel like a fetus in the womb, dismembered with sharp tools. Again and again, his eyes imprint on my skin, molding themselves around every detail of my appearance. Finally, he steps away.

He looks at his father but speaks to me: "My prayer is to one day serve you when you are our queen. On that day, I pray you forgive me. The illusion of today will be tomorrow's reality."

"My promise still stands," Ravana says. "You need never see Rama dead. All you have to do is choose me. I give you my word. No harm will befall him. I will let them all go."

"Rama will never let *you* go unharmed," I say, filling my voice with disdain. "Go and bid your wives and children farewell. There is nowhere in the three worlds that you could go to escape Rama's wrath!"

Indrajit clenches his teeth and turns away. Father and son leave. His own prophetess predicts our victory, and yet I'm not certain. I will not believe I'm saved until I feel Rama's hand in mine. If that day ever comes.

CHAPTER 23

The Siege of Lanka

As we beheld the mighty fortress, I witnessed the transformation of my people. Sugriva pricked his ears and showed his fangs again and again. Tens of millions of tawny monkeys with yellow eyes, all from Kishkinda, glared at Lanka, baring their fangs. The leaders of the four search parties were enraged. Angada stalked the Earth on his hind legs, lashing the ground with his tail repeatedly. Vinata did the same with his red, yellow, and black tail. This was all the more frightening when the 100 million under his command followed suit. Silver-hued Sushena beat his chest vigorously, as if his opponent stood before him, fangs bared. The ten billion monkeys from the sandalwood forests swarmed around him, egging him on. Shatabali threw his neck back and roared, shaking his mane. His leonine monkey followers did the same. With their four great fangs, tails arching upward, they were huge as elephants. Mainda and Dvivida, the leaders of the apes, pounded the Earth with their powerful paws.

Seeing them, my faith in our powers was cemented, for when I'd landed on Lanka the first time, I was activated the same way. Every experience, every choice of my life had groomed us for this exact moment. That was the knowing rising collectively in our consciousness: We had been born for this purpose. Our demigod fathers had mated with simians of all kinds to create us, a superbreed. We were rising to our life's purpose—heeding Daivi's command.

Vibhishana was visited by four birds that flew around him chirping and soon brought him a golden mace in their talons. Mace in hand, Vibhishana brought Rama to an elevation. From there, Rama oversaw the inflow of troops. Vanaras leaped to him and back to their delegation, directing the monkeys. Rama scrutinized the fortress, its peaks high in the clouds. I looked for signs of the mighty firestorm that had devoured half the city. Black soot stripes remained visible, but they had rebuilt the walls quickly.

"My ministers," Vibhishana said, gesturing to the birds on his shoulder, "Lanka's army consists of a thousand elephants, ten thousand chariots, and more than ten million warriors. All hand-picked by the king. When my brother went to war against the gods, he did so with six million of these troops. With six million, Ravana conquered the gods and become the sovereign of the three worlds. Now we face that same army, with an additional four million troops."

After a brief pause, Vibhishana continued, "On the other side of the island there is a colossal building. Inside, a giant sleeps: Kumbhakarna, my brother. Don't be alarmed by his enormous presence. His boon from Grandfather Brahma is forever sleep. The gods tricked his tongue. He wakes up one day a year to eat and drink. He sleeps as if dead the rest of the year. He cannot be woken."

"When comes the day of his awakening?" Lakshmana asked.

"It will not be for another six moons. He is no threat to us."

Sugriva and Angada gave me a meaningful look: *Why didn't he tell us earlier about this threat?* They were certain that Vibhishana was leading us into a trap.

"The one I fear the most is Indrajit," Vibhishana revealed. "He excels in dark magic, greater than my own or his father's. Conquering him in battle is impossible. We must locate the place where he cultivates his magic. Maybe Nala could find it with his sense of Lanka's design."

Though we had not yet been accosted, Vibhishana's spies had seen Lanka's troops beginning to mobilize. They told us that Prahasta was at the eastern gate, Mahaparshva and Mahodara at the southern. Indrajit and Dhumraksha held the western gate, and Ravana himself was at the northern gate. In response, Nala and I were sent to the western gate, along with ten million monkeys. Rama sent Angada with Yama's sons—Gaja, Gavaksha, Gavaya—to the southern gate. They brought one hundred thousand monkeys with them. To the eastern gate he sent Nila along with the superapes, Mainda and Dvivida. They brought another one hundred million of our troops there. Rama himself would guard the northern gate; the remaining ten million monkeys stayed with him and Lakshmana. Sugriva would stay at the central encampment to deploy monkeys to the four gates. Except for the two princes, none of us were fitted with weapons or skilled in traditional warfare. But the demons could not predict our moves or methods, for we had none, surprising even ourselves. We surrounded the golden fortress from all sides. More monkeys kept arriving over the bridge. They came in great waves, as inexhaustible as the ocean itself.

As our forces were distributed, Vibhishana pointed out the great defensive engines stationed on the ramparts. The gates were made of iron, but even from a distance, we were dazzled by the gold fretwork, the diamonds and rubies that covered them. The moats were wide, filled with snapping crocodiles.

Suddenly, Vibhishana dragged two Vanaras through the air and dropped them on the ground. They landed with a thud, thrown at our feet, and turned into blood-drinkers before our eyes. A host of little monkeys appeared out of nowhere and began to pester them, screeching in their ears, biting them, and pulling their hair.

"Spies," Vibhishana said. "Shuka and Sharana. My brother's best."

"Kill them!" the chimps cried out.

"We have a message," Shuka cried above the ruckus.

He was allowed to stand to deliver his king's message by mouth.

"Ravana, king of the three worlds, ruler of the blood-drinkers, says this to Prince Rama of Ayodhya:

I will lay my life down to honor Sita's wishes. She orders you to abandon your claim on her. She loves me now. Heed her desire and leave. Or else, not a single one of you will live to tell of Lanka's existence.

A shadow crossed Rama's face before his jaw was set in steel.

"Deliver this message to your king," Rama said. "In the name of my ancestor Anaranya, I challenge you. Unless you return Sita to me and seek my refuge, I will pursue you to the ends of the worlds. Prepare yourself for the next world. On the morrow, you will be stripped of your kingship and your life."

Turning to us, he said, "At sunrise, we storm the gates."

Vibhishana flicked his hand at the spies, and they took off at a run, flying away as quickly as they could. Rama issued the order that no one shape-shift during the war. Our natural forms would be our means of identification once the battle began.

As the full moon rose, Rama and Lakshmana scaled Mount Suvela, one of the three peaks. The moon marked the eleventh month of Sita's captivity. She must have been gazing up at the moon, just as we were. All the Vanara leaders gathered where Rama made camp. Sushena, our healer, would receive the wounded here. From here, we could see Lanka clearly. How could anyone sleep when daylight heralded an altercation of such proportion that the worlds had never before witnessed it?

At sunrise, all four gates of Lanka opened at once. Bugles blew as the bridges were dropped across the moats. We screeched at the top of our lungs, beat our chests, and showed our fangs. Hordes of blood-drinkers rushed forward, weapons lifted. The clamor was thunderous. At the western gate, we rushed forward, eager to kill them. We were as certain of our victory as they were of theirs. They began to slaughter us with maces, axes, cudgels, and spears. We slaughtered them back with our claws, teeth, boulders, and uprooted tree trunks.

A chariot drawn by eight steeds galloped across the drawbridge. A pack of squirrel monkeys pounced on it. With their small, sharp teeth, they attacked the warrior, pulling out his hair, clawing at his eyes. Like a grasshopper overpowered by a swarm of ants, he dropped his weapons, trying to fling them off. Too late. They tore the meat from his bones, leaving nothing but a standing skeleton. The little monkeys paid dearly for this small victory. The next champion, Dhumraksha, slaughtered them in the thousands. I rushed in with a large boulder, raising it up like a shield. From that moment, there were as many battles as there were monkeys and foes. The ground grew thick with blood and carcasses.

At the forefront of the army, Dhumraksha—Smoke-Eyes—attacked from his chariot, drawn by mules with wolf faces. His chariot crushed monkeys under its wheels. Howling, Mainda rushed toward him with an uprooted tree. Dhumraksha shattered it and pierced Mainda's body with his arrows. The great ape stumbled and fell forward, blood pouring from his neck. Dvivida leaped in, pummeling Dhumraksha with a hailstorm of rocks. He heaved his brother over his shoulder and escaped.

As Dhumraksha's chariot raced toward me, headless corpses began to wail. A storm cloud passed over him, rumbling frightfully. Ignoring these portents, he continued. The mules with their wolf faces brayed terribly. I rushed at him, hurling a boulder with the speed of the wind. It demolished his chariot: the wheels, poles, flagstaff, charioteer, and mules. He jumped to the ground with a pike in his hand. His eyes were black; it was impossible to tell where his smoky gaze was fixed. I leaped away from his pike as two blood-drinkers clung to my legs, leeching blood from my thighs. I smashed their heads with my fists, feeling their fangs sink deeper into my legs. I ripped their fangs out, disgusted. Bleeding, my battle rage was fully awakened.

Dhumraksha swung his pike above his head. He pummeled my shoulders. I moved only my upper body to dodge the next swing. My tail crept forward and wrapped around his ankle. The next time he swung, I yanked him onto his back. He thudded to the ground, the jagged pike flying out from his hand. I smashed my fist down on his head, crushing his skull. The fearsome demon was dead.

I beat my chest, encouraging my brave friends to continue their glorious battles. Angada fought Indrajit, who rode a chariot drawn by lions. Nila hurled fireballs at a blood-drinker with gigantic ears. Lakshmana fought Virupaksha, Squint-Eyes. Mainda fought Vajramushti, the one with the lightning fists. Dvivida fought Vajradamshtra, the one with lightning fangs.

Rama fought two chariot-riding archers, Agniketu and Rashmiketu. Though he was on foot, he was surrounded by four chariots.

"Suptaghna and Yajnakopa, my uncles!" Vibhishana shouted.

Rama's arrows flew faster than the eye could see. He shot down their banners and smashed their wheels. The four blood-drinkers jumped to the ground, raising their spears, then their clubs, then tridents. Rama demolished their weapons with ease. He had not yet been wounded. Golden energy vibrated around his skin, a celestial armor. The four blood-drinkers closed in on Rama despite the arrows that riddled their bodies. Rama's arrows knocked off their crowns, then their mustaches. He taunted them, inviting them to retreat,

accepting their defeat. The four demons lifted their claws and rushed at him. Crescent-moon-tipped arrows sliced off their heads. Vibhishana did not flinch seeing the heads of his uncles severed.

The sun set and rose. Set and rose. All I saw was the color red and hills of the dead. The generals Ravana sent out to command his forces were his foremost fighters. When the first drop of blood hit the ground, they grew blood-crazed and deadly. With great losses on our side, we defeated each one of them. Virupaksha, the squint-eyed one, slaughtered thousands before Lakshmana killed him in a fierce combat. Angada killed Mahodara, the big-bellied one. Sugriva slew Vajradamshtra. Angada killed Mahaparshva, the mighty one attacking from all sides. As night set in, the blood-drinkers swelled in size and power. We armed ourselves with the weapons of the dead—spiky clubs skewered with flesh, spears, swords, bludgeons, cudgels. My own determination to win increased with every monkey I witnessed dying. The victories were hard won, our glee gone. I was surprised that our bones didn't usurp our flesh to sustain themselves. All thought of the enemy's tactics was gone. Our only concern was to survive this battle, right here, right now.

The next day was the Battle of the Sons. Sugriva went to the eastern gate to combat Kumbha and Nikumbha, the sons of the sleeper, Kumbhakarna. Like their father, they had ears that protruded like wings. Angada went to the southern gate to battle Devantaka and Narantaka, Ravana's own sons. I went to the western gate to oppose Trimurdhan, Ravana's three-headed son, and Atikaya, his youngest. Rama stayed at the northern gate to battle Makaraksha, Crocodile-Eyes, the son of Khara, the leader of the battalion that Rama massacred in Panchavati. Within hours, they were no more.

As night set in, I pulled wounded Vanaras from the skirmish, delivering them to Sushena, our healer. Often, he could restore them completely. As I did this, I saw Nila fighting Prahasta, one of Ravana's closest ministers. Nila's body was covered in blood. He took a blow to the head, and blood sprayed from his ear. A discus gleamed in his left hand. He swung his right hand at Prahasta, who blocked him, unaware of the Chakra. Nila jammed it into Prahasta's neck, his own fingers sliced in half in the process. Blood spouted from Prahasta's neck. As he fell to his knees, his eyes rolled back into his skull. He slumped forward onto Nila's limp arms, eyelids closing. Nila slumped forward too. Their foreheads rested against each other as they sank to the ground. Nila followed his enemy to the land of Yama. Quickly, I leaped to his side and took him to Sushena.

The fifth day began with shadows rising from the blood-covered Earth. As I fought, I saw apes felled by an invisible hand. Showers of arrows came from nowhere. Swarms of insects descended from the skies. A terrible chaos ensued. The battlefield was ablaze with dark magic, missiles that hit us in the back, insects in our eyes, laughing shrieks in our ears—all conjured to drive us mad. The monkeys jumped here and there aimlessly, trying to escape an opponent they couldn't see. Insects crawled into their mouths and out of their noses.

At my wit's end, I leaped to Rama and saw Vibhishana and Sugriva already conferring.

"Indrajit is upon us," Vibhishana warned. "His illusions are unparalleled."

"If Lakshmana and I fail today," Rama said, "swear to me that you will continue the battle. Princess Sita must be rescued."

Tension gathered in my heart. Rama and Lakshmana released blazing missiles that challenged Indrajit's dark arts. The missiles crackled above like fireworks. One defused the other, falling like meteorites. The shrapnel fell on monkey and blood-drinker alike. But Indrajit could not be seen, and this gave him the advantage. As Rama turned about, searching the skies, his knee-long dreadlocks flew around him. Indrajit's arrows pierced Rama from all directions.

Arrow after arrow hit Rama's limbs. I threw myself in front of him, as did Lakshmana. I was hit by the most excruciating pain, an arrow in my belly. It moved, burrowing deeper into my flesh. *Nagapashas.* The snake arrow sunk its fangs into my stomach, wrapping its tail around my forearm. I roared loudly, ripping it out along with chunks of my own flesh.

Indrajit shot thousands of nagapashas at the two princes. They were pinned to the ground by venomous snakes that writhed around their limbs, binding them to the Earth. Rama's teal skin started darkening, infused by snake poison. His eyes were open but glassy, staring into the sky like a dead man's. Next to him, Lakshmana struggled to keep his eyes open, poison spreading through his veins visibly. Indrajit called out, "Victory!" with one sharp bark of laughter.

I tried to pry a snake loose from Rama's leg. It tightened its hold, digging into his flesh. Venom spread, discoloring his hue. Lakshmana's fair skin started turning green. Both of their breaths came in raspy gasps. The brothers were unresponsive, clearly on their way to Yama.

The battle slowed to a halt. Our troops dispersed at an alarming speed. Sugriva tried to rally them as we created a protective circle around the dying princes. The snakes covered every inch of their bodies, wrapped around their throats, wrists, and ankles. Sushena arrived, and torches were lit. But there was no antidote to the nagapashas. Venom darkened the ground around the princes. I felt the tearing pain in my stomach, where traces of poison had spread.

Next to me, Vibhishana was pale, and his hands shivered. Seeing this, I was stricken to the bottom of my tail. I couldn't bear to see the poison spreading in Rama's body. Could this really be the end?

CHAPTER 24

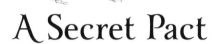

A Secret Pact

While the war rages beyond the walls of Lanka, I keep my trust in Rama close to my heart. Rama is the one. I must trust this, just as he must trust me. The loss hits us all. My nights are never restful. To my surprise, blood-drinkers come to me with their grief. I, who have no children. I remember how shattered Rama's mother was by his exile. Facing the death of your own children, is there anything more painful than that? When I lie on the ground, the Earth bruises my skin, pressing hard against my ribs and hips. I have no appetite. There is so much violence and loss. Ravana's intensely persistent attachment to me threatens to pierce my consciousness. I'm ever vigilant, ever fearful that it may take root.

Every few hours, Trijata gets a report from beyond the walls. Everyone is invested in the outcome of this battle. Instead of Lanka being split into two camps—one that wants to return me and one that wants me for queen—the feelings about me have grown more intense. Some hate me for the destruction of their families. They do not blame their king; they fault me for snaring him in my sorcery, for I am the goddess that enchants men with one glance, who needs no sustenance to live, who is worshipped even by the Pisachas.

We are all on edge, aware that anything can happen at any moment.

A flying palace descends through the sky. The Pushpaka. I know it well from

Dhanya-Malini's description. It's the very one she was abducted in, the celestial vehicle that Ravana promised would take me anywhere. The vehicle looks like an extension of Lanka, crafted exquisitely, with golden latticework and ornate pillars. True to its name, it's bursting with flowers, full of vines and blooming creepers. I never planned to set foot in it, but as the Pushpaka lands, a host of guards rush forth, herding me into it.

As my right foot steps inside the plane, alarm grips me. Victory is by no means certain for us, but Ravana must be taking me away because Rama has won!

"I will not leave Lanka!" I declare. In response, my foot receives an assurance from the vehicle: *We are not*.

I step inside, feeling the magnificence of the Pushpaka, who is aware of my presence. Did the craft join forces with Dhanya when she and the others cursed Ravana?

The guards cannot board the Pushpaka, which denies them entrance. Only Trijata is allowed in. She stays near me, suspicious of the flying mansion. The craft lifts from the ground gently. We rise up above the golden towers, leaving the ruined forest behind. Trijata grips my hand, and I entwine my fingers with her. As we fly over the city, I see the destruction. Like a dying beast, half the city is blackened and ruined, the ramparts melted to the ground. There has been no time for Lanka to recover from the fires. Only the exterior wall has been rebuilt, giving it a semblance of perfection from the outside.

As we approach the battlefield, it is strangely silent. I hear only occasional cheering sounds from Lanka's troops—not an auspicious sound. I cling to the window of the Pushpaka, straining to see. As far as my vision extends, I see monkeys in all shapes and colors. There are so many Vanaras, so like Hanuman. But countless of them stand in a large circle, and this is where the Pushpaka flies to. In the middle of the circle, two forms lie on the ground. I strain to see below, half hanging out of the window; Trijata holds me tightly so I will not fall.

In the center of the circle, I see what I'm not prepared to see. My hands fly to my eyes. Through my fingers, I peer at my beloved and his brother. I have not seen Rama or Lakshmana for eleven months. I see them now. Fallen. On the ground, breathing their last. Those two powerful sons of Dasharatha. They lie on the ground, pinned down by arrows that wriggle like snakes. I look through my fingers, taking small, fast breaths. No. No. No! It cannot be. A hundred times, I've been told he's dead. It cannot be. And yet my eyes refuse to lie.

Trijata leans out to see. "Indrajit's arrows," she concludes.

Rama's eyes are closed. His eyelids are puffy, his beautiful features twisted in pain. The venom is spread like a net across his skin, coloring it purple. I cannot see whether his chest is rising with breath.

"Down!" I order the Pushpaka, stomping my feet against floor. "Take me down!"

The craft ignores me, subservient to Ravana's will. The apology is soft but firm. It cannot. A Vanara on the ground suddenly jerks his head up and sees us hovering there. His chin is powerful, the fur on his back burned off.

"Hanuman!" I cry.

The Pushpaka responds immediately, zooming up. I see Hanuman's mouth move, but his words are lost in the wind. The Pushpaka relentlessly carries me away.

"Curse upon you!" I cry. "Your friendliness is deception! Curse upon those snake arrows! Curse upon Indrajit!"

My fury is only to avoid the truth below: the body of the one I love, dying a torturous death by snake venom. With no further apology, the Pushpaka returns me to my prison. The guards escort me back toward the center of the forest. If they say anything to mock me, I do not hear it. If Trijata says soothing words to me, they don't register. I'm beyond that. Words are nothing to me. Not even kind words reach my heart. I run to my tree. How can it bloom when the world is ending?

"Wilt!" I cry, and throw myself on the ground.

Trijata stubbornly follows me and begins to speak. She is too old to mind my outburst.

"Listen to my words, Princess," she says. "Your virtuous demeanor and pleasant conduct have won you a place in my heart. I do not lie, so listen."

I don't sit up, but I look at her.

"Your prince is not dead. Let me tell you how I know this. His troops stand in a protective circle around him. If he was dead, they would have fled. Their defiance tells me that your prince clings to life."

"May it be so," I say.

Her kindness restrains my flight to grief. Her words ring true. I beat my fists angrily at the ground. I feel so helpless. So near my end, always.

It's at this moment that Sharduli returns to me, just as she did that day when I was ready to bare my body. As she drapes herself against my chest, Trijata retreats. She alone can see Sharduli, who is neither real nor unreal. I cling to the little mongoose, warmed by her eternal love. Her coarse fur grows silky and smooth under my hands. I see feathers sprouting on her body. She looks at me reassuringly, her light-green eyes growing larger and rounder. Her black hind claws turn into three yellow talons. Her arms grow long and feathered. Her pink nose becomes a curved beak. She hops out of my lap, fluffing up her feathers. She opens what were her forelegs revealing her speckled wingspan. She flies up and comes to sit on my shoulder.

I will summon the one all snakes fear, she says.

Her weight presses into my shoulder as she prepares to launch. Then my shoulder is free, and Sharduli is in the sky. Curiosity sparks my heart, though I'm not ready to see her go. It's precisely because Sharduli seems harmless that I know she's formidable. I see what happens next through her eyes, for she was always a part of me.

An eagle emerges from the dark night, a streak of lightning: the very nemesis of all snakes, Garuda himself, the legend from ancient stories. The fierce wind from Garuda's wings churns up waves at the ocean shore, crashing over the incredible bridge. The gale swoops through the towers of Lanka, like whistling ghosts. As Garuda approaches the circle where Rama and Lakshmana lie, the windstorm from his wings throws Vanaras to the ground. Even mighty Hanuman and Vibhishana crash down. Leaves and golden feathers fly around them. Gusts of air sweep across the battleground. Garuda looks at Sharduli through one of his yellow eyes, then he tucks his wings in and plunges down.

The nagapashas panic. The snakes writhe and hiss. Faster than arrows, they extract themselves. Garuda lets out a high-pitched scream. He snatches up snake after snake in his beak and gulps them down in one swallow. Hovering in the air, he brushes his wings across the princes. The poison recedes. Rama regains his dark emerald color. The venom in Lakshmana's pores drains away, leaving him the color of the moon again. Garuda alights near them.

Rama opens his eyes, and my heart awakens. Sharduli fluffs out her feathers with joy. The fierce wind plasters Rama's hair and garments to his body as he stands up. He reaches for Garuda, placing his hand on his beak. Rama glows with strength as he communes with the great eagle. Garuda beats his wings to lift off, and Sharduli flies closer to Rama. When he looks into her eyes, I feel a burst of life, as if he is looking directly at me.

Faraway cheers erupt. Rama is alive. I seek out Trijata and thank her.

Soon, Sharduli is next to me again. An owl now—her true form, she says. I stroke her feathers: *You saved them.* She answers, *You saved them.*

I look into her eyes, seeing myself reflected there. Now, I understand who she is: an extension of me, one of my aspects embodied as a charming chameleon. How she has eased my loneliness all these months. I kiss her little beak. I'm flooded with a feeling of gratitude, as if the battle has been won. Yet my right hand shivers sporadically. It won't forget so quickly how very close to ruin we were.

A cloaked figure enters the gardens. Her shadow precedes her, spilling out from her. Though the black cloak covers her entirely, I know that walk, those staccato manners. Shurpanakha hasn't come here since the night Dhanya-Malini was murdered. Why does the enemy's sister seek me now?

I see indecision in her shoulders, and her chin droops, jutting out beneath the hood. She slouches down under a tree a distance from me. She throws the hood off and runs her fingers over her mutilated nose, muttering to herself. She acts as if I'm not here, as if she's come here by chance. I decide to go to her. She cannot see Sharduli, who flies by her and settles on a branch above her.

She has changed, Sharduli observes. Yet the least perceptive of the guards would have noted this. Shurpa is like a dog kicked once too often, cowering, anticipating the next blow. What's happened to Lanka's arrogant princess? As I approach, she huddles closer to the tree. If the fire in my eyes has been ignited, hers has been extinguished.

If she were my friend, I would have immediately asked in my softest voice, "What is the

matter?" I would have lowered my tone, quieted my tempo, turned down my velocity to vibrate as slowly and heavily as hers. But I know better than to offer Shurpanakha sympathy. She has come to me, and yet she does not want to come to me. I wait for her to speak. She huffs and squirms until I sit down next to her.

Then she blurts out, "*You* burn down our city. *You* bring the enemy to our shores. But who do they blame? *Me!* Even the ugliest of the ugly dares to point at me and call me hag, slut, *pig!*"

She covers her nose with her hands, well aware of why she's likened to that particular animal. Her hand cringes away from the slits of her nostrils.

"I am ugly!" she says. "I know that."

I want to offer some comfort, some sympathy, but a denial would be insincere. I notice that her bronze hair is white at the roots. She dyes it orange, despite the fact that she can shape-change into another form at will. She is invested, then, in the appearance of her own body. She is pained by the deformity inflicted on her. She sighs hotly and continues:

"I know my flaws. Why do you think I spent so many years perfecting my skills as a kamarupini? But to blame me now for everything? That is unfair! Everything is my fault. The food you ate yesterday did not digest in your belly, your lover didn't sleep with you, your pillow was lumpy. Everything going wrong is suddenly my fault. My brother is infatuated like a boy, our empire is on the brink of ruin, and why? Ask me why! Are you just going to sit there looking stupid, or are you going to ask me!"

"Why?" I say, not letting her anger turn me away.

"Oh, I'll tell you. It's because Shurpanakha had the stupidity to think she could win Rama for her mate. She who is so ugly, he who is so handsome. She who is pot-bellied, he who is slim. She who is aged, he who is young. She who smells like stool, he who smells like sandalwood. She who is pathetic, he who is noble.

"They spy at the walls and imagine that Rama is God come to Earth. And they ask, how could that snaggle-toothed hag make advances toward him, who is handsome as Kama, god of love? Rama is replete with every virtue, while Shurpanakha, white-haired and withered, has none. Rama, *our enemy*, is suddenly the hero, and I'm the villain. *No one* cares that those two cut off my nose and ears. How dare an ugly old hag like me set her eyes upon a young, handsome man like Rama?" She flings her cloak off, sweating in her passion. "The whole harem, all those seven thousand sluts, think they are better than me. Everyone in Lanka thinks that I am an entitled, selfish hag."

When silence descends between us, she demands, "Why don't you say anything?"

"Why have you come to me?" I ask. "You detest me."

"I do," she answers, but without conviction. "This is all your fault."

She isn't entirely wrong. So I quietly nod.

"You are the only one who has a right to blame me," she says quietly, unwillingly. "But you do not. That's why I've come to you."

A rush of emotion clouds my eyes. She acknowledges me when I least expect it. Being understood is a great gift. I didn't expect it from her at all. I press my feet into the earth, my back into the trunk of the tree. It was rewarding to focus on her struggles and not my own. Now my own emotions come flowing again. Shurpanakha glances over at the guards and then scoots out of their line of sight.

"Come," she says.

She pulls off her cape and throws it around me. A rotten smell engulfs me as her arms encircle me. She mumbles as she ties the cloak on me. "My brother is donning his armor and weapons. He will be out in the battlefield soon."

She pulls the hood over my head, then transforms into Sita.

"You are me now. And I am you," she concludes.

The cloak covers me completely, shading my face. The guards are shuffling our way, suspicious because they cannot see us and because they know Shurpa's animosity toward me. She steps out from the tree to show herself, to show them Sita. Will they recognize her as an impersonator? But the guards are appeased. I stay where I am.

"As long as I keep my mouth shut, they won't know the difference," Shurpa says. "You should hurry. Mandodari and Mother are at the court, hoping someone will listen to them. You have free access to his private shrine, the Ruby Room. The room you were first put in, remember?"

Though my heart beats eagerly, her sudden plan to assist me is suspicious. "What's in the Ruby Room?" I ask.

"The thing you need to obliterate him."

"Why don't you get it for me? That would be simpler than this ploy."

"Only those he loves can gain entrance to that chamber," she says. "Only Mandodari, Mother, and Indrajit can set foot in there. And you."

I didn't know! My breathing quickens. I turn from her and pull the cloak to me, covering my body. Heat courses through my veins, and blood pounds into my head. I pull all my impressions of Shurpanakha into me, imagining that I'm her. The only thing I want is the means to crush those skulls, to destroy his power.

I hurry along as fast as the disguise will allow. Up the palace steps, into the hallways. The walls and ceilings close in on me, but I ignore my surroundings, focusing on my goal. To make it bearable, I embody Shurpanakha—her walk, her impatient manners. No one spares me a glance, and those who do turn away in disgust or hiss at me. She is hated, as she said. I turn a corner, away from the women's quarters, away from the room with the backless throne. How long will Shurpa be content to play this game? Despite her softening, she is a fickle creature. She could be bored with the charade already.

The Ruby Room was my first prison, and therefore the most memorable. Only now can I appreciate that I know how to find it. The marbled archways are polished to a glow, framing the ruby-red drapes that bunch up, kneeling at the floor. It looks like anyone could just push the drapes apart and go inside. But Vibhishana's attempt to see me at the onset of my captivity suddenly gains new meaning. When was he cast out from his brother's heart?

I step through the red drapes. The velvet resists for a moment before pushing me into the Ruby Room. I'm dazzled by the life perceptible in each swirling gem. How could I possibly have seen it as just a room covered in rubies? Now I feel like I'm inside a giant's beating heart. The room pulses, as if connected to his breath. I pray he does not feel my intrusion. My eyes scan the room, landing uneasily on the large bed and the web of ruby garlands around it. I can barely separate the demon from these objects, accepting their beauty but not his. When I see the vina, his favorite instrument, I feel a pang in my heart for Dhanya-Malini, that dearly beloved friend who gave her life for me. For humankind. She had known how to play him until the very end.

I hear the noise of someone approaching. I stiffen and pull the cloak around me. But if I'm apprehended, what punishment can he inflict on me? None that I fear, I who have welcomed death. I fear only dying before I find the means to destroy him. The next time I hear someone passing in the corridor, I don't pause; I cannot fail at this crucial moment. The seconds tick by. I will not find what I seek with my eyes, that is clear. There is something here, yearning for me to find it!

I slow my breathing and open my hands to the room. The chamber pulsates and then whispers, *If you love me, the secrets of this chamber will be yours.*

What a clever demon! Only when he loves you can you enter. But only when you love him in return can you receive. But how can I love Ravana? He is anathema to me in every way. I will *never* love him. Not ever.

But what I've learned these months is that I'm more than Sita, more than that sheltered princess. As the goddess, I accept every single being, complete with their darkness and light. I welcome them all into my embrace. And that is the love that I flood into Sita's heart.

Love him! The feeling trickles past my resistance. *Love him!* My heart fills with the emotion. *Love him!* The room starts spinning around me. My heart brims over into my face. My being is full of love for this powerful soul who so cleverly has placed himself at the center of universal omniscience. I celebrate him.

"I declare my love!" I cry. "Now yield to me!"

Who has given this heart, and to whom?

I say the words that I last uttered in my marriage ceremony to Rama: "Love has given this heart unto love. Love is the giver, love is the receiver. Love has entered the ocean of love. I receive you through love."

O love, this heart is yours.

The transfer is instant. It yokes to my shoulders, presses me down into my feet. All that is his belongs to me. It is not an object but a title of rights, given to me in the name of love. My love will transform him. Who is more clever now, him or me?

I hurry out the way I came and return to Shurpanakha. Amazingly, she's in the same place, under the tree. Sharduli is still on the branch above her.

"Did you find it?" Shurpanakha asks eagerly, as if she will snatch it from me.

My hands are empty. "No," I say. I cannot trust her. "There was nothing."

"Maybe he doesn't love you as much has he professes." But she looks disappointed.

If only she knew . . . I take the cloak off and return it to her. "Thank you."

Her assistance has been crucial. I glance up at my faithful Sharduli, perched on the branch. She looks at Shurpanakha and me, swiveling her neck. Then we lock eyes. We both agree: A change in attitude can transform a person's entire being.

That includes you, she observes.

My recent pact has left marks, it seems. I keep my attention on Shurpanakha until she leaves. Would she have helped me if she knew what I mean to do? Would Ravana be so eager for my love if he knew what it would do to him?

CHAPTER 25

Dark Powers

A chariot charged forth from the northern gate, drawn by steeds with demon faces and red eyes: Ravana was making his first appearance. The battles at the other gates had already begun. Knowing that Ravana himself was coming into battle, Sugriva and I had stayed at Rama's side. Lakshmana also insisted on being near his brother for this fateful battle.

The chariot was wrought of heavy iron but gleamed with gold and gems. It was surrounded by malignant spirits with the faces of tigers, elephants, and camels. The banner depicted a severed human head. Behind the king's chariots, the troops marched out, decked in gold and black armor. I watched the spectacle with growing unease. My senses were being manipulated, assaulted by the grandeur of the enemy. I wanted to tell Rama that all this had been orchestrated precisely to make him feel small.

The chariot came to a halt before us. Empty. The demon horses snorted, scraping their hooves against the ground. Ravana descended through the sky, two gleaming swords across his chest. His wore golden mail, his ten heads protected by helmets. He was splendorous, fiery, and charismatic. His power shone in his eyes, and the glow from his body made him appear saintly. His fangs were huge as tusks, sharp, and glistening. His hair shone like fire, his skin dark as night, the same color as Vishnu's. Ravana could be the ruler of the worlds. That was the spell he put on all of us by his presence alone. Dark Maya seeped out from his heart, covering his entire body, oozing far beyond his physical frame. It was hard to gaze upon his blazing form. His presence dominated the battlefield. His mountain-thick neck and scarred arms were frightening. The monkey warriors around us whimpered, and my tail was subdued.

Rama stood on the ground, shining in his own right. Here was the one Sita loved, for whose sake she shunned Ravana. The two great warriors beheld each other, tied together by prophecies and by their love for the same woman. Envy tainted Ravana's many eyes.

Without a word, Rama lifted his bow and fired. His arrow knocked down Ravana's flagstaff. The human head fell to the ground. Ravana bared his fangs and lifted his bow. And the battle began. Sugriva was the first to challenge Ravana, king to king. He leaped across the sky with a great boulder and hurled it. Ravana shattered it with an arrow and shot Sugriva down. Shrieking, I rushed to his side and took him away. With boulders the size of mountains, Gaja, Gavaksha, Gavaya, Mainda, and Dvivida rushed toward Ravana at the same time. Those five heroes had destroyed Ravana's most powerful generals. But Ravana defeated them easily, like an evil man knocking down small children. Rama took his stance against his archenemy. With an arrow, Rama knocked off Ravana's dazzling crowns—all ten of them, in fact. It was like seeing a man without clothes. A king without a crown? Who, indeed, was he?

In glee, we showed our bottoms to the demon. We urinated on his chariot. Squirrel monkeys clung to the charioteer, pinching him and pulling his armpit hair. It became a circus. Caught by our mirth, Rama twirled his arrows in his hands before nocking them to his bow.

"Tell me who you really are," Ravana cried out, parrying Rama's arrows.

His oozing Maya inched closer to Rama.

"The moment you laid eyes on Sita," Rama said, "I became your death!"

"Big words from a little man," Ravana laughed, and the darkness surrounded Rama completely. Quick as lighting, it entered through the top of his head. For a split second, Rama was filled with darkness. The next moment, Ravana retreated on his chariot. No one, neither Rama nor Lakshmana, seemed aware of what had just happened.

Enraged by his trick, I leaped onto the banister of Ravana's chariot. Being so near the demon king, a chill ran down my spine, but I did not let it show. I had been this near him only once, when I played king of the fruit pile in his harem to convince him that I was just a harmless little monkey. That was before I'd found Sita. One of his eyes had watched me, half-asleep, lulled back into slumber by my ruse. Now, those same eyes looked at me again: *I know you, tiny creature.* Ravana's faces growled. He struck me on the chest with the palm of his hand. Stumbling back, I was knocked against the railing of the chariot. I shook myself, clearing away the shock.

With an open hand, I slapped his face. He reeled back, shaking like an earthquake. With the imprint of my hand on his face, Ravana was humiliated. He struck me on the head with his fist. I was stunned; I'd never been shaken by a blow like that. Dizzy, I retreated.

Moving as one, the two princes attacked Ravana's chariot. Rama's arrows crippled the right wheel, Lakshmana's the left. In retaliation, the demon flung a golden javelin at them.

The javelin soared, flying at Lakshmana. It pinned him to the ground, like a flagstaff claiming new land. My heart pounded wildly as I ran to him. Running to his brother, Rama was attacked. Three arrows pierced his back. Tears ran down Rama's face as he turned around to face his enemy. As Lakshmana's eyelids closed, he gave me a half-smile, blood pumping out from his chest. I clutched his hand, willing him to stay alive. He did not even moan as the javelin extracted itself and returned to Ravana. I guarded Lakshmana, stopping the blood flow.

Aggrieved beyond words, Rama severed the string of Ravana's bow and then split it in half. Animated by fury, Rama's next arrows severed two of Ravana's heads. Blood exploded from his necks as the heads thudded to the ground. Ravana staggered in his chariot but began to laugh. A split second later, new heads appeared. The blood continued flowing down his necks. Ravana laughed louder. The blood flowing from his necks empowered him. He swelled in size, as Vibhishana did only at night. He hurled a trident at Rama, which grazed Rama's shoulder, knocking him off-balance. On foot, Rama had a clear disadvantage: a great many of his arrows were lodged in the chariot. Ravana began to speed away, forcing Rama to give chase.

"Where in the world can you go to escape my wrath?" Rama cried, shooting a volley of arrows at the chariot's wheels.

Rama began shouting mantras to invoke his divine missiles. The chariot wobbled to a stop, but Ravana's weapons did not. The golden javelin that struck down Lakshmana pursued Rama; I leaped to his side to intercede, when a brilliant light surrounded Rama.

"You mother's blessings protect you," a melodious woman's voice sang.

A web of protection pulsated around Rama. The javelin shattered and fell into a harmless heap on the ground. Rama's breaths came out in big gasps, his stomach pumping like a bellow. Bleeding from his shoulders and thighs, Rama took a stand. With grim determination, he shot off Ravana's heads, one after the other. For hours, they fought: Ravana's headless body fell to the ground. Instantly, his heads grew back and he soared up.

Ravana opened his arms and looked at Rama, a broad smile on his faces. The message was clear: You cannot kill me! Yet he assessed Rama, a baffled look in his eyes. His hands sagged around him like a cloak. He could not kill Rama, nor could Rama kill him. Unwillingly, they watched each other, accepting this.

Blood pouring from their wounds, they begrudgingly bowed to each other. Ravana's chariot turned, taking him back into Lanka on broken wheels. Rama's face was dark with despair as he turned away from the enemy he could not kill. Then he ran to Lakshmana, clutching his brother's hand to his heart. Alarming amounts of fresh blood kept pumping out, despite my efforts to hold the wound closed. We moved Lakshmana to Sushena's camp at the top of Mount Suvela; Rama's injuries also needed attention.

As soon as Lanka's gates closed, however, Ravana unleashed his full power on us. A rainstorm descended, lacerating us with a thousand whips. The ocean smashed against the shores. Wind howled, and black smog erupted from Lanka's towers. Thunder and lightning crashed through the darkness, setting trees on fire. The final betrayal of the elements hit me in the face when a terrible wind knocked me to the ground.

I squatted down on my haunches and leaped beyond the clouds. Vibhishana soared next to me. The devastating storm moved over our troops, a hurricane rumbling with vengeful lightning.

At the highest tower of Lanka, I saw a terrible sorcerer, the black smog erupting from his hands. His black hair flowed like a cape down to his feet. He lifted his hands, and the dark mist followed. As he threw down his hands, all four gates opened. The rush of blood-drinkers howled like thunder. The sounds of slaughter hit my ears. A chilling howl rose high above the others. A golden dome, cresting the clouds, began to move. A portentous feeling seized me.

"Impossible!" Vibhishana cried. "Ravana has forced the Sleeper to awaken! Kumbhakarna!"

He flew away toward the city. I dropped back down to the Earth. I was whipped by rain lashes and could barely see through the rising black mist, but nothing could obscure Kumbha, tall as Lanka's highest towers. His hands were the size of mountains, his claws the size of the snow-peaked Himalayas. The Earth rumbled as he walked. The tip of his crown—marvel that he had one!—upset the clouds. His fangs were like upside-down mountains, his mouth a black cavern.

Kumbha stepped across the high ramparts, crushing hundreds under his feet. The hair on my entire body bristled. In one motion, he seized hundreds of monkeys, throwing them into his mouth. He devoured them as if plucking berries from a bush. Woken up in undue time, Kumbha's appetite was unstoppable. The shrieks of the monkeys were earsplitting. His laugh boomed like a thunderstorm across the plains. Seeing the gigantic demon, the entire army broke ranks and fled in sheer terror. The rain howled around us, drenching us. Within minutes, Nala's bridge was crowded with deserters.

Together with Sugriva, Angada, and Nala, I attacked Kumbha. We pounded him with our fists, using all our strength, enough to instantly kill other blood-drinkers. But he knocked me off his shoulder with a flick off his hand. I expanded to my largest size. But I was still like a doll on his forearm. He was not impressed; he mocked me, moving his thumb and fore-finger together, reaching to pinch my cheek. I leaped out of his reach. The stampede out of Lanka continued.

In three fierce leaps, I was back on top of Mount Suvela. Rama sat at Lakshmana's sick-bed. The bandages around Lakshmana's chest were soaked in blood. His breaths were strained, his body burning with fever. Sushena changed the drenched cloth, pressing herbs into the wound to stop the blood flow. Rama's face was grief-stricken.

"Ravana is stronger than me, Hanuman," he said. "I cannot kill him."

"Neither could he kill you," I said. "We will find a way."

In a rush, I told him about the giant. He gave his brother one last look, kissing his fore-head. He might never see Lakshmana alive again.

"Take me to Kumbha," Rama commanded.

With Rama on my shoulder, I leaped through the air. Rama's arm was around my neck, holding tight as we landed. He slid from my shoulder and fitted an arrow to his bow. When the arrow pierced Kumbha's hand, he lifted his foot to stomp Rama down. But twenty

consecutive arrows crushed his toes, splitting his toenails open. Kumbha lost his footing for a moment but continued to devour our troops. Rama's arrows ripped away layers of fat from his body. Blood-drinkers forgot the battle and pounced on the chunks of flesh. Irritated by Rama's arrows, Kumbha stalked away. As if we were one entity, Rama jumped onto my back and we leap-flew in pursuit of Kumbha's giant steps. Rama quickly devised a plan, one word running into the other. His relentless arrows accompanied every word. "Gather as many as you can. I will herd him toward the shore. When I use my crescent moon arrow, rush at him and tip him into the sea."

I was gone from his side before his final words were spoken. Next to Kumbha, Rama glowed like a distant star. The plan quickly spread through our troops. The monkeys who were running in fear for their lives ran faster to the shores. Dark shadows flew above us, coming closer and closer. Spooky laughter filled our ears. Indrajit's magic tricks. Invisible, he shot missiles from the sky. Rama was occupied with Kumbha and could not save us from this too. I launched into the air, chasing Indrajit. Every time he released an arrow, I saw him for a split second. He was like lightning, visible with a crack, then gone. I pursued him with the force of a tornado and pounced on him. I pounded his ribs mercilessly.

"Curse you, monkey!" he gasped.

He slammed an arrow into my thigh and muttered a mantra to overthrow me. He kicked my chest as he bounded away. Gravity pulled me back down, and the veil of smog covered me. I had to return to Rama and topple over the giant.

Kumbha destroyed us from one side and a wielder of black magic assailed us from the other. Sugriva, Nila, and Nala stayed to combat Indrajit. Angada and I rallied our troops, herding them toward Kumbha. He crushed everything in sight, his feet and his club the size of mountains. Mangled monkeys hung from his jaw, impaled on his fangs.

Rama had covered Kumbha's back with arrows. He used them to climb up the demon. With every upswing, Rama plunged his sword in to its hilt. Kumbha's hand groped for Rama, but he was out of reach. Kumbha swayed back and forth like an angry elephant. Rama reached Kumbha's shoulder and sliced off his ear. Blood squirted down Kumbha's shoulder as he howled and swatted blindly. Rama cut off the other ear. Kumbha's equilibrium was reduced by this loss.

Balancing on Kumbha's bloody shoulders, Rama slipped and tumbled down. He caught himself, grasping Kumbha's hair. Kumbha shook his head ferociously, throwing Rama right and left. I leaped up and hooked my arm around Rama's waist. I kicked off from Kumbha's back and brought Rama to the ground. Kumbha smashed the tip of his club down on us. We joined the fleeing monkeys and sprinted toward the shore. The dark mist gathered around Kumbha's ankles. The ocean lapped at our feet, steam rising from the waves. Angada leaped up from the black mist, coming toward us, followed by a throng of monkey warriors, his part of the plan underway. Kumbha pursued Rama, his footsteps crashing against the shore.

Rama invoked a spell-infused missile. It glowed like the crescent moon. As Rama released the arrow, Angada's monkeys swarmed up Kumbha. The arrow flew into Kumbha's neck. He grabbed monkeys, flinging them into the ocean. Serpents reared up with jaws open.

A red line appeared across Kumbha's neck, then blood exploded. His head began to fall forward, his body backward. As he fell into the sea, the shores swelled. Water rose high above our heads and crashed back down. Slowly, the giant's body began sinking. As the corpse momentarily floated, monkeys jumped up and down on it. When sea serpents clamped down on it, they leaped ashore. There, they continued jumping up and down, as on the first day of our victory. Only I seemed to notice the black mist engulfing us from behind.

"I have repaid my debt to the Lord of Oceans," Rama said. "His creatures feast now."

The black smog had covered the entire island. Rama threw himself into the darkness, blazing it away with his magical arrows. Monkeys rushed back from the bridge into the mayhem. But Vanara after Vanara was shot down by the invisible Indrajit. In the thick darkness, we could not see who we were fighting. Blood-drinkers slaughtered blood-drinkers, and monkeys slaughtered monkeys. Indrajit's merciless missiles lay entire sections of our army to waste. With his magic and his weapons, he felled more monkeys than Kumbha had done. As I desperately pursued him through the clouds, the corpses grew into hills around the four gates. Few and far between did I see my valiant Vanara brothers leap above the dark mist. Rama's blazing arrows chased Indrajit through the sky.

Then I saw Sugriva just as he was shot in the heart. Indrajit's barking laughter echoed in my ears as Sugriva disappeared into the black mist. Next Nila fell. Then Nala. I leaped toward them, searching for their fallen bodies, but the darkness hid them. Angada howled in pain. No! Our army was being destroyed. Still, we fought. Rama's arrows dispersed the smog, which showed us Indrajit's work: Six hundred million swift monkeys lay dead. With the black mist gone, Indrajit withdrew all his magic. Rama's eyes darted across the blue skies. He stood with his bow aimed, but the target was missing. Then we heard Sita's voice, crying for help. In a flying chariot, Indrajit held her by her hair. His other hand wielded a sword.

"Surrender!" he roared, "Or she dies!"

His voice echoed across the battlefield. Those who were still alive turned their eyes to the terrible scene. Rama was frozen, eyes fixed on his princess. I gazed with unblinking eyes at the crying woman. It *was* Sita! Every detail was right, from the dirt on her cheeks to her bright eyes.

The blood-drinkers started chanting: "Kill her! Kill her!"

The princess cried, "Rama! Thirty gods have mercy! Have mercy!"

The same words over and over again. But the ring in her voice was so authentic, I was frozen in horror. Indrajit never loosened his grip on her. Rama drew an arrow to his ear. Indrajit's sword cut through the air; he split Sita in half from hip to shoulder.

"*No!*" Rama screamed.

The two pieces of her body fell to the Earth, blood splattering on us. Blood-drinkers pounced, devouring her within seconds. Rama's bow dropped to the ground, and he fell to his knees. His eyes stared ahead in shock, arms limp by his sides. I stood in front of him, protecting him from Indrajit. The crown prince abandoned us, cackling with laughter, certain of his victory.

Lakshmana was on his deathbed. My dearest friends had all been slain. Sita was dead. All around me, monkeys moaned, breathing their last. There was nothing left to fight for. Night descended, sealing us in absolute darkness. Someone handed me a torch. A handful of desperate Vanaras scaled Lanka's walls with torches in hand. It was their turn to burn.

Garland of Nine Skulls

I am jolted awake by the most horrific wailing in the night. First, I think Ravana has been slain. That his wives cry for him. But this is not grief. It is ear-splitting panic. A thousand girls screaming at the tops of their lungs. I press my hands to my chest, calming my beating heart. My hair stands on end. My eyes fill with tears. What is happening? The entire island must be rocking at its foundation, pierced by the terrible screams. The end of the world. Then I see the licks of fire flickering in the night sky, burning inside Lanka's walls.

Quick as lightning, I descend to my core, becoming elementally fire. My essence becomes one with the fire ravaging Lanka. By the time I join my Shakti to it, thousands of women are already dying. The horror is immediate, and I shrink away, revolted. The last time I became fire, protecting Hanuman's tail, I was an exultant firestorm. But this sickening fire rages without me. The taste and smell of charred flesh nauseate me. I cannot easily assimilate. My consciousness spreads out into the flames until the entire fire is under my purview. I contain it and stop it from spreading. The flames burst angrily in protest, then resume gorging on anything within reach: beds, bodies, curtains, pillars, gold, closets with clothes, boxes of jewelry. The fire devours without discrimination.

I turn my attention to the living. The woman closest to me wails at the top of her lungs. Her hair has burned to the root. The first layer of her skin has peeled off. It is more merciful to complete what the fire has begun. But flesh is resistant to quick consumption. The flames slowly chew on her arms, thighs, and lip, then blister and blacken her skin. It shrinks and cracks open. Fat begins to leak out. Still she screams, screams, screams, until I, the fire, devour her tongue, her tonsils, her throat. Her eyes explode out of their sockets. Her innards flow out like lava. The flames grow, fueled by the fat and blood. It will take several hours to completely devour her body. Her consciousness flees.

Her subtle body hovers, distressed by its forced exit from its physical armature. This is where my real work begins: I lean closer to her soul and surround her with my warmth. My presence no longer burns or destroys, for the soul cannot be burned or cut. She settles into my embrace like a newborn, soothed by its mother. There she stays as I turn my attention to the others that need me just as desperately. The agonized souls flock to me, calmed by my presence.

Even with the fire contained, the disaster continues. The vapors and gases produced by the fire create another death trap. The noxious fumes fill the air. A few hundred are spared the horror of burning alive, suffocated instead in their sleep. I understand why the screaming voices have all been female. Their mates are already dead. They sleep alone, their husbands killed in the war. They die an almost peaceful death, poisoned in their dreams. I just have to gently beckon their souls and they come to me, tethering to me. I grow in size and stature.

From the highest point of the flame, I look beyond Lanka's walls and see a host of Vanaras on the battlefield, holding torches, glaring up at Lanka's walls. Two of them stand on the ramparts, their torches flickering black and yellow against their eyes. They have scaled the walls and set fire to the most vulnerable population! *Rama, how could you let them do this!*

This wreckage, this horror, this tragedy, this killing of innocent women, is all done in my name. For the sake of rescuing me. This heinous act is executed by the side of righteousness, and why? Why must these women pay for the evil deeds of their men? Why is the entire female population of Lanka punished because of the desire of its king? The unfairness, the atrocity, the injustice of this fuel my fire body.

I distinctly sense the outlines of the fire that is me, separate from the fire that devours, blindly following its nature. That fire will continue as long as there is fuel. Unlike it, I have a choice. Like an executioner, I move with great speed, without mercy. Yet when the end is certain, what greater mercy than instant death? The screaming carcasses combust, exploding into the fire, one after the other. When the shining souls emerge, I know their suffering has ended. Their souls rush to me, thirsty for peace. I outgrow the fire. It continues its steady mastication of the dead female bodies. There is no more work for me here. With all the souls tethered to me, I rise into the sky, my energetic body like a rising sun in the starless night. They trail behind me like a constellation.

A sentient force becomes vivid next to me: the king of Lanka.

"You saved them," he says.

He spirals up, like a serpent following his queen. Since his core was purged of victims, his spirit is flat, colorless. Yet his power remains vibrant.

"You complement me," he says. "Stay with me, and we can always be like this. King and queen of the elements. With me, you can always be who are you."

But I know one thing with fire-blinding clarity: *I am what I am.*

"I do not need you," I answer. "I am who I am. In spite of you."

His atrocious acts are already doubling back upon him; he has lost large numbers of his people and, tonight, all the bearers of their future. No more progeny will be born to Lanka for a long time. And the war is not yet over. What else will Rama and his troops do? This war is no longer about winning me back, but about vengeance, about destroying Ravana and anything connected to him. I cannot let these deaths go in vain!

Together with them, I swell and grow. I set aside my previous resolve never to use these powers. With just four souls, I had grown into the sky, large as the sorrowless garden. With these thousands eagerly serving me, I easily access the energies that have cordoned Lanka off from the rest of the world. My Shakti is wild, erratic, the fire of cosmic destruction. I break through the Maya that Ravana has created all over Lanka, denying the elements any power save in his service. I strip him of his elemental power. He is flung down into his ten-headed form. Rid of him, I breathe a sigh of relief. I gather the elements to me, channeling all their power into one of Rama's arrows, the Panchabhuta: the Five Elements. May he use this arrow at the right moment.

Then I untether myself from every soul.

Go in peace, I say as I usher them onto their next destination.

They blaze through the sky like comets and disappear into the night. Below, the last fire within the walls sputters and is drenched into nothingness. The blackened remains stare up into the quiet. To me, it looks like a giant skull, pointing me in the direction I must go.

Like a well-kept secret bursting to be told, the Ruby Room gave Ravana to me. The skulls that glow forcefully in Ravana's psyche belong equally to me now, through the Pact of Love. Did he offer himself to me, giving me the keys to his power, in just the way that one wins someone's trust by revealing vulnerabilities? Instead, like a thief, I snuck off with my knowledge, pretending I'd found nothing. And like someone planning a premeditated murder, I will not hesitate to give out the killing blow when my moment comes.

That moment is now. In a split second, I'm at the place Ravana forbade me to go. I look with my own eyes at the remote, craggy valley. A lone mountain goat grazes on meager shrubbery. A snow-chilled breeze ruffles my hair. It is uninviting and rugged. My breath puffs out frostily, and yet I'm not cold. In the center of this valley, a many-tongued fire once blazed. Only the firepit remains, black and charred. This is where I seek my treasure.

I dig through ash and charred timber until I find the skull. It is heavy in my hands, susceptible to my touch. It grins back at me, the blackened remains of his innocence. I clutch it to me and soar to the next site. My arms and body are covered in ash. I'm digging through ten thousand years of fire. Ravana endured thousands upon thousands of years completely

alone. No wonder he craves thousands upon thousands of people to affirm his earthly existence. I find another skull. I rip apart a piece of my cloth and string the skulls together, weaving the yellow strand through the eye sockets. I go to every site, seeking the skulls.

I climb out of the last black hole, smeared in ashes, like Kali, goddess of transformation. I count the skulls one more time, just to feel the satisfaction of a quest complete. Nine skulls. Save for a few cracks on the oldest two, the skulls are intact. With blackened fingers and arms, I raise the garland up high up, offering it to the elements. Then I wear it around my neck, as if they are pearls, not boulderlike skulls. The moment his skulls rest on my breast, I begin to dance. I stomp my feet against the ground and throw my neck forward and back. I stomp one foot and throw the other in the air. As I jump in circles around the dead firepit, the skulls clang together, dancing with me. I throw my hands up in the air and become the prayer.

Ravana's power was created here. May it be destroyed here.

As I jump, the garland flies up. When I land, it thumps back onto my chest, a terrible heartbeat. As if there is a great celebration and I the famed dancer, I dance. As if this is the end of the world and I am the destroyer, I dance. As if I am the center of the universe and every movement depends on me, I dance. As if Brahma is watching me and creating the original dance vocabulary, I dance. As if this is my wedding night, I dance. As if I am a shooting star granting wishes, I dance. As if I'm giving birth to new life, I dance. As if I'm a thunderstorm, I dance. As if I'm the monsoon raining on parched soil, I dance. As if I'm the first union between lovers, I dance. As if I'm every wish upon this Earth come true, I dance. I dance. And dance, and dance. The stars and the moonlit night surround me.

I dance back the way I came, into my sleeping body. Sharduli lifts her beak from under her wing and watches me come, green eyes unblinking. When I'm back in my sleeping body, she closes her eyes and keeps sleeping. Slowly, the dance comes to a natural close. I breathe heavily into the night. My last lucid thought touches on the wild goat, which long since must have scampered away. I close all my senses and sleep.

When I wake, I hear a clanging around my neck and see the garland of nine skulls. It has come with me from the spirit realm to this realm. The skulls have been ripped from their natural habit, reduced to ordinary bone. Seeing me with the garland of nine skulls, the guards are in awe. I'm Nikumbhila incarnate. If they'd forgotten I was their goddess, they know it now.

Every single one of them is prostrate before me. "Have mercy!"

I take the garland off, a great psychic weight lifting off my body. Even his dead matter is so potent. I put the skulls in a circle around me and reach for Trijata's trident. With a dance-like movement, I crash it down with all my might. The skull shatters into a thousand pieces. It does not re-form. It's destroyed with the utmost love. I, who have never wielded a weapon before, quickly shatter the next skull and the next. With each shattering, I feel an explosion of Maya, like a door closed shut and sealing itself. As I crush the last skull, a quake shakes the ground. Ravana's howl is heard far beyond the palace. I collect the bone pulp carefully.

I mix the ash with the earth, purifying it. I pour Ganga's holy water onto it. No latent power remains.

Ravana descends on me soon, screaming, "What have you done? What have you done?"

The guards flee in terror, even Trijata. Ravana needs no answer. He can feel exactly what has happened. I've stripped him of his identity. His body is not his own. Even his pain seeps out through his compromised Maya. Nothing can stay within him long. The Earth is already claiming his material for herself. He doesn't belong to himself anymore. He feels it.

"You've betrayed me!" he shouts. "You tricked your way into my heart. You've taken everything from me. The tenth offering would have given me eternal power. Now I will take yours. The head of the goddess!"

He stalks toward me with a sword, eyes mad. He lifts the sword and, without hesitation, charges. I touch Dhanya's necklace and invoke the power of a hundred women. I don't even have to say a word. The magic of their spell descends on me immediately.

He steps back, as if burned.

"The curse of one hundred women stands between you and me," I say, speaking in a voice with a hundred echoes. "I cannot be destroyed by you."

The glow of the spell swirls around me, and yet it is my innate effulgence that shines through, so bright he shades his eyes and squints, unable to see past the light that emanates from me. Madness flickers black in his eyes. If we were in the spirit realm, he would fling his madness at me, forcing me to see his vicious convictions. Here, he must concede his impotence. He surrenders at my feet, acknowledging my prowess.

"Accept me, Sita, please," he begs. His ten heads are on the ground. "I am yours. I love you so intensely, I know nothing else. I've given everything for you. And you know it. Grant me your mercy."

Why does he not flee?

Even now, he looks up at me with hope. He thinks he can win. If Indrajit doesn't conquer Rama, he is certain he will. When that happens, I must submit to the laws, offering my hand to the victor. He is willing to die for that hope.

I lift my hand in blessing. Sharduli flies to my shoulder. I am now Kalaratri, leading him to his final night. He wants nothing more than my love, nothing more than to tear my flesh apart with his claws and teeth. He wants to crush me in his embrace, to punish me for defying him. And on and on it goes, all he wants and needs from me. It can only end in death. That is the only release I offer.

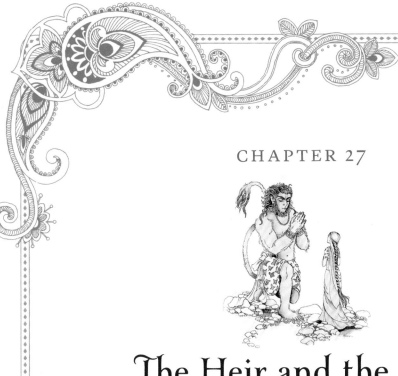

CHAPTER 27

The Heir and the King

W hen all hope was lost, Vibhishana rescued us. He knelt at Rama's side, insisting Indrajit had not killed the real Sita. In the eleven months of Sita's captivity, he argued, *no one* had been able to see her. Not by the four means of achieving one's goals: bribery, flattery, and sowing dissension, not to speak of violence. Ravana would *never* allow Sita to be harmed. Aroused from his stupor, Rama went to hold vigil for Lakshmana, whose condition was critical.

Vibhishana and I went to scour the battlefield for anyone living. The battlefield was dark and ghostly, filled by wails from within Lanka, where a terrible fire raged. The two of us seemed to be the only ones alive. I brought my torch close to many dead faces, until I finally found Sugriva, his eyes open but unseeing. I stroked his tawny hair, showing my affection in a way I could not when he was alive. I was plunged into remorse. When he most needed me, I had not protected him. Vibhishana and I brought Sugriva, Angada, Nila, and Nala back to the camp. They would be given honorable burials. On Mount Suvela, Sushena was in a panic: Lakshmana was dying. Sushena ordered me to fly across the ocean to the Himalayas. *Sanjivani,* a life-giving plant, grew on the Dronagiri Mountains. Without wasting a moment, I did so. When I landed on the mountain, the pungent smell of ripe herbs wafted over me. I could not find the right one, so I picked up the entire mountain and brought it to Lanka. I had no choice but to fully display the size of my ignorance. I placed the Dronagiri as close to Mount Suvela as I could. Sushena found the sanjivani within seconds.

When he applied it to Lakshmana's wounds, Lakshmana's breath grew steady, and his wounds healed completely. When he opened his eyes, Rama burst into such joyous tears that the hairs on my body stood on end. Within moments, my Vanara friends were also revived. That was a moment of true hope. While the magical herb worked on their bodies, the revived warriors fell into a deep slumber. The fire inside Lanka had died down, and for the first time, the night was quiet. Even our enemies were licking their wounds.

I, however, could not convince my body to rest. There were too many unsolved questions. How would we defeat Ravana and Indrajit? It seemed impossible, but there had to be a way, so I stood guard at the edge of our camp, eyes never leaving the gleaming city we had yet to conquer. Behind me, Rama sat at Lakshmana's side, leaning his forehead on his brother's chest. He had been so close to losing his brother forever.

Rama and Lakshmana's breaths were even and matching, resonant with sleep. Then Rama awoke with a start. Quickly, I scanned our surroundings. Had his warrior instinct sensed something awry? But the camp was quiet, and both of us settled down, resuming our vigils. When Rama began to murmur, I didn't hear his words at first. But then I could not stop listening, though his words were not for me.

"I had a terrible dream, Lakshmana, just now. It clings to me, filling me with shame." His voice grew muffled, his hand covering his face. "So much shame."

Did Rama forget that even at this distance, I could hear his words well?

"A terrible certainty fills me. My hands tingle, my arms feel numb. Ravana's message as the war started may be the truth: Maybe Sita loves him. We don't know what she wants. Not even Vibhishana knows what has taken place in Ravana's private quarters. Only Ravana knows. Only Sita knows. Thirty gods, to voice it makes it more real."

I could barely stop myself from intervening. There had been no time to speak to Rama, to share my suspicion that Ravana's dark magic had penetrated his consciousness. I had wondered what form it would take, and here it was—so private and terrible that Rama spoke of it to Lakshmana only because his brother was unconscious.

"The dream began with Sita," Rama whispered, "her back to me, hair loose and shining. Then Ravana's hand slid across her head, bunching her hair into his fist, pulling her head back, exposing her slender neck. Like an animal, he began to sniff her throat, her ears. She made sounds, moaning in a way that only I've heard. She lay under him, moving in ways only I have seen. She smiled in ecstasy, a smile that only I know."

He was quiet for a moment. I wanted to cover my ears: *That is not a dream! It's a ploy!*

As if hearing me, Rama asked, "Have I conjured this shameful dream? Is it my own fear made real?"

No. Ravana struck you where he knew it would hurt the most!

"Before seeing Ravana, this thought never entered my mind," Rama sighed. "But now I've seen his potency. He attracts and allures the mind. How could Sita resist him all these months?" In a barely audible voice, he whispered, "The dream was too vivid. Too detailed. After the union, Sita pulled the silks to her breast, covering herself. She started crying softly, in deep remorse. 'I will never forgive myself for this.' He gathered her hair, twisting it away from her glistening back, placing her crest jewel into the nape of her neck, tying up her hair. 'No one needs to know,' he said. 'It will be our secret.' Softly, he blew on her skin, causing goose bumps. The hair at her neck sprung into curls. She flung the crest jewel to the floor, her hair spilling over her back. She leaned back into his arms, and they began again."

That is when I no longer could keep silent. With eyes downcast, I approached quietly, apologizing profusely for invading his private moment. I told him first of Rambha and Nala-Kubera's curse. I wanted him to know that other women had refused Ravana, at great peril. Then I shared my conviction that Ravana had implanted this dream. Rama listened as I spoke. The heady smell of sanjivani mingled with the scent of Rama's perspiration. Rama kept his eyes on his brother. At times, Lakshmana's breath pushed through his nostrils with effort, as if it was his last. But he kept breathing. These sharp interruptions allowed Rama to focus on his brother instead of himself. He said nothing in response to my words. But finally, he nodded. He would take my words into consideration. As I retreated to my post, I imagined that I saw Ravana's looming shadow behind Rama. His ploy had worked, no matter my words. Something once seen could not be erased. Would that dream haunt Rama again? I was certain it would, for the darkness had not been purged. And yet Rama's shame worked as a gag on me. Even if there had been an opportunity to speak to Vibhishana, was it my right to share a dream that I had overheard? Unwillingly and against my better judgment, I left the matter behind.

We still did not know how to defeat Ravana. But Vibhishana had a plan for Indrajit's demise. We turned our sights on destroying Indrajit, the most powerful sorcerer we knew. The scheme depended on stealth and a show of strength at the right moment. Lakshmana insisted on being the one to kill Indrajit. Angada and I were appointed to aid him. And of course Vibhishana was indispensable.

With waning numbers of troops on both sides, night had naturally become a time for cease-fire. Close to midnight, the hour came that Vibhishana had waited for. The four of us gathered under a neem tree with low-hanging branches to avoid spying eyes.

"After using so much of his power," Vibhishana said, "my nephew must renew his pact with the goddess Nikumbhila. She is the protector of our clan. She has favored Indrajit since he was a child. He regularly makes offerings to her, but especially before and after a battle. We will enter his secret cavern and extinguish the fire before his ritual is complete."

"If it's so secret," Angada shot in, "then how come you know about it?"

Vibhishana ignored Angada's question. He understood it rightly as another fit of pique, naming Vibhishana a betrayer. As if any of us could forget. Lakshmana nodded as Vibhishana spoke, sharpening his arrows with a rock. By his own power, Indrajit had slaughtered six hundred million of our monkeys, including our mightiest. It was an unspoken fact that we relied on Vibhishana's prowess. We had never seen a single weapon pierce his skin. Despite fighting ferociously, he was probably the only unbloodied one among us.

"How many in total must we prepare to defeat?" Lakshmana asks.

"I cannot answer that," Vibhishana answered. "Indrajit seems thoughtless during battle, striking like a hungry snake. But that swiftness is the result of many, many hours of strategic planning."

"It sounds like you admire him," Lakshmana said. He examined the tip of his arrow.

"I was there the day he was born. His only fault is pride, which I fear he's inherited from his father. Be prepared to match his ferocity. We will come upon him in his most vulnerable state. He must approach the goddess unarmed. Attack immediately." Vibhishana put a hand on Lakshmana's shoulders. "Prince, don't waste your second chance."

Lakshmana packed his arrows into his quivers. He would focus on Indrajit, while Angada and I would extinguish the ritual fire. That was the plan.

"I learned the directions from my mother," Vibhishana says, "when she was drunk one day. She was certain I would never find the location."

"How did you?" I asked.

"For days, I observed the pure black goat he needs for the sacrifice. When the dark mist covered Lanka, it was sent to that mountain."

He pointed to the mountain opposite Mount Suvela. We turned from the golden city, heading toward the third peak on the island. We were forced to travel on foot, and finally the mountain stopped us. We would never have detected this place on our own. Vibhishana looked at me.

"Even if Indrajit escapes or we are forced to flee, extinguish the fire!"

Following Vibhishana's lead, we began our ascent of the mountain silently. We placed our toes and fingers meticulously against the rock wall. Our nimble feet quietly ascended the cliff. Lakshmana slipped once, loose rocks spilling over the edge. Nothing could be done about the rocks clattering down. There was only a handful of them, but to our ears, they sounded like an avalanche. Quietly, we pressed our bodies into the wall, only our eyes moving.

Two guards clad entirely in black leaned forward to inspect the noise. Then I saw the gaping entrance they were protecting. My fur bristled with tension as we waited for them to stand at ease again. The seconds ticked by into minutes. Quietly, we continued our ascent. On Vibhishana's signal, Angada and I shrank into our smallest forms and snuck past the two guards and into the tunnel. Inside, we transformed into blood-drinkers and returned to the guards, pretending to be guards ourselves. Swiftly, we covered their mouths and twisted their necks. Vibhishana caught the two bodies and slipped them down to the bottom of the mountain.

It was pitch-black in the maze. Vibhishana took the lead. Only once did he take a wrong turn and mutter, under his breath, "Exactly at this point, she got confused."

I was inundated with the tension emanating from him. The queen mother's directives could have been the nonsensical ramblings of a drunk woman. This seemed to be Vibhishana's sudden fear. But then a flickering light up ahead slapped the walls of the tunnel with

a silent whip. The force got darker and angrier the closer we got. Nikumbhila was not a gentle goddess. I heard a goat bleating. Our tension mounted as we silently moved closer. Fire crackled, and Indrajit's voice chanted. The guards posted at the entrance were dispatched by Vibhishana. Then we crept into the heart of the mountain, a large cave.

Indrajit, draped in red silk, long hair unbound, poured red liquid into the fire with a black iron ladle. The cave walls were lined with male and female guards wearing red turbans, their eyes fixed on their prince. A pure black goat lay beheaded, blood pooling around its neck. Painted skulls and half-melted golden pots surrounded him. Heaps of wilted red flowers decorated the shrine. Indrajit's weapons, gleaming by the fire, were smeared with goat blood.

Sweat poured down his neck and chest. Then he sensed our intrusion. His blood-red eyes snapped open and his head whipped toward us. Lakshmana and Vibhishana faced him. Angada charged to the left and I to the right. I used my fist to smash the heads of the guards, as easily as crushing coconuts; the pulp of their brains was crushed against the wall. One guard clawed at my chest, ripping up my skin. I grabbed his arm and swung his body as I would a club. The fire crackled, the goddess demanding her offering.

Parrying Lakshmana's arrows, Indrajit retreated to the far wall, but he had eyes only for his uncle, the betrayer.

"These humans are not our true foe," Indrajit seethed, letting loose arrows. "I curse the day I called you uncle!"

Vibhishana seemed unfazed but continued to make gestures with his hands to keep Indrajit's magic at bay. When Indrajit hurled another insult at him, Vibhishana spoke: "Your father's defects are carried on by you, whelp. His horrific murders of the holy ones, warring with the gods, his wrathfulness, hostility, and perversity, have become yours. Neither of you will endure!"

Indrajit's rage increased. How to kill this fire that was roaring so hungrily?

The mountain rumbled in protest as arrows crashed into the walls. But instead of attacking, Vibhishana dropped his bow. Soon, he had arrows lodged in his arms and legs. If it weren't for Lakshmana, he would have been dead. Snarling, Angada threw a dripping head into the fire. It sizzled and burned brighter, only to die down: The goddess was not pleased with that offering! We threw dead and alive blood-drinkers into the hungry flames. With every corpse, she grew smaller and smaller. We piled bodies on top of the fire, suffocating the flames with flesh. It stank of burning meat.

A sharp pain hit my left arm as an arrow ripped through it. Indrajit's eyes were on me. The presence of the dark goddess was diminishing. Another arrow pierced my shoulder. I ripped it out with a roar. An arrow grazed Vibhishana's forehead, knocking him off his feet.

"Die, traitor!" Indrajit screamed.

Tears ran in streams down Vibhishana's cheeks. His warding movements were half-hearted. Lakshmana too was flung back by the force of Indrajit's arrows. His head crashed against the rock, blood flowing from the back. Only tiny tendrils of fire burst forth, like a dying man's gasps for air.

"Soon you will be dead, prince," I promised.

I hurled another blood-drinker onto the pyre. Behind me, I heard a terrible crash as Lakshmana and Indrajit were both thrown backward by each other's arrows. I held the last demon high in the air, running to the firepit. As arrows flew past me, I shielded myself with the body. I jumped on top of the fire, crushing the bodies with my feet. There was no place for the fire to breathe anymore. Lakshmana charged, smashing his fists into Indrajit's ribs. The two archers abandoned weapons and clubbed each other with their fists. Blood ran down Lakshmana's nose. Indrajit flung him away. The final flame died. Smoke filled the cave.

Lakshmana grabbed his bow and released an arrow with a mantra to Brahma the creator. There was nothing to protect Indrajit; the arrow flew through the air so clearly, I was sure Indrajit would move away in time, but he was looking at his uncle, who was aiming an arrow at him. When Lakshmana's arrow hit his heart, he stumbled back, and his arrow flew past Vibhishana. Indrajit looked down at the missile in his nephew's chest.

Vibhishana sobbed, covering his face with his hands. Indrajit spat in his uncle's direction and sagged against the wall, glaring at us. The stuff oozing from his fatal wound was as black as his hair, which clung to his sweaty chest and face. Lakshmana held his bow ready, panting from the exertion. His left eye was swollen shut. He was bleeding everywhere, and his broken ribs protruded.

Time slowed as Indrajit took his last breath. His dark goddess had deserted him, displeased by the offering. I was grateful I didn't serve such a fickle master. Indrajit's eyes rolled back, his eyelids fluttered closed. But he had tricked us so many times that we stared at him, expecting him to shoot up with a cackle or vanish.

"He's dead," Angada finally announced, arms crossed, drenched in sweat and blood.

"Compose yourself," I said to Vibhishana, kneeling at his side.

Vibhishana stood up and kneeled at Nikumbhila's shrine. A chilly wind knocked down the wilted flowers.

"My brother's powers have been compromised," he said.

I didn't know if he meant because Indrajit was dead or something else. Gently, as if handling a baby, Vibhishana lifted his nephew up into his arms, embracing him tightly before slinging him across his shoulder. Lakshmana could not move without the help of Angada and me. He was barely conscious. Sometimes his feet stumbled along; mostly, his toes dragged across the ground.

As we neared our camp, I saw Rama's silhouette outlined against the torchlight at his tent. When he saw Lakshmana's crushed face and broken body, he cried out. He pulled his brother onto his lap and kissed his face gently. Lakshmana smile was barely detectable through his swollen features. "I did it," he mumbled. "I did it."

Vibhishana lay Indrajit at Rama's feet. "The heir to Lanka's throne."

A tear trickled down his cheek. Otherwise, his remorse had vanished. Rama placed his hand lightly on Vibhishana.

"Your loss will be rewarded," he promised. "You will lead your people to prosperity."

The mighty sorcerer at our feet looked like a sleeping boy, his black hair spread out around him. Vibhishana's love surrounded the lifeless body.

"Nikumbhila assures me that Ravana has been weakened," Vibhishana said. "Kalaratri leads him away."

I didn't fully understand this, but Rama turned to me.

"Take the crown prince to Lanka's gates."

As I carried away his nephew, Vibhishana's eyes bored into my back. The dead prince would be our silent messenger. The only warrior left now was Ravana himself.

When Ravana's howl filled Lanka, the sun above us quivered slightly. I understood how monumental this final battle would be when Agastya and other all-seeing sages appeared. In turn, they blessed Rama with victory, then remained in the sky as spectators, hovering at a distance. Rama began to worship the sun, praying for victory. Sugriva was nearby, doing the same, calling for his father's support. I could not forget how Indra brought down rain to mourn Vali's death. Sugriva's prayers had the same potential.

It was new moon day, the fourteenth day of the battle—just days from the moment when Rama's exile would be complete. For fourteen years, he had been separated from his kingdom. He had left as a boy of eighteen and soon would be a man of thirty-two. Today, he would gain everything—or lose everything.

First, Ravana's queens appeared on the ramparts. They lined themselves up along the city's walls to be his witnesses. Their jewelry and splendor sparkled in the sun. As usual, Ravana wasn't above wanting an audience. Rama stood barefoot in the center of the battlefield. He faced the northern gate, a black tunnel from which anything might emerge. We had taken our place at Rama's back, with Lakshmana and Vibhishana at our sides.

Ravana charged forth, his chariot drawn by demon-faced mules. We had never seen him so angry, so terrible in his wrath. His ten-headed, twenty-armed form chilled us with its power. The two heroes exchanged heated insults, but soon their weapons spoke for them. Rama's arrows were relentless, and he was swift on his feet. He ran fast like the wind. He fought like no warrior I'd seen before or since. Within seconds, he had pierced Ravana's hands, an arrow through each one. Ravana roared with all his ten mouths, like a pack of infuriated lions. Still, he parried Rama's arrows. For us who could only watch, it was excruciating. I cheered for Rama, but it cost me to simply stand there.

In the first hours, they seemed to just play with each other. I could not have said who was the hunter and who the prey. The crash of arrows was steady and persistent; they circled one another without ever diminishing the incessant attack of arrows. As the sun traveled past its zenith, the mood changed. The rivals had assessed each other's power, and it was time to attack. I didn't know who initiated the change, but both were quick to respond, like vipers rising from their hiding places. Rama transformed into Death himself. I expected Ravana to conjure an illusion of Sita or to rope Rama into some trap, but like a drunken man, he seemed unable to fully direct his powers. There was something very unbalanced in his entire presence, like a man walking on a wounded leg, yet I saw no fatal wounds on him. Like Rama, he was bleeding, but neither had sustained grievous harm.

An arrow now hit Rama midstride, throwing our prince into the air and dashing him to the ground. We gasped. Lakshmana flinched, ready to run to his brother's aid. But Ravana stopped us with mocking words: "Let it not be said that I brought you to Yama only because you were exhausted! Stand up, prince!"

Ravana wanted to win this on his own merit, and so did Rama! He got back onto his feet, but the vigor he'd displayed earlier had diminished. The place where he'd fallen was slick with blood, and his back was entirely covered in blood-soaked dirt. If Rama faltered, would I be able to stand by as a spectator? Rama's arrows pounded against his enemy's armor, denting it. Yet Rama's armor was dented too. Blood flowed from wounds on his arms, shoulders, and thighs.

The demon-faced mules charged at Rama. At the last second, Rama lunged aside, bow lifted. The chariot thundered past him. Arrows lodged into the ground around him. Rama jumped to his feet and attacked Ravana from the back. This was not foul play, since Ravana's heads could see in all directions. Rama's arrow pierced Ravana's neck, and a head went crashing to the ground. I waited for the sickening sound of a new head emerging. But it never came. Ravana's remaining heads stared at the headless neck. He was as stunned as we were. Rama severed another head; it flew off in another direction. A new head did not appear.

Rama sprinted around the chariot, releasing arrow after arrow. Ravana put all his focus now into saving his heads, hiding behind shields, but Rama was quicker. When only three heads remained, Ravana soared up, abandoning his chariot. Blood poured down his back. The pain must have been unbearable. As he swooped down with claws lifted, Rama let go of an arrow. It split into three and severed Ravana's remaining three heads.

Ravana fell to the ground headless, the severed heads screaming so loudly the Earth shook. We cheered loudly, but Vibhishana lifted his hand, demanding silence. Beheaded, Ravana was still alive. His threatening presence remained as strong as ever. He lunged to his feet: One head had grown back. Rama's arrow cut it off. A sickening pop resounded as it emerged anew.

"I cannot be killed!" Ravana roared. "Grandfather Brahma's boon protects me!"

Dashamukha, the one with ten faces, stood before us with just one face. Dashagriva, the ten-necked one, stood before us with blood pumping out from nine necks. Ravana, the one who made the universe wail, stood before us, wailing. His end was near.

"From this day, the name Vibhishana will mean one's worst enemy!" Ravana shouted. "If Rama wins today, it's only because of your treachery."

But Vibhishana was not the one who had compromised him. That had been someone else. With sharp movements, Ravana hissed and sealed his necks, absorbing them into his body, accepting a reduced form. The dark Maya vibrating around him grew closer to his body. His final head was impervious to Rama's arrows, however. It grew back, again and again. He soared up, claws lifted, fangs bared. He tore a deep gash on Rama's chest and then on his back before Rama could stave him off. As on their previous battle, the two circled each other, unable to strike the death blow. Eyes on each other, they retreated to separate sides of the battlefield to recuperate.

We rushed to Rama. Vibhishana and I were allowed near our prince, while the rest watched from a distance, keeping an eye on Ravana. He had his own defense team tending to him. Sushena pressed sanjivani on Rama's injuries, while Lakshmana cried out, "Why do you hold back, Rama? Why do you match him blow by blow? I can see that your heart is not in it to kill him!"

Rama drank water and poured the rest over his face. He whispered fiercely, "I'm not sure what she wants!"

"Rama! How can you say this?" Lakshmana's incredulity was all of ours.

"What if his message was true?" Rama said. "What if Sita doesn't want him dead?"

Lakshmana sputtered, "Rama, I can't . . . I don't . . . No! Even if that wasn't the most ridiculous query, it's far too late now! It's your life or his. We will never allow you to die. How can you even think that Sita would want that!"

A shadow crossed Rama's face, curling his lips down in a way I'd never seen. My heart beat rapidly. Couldn't Rama feel how foreign that shadow was, how alien the intrusion?

Just then, a chariot descended from the sky and landed in front of Rama, magnificent and heavenly, Indra's own chariot, drawn by Matali, his charioteer. The holy ones in the sky hailed Rama, blessing him with victory.

Lakshmana knelt at his brother's side, growing earnest. "Rama, dear brother, you must put aside your personal feelings. Walk the path of duty, which you treasure. You, of all people, recognize dharma as the highest path. Yours is to slay Ravana."

Rama got onto the chariot; it thundered away to meet Ravana, whose steeds had been replaced with black stallions. Ravana's body was now that of a perfectly two-handed man, whose similarity to Rama was uncanny. For Rama, it would be like killing himself. The tricks of these demons never ended, but Lakshmana's words pushed Rama. His fight was relentless, and it was clear from the first arrow that he was winning. The demon king's laughter was forced as he struggled to match the pace of Rama's arrows. He resorted to magical missiles, sending hailstorms, fires, and black mists. Rama countered these easily.

The chariots pursued each other in turns, crushing the dead under their wheels. All the other spectators and I grew grim, the thrill of a good battle between equals gone. This was like watching a boxer bludgeoning his fallen opponent. Though Ravana refused to fall, he stumbled through the motions of defense in a grotesque, graceless way. He wore his bravado like a tattered mask. He had to see death rising up for him, but he refused to accept what was before his eyes.

"In the name of Sita!" Rama cried, invoking a missile imbued with the five elements.

The golden arrow soared through the air, propelled by fire, water, earth, air, and ether. Nothing could stop it. I heard the crash of Ravana's body before it occurred. The golden arrow plunged into Ravana's heart, ripping him apart. His last cry was drowned out by blood bubbling up through his mouth. Ravana fell—like a mountain, a meteor, a planet—smashing the Earth's surface.

We were quiet, unblinking, hardly breathing. Not a single cheer celebrated Ravana's fall. Rama approached the heaving body of his bitter enemy. Blood and subtle dark matter poured into the Earth. As Ravana's soul sought its exit, he began to convulse. Rama placed one foot on Ravana's chest, pushing his body to the ground, stilling him. The two faced each other a final time. Ravana's eyes were fixed on Rama. His lips moved. Neither I nor anyone else heard what passed between them.

A glowing fire of light surrounded them both. Then it was gone. The king was dead.

Showers of flowers rained down on Rama from the sky. He remained near the body until Ravana's consorts spilled out of Lanka's gates. They cried desperately for their fallen king. Mandodari was the first to reach him, her face drenched with tears, her hair scattered across her back. She flung off her jewelry as she wailed.

Rama's eyes swept across the group of grieving women again and again. Surely, he could not think that Sita would be among them? Yet Rama did not order us to bring Sita. I waited for the command, but it did not come. I expected Rama to rush to the sorrowless forest to reunite with her, but he didn't. Why did it feel like Ravana was still alive, still tormenting and oppressing us?

Rama walked back to us slowly, a man returning from death's embrace. The wrenching cries of the women filled our ears. There was no room for celebration yet. Rama embraced Vibhishana tightly. The new king of Lanka wept, mourning his elder brother, whose secrets he'd betrayed, whose life he'd offered into the hands of Rama.

My eyes were fixed on Rama, my master, whom I was determined to serve until the end of time. Ever since I had met Rama, I had understood how deeply bonded he was to Sita. I searched and searched for the Rama I knew—my master, my friend, the possessor of the deepest wisdom. All I could see was a pale, lusterless man brought to a sickness of the soul. I prayed that Sita's presence would dissolve the pain I saw etched in Rama's face. If I knew anything for certain, it was that this was just the beginning of Sita and Rama's love story. Whatever trials they would face, their love would persist. And so it would be until the Earth shattered, the sun died, and the wind faded.

United at Last

I feel the moment he dies as viscerally as if I am shot in the heart myself. I'm slammed backward into the trunk of the tree. That is when I do my worst: I blast my Shakti body into his, exploding, destroying the boundaries of his being with my own. I tear open the leaks, pulling apart his energy body at the seams. As if his body is a chalice knocked over, his spirit drains out. He clutches onto me, trying to pull me into the Earth with him, but now he has little control over his Maya, for it was never truly his, but borrowed from the elements. His essence returns to the Earth, his spirit set free by Rama. The power he's held over me releases. My archenemy is gone.

After that, everything is quiet. Only Trijata seems to have an inkling as to what has happened. She nods, peering at me with her good eye. The others stand about, clutching their tridents as usual. When the wailing begins, they shuffle their feet, scrunching their mouths together. They suspect what this means, but they don't want to believe it. The heartbroken wailing of women declares our victory. Hearing their grief, it's impossible to feel overjoyed. But the battle is over.

As time ticks by, I'm filled with unease, more than ever before, bound by the protocol of a queen. Rama will send someone to escort me, to bring me to him. Why does he tarry? The reunion with Rama is so delayed that other people claim my time.

As Kaikasi stalks toward me, I understand that a layer of protection has left me with Ravana's death. I especially don't want to see the queen mother. Her ominous habit of finding sorrow in relationships threatens me now that my reunion with Rama is imminent. Her painted face is destroyed by tears. Her hair is in disarray, her clothing mismatched.

"He sacrificed everything for you," she seethes. "Why did you refuse to see this! You sacrificed all our sons for your selfish reasons! Fie upon you!"

Her refusal to take any responsibility for all that has happened angers me, and I cry out, "Curse your son, not us!"

"No, I curse you!" she hisses. "I curse your love for Rama! May it be fraught with the same loss and pain I feel. You could have submitted and sent Rama away. You could have prevented this entire war from happening with just one little nod of your head! But you care nothing for the blood that has been shed because of you! All the people who have been killed, just for you! You are the most selfish person I've ever known!"

She continues ranting and wailing until Trijata leads her away.

Her grief and unfair words feel heavy. I consider sending Sharduli to find out what's happening, but I'm afraid—afraid that one small misstep by me will disrupt the fragile balance of human custom. I have to be queenly and wait. When, finally, I see my golden friend, Hanuman, my face beams, my heart delighted. My guards immediately fling their weapons to the ground, announcing their surrender. While my destiny has become certain, theirs has become uncertain.

Hanuman bows at my feet. Unable to contain my joy, I start ahead before him. I feel almost sick with the relief and power surging through me. "Take me to Rama."

Behind me, Hanuman hesitates. "Prince Rama has requested that you adorn yourself as a princess before you appear in the public eye. Millions have lost their lives in battle to rescue you. They are ordinary monkeys. They will not recognize a princess in you."

My hands are pale and streaked with dirt. Leaves and clumps of dirt are caked into my hair, under my fingernails, and in the crevices of my ears. I don't have to look further to know that the rest of my body and the Cloth of Essence are in the same state.

"I made a vow, Hanuman," I say, "to return to Rama in the same state and same dress that I left him in."

"And yet you did not look like this on the day of your abduction, Princess."

Hanuman's discomfort is obvious.

"My heart tells me to go at once," I say.

"As you wish, my princess," Hanuman says, but adds, "I was shocked when I first saw you. Our prince will suffer all the more, seeing you like this. The order comes from Rama. The battle is over. The time for cleansing is here."

I hear the reason in his words. It is selfish to want to run into Rama's arms like a young girl, careless of all appearance. Having shunned externals all these months, I find no reason to indulge in it now. Perhaps I've been alone too long; I've forgotten what's required of a princess. But I see that Rama is right: An unspeakable war has been fought in my name, and I must become a princess worth dying for in the eyes of our allies.

Seeing the assent in my eyes, Hanuman takes charge. He might not be an expert in the ways of a princess, but he certainly knows who is. He takes me directly to a place I've never been before: the women's quarters. We go through the Lotus Hall and into the private residence. It's equipped to answer every need a princess might have. Being inside the palace makes breathing difficult, and I feel extremely uncomfortable.

But Ravana is dead. I do this for Rama.

The maidservants gather around me. Save for them, the palace is empty. Ravana's wives are mourning for him on the battlefield. Accepting a favor under his roof is different now because Ravana is gone. Lanka is no longer his. Vibhishana is king. So I let the maidservants immerse me in a hot pool of rose-scented water. The water turns black around me as they scrub me clean. I see them wrinkle their noses, but I don't find the murky water offensive. As they reach for my hands, I unwillingly unclench my fist, revealing Rama's ring. I transfer it to my other hand while they scrub my fingers and nails clean. Being in the heart of Ravana's residence, yielding to their services, makes a deep unease persist.

They wash my braid again and again, hoping to untangle its matted coils, until I have to insist it's good enough. They lift me out of the bath and massage scented oils into my skin and hair. I've not been pampered like this for fourteen years. The rituals of it are not familiar to me anymore. And to think all these things were part of my daily life in the past. I look at their faces. Do they mourn their king? Do they know that Vibhishana will be a better king?

As my body is decorated, all I can think of is Rama. My heart flutters, and I feel the flush in my skin. *He is your husband. You are his wife. Nothing has changed.*

Yet everything has. I've been broken. Has Rama changed too?

"You are ready," a servant girl declares.

They turn me to the full-length mirror so I can admire myself. I see a woman wrapped in heavy, blood-red silks. Her eyes are outlined with black kohl, her lips red like cherries. She wears rubies, pearls, and gold on every possible place on her body. Every movement sparkles. Her hair is bound up with jewels and flower buds into a crown on her head. What I see is a queen, majestic and opulent. I look at her as one might look at a mysterious painting. All I can think is how pleased Ravana would be if he saw me. How very pleased. I shake off the feeling that he is watching me.

Leave, malevolent spirit!

"Thank you," I tell the maids.

Hanuman greets me at the doorway, where I left him. When he sees me, he kneels to the ground, bowing deeply.

"Take me to Rama at once," I command, and I do sound like a queen.

Too many precious seconds have been wasted!

Hanuman brings forth a palanquin, lavishly decorated, not knowing how detestable that conveyance is to me. I would have preferred the familiar ground under my hardened feet. But seeing Hanuman's eagerness, I stifle my dismay. He has brought four of his people to carry me, and they too are on the ground, worshipping my feet.

"These are my trusted friends," Hanuman says. "Nala, Nila, Mainda, and Dvivida."

I lift my hand in benediction, just as a queen would. As I climb into the palanquin, I calm my beating heart. I don't trust myself anymore to know what's best. The knots in my stomach grow. I squeeze Rama's ring into my palm and beg them to hurry. As we exit the northern gate, the sounds of cheering monkeys crash against my ears. My hands shiver, and I search for Rama. I press the ring to my lips and imagine again the moment I will slip it back onto his beloved hand. My lips quiver with a smile that comes and goes. I am more nervous today than I was as a bride.

Across the vast body of boisterous monkeys, I see the outlines of two men standing on a hill, leaning on their bows, and my breath quickens. It has to be Rama and Lakshmana. My eyes never waver after that. Although I cannot see his eyes, I feel Rama's full attention fix on me. My soul rushes forth from my body to meet my beloved. Our souls collide with such force that we shoot up into the sky, becoming one. United at last, our spirits dance—a dance that few can see but everyone feels. Their collective cheer erupts louder than ever.

All is forgotten, the months of pain and longing. The reunion is more complete than I ever imagined. I feel like we're dancing in the stars, fingers intertwined. We're joined together in such a way that no one can ever tear us apart. We dance as we've always done, skipping on stars, hand in hand. We become as fathomless and deep as the universe itself, having neither beginning nor end: no time for time. Intense joy fills us both. His tears are like hot embers on my hands. We succumb to the laws of this world and are pulled apart. A deep, tearing pain staggers me. Back on the Earth, in my palanquin, my eyes spill over with tears of joy. With his nearness, Rama washes away Ravana's intrusion into my Shakti. I'm free! He's come to my rescue!

Sitting in the palanquin, I squirm and long to run into Rama's arms.

"Stop!" I call out.

I dismount from the palanquin and turn to my beloved. The moment my feet touch the Earth, however, a jolt hits me so forcefully that I stumble. I meant to run to him with all the speed I could muster. Instead, I resort to a slow lumber, one foot before the other. A regal way to move forward, no doubt, but not the passionate run that had urged me off the palanquin. Something is not right. Something is terribly wrong.

If I didn't know Ravana was dead, I would have suspected he was oppressing me. I hope my discomfort is caused by the attention I'm receiving. There are monkeys in all shapes and colors as far as my eye can see, their round eyes trained unblinkingly on me. I still can't see Rama's face, but there's something stiff in his stance. He does not take a single step toward me.

With every step, I feel more awkward. The anklets on my feet feel like chains. The ornaments that tinkle sound shrill and out of place. Hanuman was wrong, I know it now. It's all wrong. I shouldn't have dressed up. I should have come straight here and thrown myself into Rama's arms. That is what my heart had urged me to do. Why didn't I listen?

Every step forward wants to push me back. I feel Rama's emotions push me away forcefully. I'm not imagining that Rama is rejecting me. He turns his face from me. But if he does not love me, why did he shed the lives of millions to rescue me?

The pain is sharp, yet there's a sweet joy in just seeing Rama, his strong arms holding his bow. I long to touch him and be near him. But when he refuses to look at me, I cannot approach him. The masses have fallen silent, eager to see the reunion between Prince Rama and his princess. But Rama appears to be a statue carved of stone, not a man.

I hear the echo of a laughter rise up from within my own mind. Ravana's voice! Although dead, he's alive within me. His shadow rises up from the Earth. It crawls out from my heart and winds itself around my body. My eyes widen with anger and recognition. So this is what he did while I liberated the souls trapped in his body! This is the price I must pay. *Demon, begone!*

I flare up the fire at my core and blast his dead touch away, just as I've done so many times while he was alive. The shadow that cloaks me slithers away. His laughter dies down. But Rama has already seen it, felt it, recognized it. Before the spell was activated, Rama knew it was there. Like a dog marking his territory with urine, Ravana has marked me in his own way.

I stop, unable to take another step. Hanuman urges me forward. No matter what Ravana may have done to me, I've counted on Rama's benevolence. This seething silence is something I expected from Lakshmana, yet

when Rama keeps his face averted, it's Lakshmana who comes forward to greet me. My eyes fill with tears again.

"Lakshmana," I say, through tears. "Forgive me." I have to say the words.

He is overjoyed to see me. If he was my true brother, he would have picked me up and thrown me into the air! Instead, he touches my feet. All is forgiven between us. Whatever ails Rama is not shared by Lakshmana. He looks at his brother and frowns. I've seen that look before: He doesn't agree with his brother. Lakshmana puts his hand on Rama's arm, as if to awaken him from a stupor. Rama looks at me then, so briefly I might have imagined it. His glance touches me from the corner of his eye. This is a face of his I've never seen. He looks sick, strained, as if he might retch. Am I so revolting? I hold my stomach.

"Rama?" I ask softly, my whole being a question.

His lips turn down, as if some disgusting smell is in the air. Then he speaks.

"Bless you, my good woman," he starts. The words sound like a curse. "I have waged a war in your name, Princess. I have won you back from the enemy. In wiping away this affront, Sita, I have accomplished all that a man can do. But it was not for you that I undertook this war. I did this to wipe away the disgrace to my illustrious dynasty.

"Your virtue is now in doubt. Your presence has become profoundly disagreeable to me, like a bright lamp to a man afflicted with eye disease. What man of respectable family would take back a woman who has lived in the house of another man? How could I possibly accept you, who has just risen from Ravana's lap?"

Tears roll down my face unchecked. My heart lies shattered at his feet.

"Go, therefore, wherever you please, daughter of Janaka. You have my permission. Go."

The pearls and gold burn my skin, the red silk cloth heavy, like a cloak of shame. I want to tear off my borrowed regalia and shout, *Do you see me now?* If I'd followed my heart and my resolve—to return to him in the same way I left—would he look upon me differently?

"Rama," I plead. "Look at me."

I hold out my hand, palm open, offering his signet ring to him. What happened to the Rama that Hanuman described to me, the one whose only goal was to find Sita again?

The Rama before me is an utter stranger, a man with a face that is too perfect, cast in stone, chiseled out of marble. Despite the pallor on his face, there is no sign of true life. His eyes are vacant and unseeing. He looks like one of the statues in Ayodhya, immortalizing the glorified ancestors. And he speaks like one.

"With your heavenly beauty, Princess," he says, "Ravana would not have left you unmolested for long while you were dwelling in his house. I have made up my mind in saying this, my good woman: I have no further use for you. Turn your thoughts toward Lakshmana or any other man as you please."

"You cannot mean this!" Lakshmana cries.

"Give your heart to Sugriva, lord of the monkeys," Rama continues, "or to Vibhishana, the new king of Lanka."

In captivity, I was reduced to a helpless victim. But my heart was alive with love for Rama. Can't he feel how that love embraces us both?

A wave of restlessness sweeps through the crowds as they realize our reunion is not going as expected. My breath comes in small spurts, and I speak.

"Even in my darkest doubts, I did not anticipate this cruelty from you, Rama. I've combated our enemy with every power at my disposal. And yet my chastity has never been compromised, neither mentally nor physically. I've been so lucky. Most women in my situation cannot say the same. Don't you see how fortunate we are, Rama?"

He does not look at me as he says, "I do not love you anymore."

This strangely dries my tears. That's all he needed to say. I grow clear and steel sharp. I will not beg. I know that my conduct has been impeccable. I've faced death by my own hands and Ravana's several times. Only Rama's arrival turned the tide and gave me the desire to cling to life. Now that he's turned from me, there is only one path open. But first I must speak words I have not rehearsed.

"You, Rama, are turning our victory over into the hands of our enemy. The coward who stole me from you is winning after all. By rejecting me, you set a curse on womankind, that we will be blamed for the crimes men commit upon us. With the Earth as my witness, I stand faultless in the face of your accusations. With the fire as my witness, I reject your pronouncement!"

My royal garb reminds me that I don't belong only to myself or to Rama. I am the princess that all these brave souls have fought and died for. I will not disappoint them. I am the princess they crossed the ocean to save. The fire between my brows pulsates with angry Shakti. As Vedavati, I consumed my own body within minutes. I can do the same now, but I will do nothing impulsive. Too much has been snatched from me. I want to be sure that this is Rama's wish. I want to know if Lakshmana will agree with his brother's decree, he who always speaks so fervently about overthrowing the unrighteous! And so, with a voice that I can barely command, I say to Lakshmana, "Brother, build me a pyre so that I may enter a fire, my only recourse."

Lakshmana is swollen with anger at his brother. His face is flushed with disbelief as he studies Rama's face. The scar on his chest, where Ravana's javelin nearly killed him, throbs red, as if it will reopen and begin to bleed again. But he obeys. And for that, can I ever forgive him?

Hanuman is so distressed that he turns into a little monkey and chases his own tail in circles. He tugs at Lakshmana's foot. But Lakshmana has made his brother's will his own. How can he then resent Rama or anyone else for following orders blindly?

I throb with righteous anger, waiting, waiting for Rama to intervene. But he does not. Soon enough, the pyre is ready for me. Even then, I give Rama a last chance. Slowly, I circumambulate him. I touch his feet. His face is downcast. He refuses to even look at me.

I wait until the orange flames dance high and the fire is hot. It will burn and melt my broken heart. I have been within fire. Yet I've never even burned my own finger accidentally. My consciousness is eager, but my body is not. As I walk toward the fire, stoked so expertly by my brother-in-law, my entire body trembles. Drops of sweat, like my own blood, pour down my skin. I have intimately experienced what fire does to a human body. The screams of a thousand women burning alive plague me still. Maybe this is my punishment.

The sounds from the blazing fire and crackling wood are drowned out by the loud wails of millions of monkeys. I grit my teeth and take the next step. I will be brave. There is a huge ruckus of noise, monkeys protesting, Hanuman among them. Everyone cries for me to stop, but not the voice that matters. The heat from the flames begs me to turn away. Every instinct tells me to run. The fire sears the skin on my arms, my hair is like a wick, drawing the flames to me. I stifle my cry of pain and throw myself—my body, my consciousness, my soul, everything—into the fire. And I do not look back. I cannot stop the horrible cry, the way my voice squeezes through terrified lungs and my constricted throat. Like on the day I was abducted, I shout at the top of my lungs, "Rama!"

CHAPTER 29

Fire Born

As my body burns and turns to ash, I spread like wildfire among those present. There are millions of monkeys, thousands of blood-drinkers, the Vanaras, and the royalty of Lanka, including Vibhishana. I enter into each of them, feeling the fire of their desires, their aspirations, their horror at my burning. Their beings are kindled, their eyes fixed on the immolation at the center. Each soul carries an array of dark material: so much anger, vengeance, jealousy, hatred, and secret sexual desire. Truly, it is not for me take this from them. But all has been taken from me, and nothing can stop me. I sweep through their psyches, setting ablaze the unwanted, purging the darkness.

In Kaikasi, I burn her sorrow that her husband never loved her. I burn the long string of evidence she has collected over the years, her conviction that all relationships end in misery. The grief over her son's recent death—that too, I take from her. Be free!

In Vibhishana, I burn his self-hate, his belief that he is a shameful traitor. Guilt is plastered thick, covering all else. Because of him, so many blood-drinkers are dead, he believes. Anger at his dead brother and nephew still pulsates like an echo. I free him from all this.

In Lakshmana, I burn up his anger toward Kaikeyi and his father. His resentment toward Rama, that he didn't fight for the throne, and at me, for suspecting him, when in his mind he never gave me reason to. His guilt for building the pyre, I leave.

In Shurpanakha, I burn her horror over her own appearance. Her disgust at her mutilated form, her desire for vengeance for all the misery inflicted on her.

I flare up inside Trijata only briefly. With the grace of the enlightened, she swats me away. She will take care of her own demons.

Hanuman's heart is pure joy, all fierce winds and awaiting adventures. The only thing I burn is his despair at my state. He is the one who stands closest to the fire, as if at any moment, he means to jump into it himself and pull me out.

In Sugriva, I flush out his dark feelings toward his dead brother, Vali. I burn his attraction to Tara, his brother's wife, so that he may not inflict the burden of his attention on her, the way Vali did to Ruma. I burn his distrust of Angada, leaving only the love intact.

In Angada, I leave the pain of his father's untimely death. It matures him. But I burn away his fantasies about overthrowing Sugriva, taking Kishkinda by force, giving Sugriva an untimely death. The desire for vengeance would have suffocated all the brilliance of this young Vanara.

In Mandodari, I burn her covetous anxiety about her position—her obsession with being the primary queen and all the dark deeds she has done to remain there. I burn her remorse for the way she supported her husband's appetites. I burn her self-hatred at the way she compromised herself for the sake of power. But her love for her dead husband, I leave.

In the wives who sit and weep at Ravana's dead body, I burn their passion for him, their desire to be satiated by his hands, his affection. I burn their obsession with their appearance, their desire to be eternally beautiful.

I sweep through the millions of souls present, awakening them to their higher potentials, thanking them for all their right choices, imbuing their good deeds with glow and power. Like candles in the night, they light up one by one.

I do not touch Rama. Like Trijata, he will handle his own shadows.

And finally, I see the dead women of Lanka who burned in the fire. I see Dhanya-Malini, that brave woman, and Sharduli, my eternal animus. In their glowing soul forms, they stay behind me, the way old friends touch you only lightly to see if you need support while fully knowing just how strong and capable you really are. All the while, my body burns and burns, just as slowly and meticulously as the women of Lanka burned, one layer of flesh at a time.

And what do I burn in myself? Everything. Every last particle. Flesh, bones, heart, mind, psyche, everything. My love for Rama. My hate toward Ravana. My remorse for all I could not do. My feeling of being a victim. My fear of being different. My fear of never deserving Rama's love again. My anger at Lakshmana for not allowing me into his heart. All that is human about me, I tear out from my soul. I return to the elements. I return to my mother, the Earth. I'm ash. Fire-bright, I seep into the Earth.

And yet, even as I dissolve into her, my mother begins to form me. Just as she did when I was about to be born. Expertly, she creates my skeleton, my nerves, my body, filling it with all the right organs. With the flair of a fervent artist, she remakes me just as I was but adds

more beauty, more vitality. There will be no doubt now that I'm a goddess made flesh. My black hair crackles with curls and life, tinged bronze, the color of fire. My curves are shapely, the form of a woman living in luxury. My skin glows molten gold. My womb is remade, fertile, and vibrant with the promise of new life. The Cloth of Essence finds me again, and instead of the golden color that once reflected my essence, it wraps itself around me now, amber, bright as a flame.

The fire consuming my skeleton becomes the cover, shielding my mother's work. I stand within the fire being remade, just as I stood tolerating Lanka's maidservant decorating me. When she is done, she pulls the fire into the Earth—dramatically, quickly, the way one pulls apart the drapes at the climactic scene. The fire is nothing but ash at my feet. And I'm nothing but Sita, the unburned, the pure.

Before I open my eyes, I hear them, the millions I have purged of their own trappings. When I stand there, remade, unburned, glowing with ferocious Shakti, one by one they fall to their knees, heads to the ground. Like trees felled, they fall, offering their reverence. Nearest to me, Vibhishana and his family cry out in their mother tongue, naming me their goddess. No more will Nikumbhila be worshipped by them. The simians howl with abandon, chanting my glory in their own unique way. The love they feel for me is so intense, I'm engulfed in another type of fire. Wave after wave of their devotion assaults me so intensely that I'm warned of the zealot's zest. In their devotion, they may devour me and bury me just as quickly as they did in their distrust. But it's not yet time for such darkness to reassert itself. Lifting my hand in blessing, I beckon them to rise. As if one, they get up from the Earth, beholding me. Faces smeared by my mother's touch, they resemble me during my months of captivity.

I feel like the goddess I am. Fire can never slay me. The elements can never conquer me. Time is my invention. And yet, when I finally turn my eyes to Rama, my heart beats faster. Blood rushes to my face. I'm embodied, and I cannot deny what I feel. There will always be those who deny their humanity, but I cannot deny mine. I am weak with hope, with desire, that Rama will love me once more. A hundred women's voices echo as I cry out in Sita's.

In this body, I can only be Sita—no more, no less. Sita's every memory is within me again, crowding out all other awareness. For more than fifteen years, our marriage was my sanctuary. Rama cherished me and sheltered me. He loved me with passionate and unwavering loyalty. Despite being a prince of great importance, he never made me doubt my importance. Not until this day. I look at Rama, and he looks at me. The glow around Rama sparkles with a million rainbows. I press my hand against my chest. I feel the rhythmical pattern, every beat solidifying my presence within my physical body. My breath quickens. Ravana broke my spirit, but Rama broke my heart. *I do not love you*, he said. Every lover's ultimate weapon. Will he reject me once again?

The vast host of beings assembled hold their breaths as they watch us.

Rama falls to his knees. "Sita, forgive me! My mind turned dark, like the blackest night. I could not see anything but you in Ravana's arms. You were gazing at him the way you used to look at me. I could not bear it. I saw you as others would see you. As one of Ravana's women,

emerging from his palace, bedecked from head to toe. I could hear their words in my ear, calling me a fool, a slur on the Sun dynasty, a man hopelessly in love, naively trusting his wife. Like my father, I would be made a fool because of a woman. They would ask, 'How could Sita withstand the powers of the most notorious womanizer?' Women of all kinds, married and unmarried, human and celestial, succumbed to him. What if your heart had softened toward him? What if you too grieved his death? Once that doubt took root in my mind, I knew nothing else."

He looks up at me. "No one can doubt you now. No ordinary woman can do what you've just done. You embody every virtue, every strength. You have illuminated my heart with your blazing power. Open your heart to me once again. I will love you until the end of time. Let me love you as you deserve. Become mine again."

I long to touch him, to feel his hands on my skin. But is it enough? Is his apology enough? My intelligence says no. He will die with his guilt around his neck.

But my heart sings a different song. *Yes, yes, yes! It's enough!*

My heart sees only the love in his eyes, his face, his uplifted palms. His despair, his agony, his incompleteness. And with each step I take toward him, I pave a path for every woman after me to forgive the unforgivable, to set aside a man's cruelty, the price we become willing to pay for just a drop of their love. I am willing. Women may follow me into fires they can never survive. But just as surely as a river flows to the ocean, I flow toward Rama. Just as a moth cannot resist a flame, I cannot resist Rama. Just as the earth must go around the sun, so too I must go to Rama. All the pieces of this tale were ordained, and so too my part. No power in this world or the next can keep me from him. Our union is inevitable, no matter how far apart we appear to be.

Rama surges to his feet, closing the distance between us, crushing me to his heart, and as I taste the salt of his tears, my heart heals. Rama's love has that power. It's all I need. My feet lift off the ground as Rama embraces me. After a long time, he sets me back down.

When my toes touch the Earth, I feel the many paths we yet must walk.

May we never be separated again.

May we always be together.

Sita and Rama.

Forever.

The Homecoming

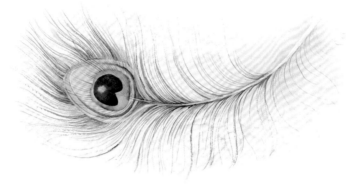

We make quite a sight, descending from the aerial Pushpaka. Our entire retinue is testimony to our strange adventures. Hanuman, a golden Vanara, so spectacular. A collection of freed prisoners and former consorts. But perhaps they are most shocked by Anala, Vibhishana's daughter, striking with her bronze hair, fangs, and midnight skin. Has a blood-drinker ever been allowed within Ayodhya before? Only as a prisoner. The threat to Ayodhya has been averted, and now we are allies. Mostly, they are shocked by me—by my changed appearance, my deific presence.

Is that Sita? They whisper. *She looks so different. Like touched by magic.*

I had lived in Ayodhya for barely a year before we were exiled, so to me, it does not feel like a homecoming. Too much has happened. I have changed. Even my hold on Rama is tenuous. I left as a girl of sixteen and return as a goddess made flesh, although they may not have those words for it. I can see how overwhelming my presence is to them all. And yet Rama, of course, is the long-lost son, the one they truly have waited for. He too is no longer the seventeen-year-old boy they sent into exile. To think how capable and mature we felt ourselves to be at that age. Now I recognize that we were but children. Rama's manhood has etched lines into his face. His nobility is sharper, more cutting, less tolerant, which gives him added gravitas and power. This too intimidates our family. Rama is not as approachable as he once was. And why should he be? He was expunged from the place he loved the best by the people he loved the most. He had everything taken from him, and Ravana was not an enemy any of us had ever thought we would face. Rama has pulled up power from depths he didn't know he had. And who knows when his nightmare will stop? I know that I am in it because he will not share the details of it with me. But I've understood it's the same dream, over and over again. Ravana and me, I suspect. Chills run down my spine when I think of it. That monster might be dead, but the spell he cast outlives him.

Bharata greets us on the thoroughfare, surrounded by an entourage of people, including Vasishta, the all-seeing priest of the Sun dynasty. Shatrugna stands behind Bharata as his shadow. But Bharata's matted hair has grown for fourteen years, while Shatrugna has groomed himself according to Ayodhya's standards, hair curling at his shoulders. The four brothers behold each other for seconds before they form a circle, embracing, heads huddled together. They stand like that so long, it's as if Rama is telling every details of our travails to them. And yet I don't overhear a single word as I'm welcomed by the women of the city.

Rama's mother is the first to greet me. Her scrutiny tells me I do not look like a woman who has struggled in exile and then captivity. I cannot withhold the power that swirls at my fingertips. I cannot change the Cloth of Essence that insists on declaring my affinity to fire, the most powerful element. How much of what has occurred does she know? How much will I need to reveal?

Queen Kausalya's hair is steel-gray, as unruly as I remember it, though every effort has been made to tie it back behind her crown. She is thin and pale, her lined face clearly declaring her seventy-seven years of life. Her mouth is set in a line that has allowed few smiles in the past fourteen years. I'm not the only one who has suffered. Only the time in Lanka makes me appreciate the depth of her sorrow. I hold her to me tenderly, offering her my empathy. She leans into me for but a moment before she continues to her son. Her brusque efficiency tells me that she has, for all purposes, been the ruler of Ayodhya with Rama gone and Bharata ruling from the outskirts of the city. This much we've learned from sending Hanuman ahead to ascertain that our return is welcome.

Sumitra, Lakshmana's mother, touches me once, almost in apology, her eyes on Kausalya. But she withdraws her hand quickly, as if burned. I never knew her well and don't detain her from reunion with her son.

Kaikeyi strides up to me. Two years past fifty, she is luminous. As she smiles, the creases crinkle around her eyes, but otherwise her face is unlined. Her hair is cropped close to her scalp. She is dressed simply, in leathers and pants. It's clear that she no longer takes stock of her own attractiveness as a woman. She has withdrawn from all palace obligations and spends her days on the plains, tending to Ayodhya's horses. The equestrian collection now rivals that of Kekaya, she tells me proudly. She visits the palace only once weekly to visit Manthara, the old hunchback, who is now eighty-four, quite a miracle for one who is deaf, blind, and infirm. Kaikeyi looks content, but her affection lacks engagement. She truly has cut herself off from matters of this world. As soon as she can, she excuses herself and returns to the fields beyond the walls. I look longingly after her receding figure. The walls around Ayodhya do not give me a sense of protection—quite the opposite. I do not look forward to the moment when we must step into the palace.

Before anyone else can demand my attention, I seek my sister. My beloved Urmila, whom

I did not even get to bid farewell. My vivacious sister, robbed of the life she envisioned, the love of her husband. I see her standing at the helm of a group of noblewomen. As I walk toward them, they whisper among themselves. She is reserved toward me and even more so toward Lakshmana. I understand that it will take time for her to trust us, to feel assured that we will not leave her suddenly again. The life of a woman without a husband in Ayodhya has squashed some of the light from her eyes. One year younger than me, at thirty, my sister looks like a matron. She has grown plump, having taken comfort in food. I sense that her mind is full of gossip. Like Kaikasi, the indomitable queen mother of the blood-drinkers, Urmila has resorted to living through others. I hope to rectify that. She is not cruel or vicious by nature. With me here, and Lakshmana, I hope that she once again will use her social affability to spread goodness.

Rama's father is conspicuous in his absence. Ayodhya is in so many ways synonymous with him and his warmhearted rule. He would have been one year past eighty. Many of his peers are still alive and hale, including Kaikeyi's father, Ashvapati, who only recently anointed his son Yuddhajit as heir apparent of Kekaya. It pains Rama to see Ayodhya without his father. Perhaps only Lakshmana and I can see it flash past his eyes as he greets our noble family.

Both Rama and Lakshmana have shorn their long, matted hair, and all arrangements for Rama's immediate coronation are made. I'm to be the queen of Ayodhya, and yet I cannot step inside the palace without my lungs constricting, without my emotions spiking. The fire could not cleanse me of those deepest impressions. Four walls means prison and Ravana. Uneasily, I walk into the palace, gripping Rama's hand. I hope that the people do not notice the droplets of sweat on my forehead, the rapid breaths I take to calm myself.

In front of everyone, Rama places me on his lap. We remain like that as the proceedings continue. There is a desperate love in Rama's hold on me. We need this physical contact to heal, to stay sane. Ayodhya is swept away with joy and merriment. Everyone is so happy. So happy. Only I seem aware of how short-lived happiness can be. I refuse to take anything from the people of Ayodhya, so I become even more separate from them.

When Rama and I unite as husband and wife, our ecstasy calls our children to us. I'm filled with Rama's love and our future. I can hear the laughter of my unborn children—I, who thought I would have none. I don't know what the future will bring. I am the prayers of my supplicants, and I've come in the form of a woman. I know that I will meet every adversity with power, strength, and fierce fortitude. This is my blessing on all womankind, a fire I've kindled in their hearts:

May you persevere.

May you know your own glory.

May you feel my presence within your heart.

Know that I see all of you. I know your heart, your darkest dreams.

May you be blessed. Close your eyes and you'll know.

I will never ever leave you.

I'm here.

Acknowledgments

I first wish to acknowledge my mom and collaborator, Anna Johansson, the illustrator. I really would not have mustered the determination or courage to complete this project without her steady presence; the artwork she has created is the force that coaxed it all into completion. Next, I offer my gratitude to my husband, Visvambhar Sheth, for being so unconditionally supportive of anything I set my mind on doing; my mother-in-law, Elaine Ananga Sheth, for being such an exemplary woman of strength and cheerfulness; Ganga and Jamuna, for being loving aunties to my kids; my weekly women's circle, for sharing my joys and woes, a process that radically transformed my self-understanding; Narada Bradman and Mira Rose-Dewil, for reading the final draft and giving me valuable feedback; and Mirabai Lee Harrington, my editor, whose astute engagement with this work pushed me to grow so much as an author.

Books that have influenced me in this creative endeavor include the following:

The Ramayana of Valmiki, translated by Robert P. Goldman, Sally J. Sutherland Goldman, and team—I: Balakanda, II: Ayodhyakanda, III: Aranyakanda, IV: Kishkindakanda, V: Sundarakanda, VI: Yuddhakanda, VII: Uttarakanda
The Artist's Way: A Spiritual Path to Higher Creativity, by Julia Cameron
Women Who Run with the Wolves: Myths and Stories of the Wild Woman Archetype, by Dr. Clarissa Pinkola Estes
Sita: An Illustrated Retelling of the Ramayana, by Devdutt Pattanaik

Many Ramayanas: The Diversity of a Narrative Tradition in South Asia, edited by
Paula Richman

In Search of Sita: Revisiting Mythology, edited by Malashri Lal and Namita Gokhale

Ramayana: India's Immortal Tale of Adventure, Love, and Wisdom, by Krishna Dharma

Valmiki's Uttara Kanda: The Book of Answers, by Arshia Sattar

Hanuman's Tale: The Messages of a Divine Monkey, by Philip Lutgendorf

The Ramayana dance dramas by Rukmini Devi Arundale, performed by the
Kalakshetra ensemble

Finally, thanks to everyone at Mandala Earth: Raoul Goff, for his friendship and encouragement; Mark Nichol and Lauren LePera for fine-tuning the final manuscript and design; and Courtney Andersson, Tessa Murphy, Phillip Jones, Mariah Bear, and the entire team that has overseen the project to produce such a high-quality series. To Raghu Consbruck at Eight Eyes for her elegant design, attention to detail, and dependability. All three books follow the template she designed, and we are so pleased.

If I've missed anyone, I'd like to thank my kids for crowding out important memories with their larger-than-life presence and demands ☺ : Naimi, Luvi, and Khol, for encouraging me to reach my highest potential by their delightful presence.

Author's Note

All fairy tales, myths, and tales that have been passed down over time contain the bones of forgotten stories. This is especially true when it comes to the legends of our female ancestors. Clarissa Pinkola Estes introduced me to this idea in her seminal work, *Women Who Run with Wolves*. When she spoke of "the bones of a story," I knew exactly what she meant. And so, for me, reconstructing Sita's story has been very much like looking at the bones, the fragments, of what has been passed down to us about her and imagining not only the body around the bones but also its actions, its sentiments, its rich, complex, contradictory, challenging life. We all have one—all of us human beings, women and men. Why should the women of the past be denied theirs?

An important impetus was seeing how Sita was transmitted to my own daughter. When she was a girl of four, she loved acting out stories. When she acted as Sita, she would inevitably sit down and sob into her hands. And that was it. There was no more. That is sadly what Sita has been reduced to over the years: the quintessential and archetypal damsel in distress. A question remains: Did I go too far, creating a manifesto of my own? Or did I not push the boundaries far enough? All readers will have their own opinion regarding this. I can only pray that I have been able to walk that fine balance of reimagining the text without hijacking it completely. I don't know if my effort will feel authentic to every reader. But I have put my energy into giving Sita more than monochromatic sorrow.

On that note, a word on the title. Naming the books and the trilogy as a whole was a challenge. I've always struggled with brevity in writing. How to condense my massive manuscripts into a short title? It was something I mulled over for a long time. Then I was in a kirtan with well-known singer Krishna Das at the Omega Institute in upstate New York. He was singing a hymn to Hanuman, and one phrase stood out to me: "*Janaki shoka nashanam*," which means "destroyer of Janaki's sorrow" (Janaki being another name for Sita). And that was it: I knew that Book 3 was going to be entitled *Destroyer of Sorrow*.

People often ask why I wanted to retell this particular legend. I've answered that it was because of my mom, the artist and backbone of the project. I say that I didn't really choose this, that I didn't have a vision of my own, and that is partially true. But what I've learned over the years is that I was not willing to see what was in front of my eyes. Very early on in this work, I had a vision of a girl walking into a sunny meadow, her anklets tinkling. She was picking flowers when Ravana appeared, and ravished her sexually while drinking her blood. It was a chilling scene. I think I frightened both myself and my mother.

So I ended up writing instead about Kausalya, Rama's mother: a scene where she's watching her sleeping son, loving him while fearing for his future. A safe scene, a scene without controversy. Who doesn't love their child? Who could argue with this fictional scene? Not only is it plausible, but it also brings up very little charged emotion. A rape scene, however, is uncomfortable from almost every angle. I was not comfortable with it, so I put it aside and forgot about it. (A version of the assault scene found its way into the prologue of Book 1. But, again, it's a mother, and her fate is left very vague. It wasn't until I tackled Book 3 and really stepped into my acceptance of my creativity that I dared to include it.) Thus, it resurfaced many years later in this final book. And, what's more, it has undeniable textual authority: There is just such a scene in the Uttarakanda, the final book of the Ramayana.

I began this in the traditional way, telling a known story in my own words. Over the years, however, I found myself most fascinated with the gaps in the story, particularly in regard to Sita and the other female characters. My main focus became filling in the missing gaps of the story, the unknown parts. Many times, I felt that whatever attempt I made would be dwarfed by the excellence of the original. I certainly cannot hope to capture this complex story better than Valmiki did. But again, Sita's story and the women's perspectives are sorely missing.

In this book specifically, the challenge was to create new material for Sita that was congruent with what we know about her, which is quite little. To illustrate my challenge, let me outline the instances in Sundarakanda and Yuddhakanda (the two sections reenvisioned here) where Sita appears. There are three major scenes: (1) Sita arrives in Lanka, (2) Hanuman and Sita meet, and (3) she is reunited with Rama after the war. There is also a minor scene when she is taken over the battle to see Rama and Lakshmana bound by Indrajit's arrows. The material, from the original, is enough for perhaps three chapters, functioning very much as the beginning, middle, and end. Yet what happens to Sita in her eleven months and fourteen days of captivity?

Destroyer of Sorrow is my effort to answer that.

After years of contemplation, many pieces still elude my understanding. For example, in a setting that ordinarily features male ascetics and their powers, two rare female ascetics are mentioned: Shabari and Svayamprabha. Both women seem significant and important. Their appearance in the text, however brief, serves a purpose that I cannot see. Sally J. Sutherland Goldman shares some great insights regarding this in her excellent essay, "Women at the Margins: Gender and Religious Anxieties in Valmiki's Ramayana." Still, I was not able to substantially develop their presence in the text and have therefore not included them, which feels like a disappointment.

As I complete this trilogy, I must share a little bit about my process and my relationship to the Ramayana itself. As in my previous books, I warmly recommend reading a close translation of Valmiki's Ramayana, which is truly inspiring. I cannot emphasize enough how delightful it was to read Valmiki's Ramayana and rediscover Rama, Sita, Lakshmana, and Hanuman for myself. My understanding of the text and my writing process has been deeply informed and enriched by the work of the Princeton team led by Robert P. Goldman, whose translations I studied. Their delightful introductions to each of the seven volumes contain a scholarly overview as well as an in-depth analysis. I owe a debt of gratitude to their impeccable work, which revived and solidified my love for this truly *epic* epic! I conclude with some verses that directed my creativity:

Valmiki's purpose: A man who always fulfilled his vows, he [Valmiki] taught them the whole of this great poem, the Ramayana, which is the tale of Sita and the slaying of Paulastya [Ravana]. 1.4.5

Sita's power: Employed by the gods, this destroyer of the *rakshasas*, Sita, will devour us along with Ravana, just as, long ago, famine was used to devour the *danavas*. 6.82.36

Ravana shivered with delight as he carried her off, though it was his own death he was embracing, a sharp-fanged, poisonous viper. 4.52.6.

For you should realize that she whom you know as Sita and keep under your control is really Kalaratri—the dark night of universal destruction—who will bring ruin to all of Lanka. 5.49.33

Otherwise, you shall witness your city, along with its stress and its palaces, crushed by the wrath of Rama and consumed by the blazing power of Sita. 5.49.35

Ravana's energetic body: The violent force of the expansion of his body threw the ten directions into confusion, for he looked like an incarnation of the wrath that fills the body of Rudra. 6.62.36

Vibhishana says about Sita, "But no one can so much as get a glimpse of her, whether through conciliation, sowing dissension, bribery, or any other means, much less through violence." 6.71.12

Ravana's other wives: "On the other hand, that innocent, black-eyed lady may have been devoured by the malicious wives of the lord of the *rakshasas*." 5.11.12

Rama's faith in Sita: When will she outwit the *rakshasas*, evade them, and escape, like the crescent of the hare-marked autumn moon emerging from the midst of dark storm clouds? 6.5.16

After burning Lanka, Hanuman says, "On the other hand, that auspicious lady, lovely in every limb and protected by her own blazing energy, cannot have died; for fire cannot prevail against fire." 5.33.18

And in Sundarakanda, of course, it's Sita who protects Hanuman's tail from burning.

Warmly,
Vrinda

April 23, 2019

Artist's Note

I just dropped off the digital art files for the last book in the Sita's Fire trilogy to Raghu, our graphic designer. I breathe a sigh of relief as I realize that finally, this project has come to completion. It has been my constant companion for decades. When I was in my early forties, I thought I would have enough time to finish by the time I was fifty. Well, that didn't happen. I am now in my sixties and have three grandchildren, but my daughter, Vrinda, and I did at last reach the goal line.

My motivation for this project has been to illustrate this Indian tale mainly for the benefit of a Western audience that has little knowledge of this great epic tale. I have also felt great inspiration from my daughter's creative writing, which presents this story in a new light, describing the different characters, especially the women, in a unique perspective and with exceptional depth.

My favorite section is the Sundarakanda. This is where the intelligent and heroic Hanuman finds Sita in the Asokha garden. Vrinda describes Sita's persona in a riveting way that is both inspiring and encouraging to all women who seek a timeless model of feminine power and endurance. I also got a lot of inspiration from the exquisite translation of the Ramayana by Robert P. Goldman and his team of Sanskrit scholars. I thought I knew this story well, but that translation transported my mind to new and previously unimaginable blissful places.

I am a traditional artist whose stylistic inspiration comes from mentors that were active during a period called the Golden Age of Illustration, generally considered to be the period between 1880s and 1920s, during which artists like Arthur Rackham, Warwick Goble, and Edmund Dulac flourished. Many of the greatest American illustrators of this period followed the teachings of Howard Pyle, and collectively became known as the Brandywine School. I am still surprised that this dynamic period in the art world was not even mentioned in my college Art History 101 course. But to ignore this dynamic body of illustrative work and the amazing group of artists who created it would be to miss out on a vital contribution to art and culture.

Over the years as a watercolor painter and illustrator, I have struggled through obstacles both material and spiritual. Fine art is a craft, and the skills to master drawing and water-color come only after years of unfruitful trials and tedious, exacting practice. When I under-took this project, every piece of blank watercolor paper in front of me presented a challenge and a great opportunity.

My intention with each piece was to create a masterpiece, to do my absolute best work without compromise. This desire for perfection is hard on many artists, including me. It is ironic that it is not until I let go of this ambitious desire for perfection that the work can actually begin to materialize and flow. Did I always achieve this level of flow? By no means. But I believe that through God's grace, I was able to capture some of the beauty and truth of the Ramayana.

So, what comes next for me, now that the Sita's Fire trilogy is complete? I honestly feel I could continue to make art-work from the Ramayana for eternity. To be immersed in trying to artistically capture the transcendental mood and character of this classical Indian epic has been an intrigu-ing pathway to some incredible spiritual healing and a lim-itless source of bliss. This journey doesn't seem to be over for me. Rather, it is a new beginning.

My heart is full of gratitude for all people who have been with me on this journey. I am especially grateful for Elaine Ananga Sheth, my friend and indefatigable cheerleader; Kosarupa Ely, who shares my passion for book illustration and always encouraged my artistic endeavors; and Vrinda, my beautiful daughter, who joined me and did a stellar job with the writing of the Sita's Fire trilogy. I will not forget to mention my greatest supporter, Len, my best friend, life companion, husband, and adviser. I doubt I could have accomplished what I did without him. My wish is that many people will find encouragement and inspiration from Vrinda's and my work.

Characters and Terms

Agastya – one of most well-known and powerful holy ones; who gifts Rama a celestial bow and golden arrow

Agni – lord of fire

Ahalya – "Flawless," the stone-woman, Gautama's wife, a mind-born daughter of Brahma

Aja – Dasharatha's father; king of Ayodhya before him

Akampana – "Unshakeable," blood-drinker, one of Ravana's ministers

Aksha – prince of Lanka, a blood-drinker, slain by Hanuman after he finds Sita

Anala – Vibhishana's daughter

Ananta-Sesha – thousand-headed serpent on whom Vishnu rests, guardian of the Eastern quarter

Anaranya – king of the Sun dynasty more than twenty-five generations before Rama; killed by Ravana in a legendary battle

Anasuya – a rare female ascetic, who gifts Sita the Cloth of Essence

Angada – Vanara, son of Vali and Tara, heir to Kishkinda

Apsara – Celestial nymphs, known for their beauty, and their singing and dancing

Asamanja – the only son of the Sun dynasty who disgraced his line; known for drowning his playmates in the river Sarayu

Ashram – a secluded dwelling or hermitage in the forest

Ashvapati – "Lord of Horses," king of Kekaya, father of Kaikeyi and Yuddhajit

Atibala – one of the sentient mantra-weapons Rama receives from Vishva-mitra, healer of wounds, sister to Bala

Atri – a sage and a mind-born child of Brahma, husband of Anasuya

Ayodhya – the indestructible capital city of Earth; Rama's birthplace and rightful kingdom

Bala – one of the sentient mantra-weapons Rama receives from Vishvamitra, reliever of fatigue, sister to Atibala

Bhagiratha – Rama's ancestor who brought down the sacred Ganga from the heavens

Bharadvaja – an all-seeing sage

Bharata – Rama's half-brother, second in line to the throne; Kaikeyi's son

Bhumi – the goddess of Earth, considered to be Sita's real mother

Bilva – a tree whose leaves are used in worship and for decoration

Brahma – father of the universe, the creator of all, and granter of boons

Chakra – Vishnu's legendary discus, one of the weapons Rama receives from Vishvamitra; also, an energy center in the body

Chakora – rare moon-gazing bird

Chaya – "Shadow," the exiled queen, mother of Yuddhajit and Kaikeyi

Chikoo – a small, round fruit

Chitrakuta – the mountain peak where the royal trio created their first home

Dashagriva – "Ten-Necks," one of Ravana's original names

Dasharatha – "Ten-Chariots," emperor of the Earth, Rama's father

Daivi – "Destiny," the goddess worshipped by the Vanaras

Dandaka – the terrible borderland, a jungle within a jungle, haunted by beasts, blood-drinkers, and spirits

Dashamukha – "Ten-Heads," the name given to Ravana at his birth

Devahuti – mother of Anasuya

Dhanya-Malini – the Brave One, a blood-drinker, Ravana's favorite consort, one of Sita's foremost friends in Lanka

Dhumraksha – "Smoke-Eyes," a blood-drinker, one of Ravana's ministers

Dundubhi – a bull monster killed by Vali, the son of Mayavin

Dushana – a blood-drinker and a general posted in Dandaka

Dvivida – a supernatural ape, part of Rama's army

Gandharva – godly masculine beings known for the light, beauty, and power

Ganga – the holy river, as well as the goddess of the river herself

Gautama – one of the seven sages, author of the most ancient Vedic hymns

Garuda – a gigantic magical eagle, known as Vishnu's carrier

Gaja – Vanara, in Angada's search party

Gajapushpi – a red-flowering creeper that Rama garlands Sugriva with to distinguish him from Vali

Gandhamadana – Vanara, in Angada's search party

Gavaksha – Vanara, in Angada's search party

Gavaya – Vanara, in Angada's search party

Guha – king of the Nishadas, Rama's friend; king of the Nishada forest tribe

Hanuman – Vanara, son of the wind

Indra – lord of Heaven, king of the gods

Indrajit – a blood-drinker, the son of Ravana and Mandodari, an unparalleled magician, known for his victory over the king of the gods

Indumati – Dasharatha's mother, queen of Ayodhya

Jambavan – Vanara, son of Brahma, the oldest Vanara in Angada's search party for Sita

Janaka – king of Mithila; Sita's adoptive father, who found Sita in a furrow

Jatayu – the king of the vultures, a loyal friend to King Dasharatha and later Rama and Sita, who gives up his life in his attempt to protect Sita

Kaikasi – a blood-drinker, the queen mother, mother of Ravana, Vibhishana, Shurpanakha, and Kumbhakarna

Kaikeyi – third and favorite wife of King Dasharatha; queen 3; mother of Bharata

Kalaratri – the Goddess of the Dark Night, a form of universal destruction

Kama Deva – Cupid, god of love

Kama-Rupini – one who is able to take any form at wish; a shape-changer

Kardama Muni – father of Anasuya

Karnikara – an evergreen tree with thick ascending branches and bright yellow blossoms

Kashi – king of Kashi, one of the most persistently aggressive kings under Dasharatha's rule, slain by Rama in his first battle as prince in command

Kausalya – first wife of King Dasharatha, the Great Queen, mother of Rama

Kekaya – Kaikeyi's birth kingdom

Khara – a powerful blood-drinker; one of Ravana's relatives and a most trusted general

Kinnaras – celestial creatures, half-human, half-animal, known for their mischievous pranks

Kishkinda – the mighty stronghold of the Vanara clan, nestled within the mountains

Kubera – demigod known as the god of wealth, as he's the treasurer of the gods; half-brother to Ravana and his siblings

Kumbhakarna – a blood-drinker, Ravana's giant brother, who sleeps all year except for one day due to a boon

Kusha – an auspicious grass used to decorate altars and for fire sacrifices

Koshala – the land surrounding Ayodhya

Lakshmana – Rama's closest friend and half-brother; Shatrugna's twin brother; son of King Dasharatha and Queen Sumitra, husband of Urmila

Lakshmi – the goddess of wealth and prosperity, Vishnu's eternal consort

Lanka – the golden island appropriated by Ravana from his older brother Kubera

Mahaparshva – "Mighty-on-All-Sides," a blood-drinker, one of Ravana's ministers

Mahodara – "Mighty-Abdomen," a blood-drinker, one of Ravana's ministers

Mainda – a supernatural ape, part of Rama's army

Makaraksha – "Crocodile-Eyes," a blood-drinker, the son of Khara

Malyavan – a blood-drinker, Ravana's great-uncle, who counsels him to return Sita to Rama

Mandodari – "Soft-Bellied," a blood-drinker, queen of Lanka, Ravana's foremost consort, mother to Indrajit

Manu – the first man; established Ayodhya and created the laws for mankind

Manthara – "the Hunchback," Kaikeyi's hunchbacked confidante

Mandavi – wife of Bharata, Sita's cousin, Kushadvaja's daughter

Marichi – Ayodhya's blood-drinker prisoner; son of Tataka, who takes the form of the golden deer to allure Sita

Matali – Indra's charioteer

Matanga – the sage whose curse bars Vali from Rishyamukha

Maya – Ravana's illusory magic powers

Mayavin – a bull-monster killed by Vali

Menaka – Apsara, one of the famous four celestial dancers

Mithila – the capital city of Janaka's kingdom, and Sita's birthplace

Mridanga – a two-headed drum, a rhythmical instrument

Nagas – supernatural creatures from the underworld with half snake bodies

Naga Pashas – snake arrows, one of Indrajit's magic missiles

Nala – Vanara, bridge-maker, son of Vishvakarma, the divine architect

Nala-Kubera – the son of Kubera, and Rambha's lover, who curses Ravana

Nikumbhila – the dark goddess worshipped by the blood-drinkers

Nila – Vanara, son of Agni, the god of fire

Nishadas – a forest tribe loyal to Ayodhya, ruled by Guha

Patala – an underworld of torture and hellfire

Panchabhuta – "Five Elements," a magical golden arrow wielded by Rama

Panchavati – "Five Groves," the final dwelling in the forest of their royal exile

Parashuram – the notorious warrior hater, avatar of Vishnu

Pisachas – demonic beings with the heads of various animals

Prahasta – "Hands-That-Take," a blood-drinker, one of Ravana's ministers

Pushpaka – a sentient, celestial airplane under Ravana's command

Rama – firstborn son of King Dasharatha; son of Queen Kausalya; next in line to the throne and wed to Sita

Rambha – Apsara, one of the famous four celestial dancers, violated by Ravana and inciting the curse upon his heads

Rasatala – the hellish planet below Earth where the blood-drinkers were cursed to live

Ravana – "Loud-Wailing" or "The One Who Makes the Universe Wail"; king of the blood-drinkers, Sita and Rama's foremost nemesis

Rishyamukha – an area in the forest adjacent to Kishkinda, the only place on Earth where Vali cannot go

Rishyashringa – son of Vibhandaka, mysteriously conceived by a deer

Romapada – king of Anga, close friend of King Dasharatha

Ruma – Sugriva's wife

Sagara – Rama's ancestor, father of Asamanja

Sala – a type of tree known for its strong wood

Sampathi – a supernatural vulture, brother to Jatayu

Sanjivani – a life-giving plant, which saves the lives of many of Rama's troops

Sarama – Vibhishana's wife

Sarayu – the river running alongside Ayodhya

Shakti – Sita's intrinsic powers

Shalakatankata – the ancestral mother of the blood-drinker race

Sharabhanga – a holy one, a disciple of Agastya

Sharduli – a magical mongoose that Sita keeps as her pet during captivity

Shatabali – Vanara who leads a search party north looking for Sita

Shatrugna – Lakshmana's twin brother; Bharata's constant companion; son of King Dasharatha and Queen Sumitra

Shigraga – one of Sita's distant uncles

Shiva – lord of dissolution, who dances vigorously as the world comes to its end

Shurpanakha – "Sharp-Nails," a blood-drinker, Ravana's sister; a skilled kama-rupini, the catalyst for the abduction of Sita, in revenge of her rejection and mutilation by Rama and Lakshmana

Sushena – Vanara leader who takes his search party for Sita west; also, a gifted healer with vast knowledge of medicinal herbs

Subahu – a blood-drinker, the impersonator who sets Marichi free; son of Tataka, brother of Marichi

Sutikshna – a sage in whose ashram Sita encounters Ravana's spirit

Shrutakirti – Shatrugna's wife, Sita's cousin, Kushadvaja's daughter

Sita – "Furrow," born from the Earth, adopted by King Janaka, wife of Rama

Sugriva – king of the Vanaras, son of Indra, brother of Vali

Sunayana – King Janaka's wife, mother of Urmila and Sita's adoptive mother

Sumantra – one of King Dasharatha's eight ministers and a loyal friend

Sumitra – princess of Maghada, second wife of Dasharatha; mother of the twins, Lakshmana and Shatrugna

Surya – lord of the sun, father of Sugriva

Suvela – one of Lanka's three mountain peaks, the place where Rama sets up camp before the war

Tara – wife of Vali and mother to Angada, sits on the king's council because of her wisdom

Tataka – the first blood-drinker Rama kills; a female monster

Tillottama – Apsara, one of the famous four celestial dancers

Trijata – a blood-drinker who guards Sita, a prophetess who can see the future in dreams

Trishira – an arrogant three-headed demon, slain in the massacre at Panchavati

Tulsi – the holy basil plant, an essential component in the temple's rituals

Urmila – Sita's sister, daughter of Janaka and Sunayana; wife of Lakshmana

Urvasi – Apsara, one of the famous four celestial dancers

Vajradamshtra – "Lightning-Fangs," a blood-drinker, one of Ravana's ministers

Vali – one of the mightiest Vanaras to ever live; son of Indra, father of Angada, husband to Tara

Vanara – a supernatural race of creatures, half-monkey and sired by the gods

Varuna – the ocean god

Vasishta – the royal priest; preceptor of the Sun dynasty through countless generations, and one of the nine mind-born children of Brahma

Vayu – lord of the wind, father to Hanuman

Vedas – the sacred ancient text, divided into four divisions: Rig, Sama, Yajur, and Atharva

Vedavati – incarnation of the goddess Lakshmi, who cursed Ravana when he accosted her

Vina – a plucked string instrument mastered by Ravana

Vibhandaka – ascetic, grandson of Brahma, father of Rishyashringa

Vidyadhara – beautiful supernatural creatures with wings and magical powers

Vidyujjihva – a blood-drinker, Shurpanakha's deceased husband, accidentally killed by Ravana in battle

Vinata – Vanara leader who takes his search party for Sita east

Viradha – the first blood-drinker the trio encounters in the forest

Virupaksha – "Squint-Eyes," a blood-drinker, one or Ravana's ministers

Vishravas Paulastya – grandson to Brahma the creator, a great sage, father of Ravana and his siblings

Vibhishana – a blood-drinker, brother of Ravana, minister on Lanka, who deserts his brother to join Rama

Videha – the province of King Janaka

Vishnu – the maintainer of the universe, present in every molecule of creation

Vishvakarma – the divine architect who built Lanka and crafted many of the most famous deadly missiles; father of Nala

Vishvamitra – Rama's mentor, exalted from warrior to sage

Yama – lord of death

Yuddhajit – prince of Kekaya, brother to Kaikeyi

Rama's Family Tree

The Sun Dynasty – House of Ikshvaku

1. Brahma
2. Marichi & *Kala*
3. Kashyapa & *Aditi*
4. Vivasvan & *Saranyu*
5. Manu & *Sraddha*
6. Ikshvaku & *Brahmani**
7. Kukshi & *Akuti**
8. Vikukshi & *Padmavati**
9. Bana & *Priyamvada**
10. Anaranya & *Hemabindu**
11. Prithu & *Prithvi*
12. Trishanku & *Kaushiki**
13. Dhundhumara & *Shaivya*
14. Yuvanashva & *Poulami*
15. Mandhatri & *Bindumati Chaitrarathi*
16. Susandhi & *Devayani**
17. Dhruvasandhi & *Sundari**
18. Bharata & *Aprameya**
19. Asita & *Kalindi*
20. Sagara & *Kesini*
21. Asamanja & *Ambujakshi*
22. Anshuman & *Hri Devi**
23. Dilipa & *Sudakshina*
24. Bhagiratha & *Jahnavi**
25. Kakutstha & *Gomati**
26. Raghu & *Dakshina**
27. Kalmashapada & *Damayanti*
28. Shankhana & *Chitralekha**
29. Sudarshana & *Sri Devi**
30. Agnivarna & *Kamalakshi**
31. Shighraga & *Bhadravati**
32. Maru & *Urmila**
33. Prashushrukha & *Girija**
34. Ambarisha & *Ekadashi Vrata**
35. Nahusha & *Viraja*
36. Nabhaga & *Padmavati**
37. Aja & *Indumati*

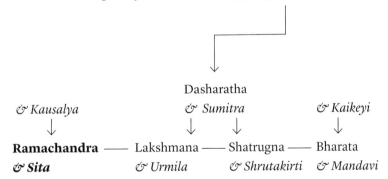

Dasharatha

& Kausalya   *& Sumitra*   *& Kaikeyi*

Ramachandra — Lakshmana — Shatrugna — Bharata

& Sita   *& Urmila*   *& Shrutakirti*   *& Mandavi*

Ikshvaku's lineage: Male progenitors as recorded in the Ayodhyakanda by Valmiki.

* Provided by the author.

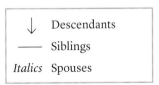

↓	Descendants
——	Siblings
Italics	Spouses

Sita's Family Tree

The Moon Dynasty – House of Videha

1. Nimi
2. Mithi
3. Janaka (the first of that name)
4. Udavasu
5. Nandivardhana
6. Suketu
7. Devarata
8. Bhrihadratha
9. Mahavira
10. Sudhriti
11. Dhrishtaketu
12. Haryashva
13. Maru
14. Pratindhaka
15. Kirtiratha
16. Devamidha
17. Vibudha
18. Mahidhraka
19. Kirtirata
20. Maharoma
21. Svarnaroma
22. Hrasvaroma *& Samapriya**

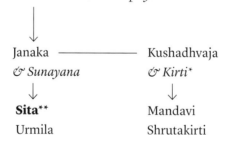

Janaka	———————	Kushadhvaja
& Sunayana		*& Kirti**
↓		↓
Sita**		Mandavi
Urmila		Shrutakirti

Videha's lineage: Male progenitors as recorded in the Balakanda by Valmiki.

* Provided by the author.

** Since Sita was found in a furrow, legend holds her true mother as Bhumi, the Earth goddess herself.

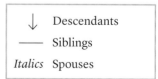

↓	Descendants
———	Siblings
Italics	Spouses

Ravana's Family Tree

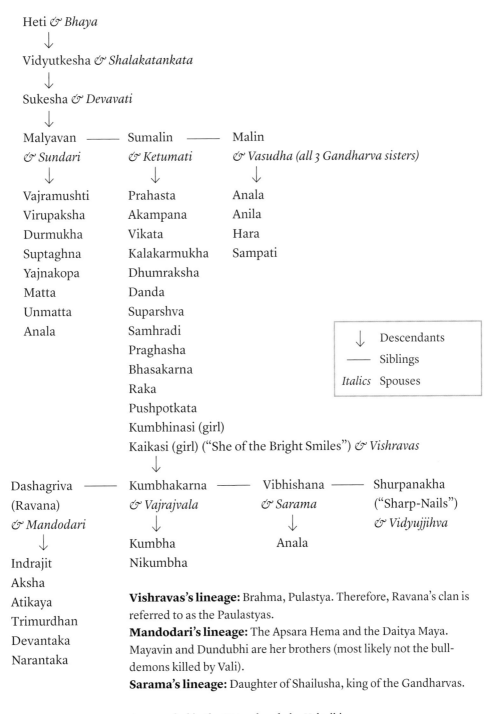

Heti & *Bhaya*
↓
Vidyutkesha & *Shalakatankata*
↓
Sukesha & *Devavati*
↓

Malyavan ——— Sumalin ——— Malin
& *Sundari* & *Ketumati* & *Vasudha* (all 3 Gandharva sisters)
↓ ↓ ↓

Malyavan's descendants	Sumalin's descendants	Malin's descendants
Vajramushti	Prahasta	Anala
Virupaksha	Akampana	Anila
Durmukha	Vikata	Hara
Suptaghna	Kalakarmukha	Sampati
Yajnakopa	Dhumraksha	
Matta	Danda	
Unmatta	Suparshva	
Anala	Samhradi	
	Praghasha	
	Bhasakarna	
	Raka	
	Pushpotkata	
	Kumbhinasi (girl)	
	Kaikasi (girl) ("She of the Bright Smiles") & *Vishravas*	

↓ Descendants
——— Siblings
Italics Spouses

Kaikasi (girl) ("She of the Bright Smiles") & *Vishravas*
↓

Dashagriva ——— Kumbhakarna ——— Vibhishana ——— Shurpanakha
(Ravana) & *Vajrajvala* & *Sarama* ("Sharp-Nails")
& *Mandodari* ↓ ↓ & *Vidyujjihva*
↓ Kumbha Anala
Indrajit Nikumbha
Aksha
Atikaya
Trimurdhan
Devantaka
Narantaka

Vishravas's lineage: Brahma, Pulastya. Therefore, Ravana's clan is referred to as the Paulastyas.

Mandodari's lineage: The Apsara Hema and the Daitya Maya. Mayavin and Dundubhi are her brothers (most likely not the bull-demons killed by Vali).

Sarama's lineage: Daughter of Shailusha, king of the Gandharvas.

As recorded in the Uttarakanda by Valmiki.

Illustration Index